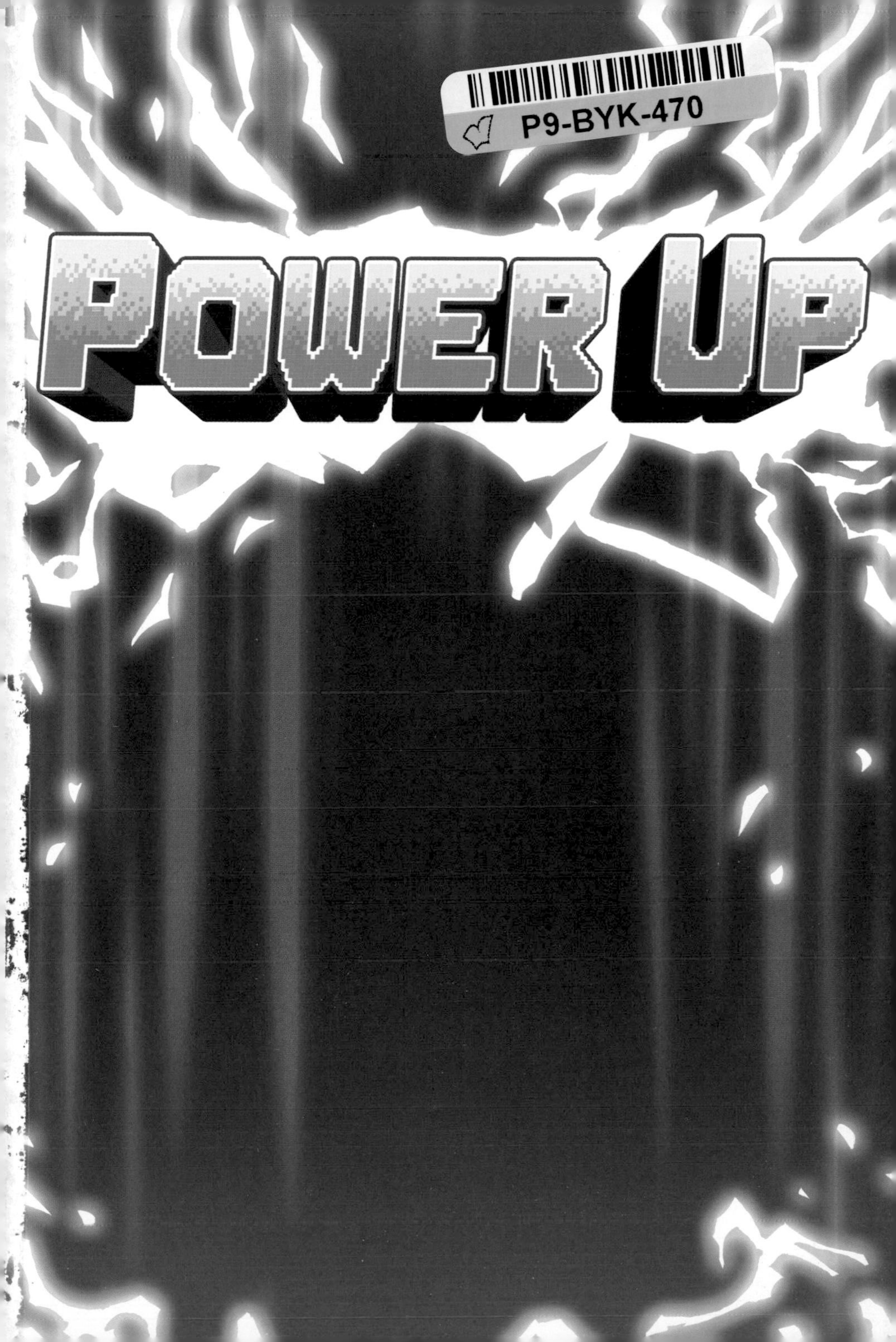
POWER UP

FOR ROY, NORA, AND THOMAS—THREE KIDS RAISED TO BE GAMERS —S.N.

TO ALL THE YOUNG ARTISTS. DON'T BE AFRAID TO GROW IN FRONT OF THE WORLD. —D.J.

ETCH IS AN IMPRINT OF
HOUGHTON MIFFLIN HARCOURT PUBLISHING COMPANY.

HMHBOOKS.COM

THE ILLUSTRATIONS IN THIS BOOK WERE CREATED DIGITALLY.
THE TEXT WAS SET IN A FONT BASED ON DARNELL JOHNSON'S HANDWRITING.

COVER DESIGN BY PHIL CAMINITI
INTERIOR DESIGN BY PHIL CAMINITI
COMPOSITION BY LIZ CASAL

ISBN: 978-0-358-32571-0 HARDCOVER
ISBN: 978-0-358-32565-9 PAPERBACK

MANUFACTURED IN CHINA
SCP 10 9 8 7 6 5 4 3 2 1
4500813726

POWER UP

WRITTEN BY
SAM NISSON

ILLUSTRATED BY
DARNELL JOHNSON

HOUGHTON MIFFLIN HARCOURT
BOSTON   NEW YORK

CONTENTS

CHAPTER 1

PUSH

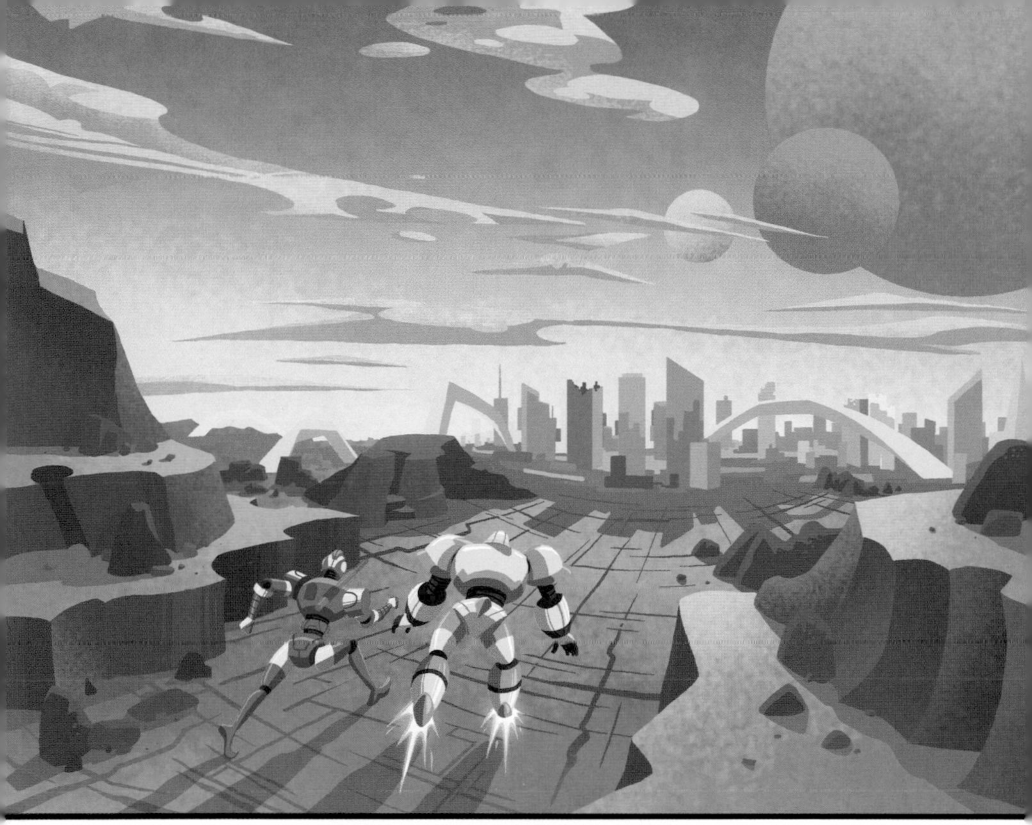

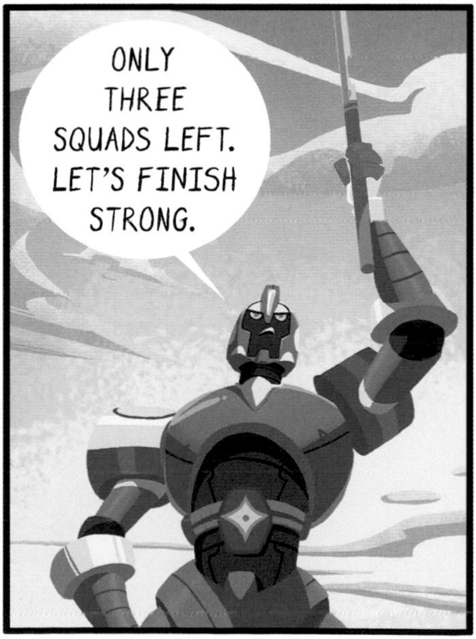
ONLY THREE SQUADS LEFT. LET'S FINISH STRONG.

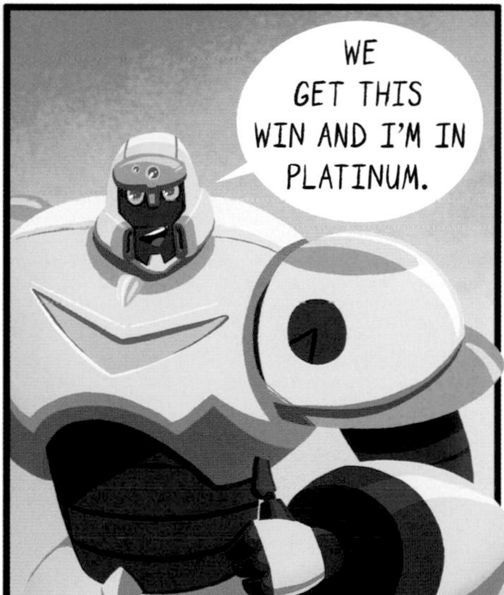
WE GET THIS WIN AND I'M IN PLATINUM.

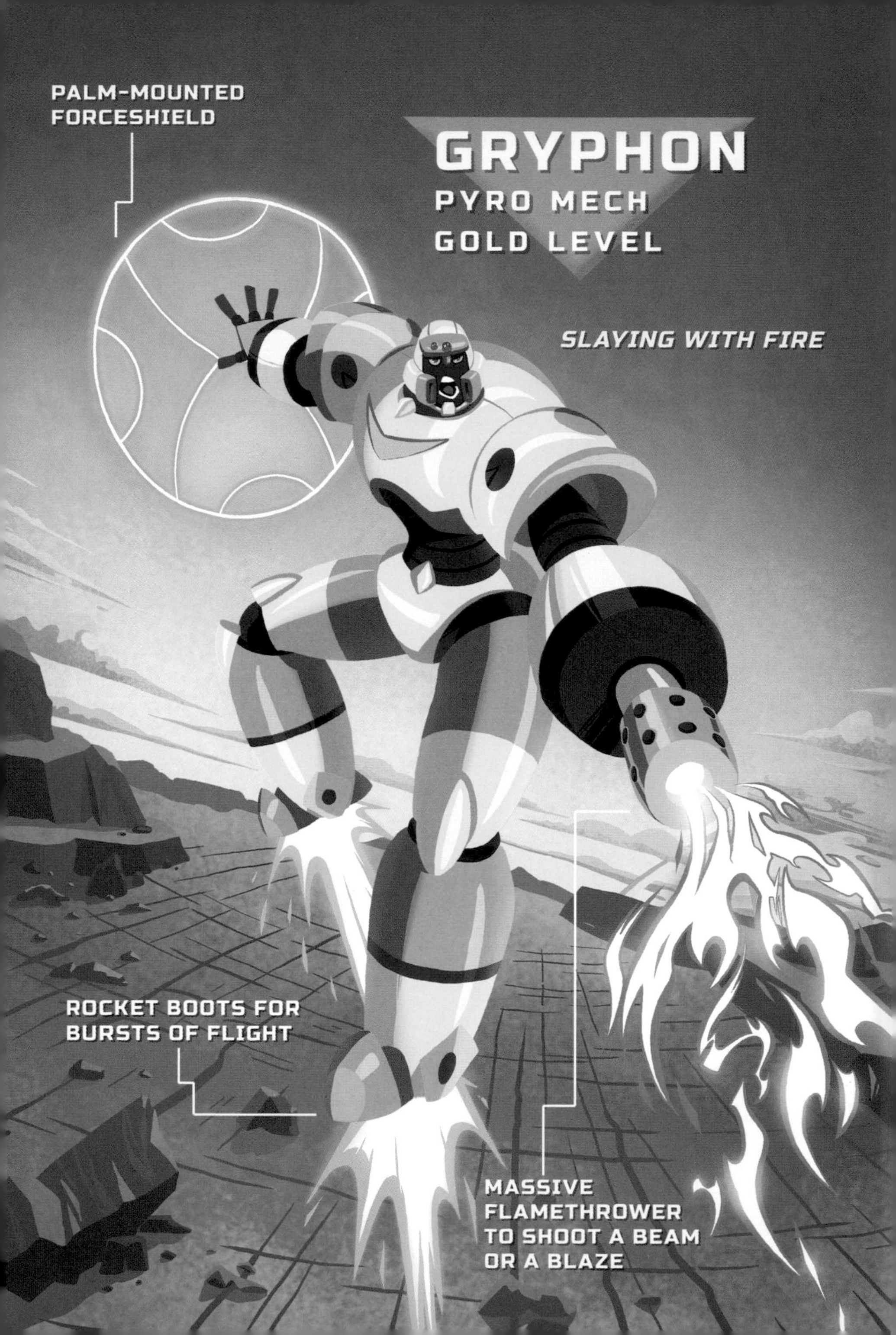
PALM-MOUNTED FORCESHIELD
GRYPHON
PYRO MECH
GOLD LEVEL
SLAYING WITH FIRE
ROCKET BOOTS FOR BURSTS OF FLIGHT
MASSIVE FLAMETHROWER TO SHOOT A BEAM OR A BLAZE

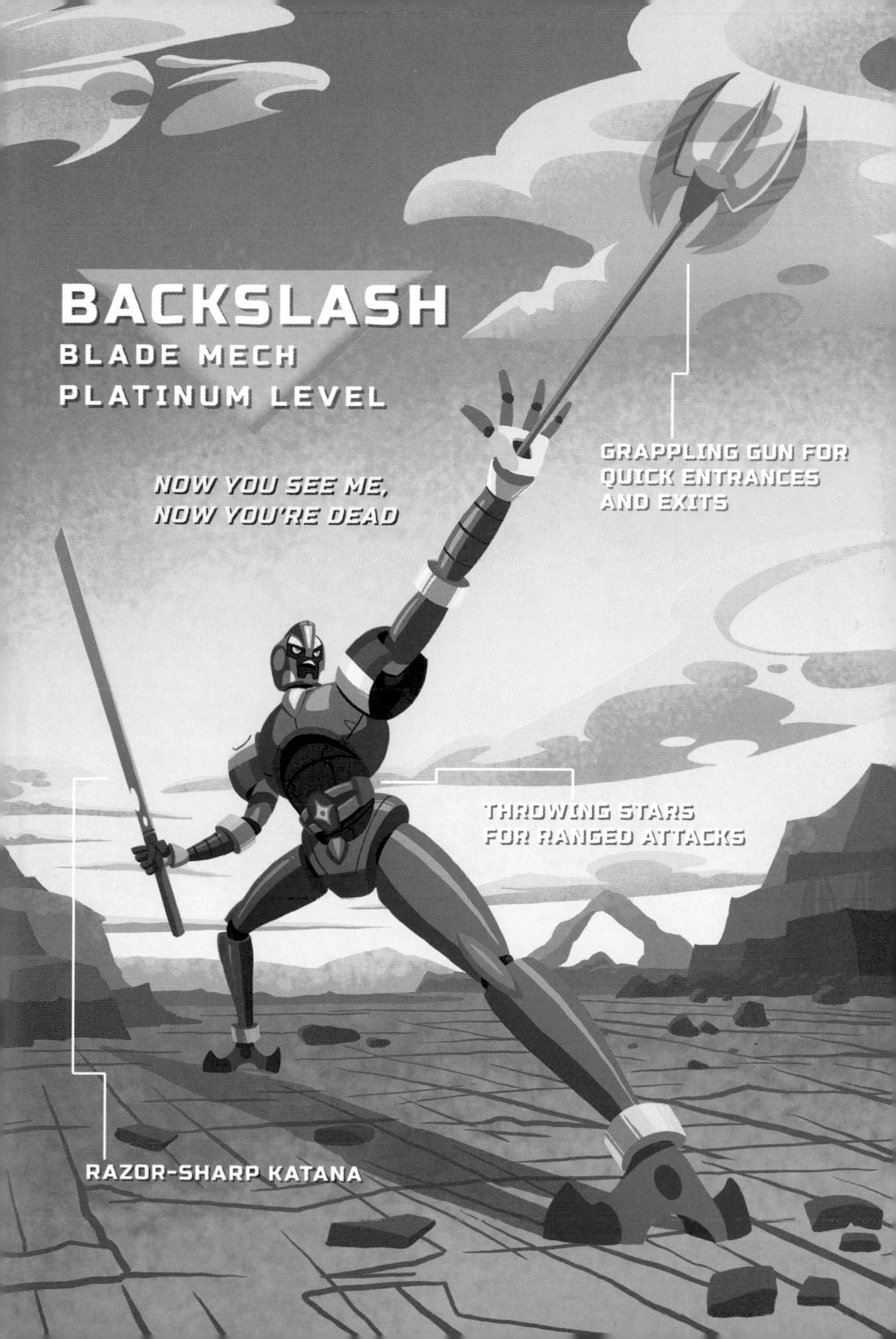
BACKSLASH
BLADE MECH
PLATINUM LEVEL
NOW YOU SEE ME, NOW YOU'RE DEAD
GRAPPLING GUN FOR QUICK ENTRANCES AND EXITS
THROWING STARS FOR RANGED ATTACKS
RAZOR-SHARP KATANA

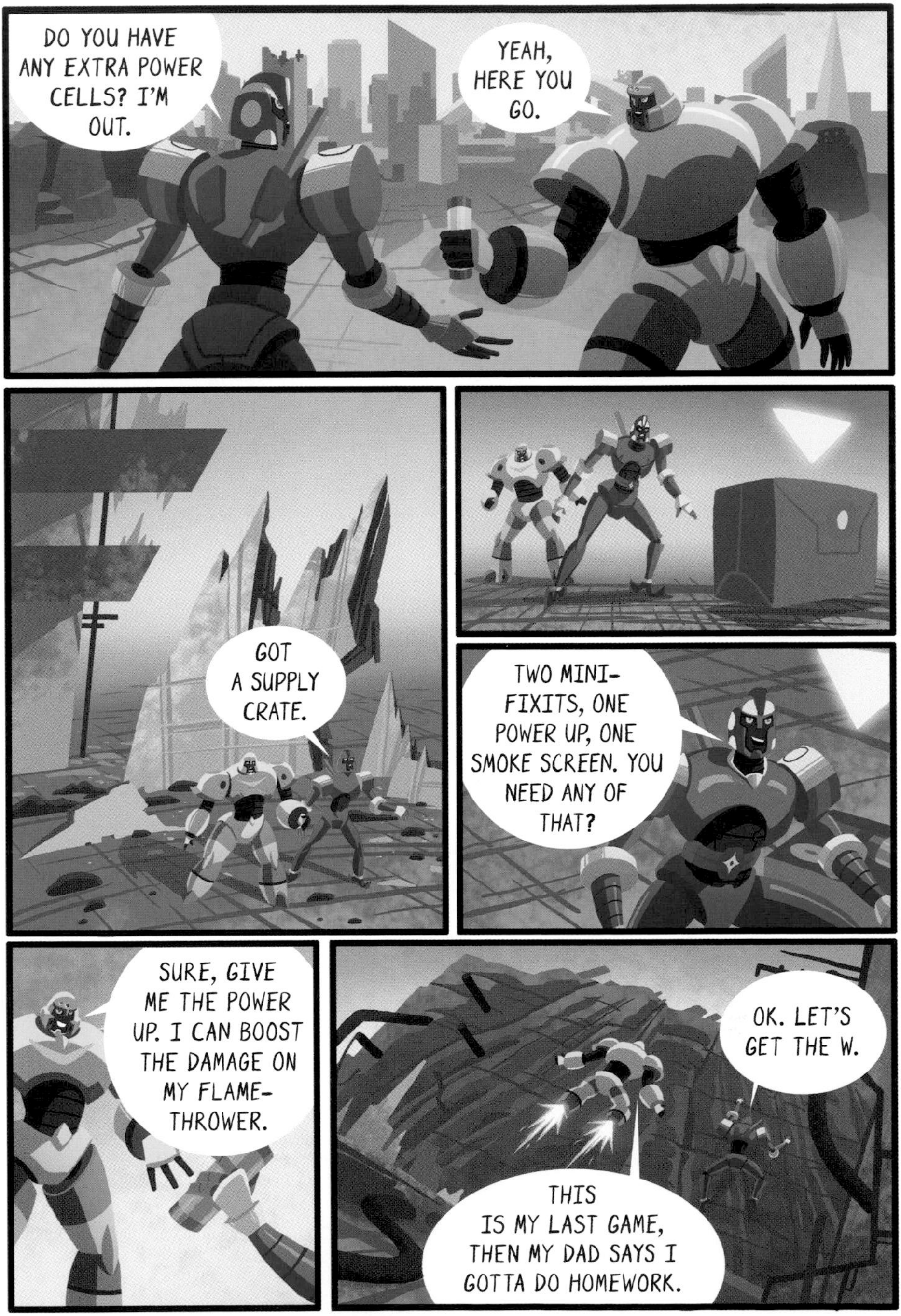
DO YOU HAVE ANY EXTRA POWER CELLS? I'M OUT.
YEAH, HERE YOU GO.
GOT A SUPPLY CRATE.
TWO MINI-FIXITS, ONE POWER UP, ONE SMOKE SCREEN. YOU NEED ANY OF THAT?
SURE, GIVE ME THE POWER UP. I CAN BOOST THE DAMAGE ON MY FLAME-THROWER.
OK. LET'S GET THE W.
THIS IS MY LAST GAME, THEN MY DAD SAYS I GOTTA DO HOMEWORK.

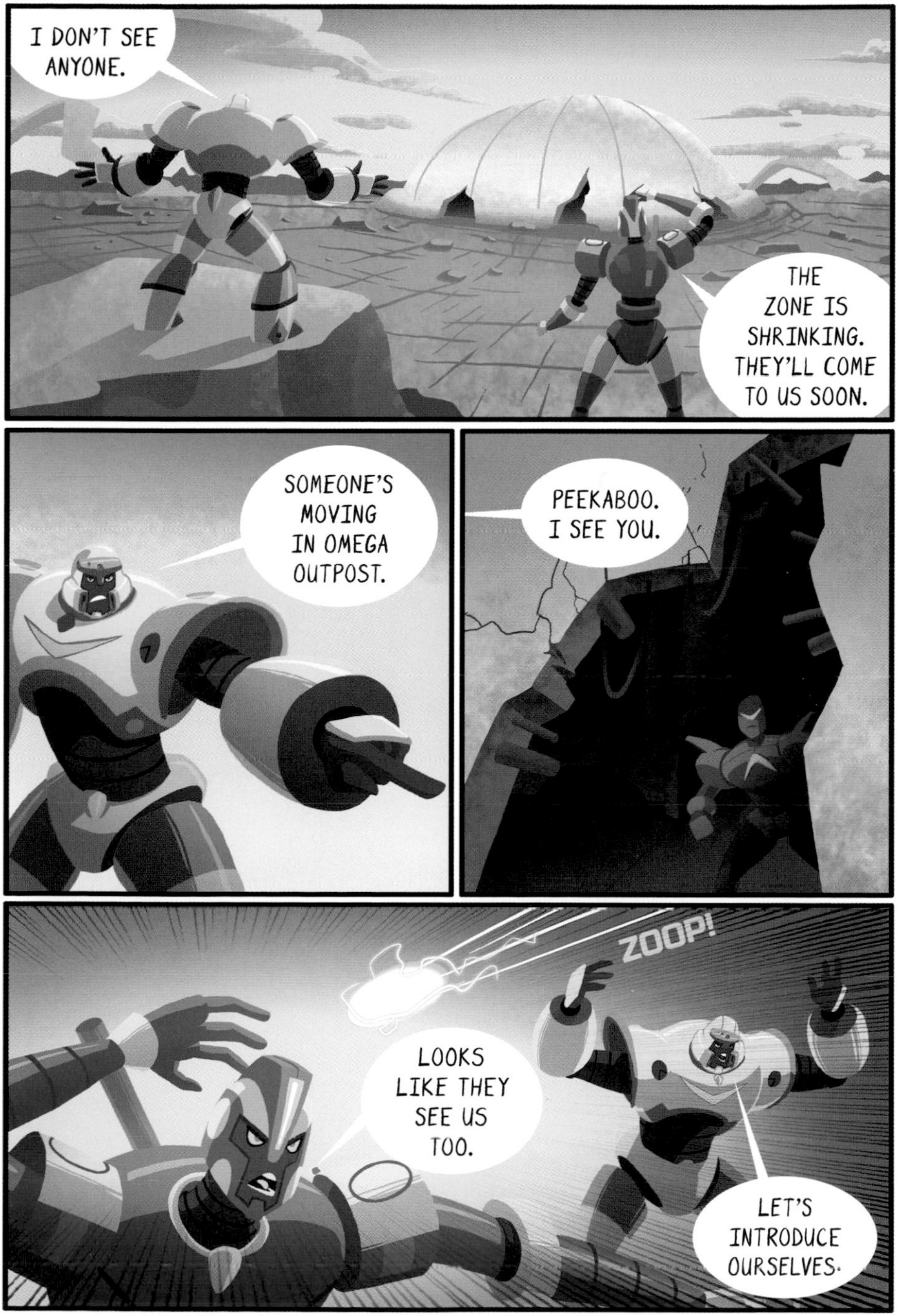
I DON'T SEE ANYONE.
THE ZONE IS SHRINKING. THEY'LL COME TO US SOON.
SOMEONE'S MOVING IN OMEGA OUTPOST.
PEEKABOO. I SEE YOU.
ZOOP!
LOOKS LIKE THEY SEE US TOO.
LET'S INTRODUCE OURSELVES.

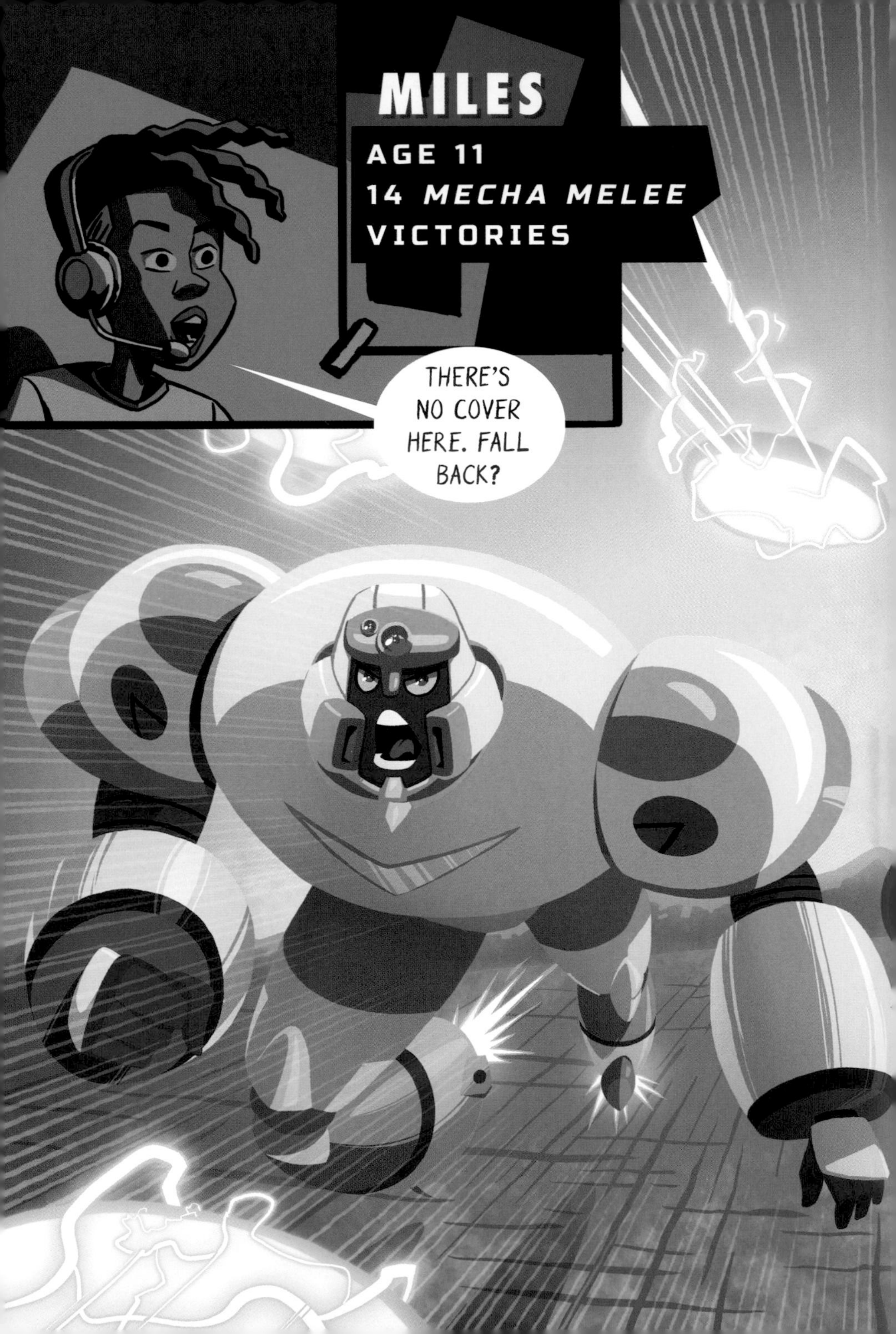
MILES
AGE 11
14 MECHA MELEE VICTORIES
THERE'S NO COVER HERE. FALL BACK?

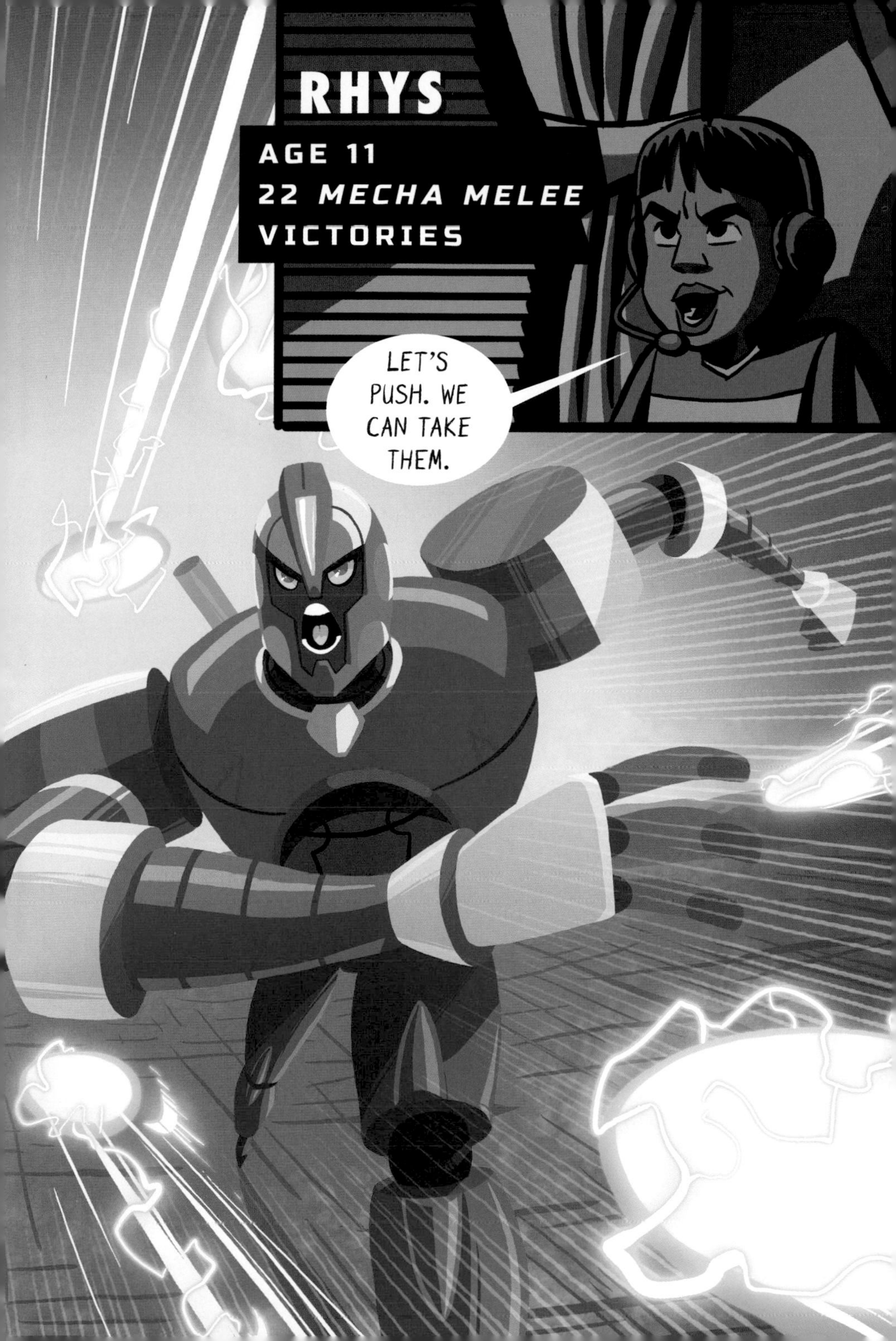
RHYS
AGE 11
22 *MECHA MELEE* VICTORIES
LET'S PUSH. WE CAN TAKE THEM.

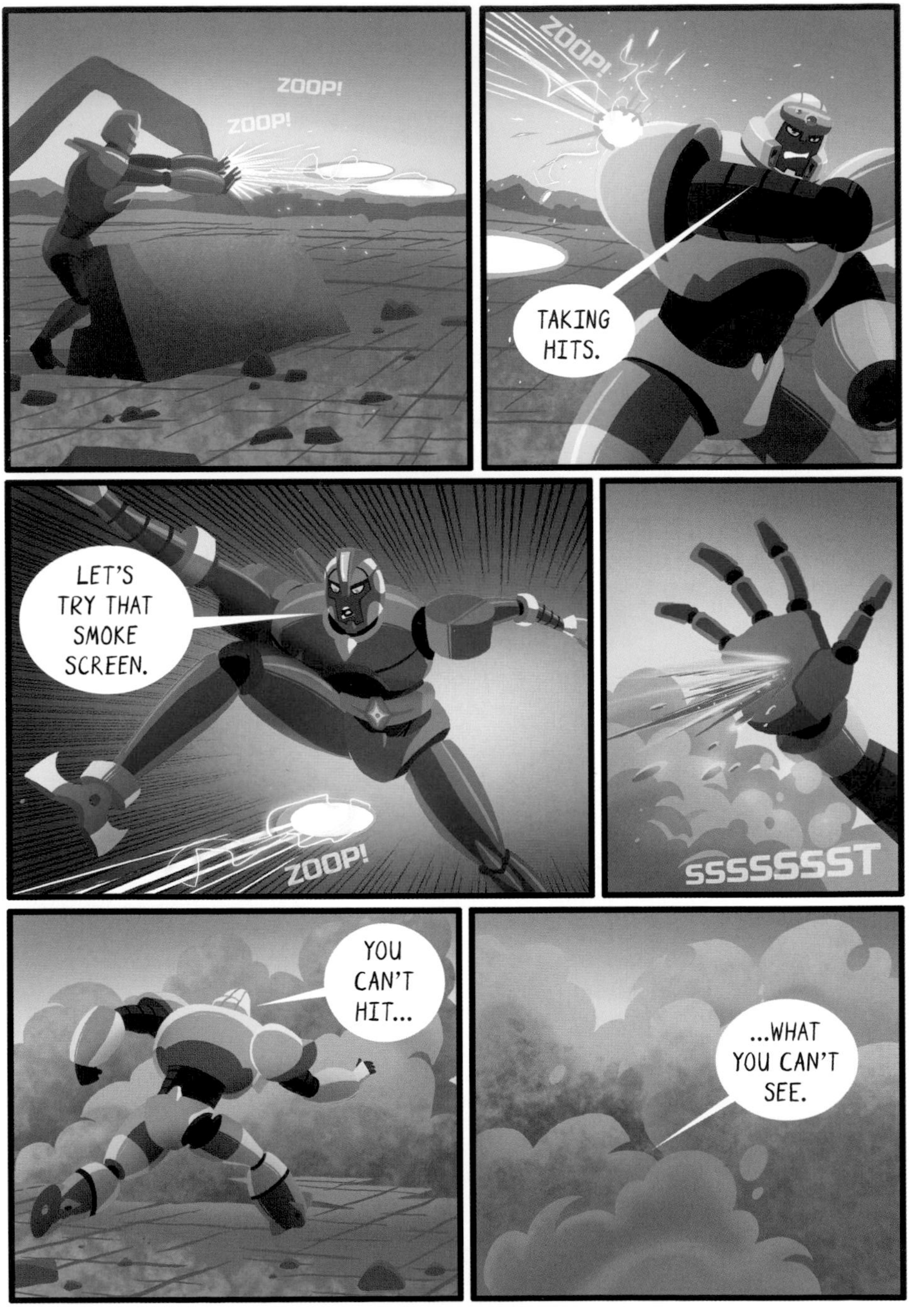
ZOOP!
ZOOP!
ZOOP!
TAKING HITS.
LET'S TRY THAT SMOKE SCREEN.
ZOOP!
SSSSSSST
YOU CAN'T HIT...
...WHAT YOU CAN'T SEE.

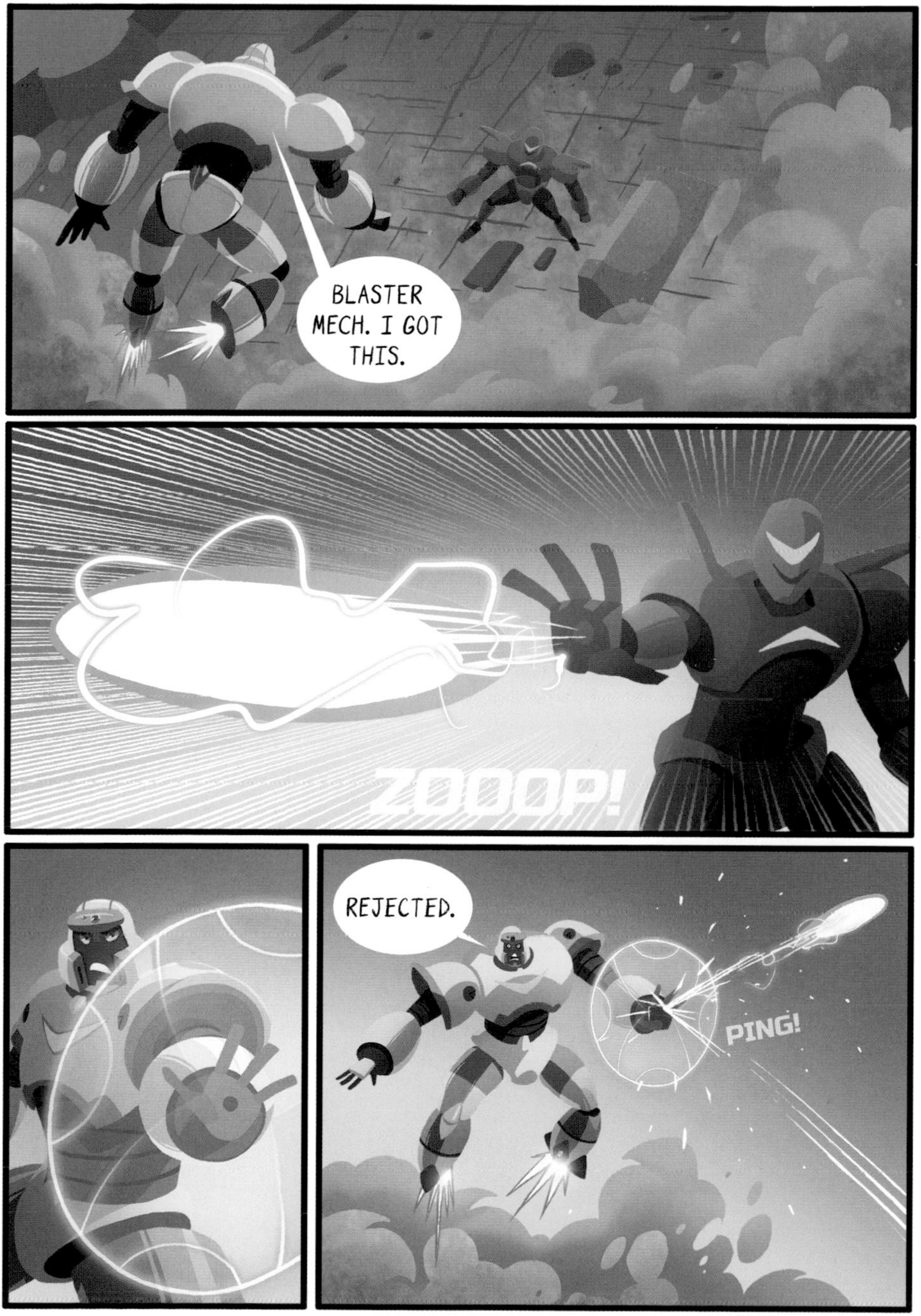
BLASTER MECH. I GOT THIS.
ZOOOP!
REJECTED.
PING!

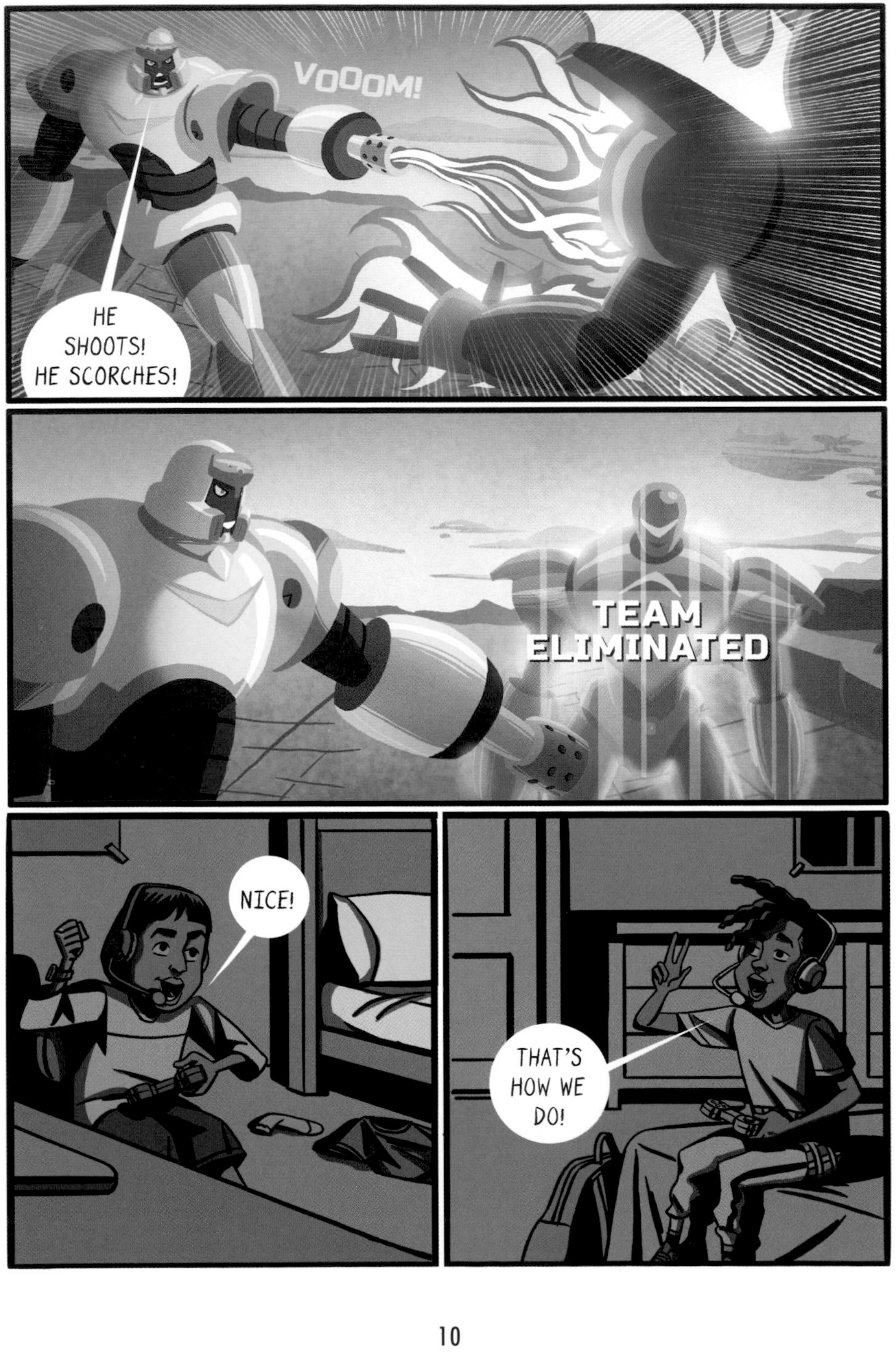
VOOOM!
HE SHOOTS! HE SCORCHES!
TEAM ELIMINATED
NICE!
THAT'S HOW WE DO!

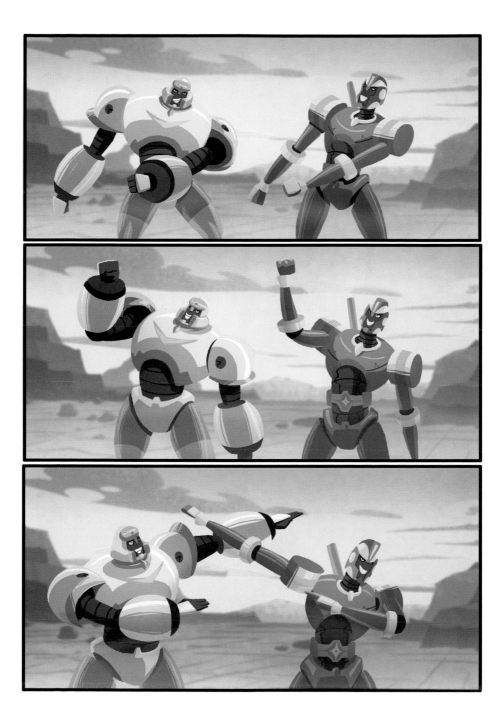

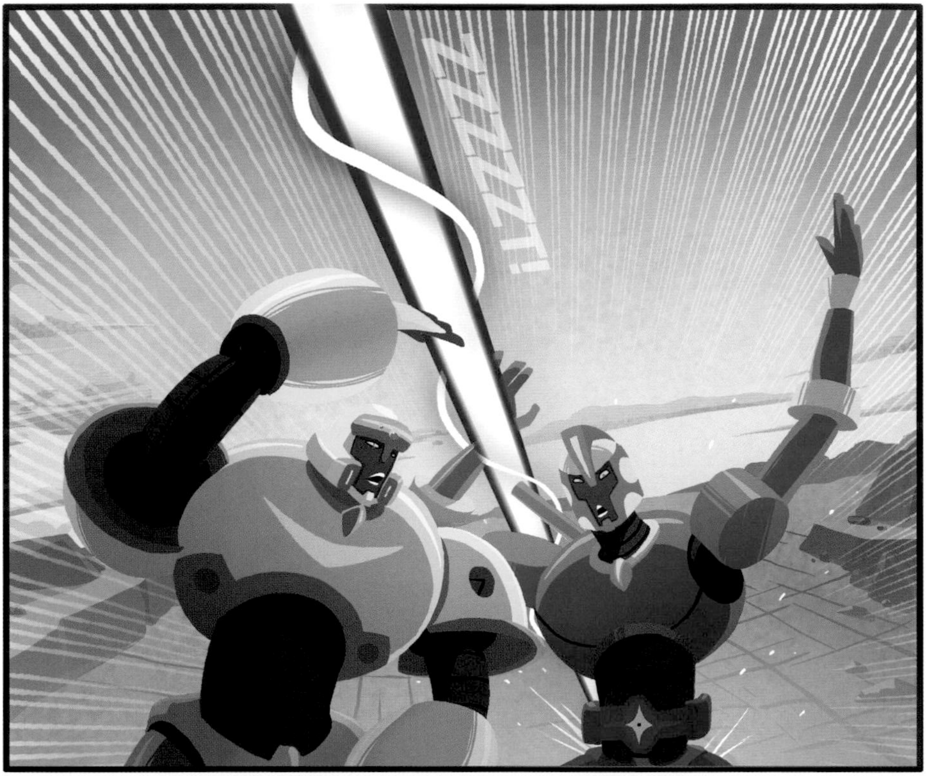
ZZZZZT!

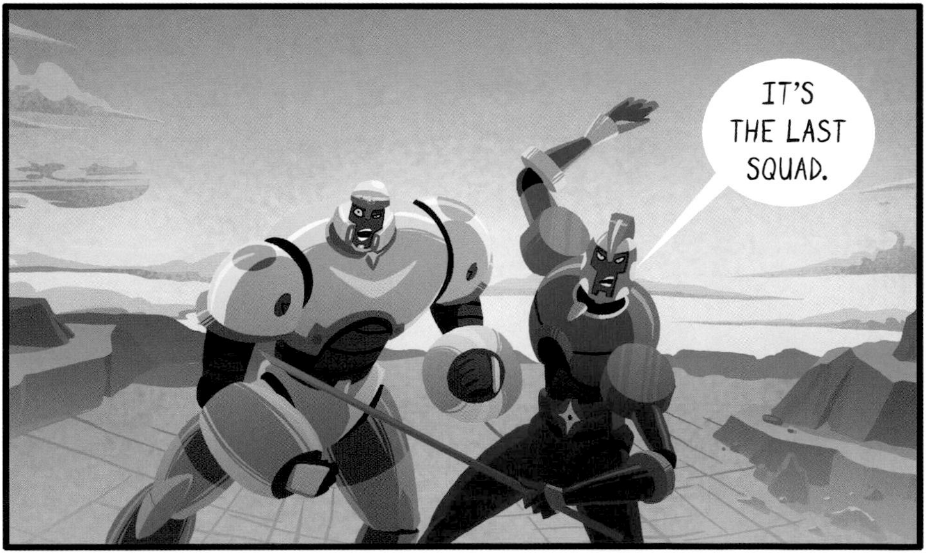
IT'S THE LAST SQUAD.

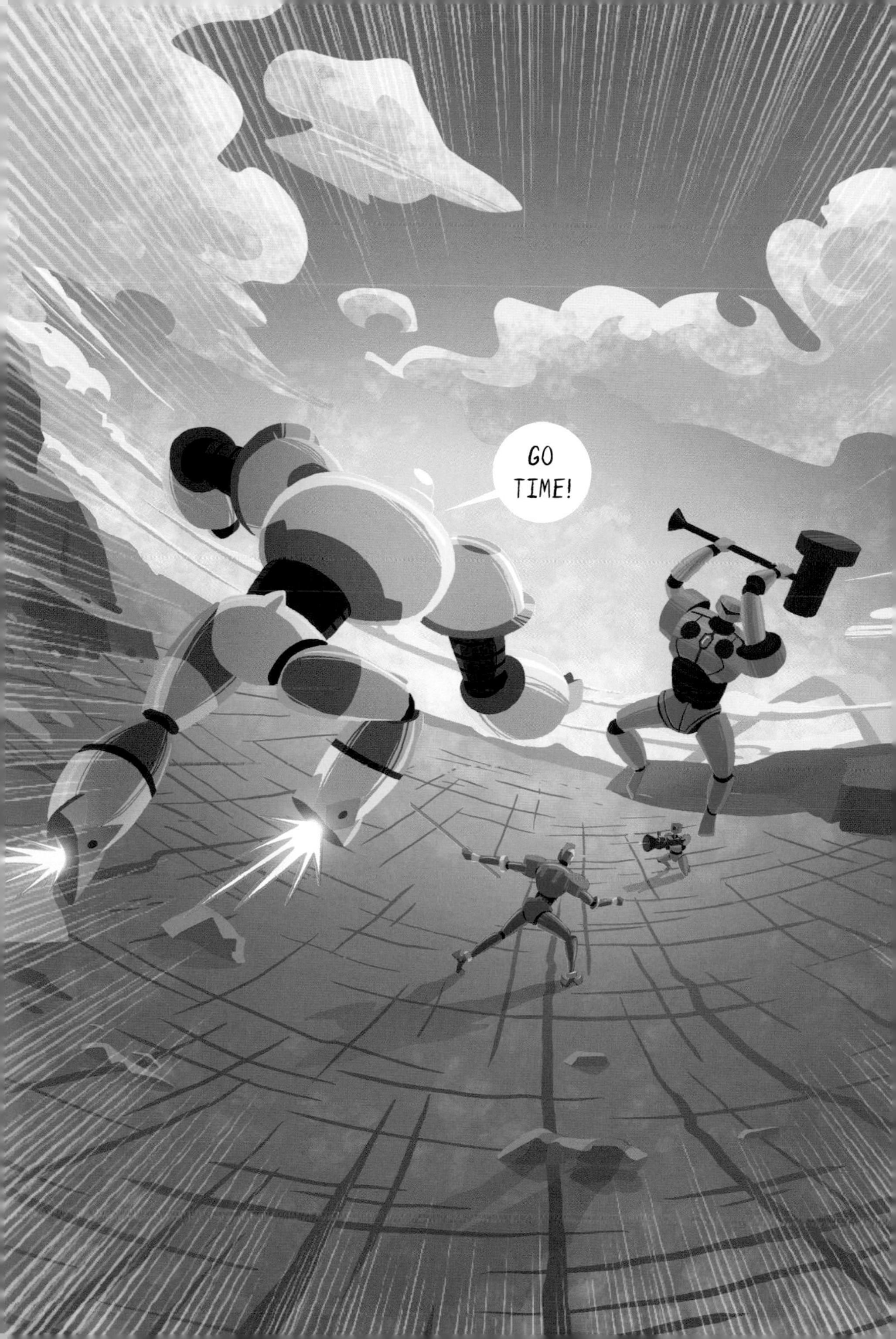
GO TIME!

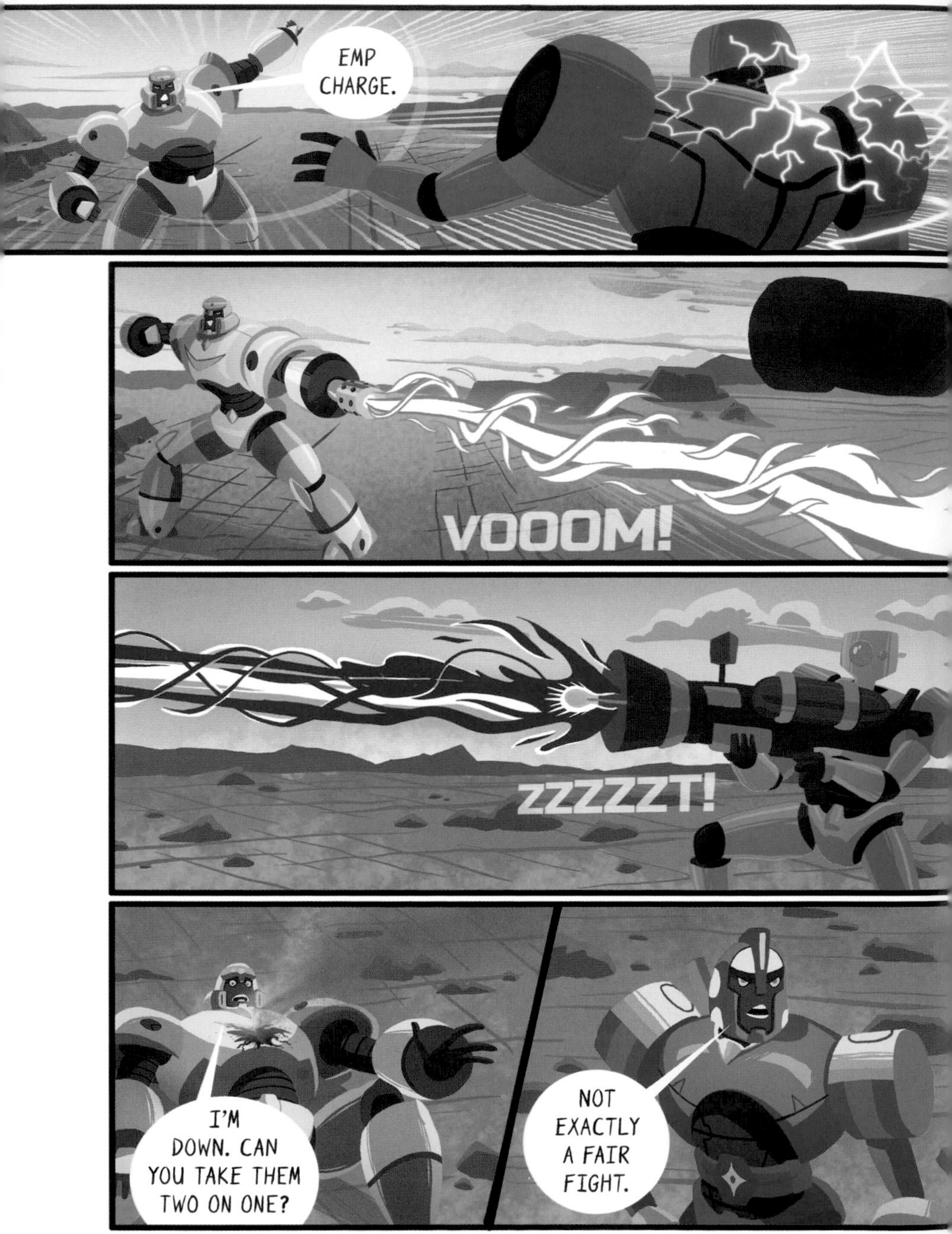
EMP CHARGE.
VOOOM!
ZZZZZT!
I'M DOWN. CAN YOU TAKE THEM TWO ON ONE?
NOT EXACTLY A FAIR FIGHT.

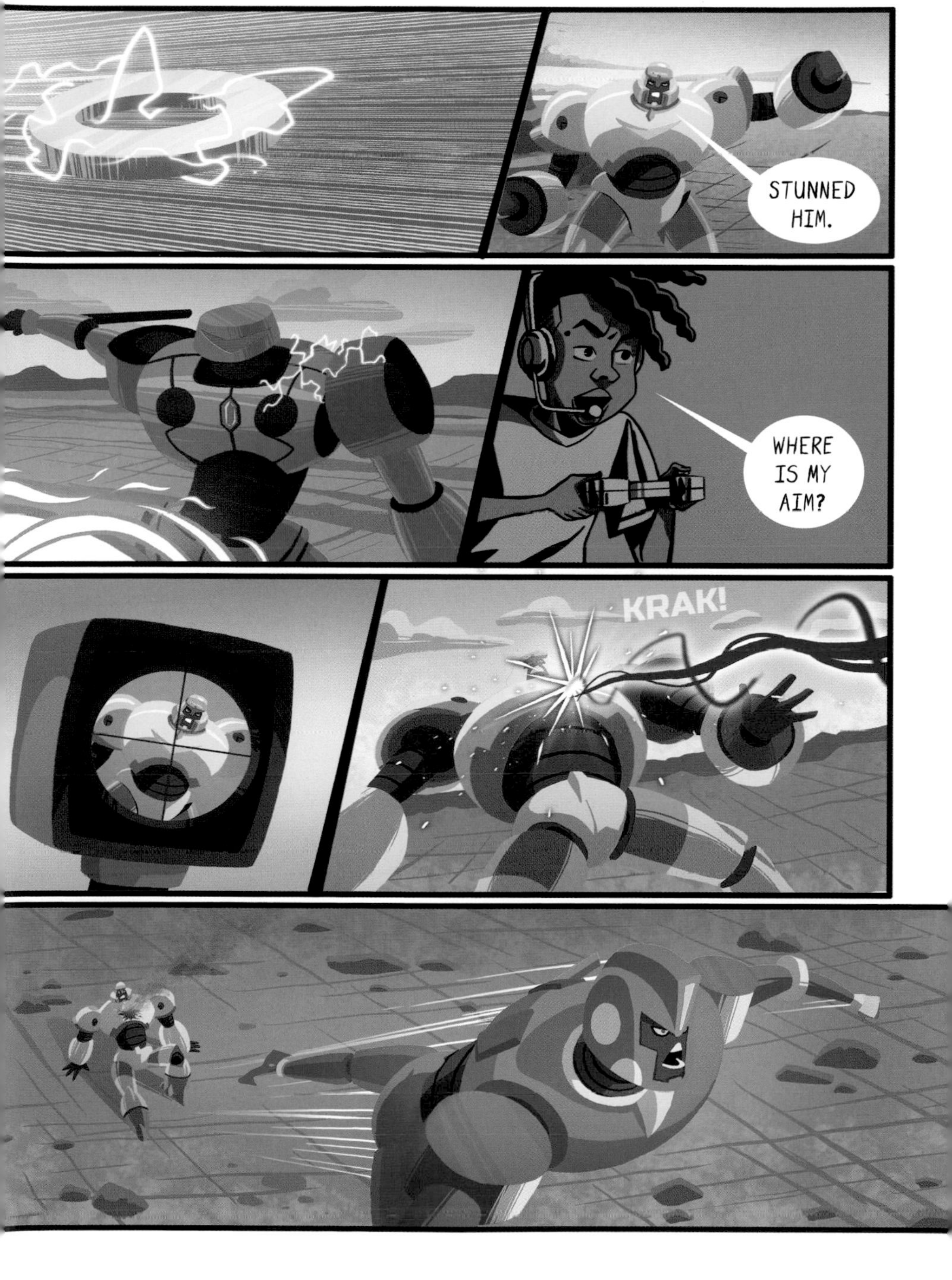
STUNNED HIM.
WHERE IS MY AIM?
KRAK!

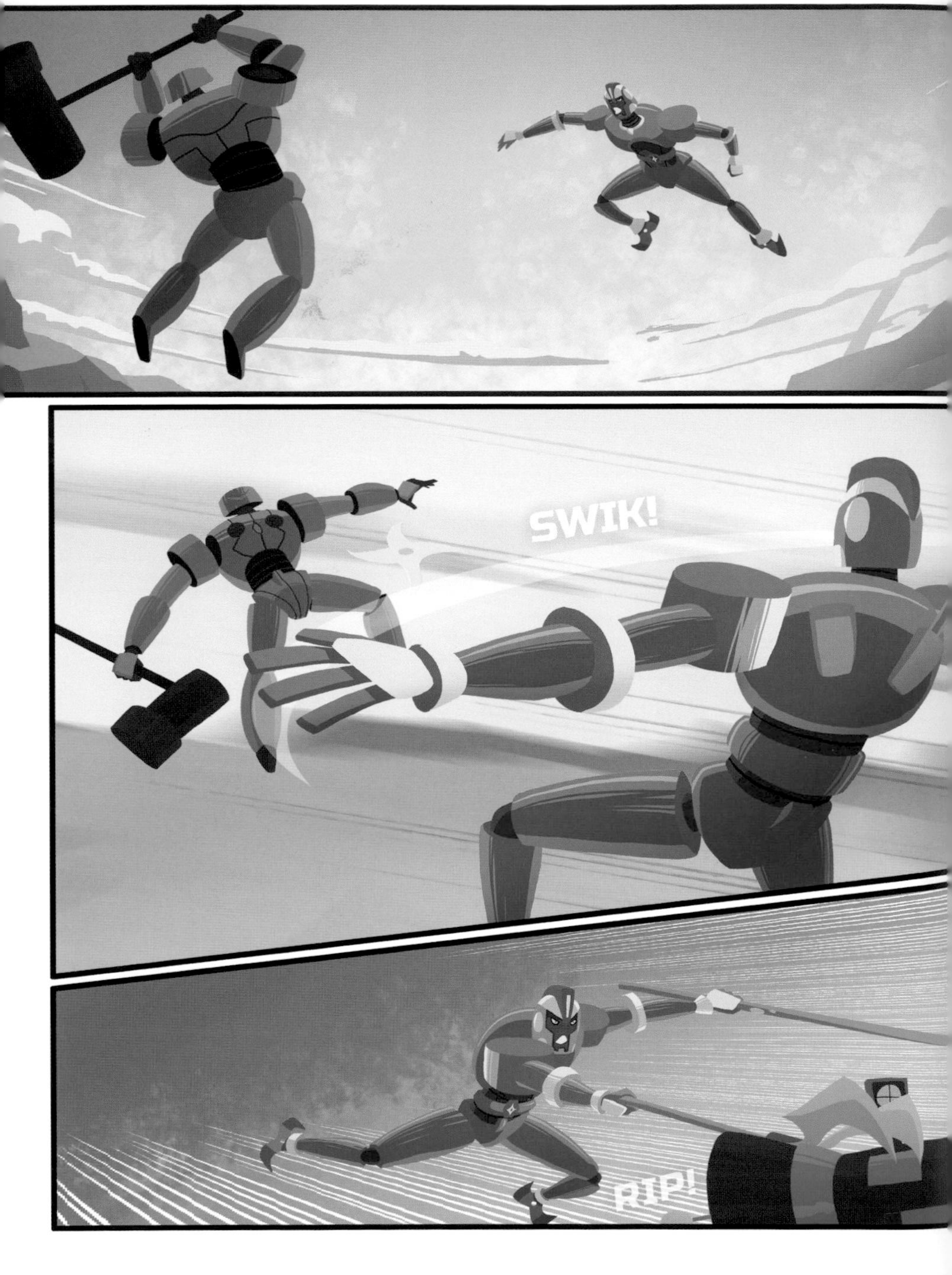
SWIK!
RIP!

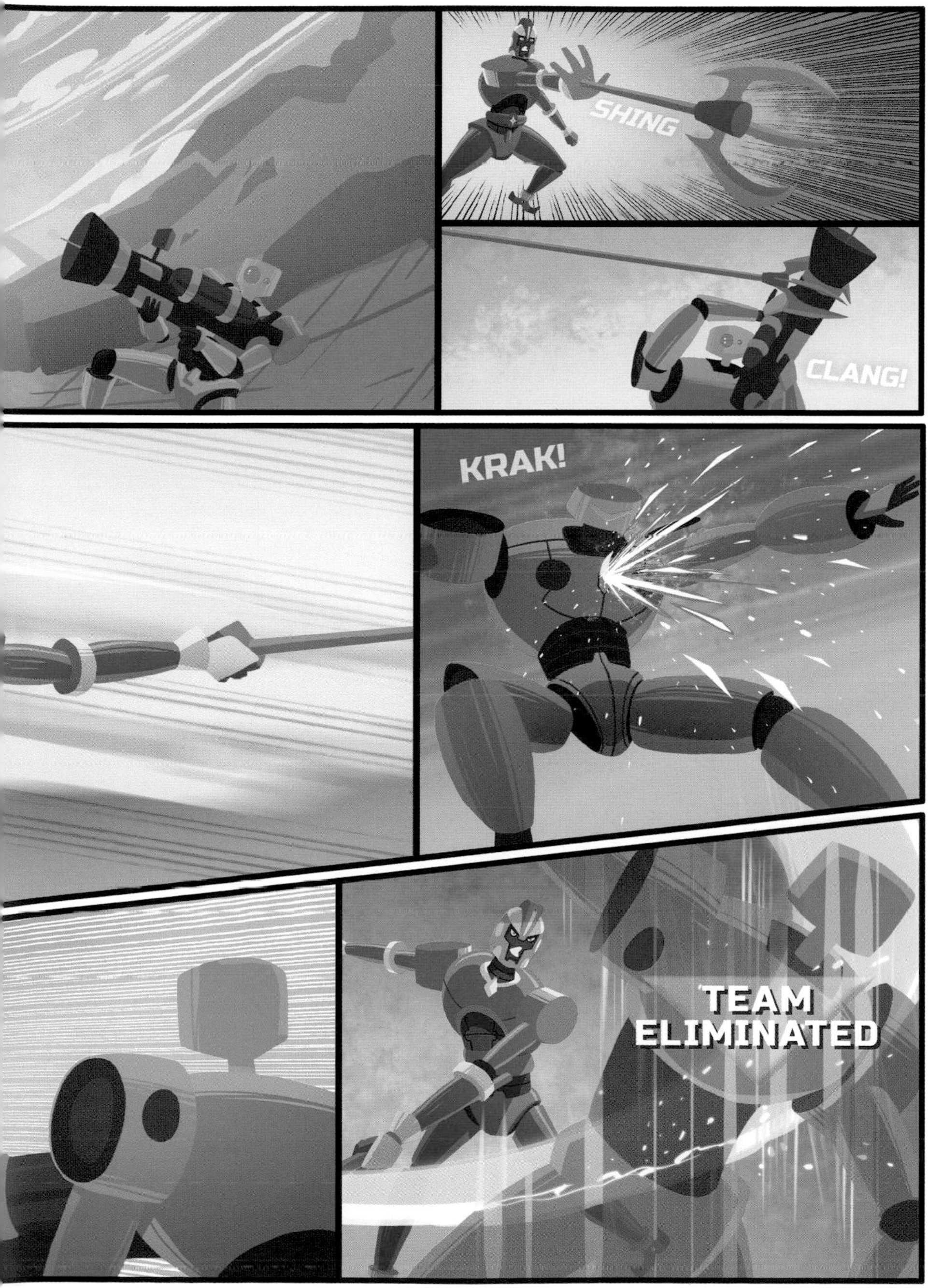
SHING
CLANG!
KRAK!
TEAM
ELIMINATED

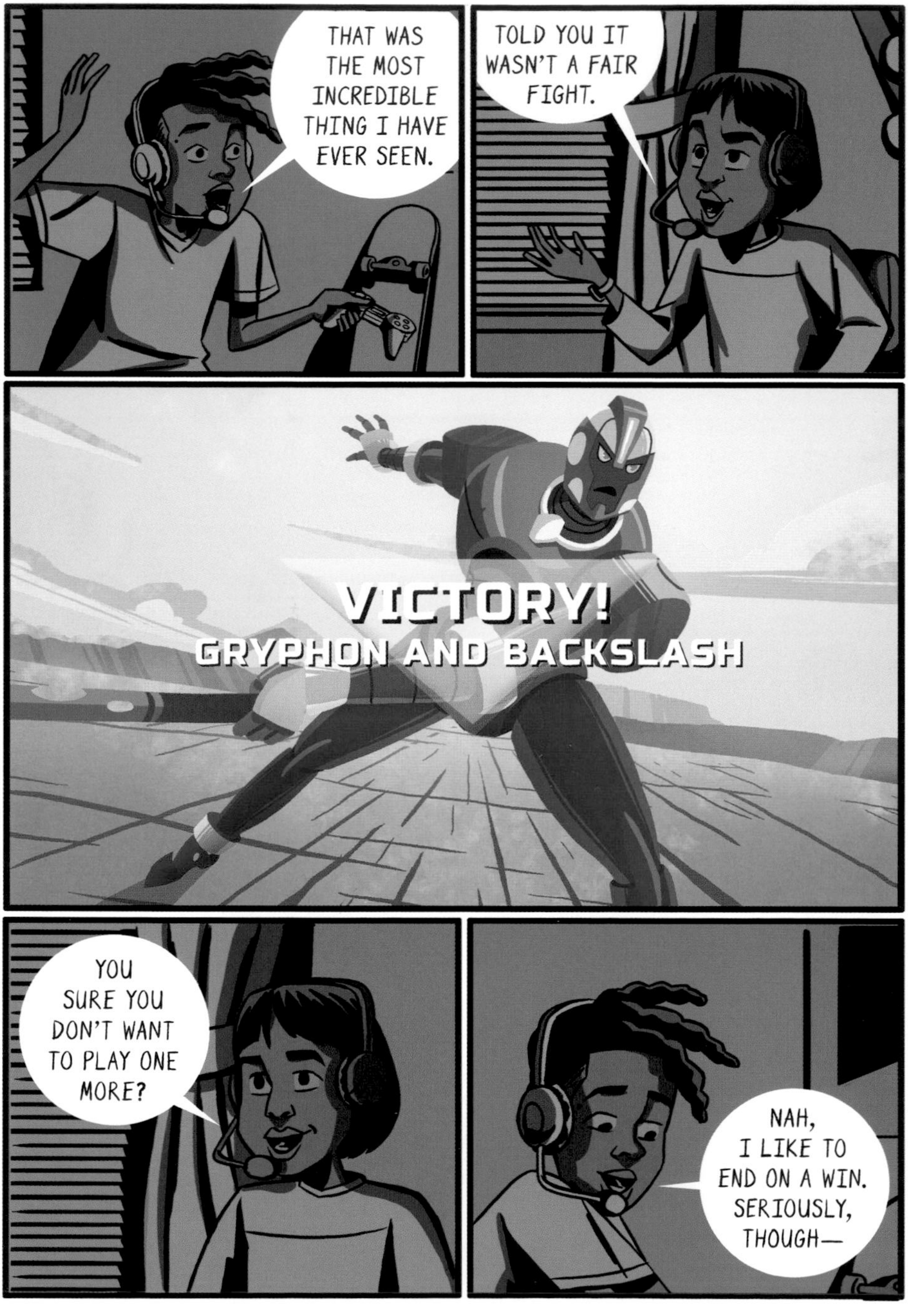
THAT WAS THE MOST INCREDIBLE THING I HAVE EVER SEEN.
TOLD YOU IT WASN'T A FAIR FIGHT.
VICTORY!
GRYPHON AND BACKSLASH
YOU SURE YOU DON'T WANT TO PLAY ONE MORE?
NAH, I LIKE TO END ON A WIN. SERIOUSLY, THOUGH—

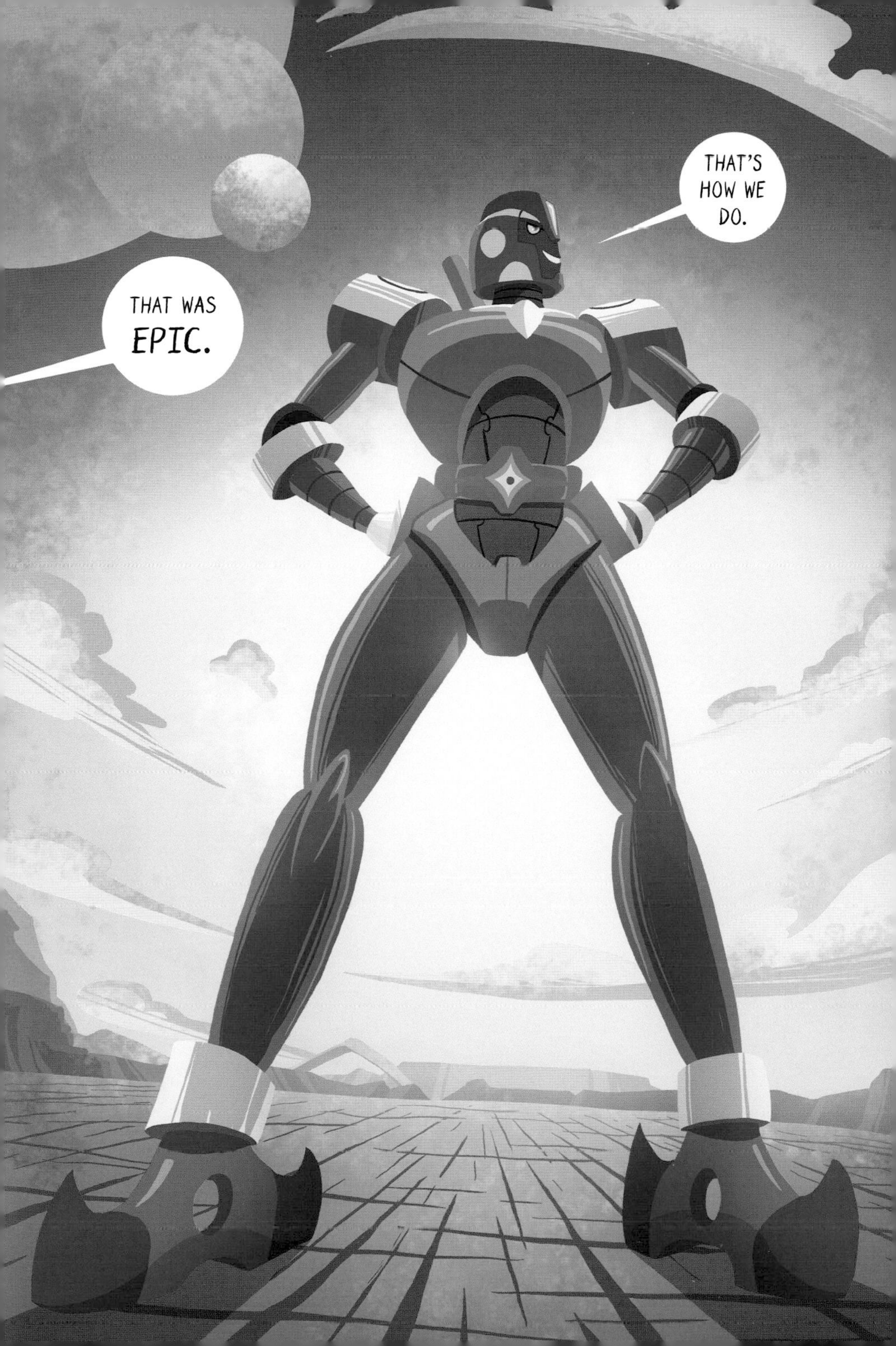
THAT WAS EPIC.
THAT'S HOW WE DO.

CHAPTER 2
IRL

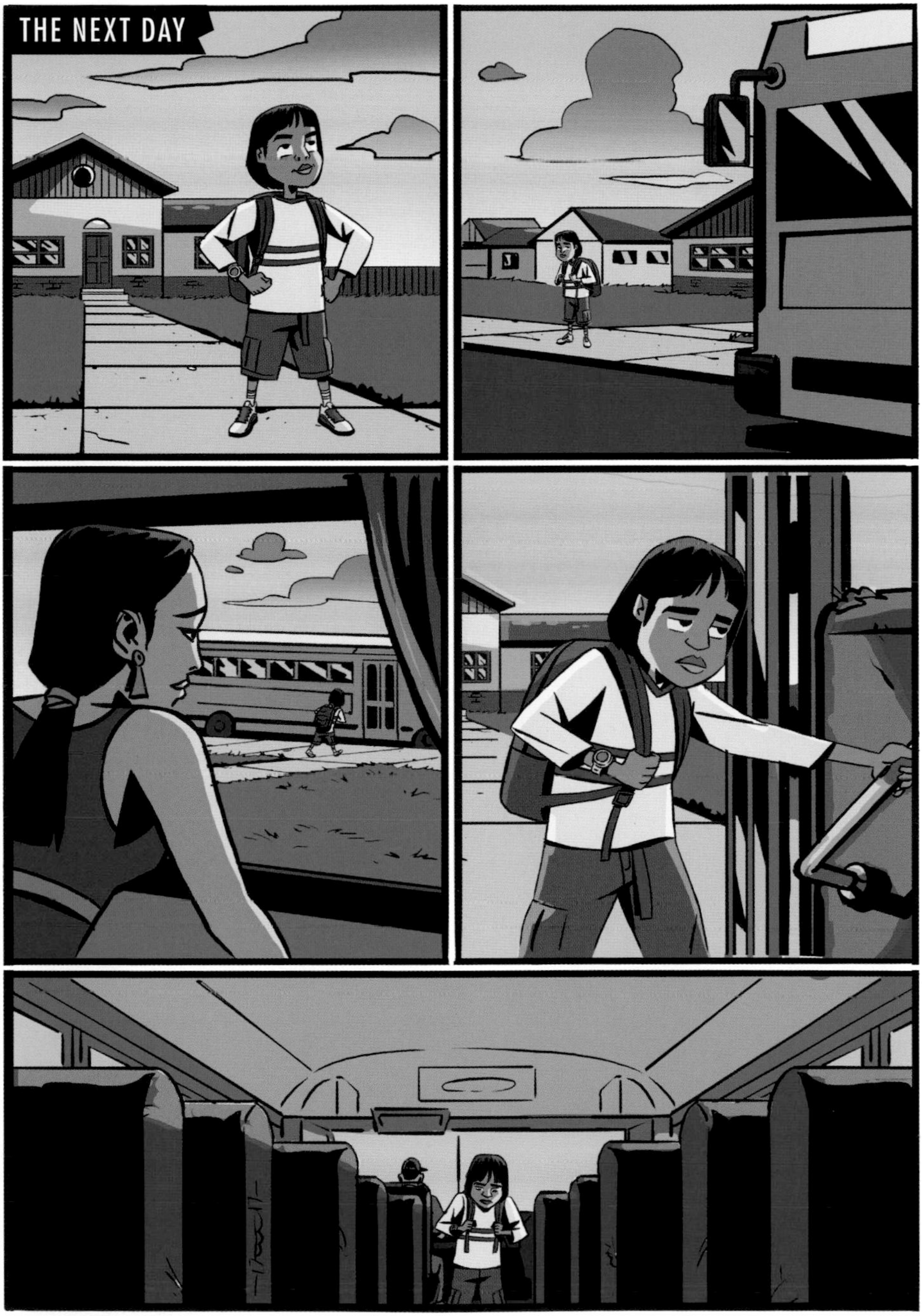
THE NEXT DAY

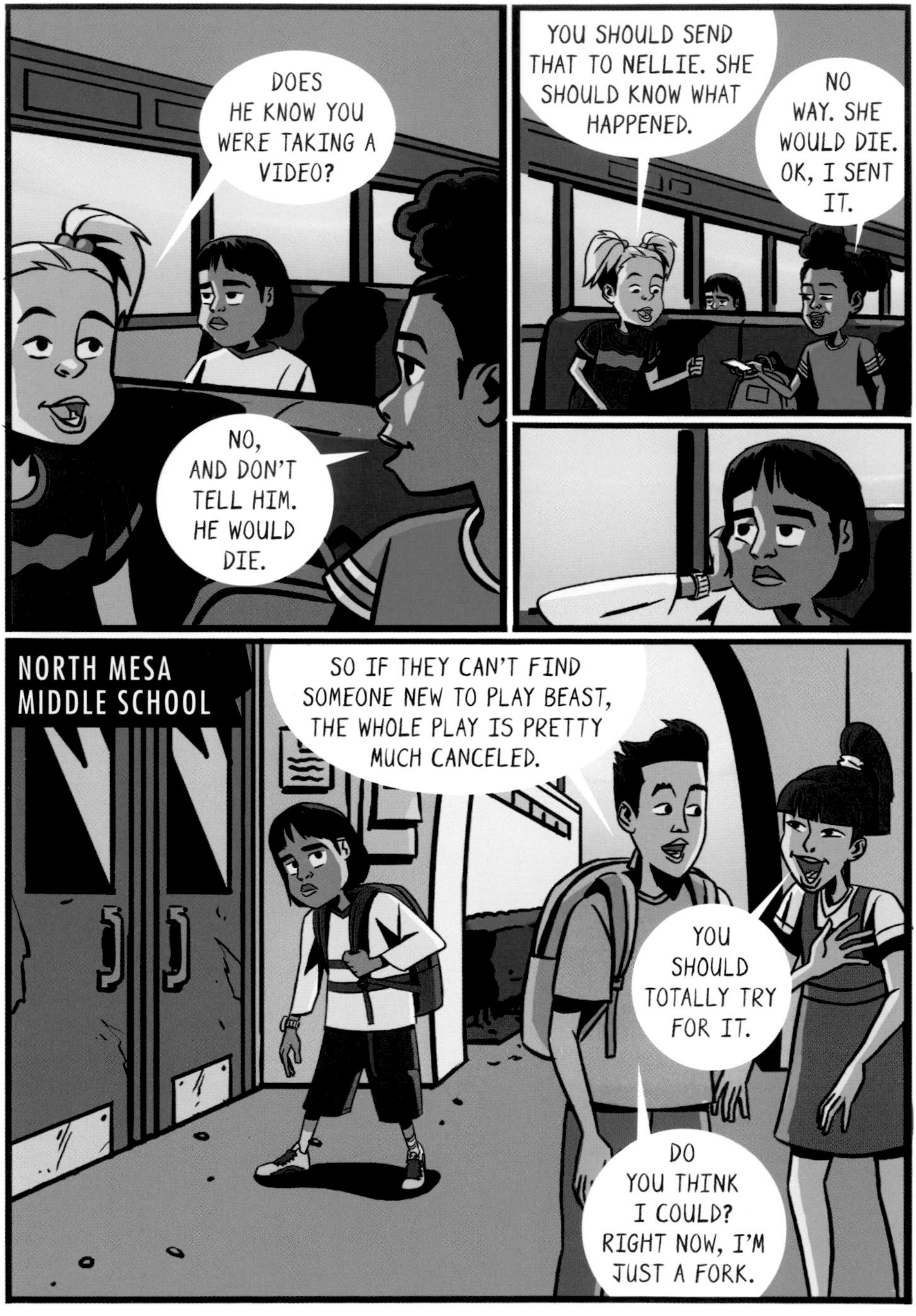
DOES HE KNOW YOU WERE TAKING A VIDEO?
NO, AND DON'T TELL HIM. HE WOULD DIE.
YOU SHOULD SEND THAT TO NELLIE. SHE SHOULD KNOW WHAT HAPPENED.
NO WAY. SHE WOULD DIE. OK, I SENT IT.
NORTH MESA MIDDLE SCHOOL
SO IF THEY CAN'T FIND SOMEONE NEW TO PLAY BEAST, THE WHOLE PLAY IS PRETTY MUCH CANCELED.
YOU SHOULD TOTALLY TRY FOR IT.
DO YOU THINK I COULD? RIGHT NOW, I'M JUST A FORK.

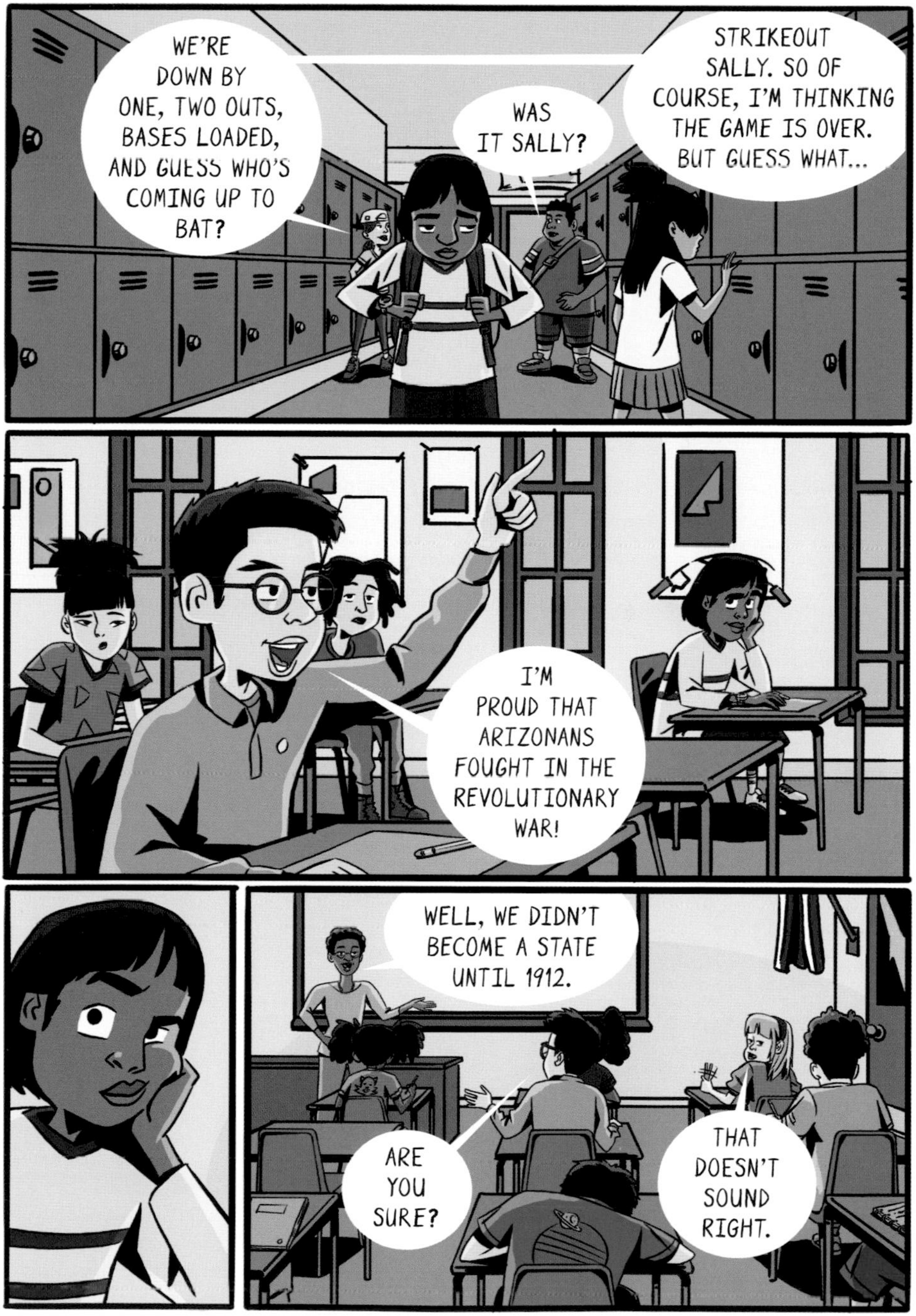
WE'RE DOWN BY ONE, TWO OUTS, BASES LOADED, AND GUESS WHO'S COMING UP TO BAT?
WAS IT SALLY?
STRIKEOUT SALLY. SO OF COURSE, I'M THINKING THE GAME IS OVER. BUT GUESS WHAT...
I'M PROUD THAT ARIZONANS FOUGHT IN THE REVOLUTIONARY WAR!
WELL, WE DIDN'T BECOME A STATE UNTIL 1912.
ARE YOU SURE?
THAT DOESN'T SOUND RIGHT.

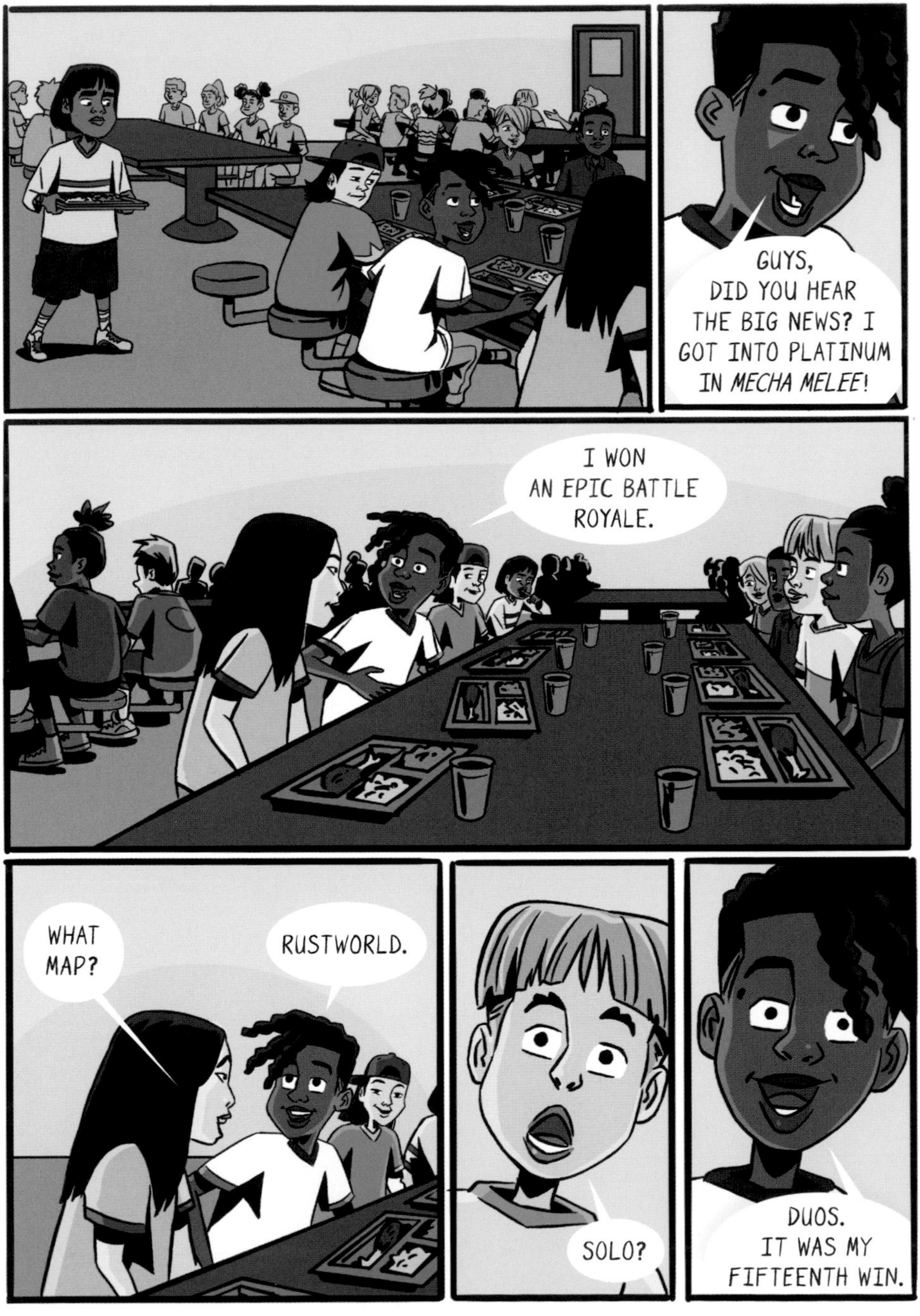
GUYS, DID YOU HEAR THE BIG NEWS? I GOT INTO PLATINUM IN *MECHA MELEE*!
I WON AN EPIC BATTLE ROYALE.
WHAT MAP?
RUSTWORLD.
SOLO?
DUOS. IT WAS MY FIFTEENTH WIN.

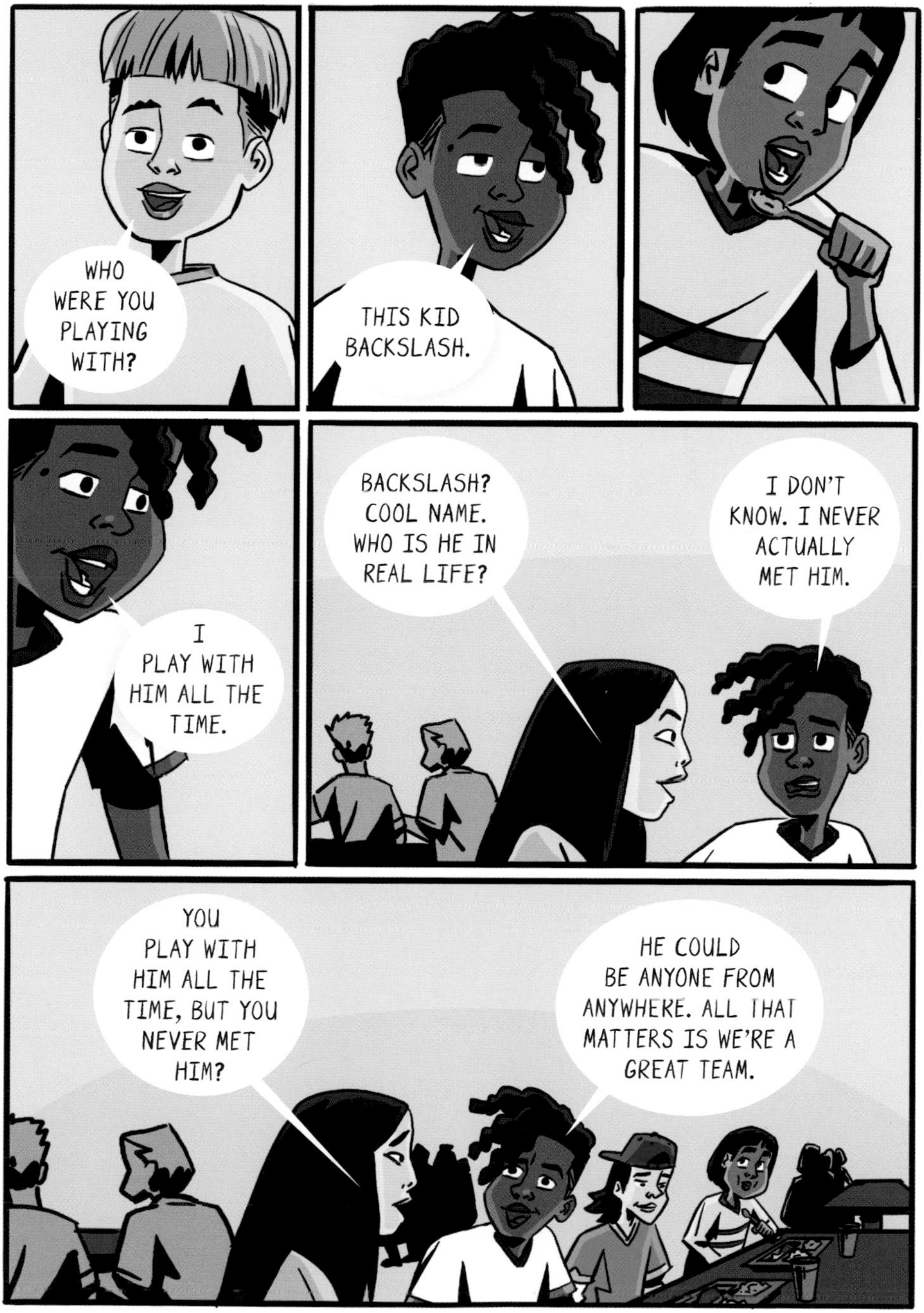
WHO WERE YOU PLAYING WITH?
THIS KID BACKSLASH.
I PLAY WITH HIM ALL THE TIME.
BACKSLASH? COOL NAME. WHO IS HE IN REAL LIFE?
I DON'T KNOW. I NEVER ACTUALLY MET HIM.
YOU PLAY WITH HIM ALL THE TIME, BUT YOU NEVER MET HIM?
HE COULD BE ANYONE FROM ANYWHERE. ALL THAT MATTERS IS WE'RE A GREAT TEAM.

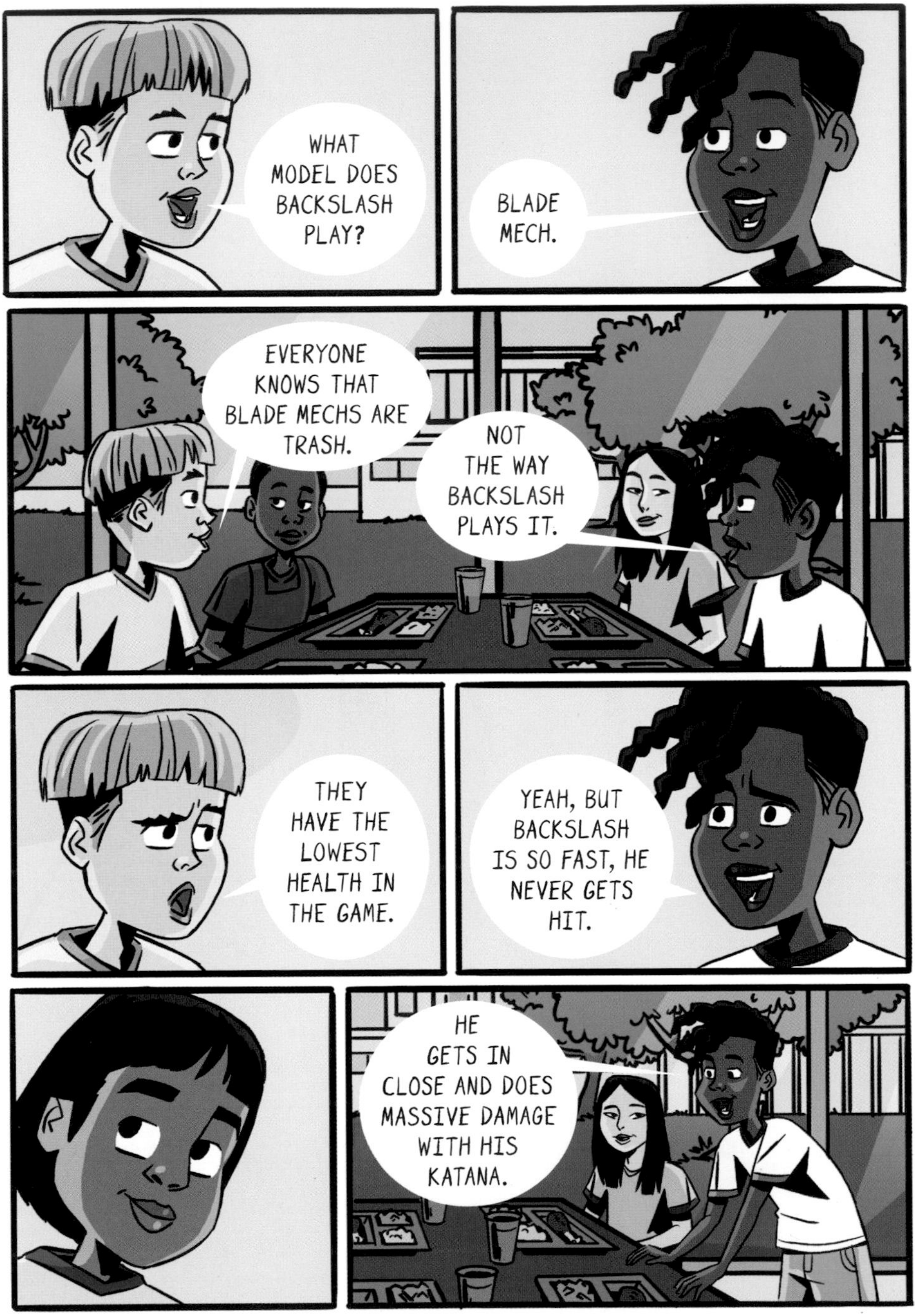
WHAT MODEL DOES BACKSLASH PLAY?
BLADE MECH.
EVERYONE KNOWS THAT BLADE MECHS ARE TRASH.
NOT THE WAY BACKSLASH PLAYS IT.
THEY HAVE THE LOWEST HEALTH IN THE GAME.
YEAH, BUT BACKSLASH IS SO FAST, HE NEVER GETS HIT.
HE GETS IN CLOSE AND DOES MASSIVE DAMAGE WITH HIS KATANA.

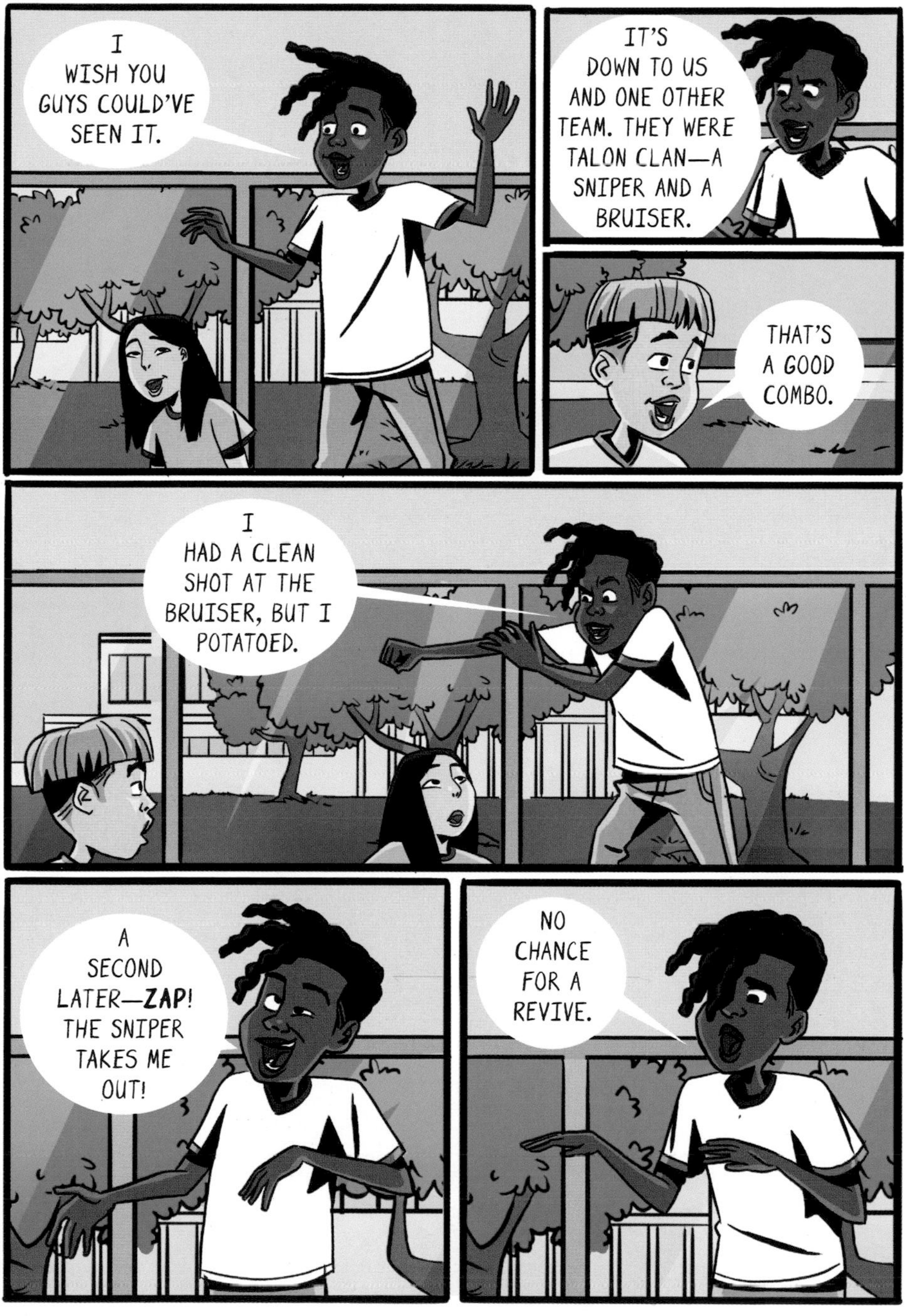
I WISH YOU GUYS COULD'VE SEEN IT.
IT'S DOWN TO US AND ONE OTHER TEAM. THEY WERE TALON CLAN—A SNIPER AND A BRUISER.
THAT'S A GOOD COMBO.
I HAD A CLEAN SHOT AT THE BRUISER, BUT I POTATOED.
A SECOND LATER—**ZAP**! THE SNIPER TAKES ME OUT!
NO CHANCE FOR A REVIVE.

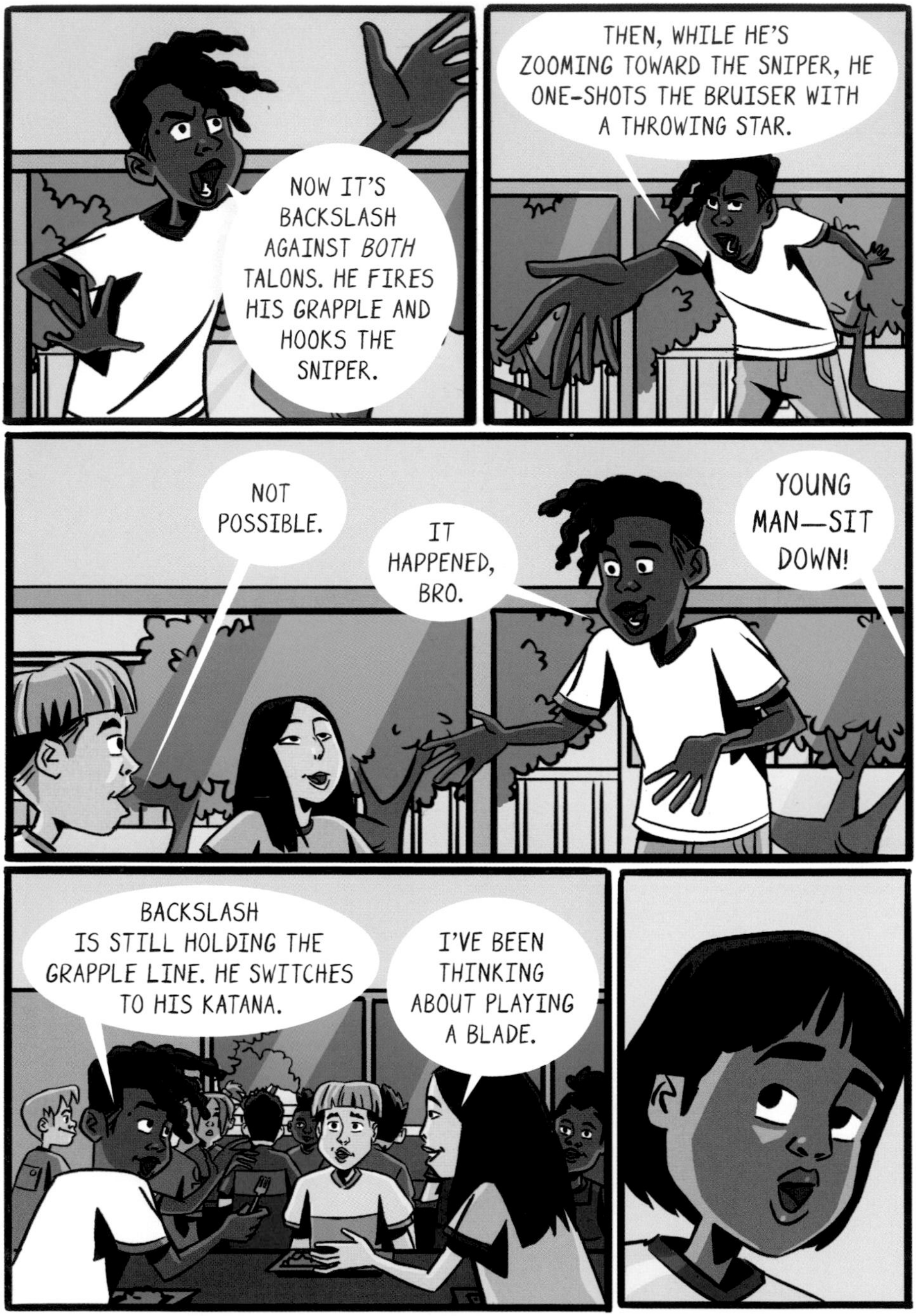
NOW IT'S BACKSLASH AGAINST *BOTH* TALONS. HE FIRES HIS GRAPPLE AND HOOKS THE SNIPER.
THEN, WHILE HE'S ZOOMING TOWARD THE SNIPER, HE ONE-SHOTS THE BRUISER WITH A THROWING STAR.
NOT POSSIBLE.
IT HAPPENED, BRO.
YOUNG MAN—SIT DOWN!
BACKSLASH IS STILL HOLDING THE GRAPPLE LINE. HE SWITCHES TO HIS KATANA.
I'VE BEEN THINKING ABOUT PLAYING A BLADE.

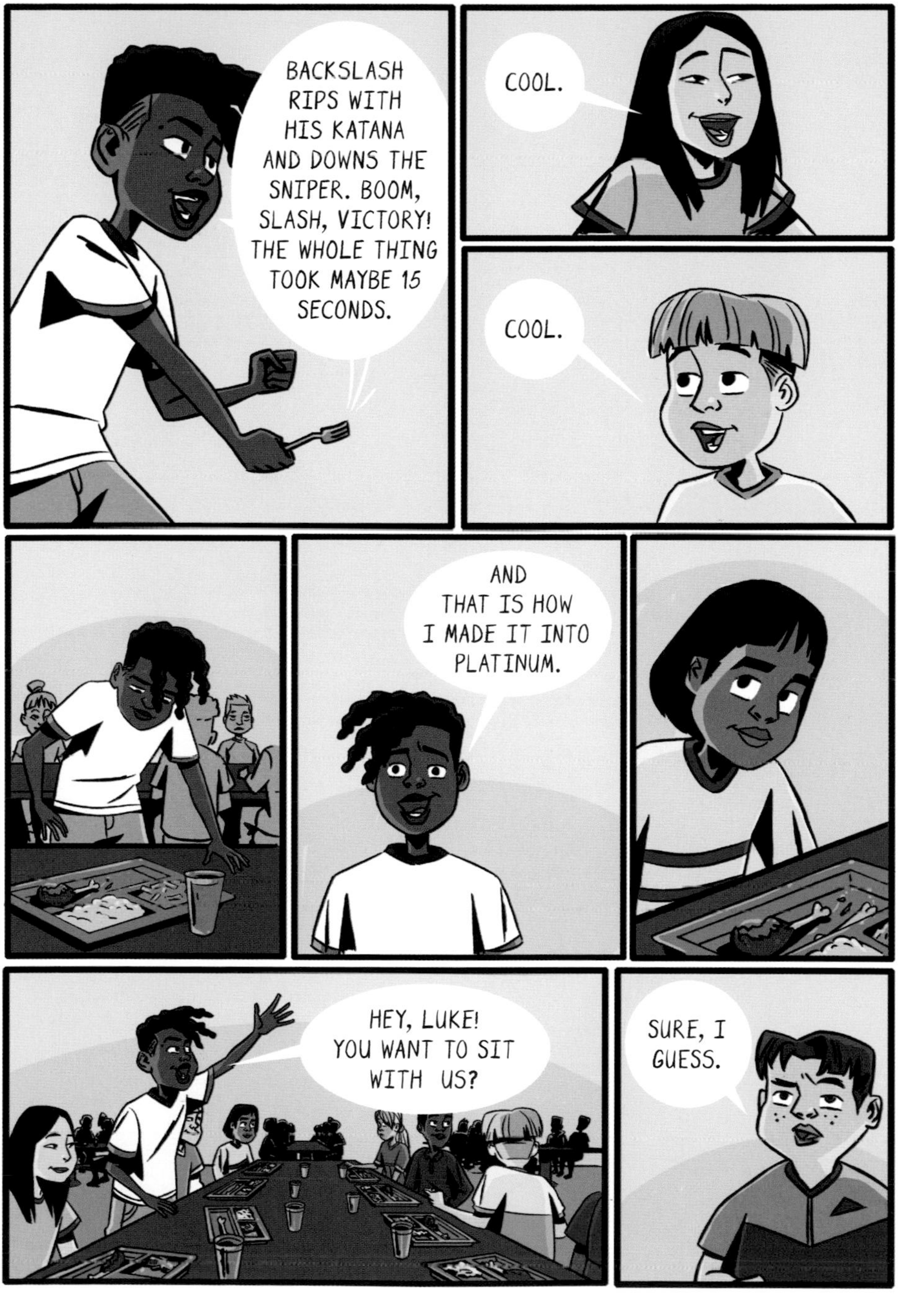
BACKSLASH RIPS WITH HIS KATANA AND DOWNS THE SNIPER. BOOM, SLASH, VICTORY! THE WHOLE THING TOOK MAYBE 15 SECONDS.
COOL.
COOL.
AND THAT IS HOW I MADE IT INTO PLATINUM.
HEY, LUKE! YOU WANT TO SIT WITH US?
SURE, I GUESS.

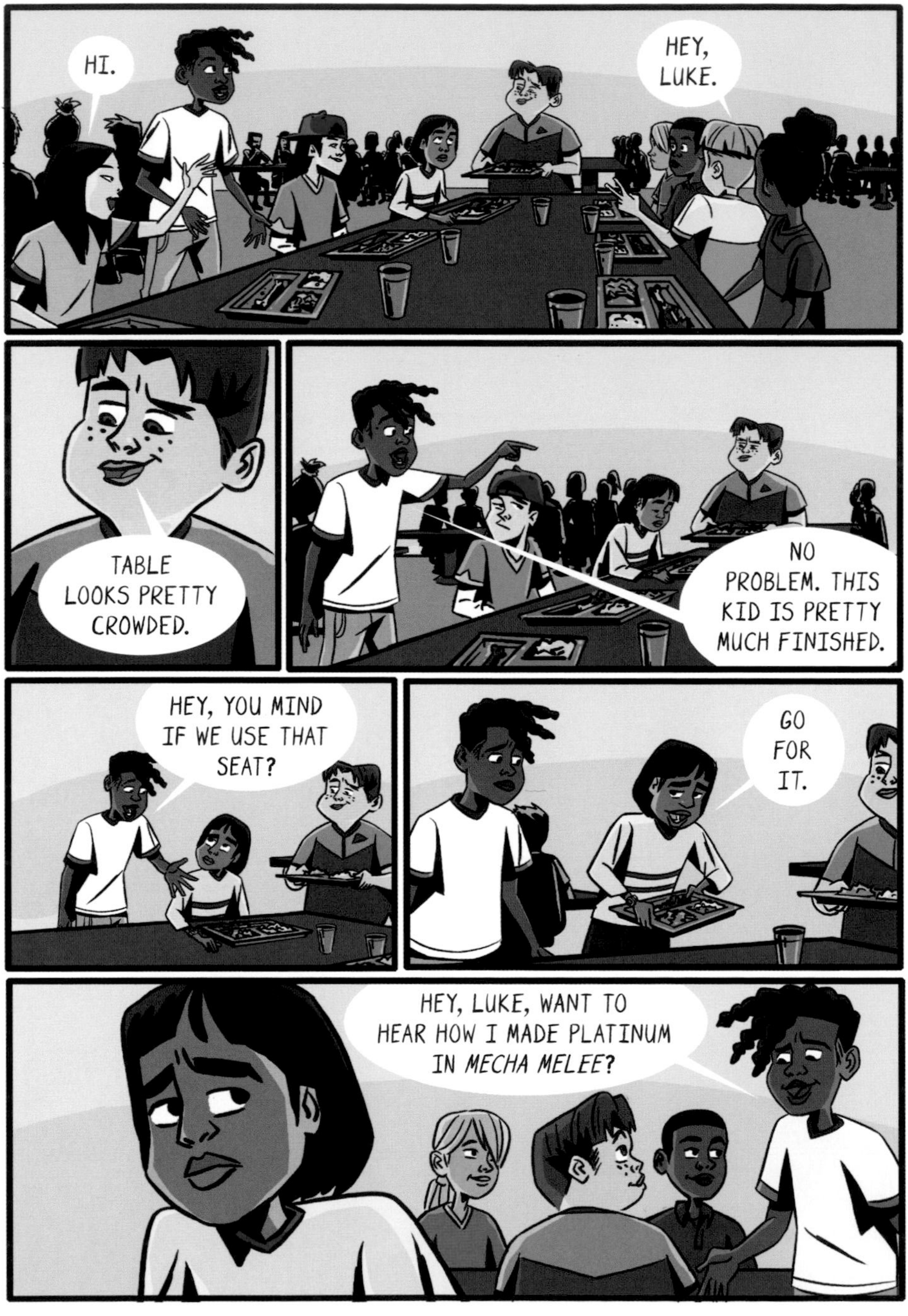
HI.
HEY, LUKE.
TABLE LOOKS PRETTY CROWDED.
NO PROBLEM. THIS KID IS PRETTY MUCH FINISHED.
HEY, YOU MIND IF WE USE THAT SEAT?
GO FOR IT.
HEY, LUKE, WANT TO HEAR HOW I MADE PLATINUM IN *MECHA MELEE*?

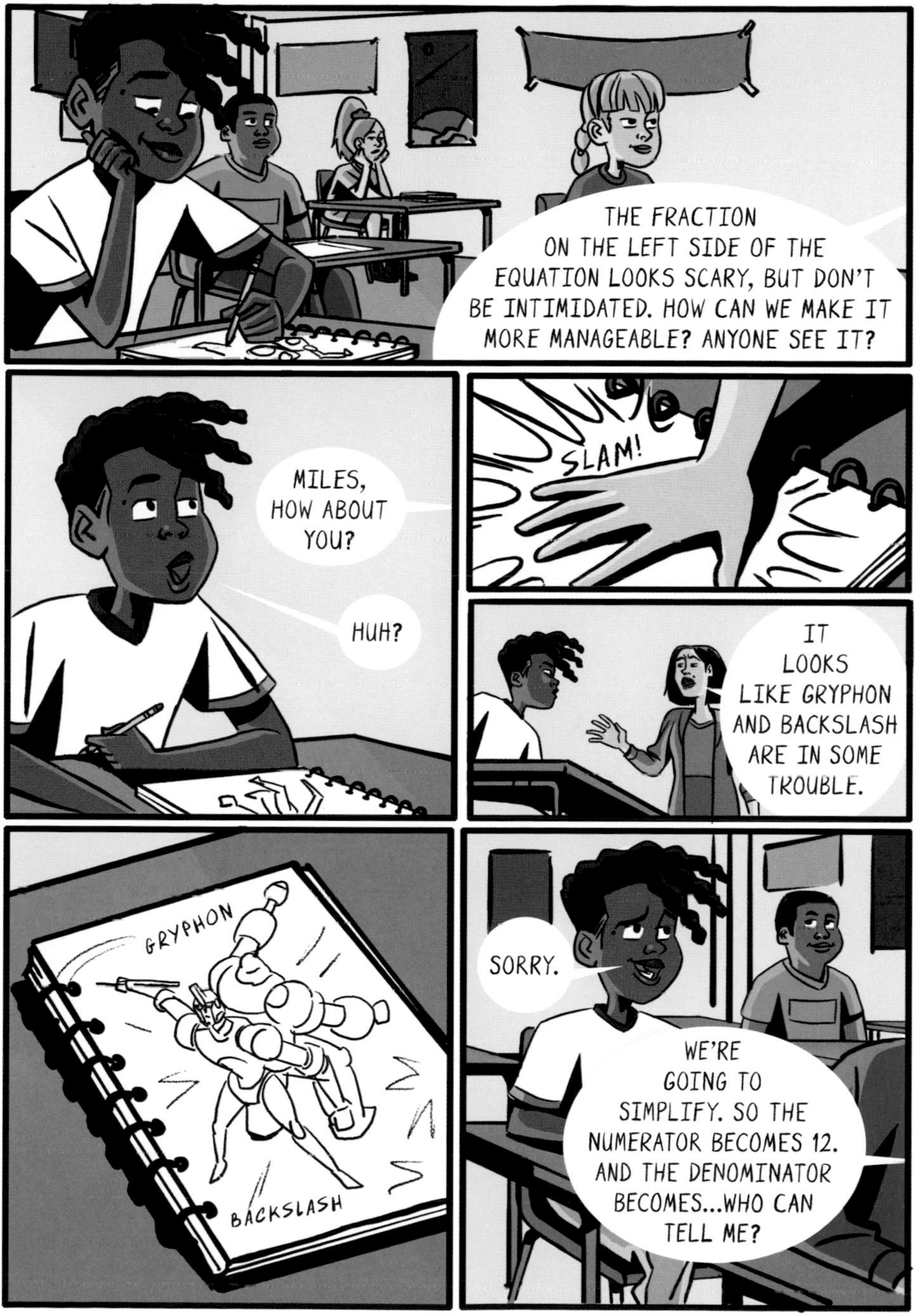
THE FRACTION ON THE LEFT SIDE OF THE EQUATION LOOKS SCARY, BUT DON'T BE INTIMIDATED. HOW CAN WE MAKE IT MORE MANAGEABLE? ANYONE SEE IT?
MILES, HOW ABOUT YOU?
HUH?
SLAM!
IT LOOKS LIKE GRYPHON AND BACKSLASH ARE IN SOME TROUBLE.
GRYPHON
BACKSLASH
SORRY.
WE'RE GOING TO SIMPLIFY. SO THE NUMERATOR BECOMES 12. AND THE DENOMINATOR BECOMES...WHO CAN TELL ME?

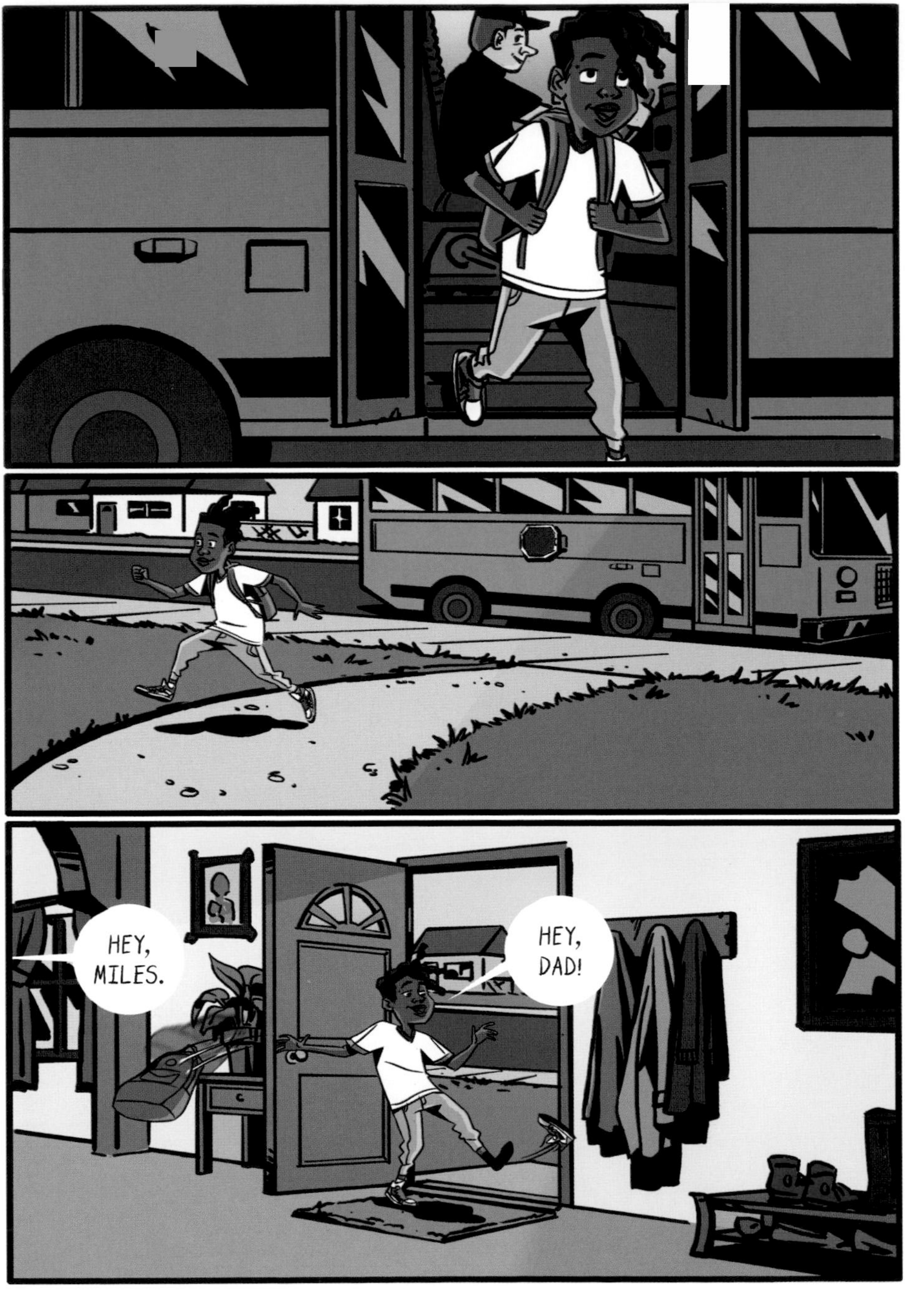
HEY, MILES.
HEY, DAD!

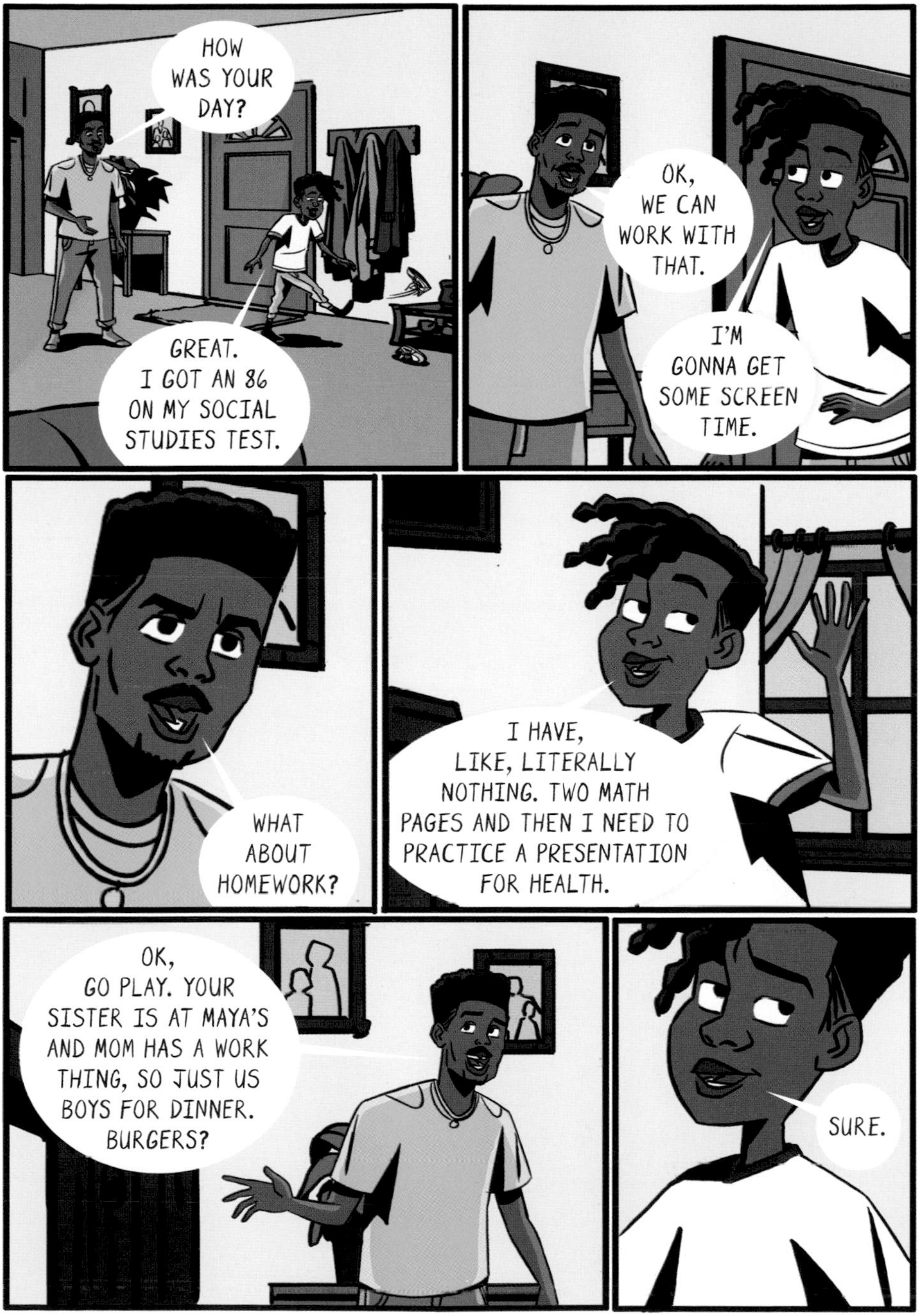
HOW WAS YOUR DAY?
GREAT. I GOT AN 86 ON MY SOCIAL STUDIES TEST.
OK, WE CAN WORK WITH THAT.
I'M GONNA GET SOME SCREEN TIME.
WHAT ABOUT HOMEWORK?
I HAVE, LIKE, LITERALLY NOTHING. TWO MATH PAGES AND THEN I NEED TO PRACTICE A PRESENTATION FOR HEALTH.
OK, GO PLAY. YOUR SISTER IS AT MAYA'S AND MOM HAS A WORK THING, SO JUST US BOYS FOR DINNER. BURGERS?
SURE.

CHAPTER 3
RAID

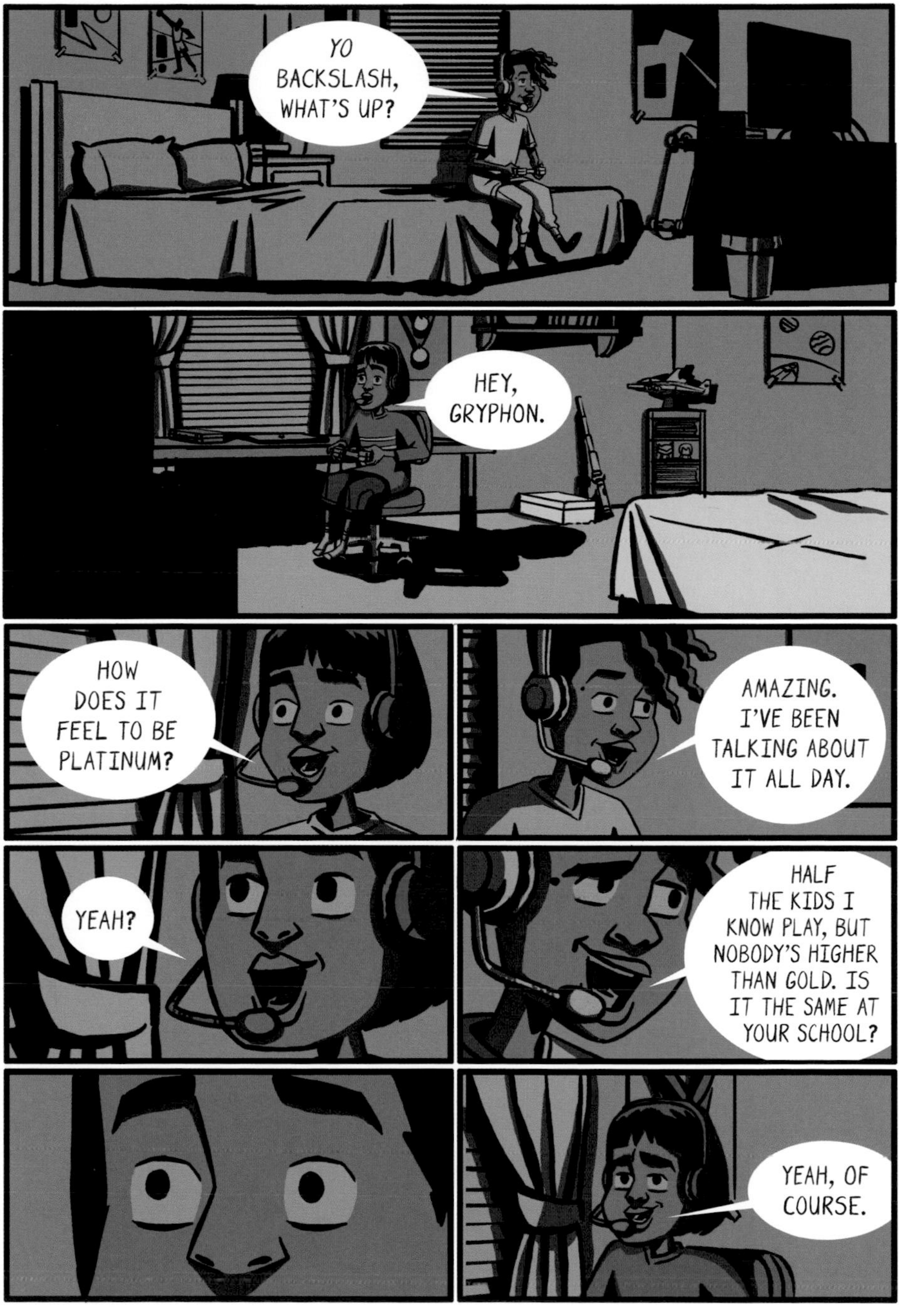
YO BACKSLASH, WHAT'S UP?
HEY, GRYPHON.
HOW DOES IT FEEL TO BE PLATINUM?
AMAZING. I'VE BEEN TALKING ABOUT IT ALL DAY.
YEAH?
HALF THE KIDS I KNOW PLAY, BUT NOBODY'S HIGHER THAN GOLD. IS IT THE SAME AT YOUR SCHOOL?
YEAH, OF COURSE.

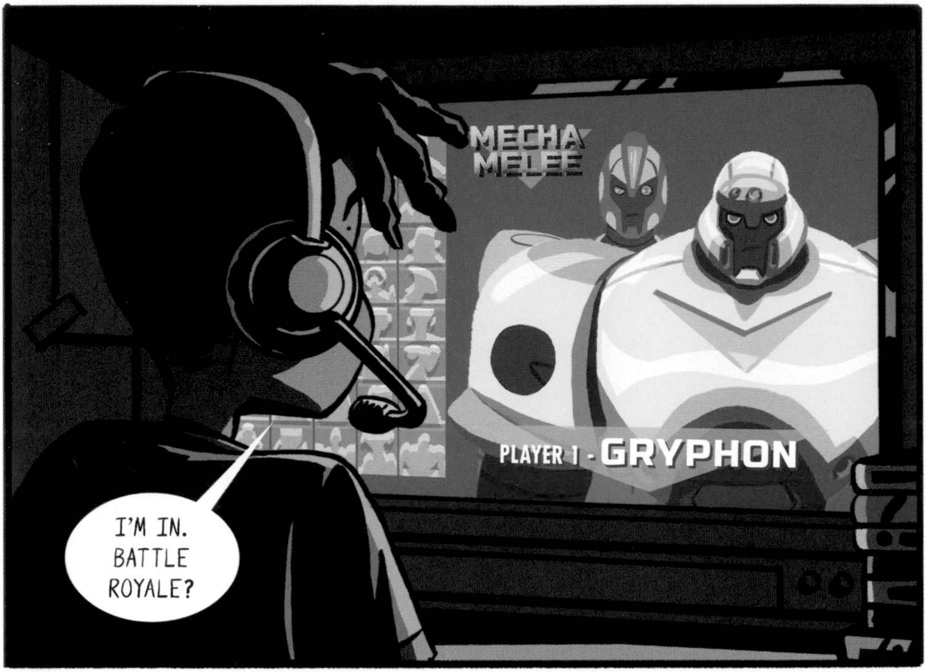
MECHA MELEE
PLAYER 1 - GRYPHON
I'M IN. BATTLE ROYALE?

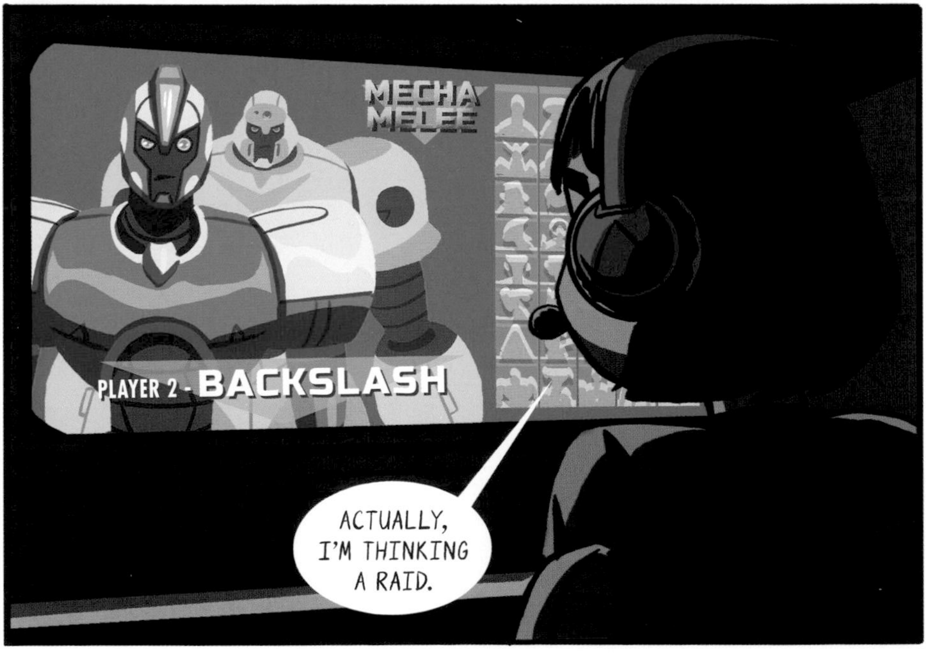
MECHA MELEE
PLAYER 2 - BACKSLASH
ACTUALLY, I'M THINKING A RAID.

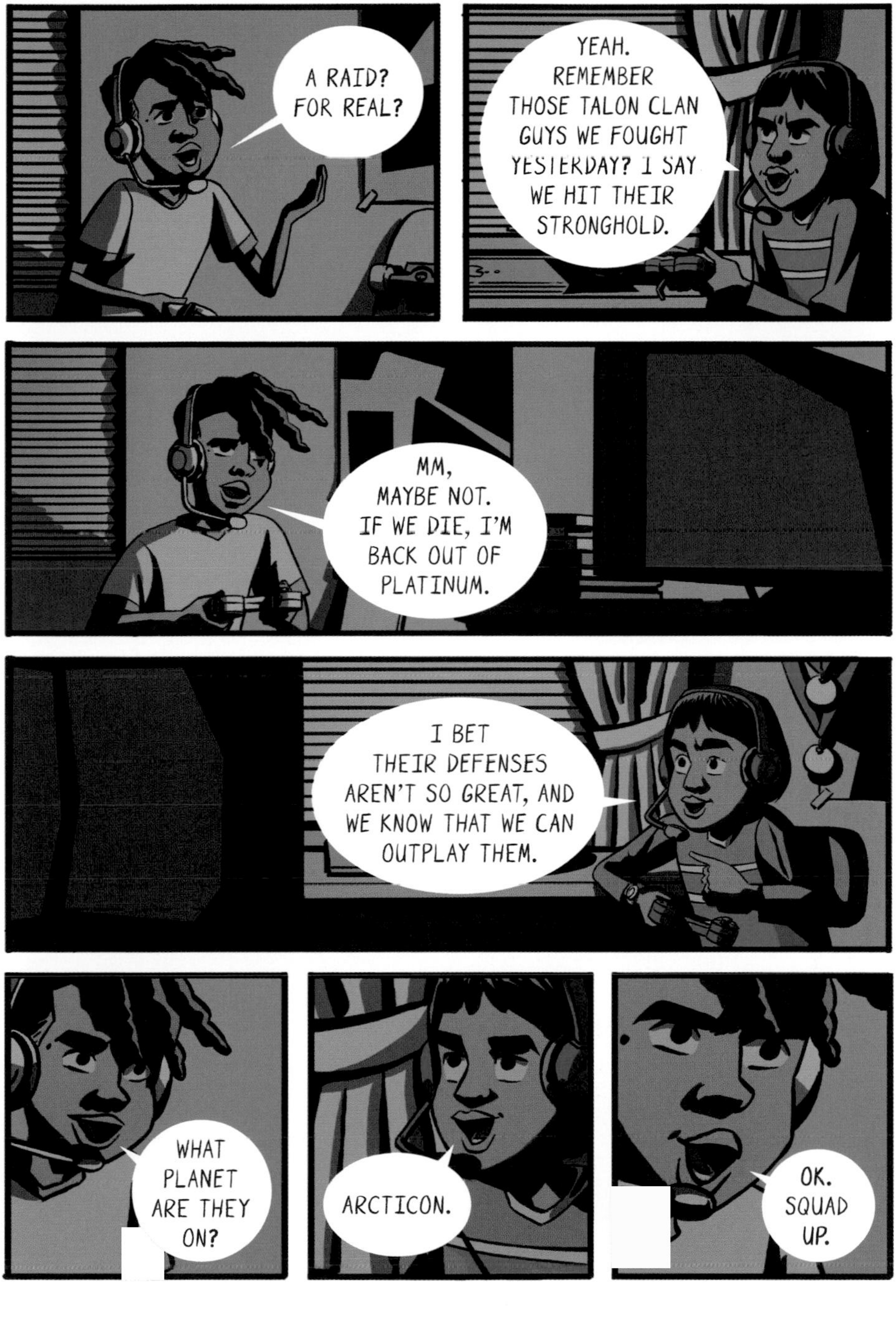
A RAID? FOR REAL?
YEAH. REMEMBER THOSE TALON CLAN GUYS WE FOUGHT YESTERDAY? I SAY WE HIT THEIR STRONGHOLD.
MM, MAYBE NOT. IF WE DIE, I'M BACK OUT OF PLATINUM.
I BET THEIR DEFENSES AREN'T SO GREAT, AND WE KNOW THAT WE CAN OUTPLAY THEM.
WHAT PLANET ARE THEY ON?
ARCTICON.
OK. SQUAD UP.

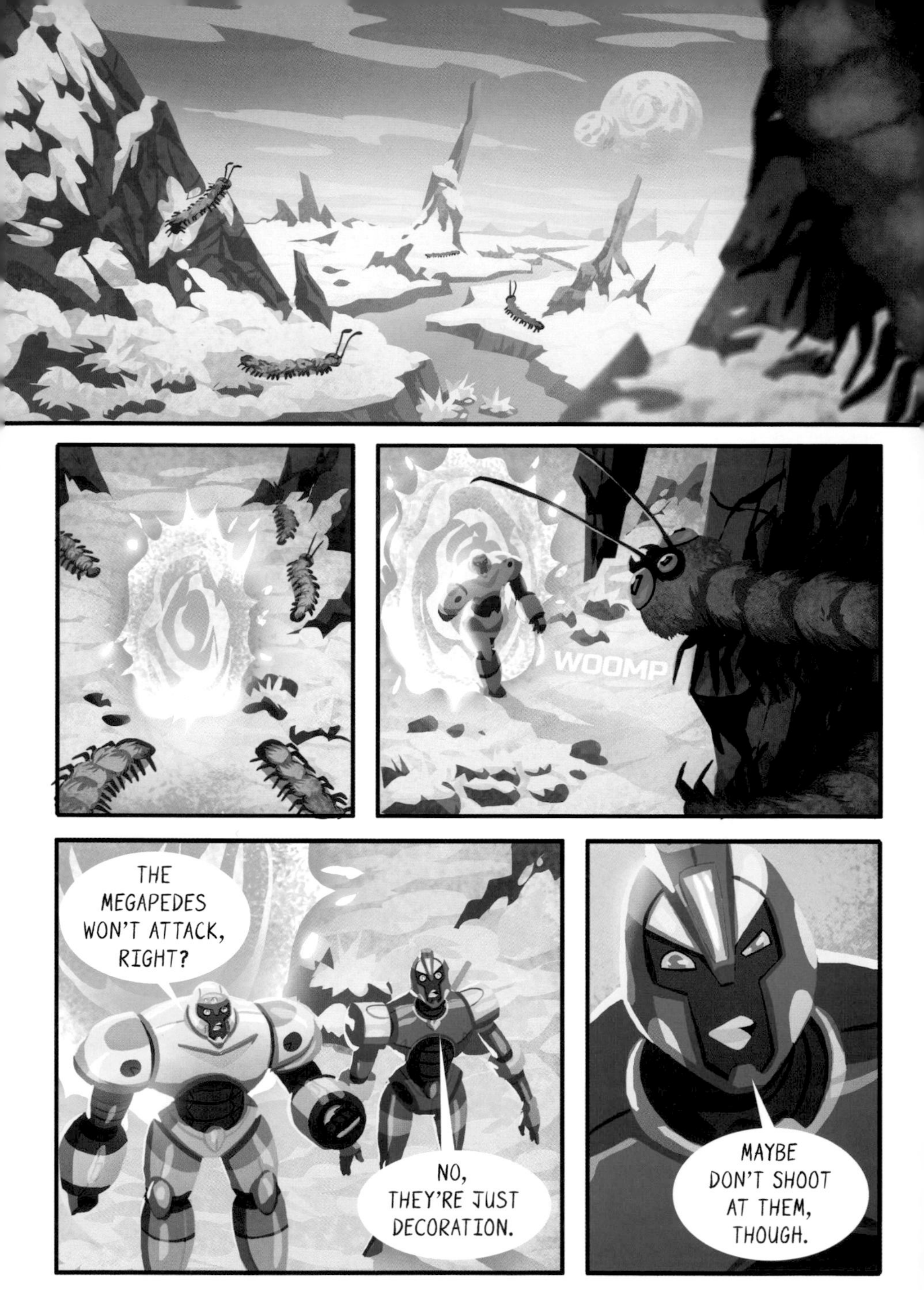
WOOMP
THE MEGAPEDES WON'T ATTACK, RIGHT?
NO, THEY'RE JUST DECORATION.
MAYBE DON'T SHOOT AT THEM, THOUGH.

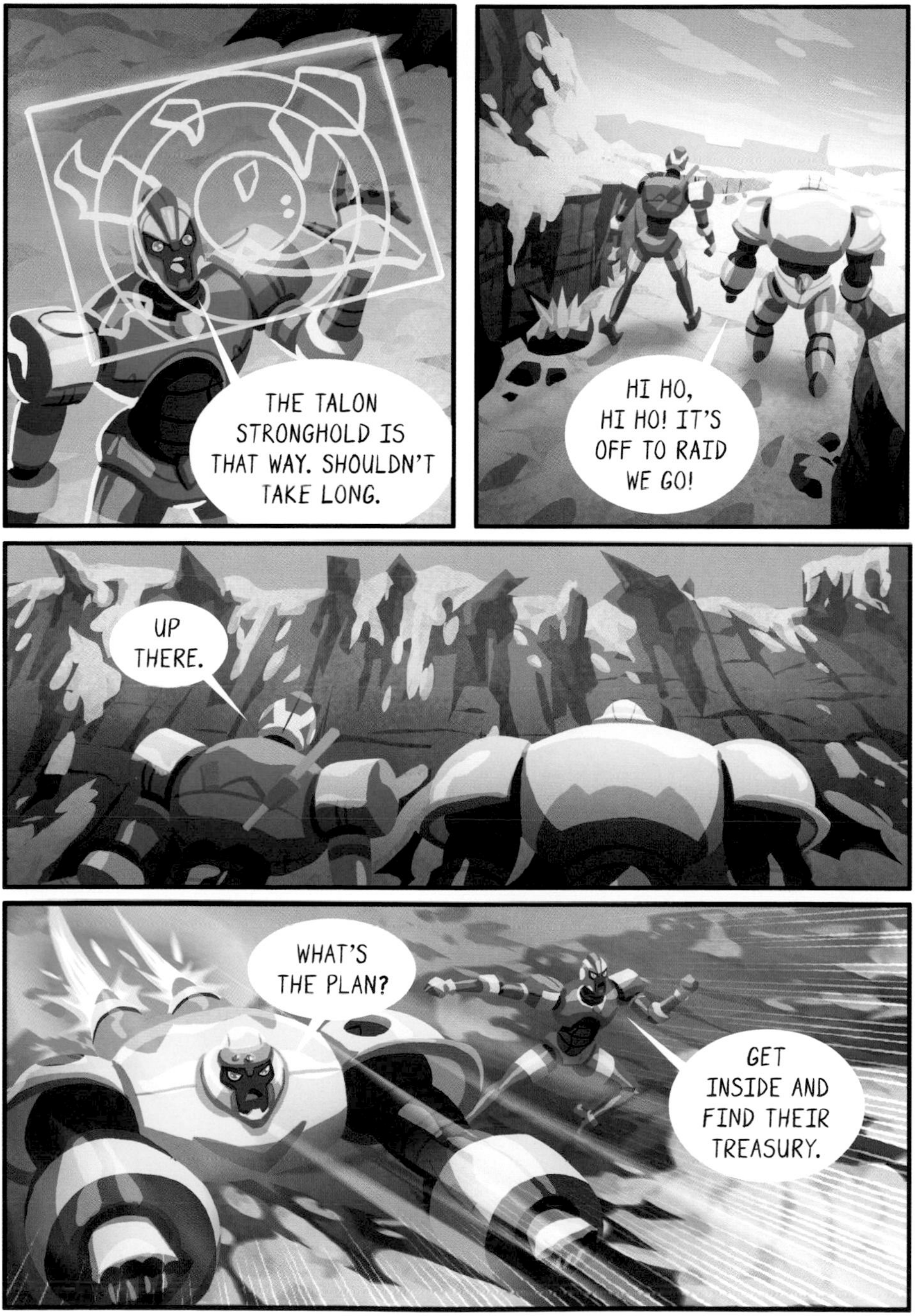
THE TALON STRONGHOLD IS THAT WAY. SHOULDN'T TAKE LONG.
HI HO, HI HO! IT'S OFF TO RAID WE GO!
UP THERE.
WHAT'S THE PLAN?
GET INSIDE AND FIND THEIR TREASURY.

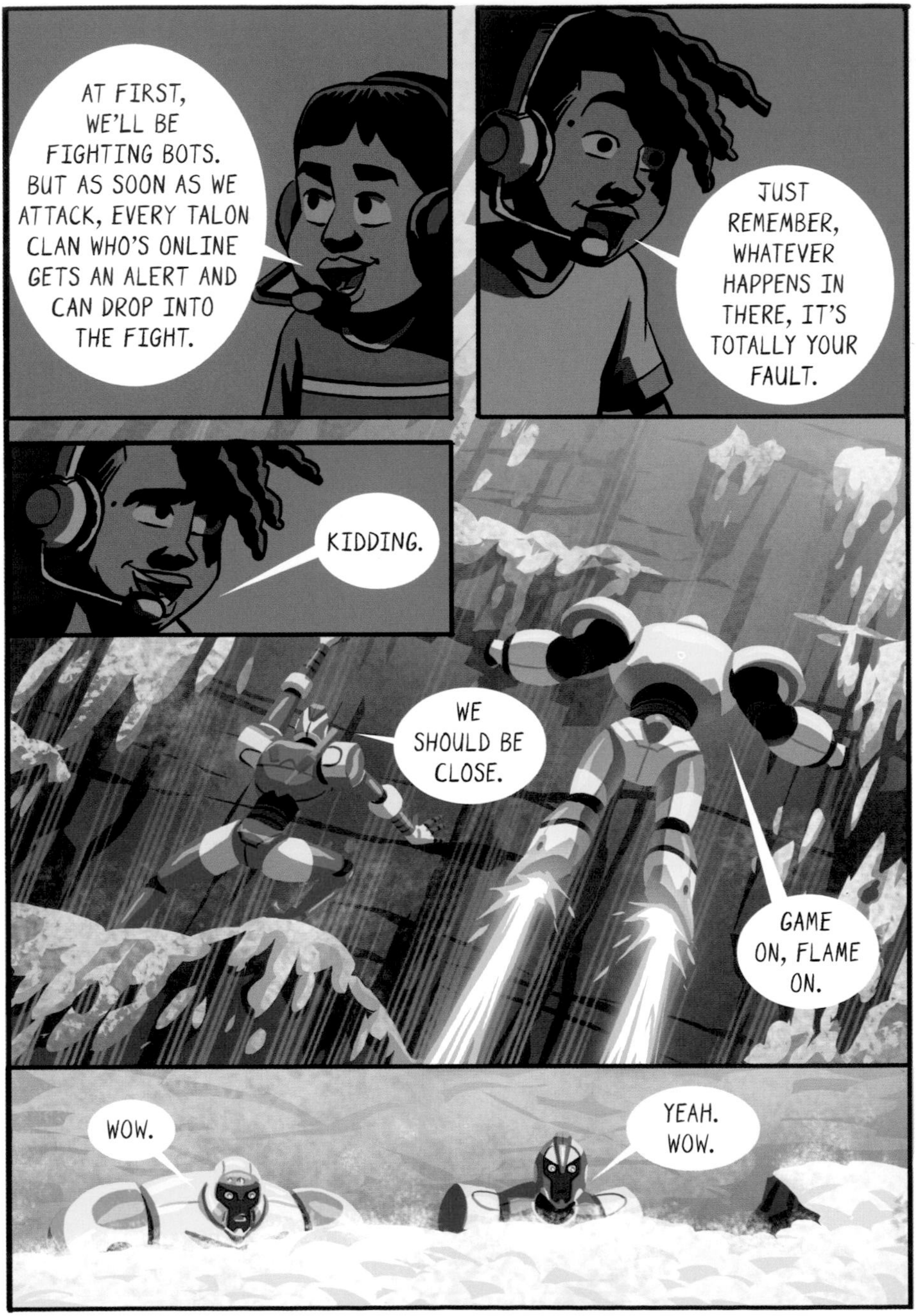
AT FIRST, WE'LL BE FIGHTING BOTS. BUT AS SOON AS WE ATTACK, EVERY TALON CLAN WHO'S ONLINE GETS AN ALERT AND CAN DROP INTO THE FIGHT.
JUST REMEMBER, WHATEVER HAPPENS IN THERE, IT'S TOTALLY YOUR FAULT.
KIDDING.
WE SHOULD BE CLOSE.
GAME ON, FLAME ON.
WOW.
YEAH. WOW.

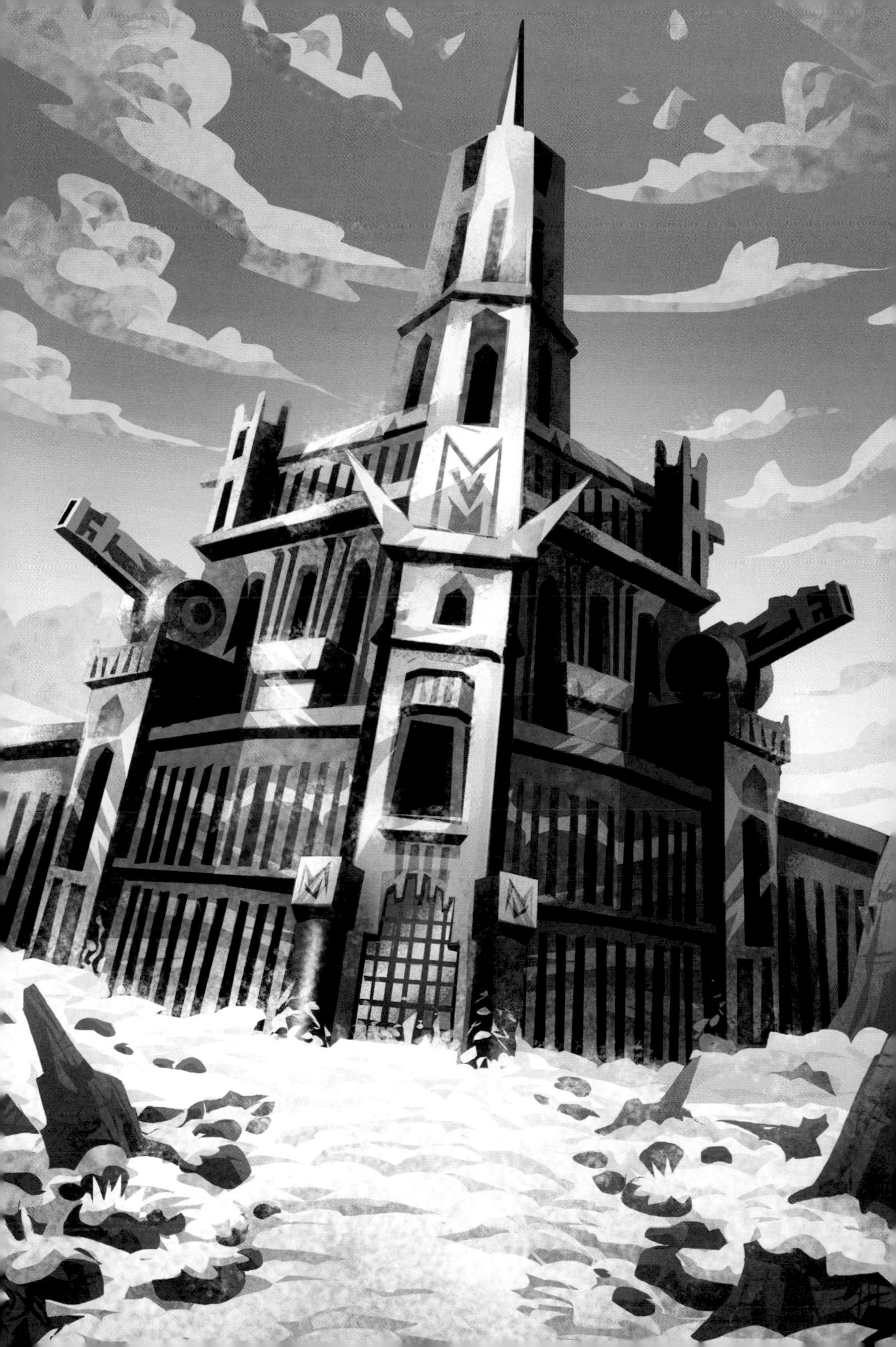

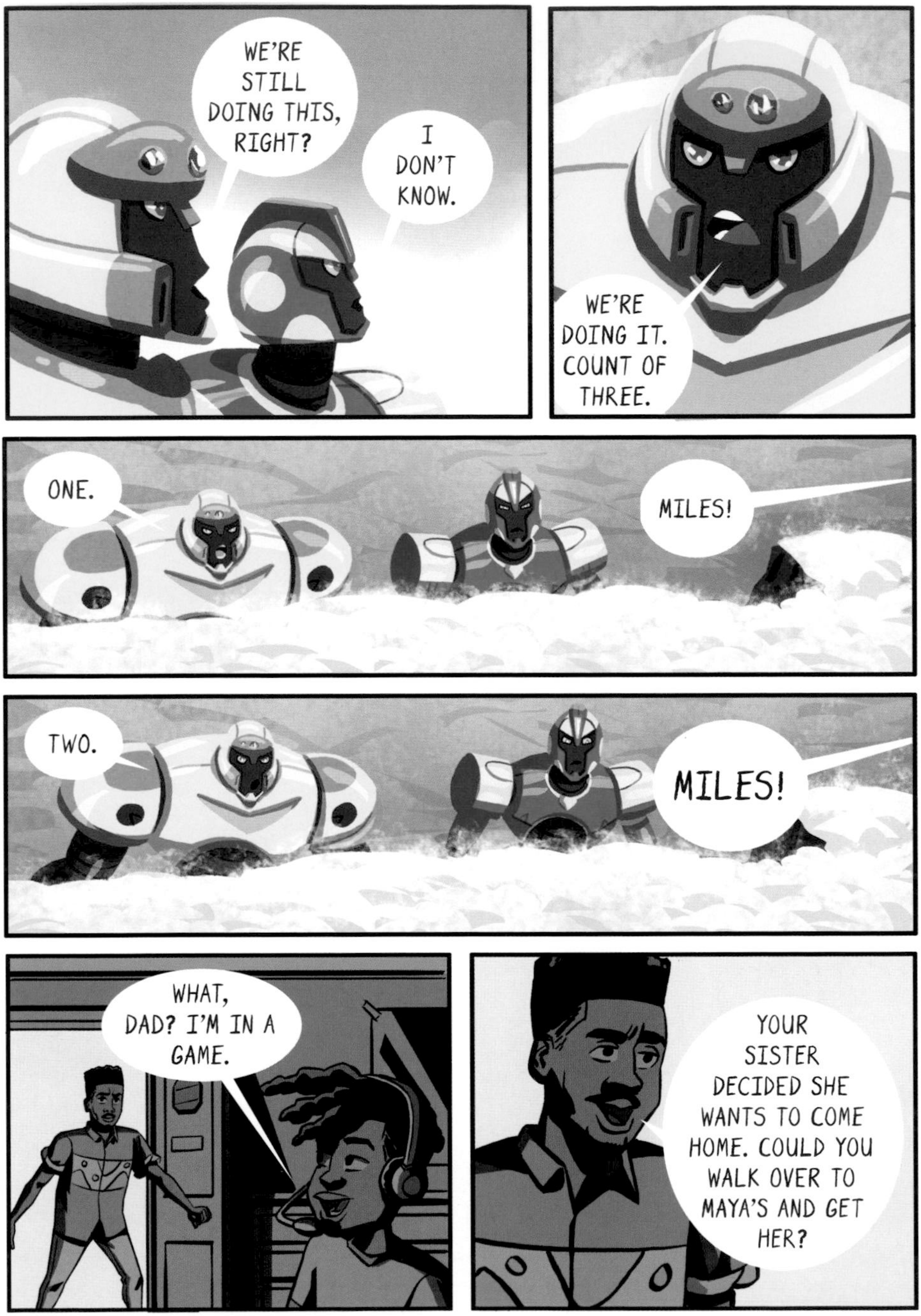
WE'RE STILL DOING THIS, RIGHT?
I DON'T KNOW.
WE'RE DOING IT. COUNT OF THREE.
ONE.
MILES!
TWO.
MILES!
WHAT, DAD? I'M IN A GAME.
YOUR SISTER DECIDED SHE WANTS TO COME HOME. COULD YOU WALK OVER TO MAYA'S AND GET HER?

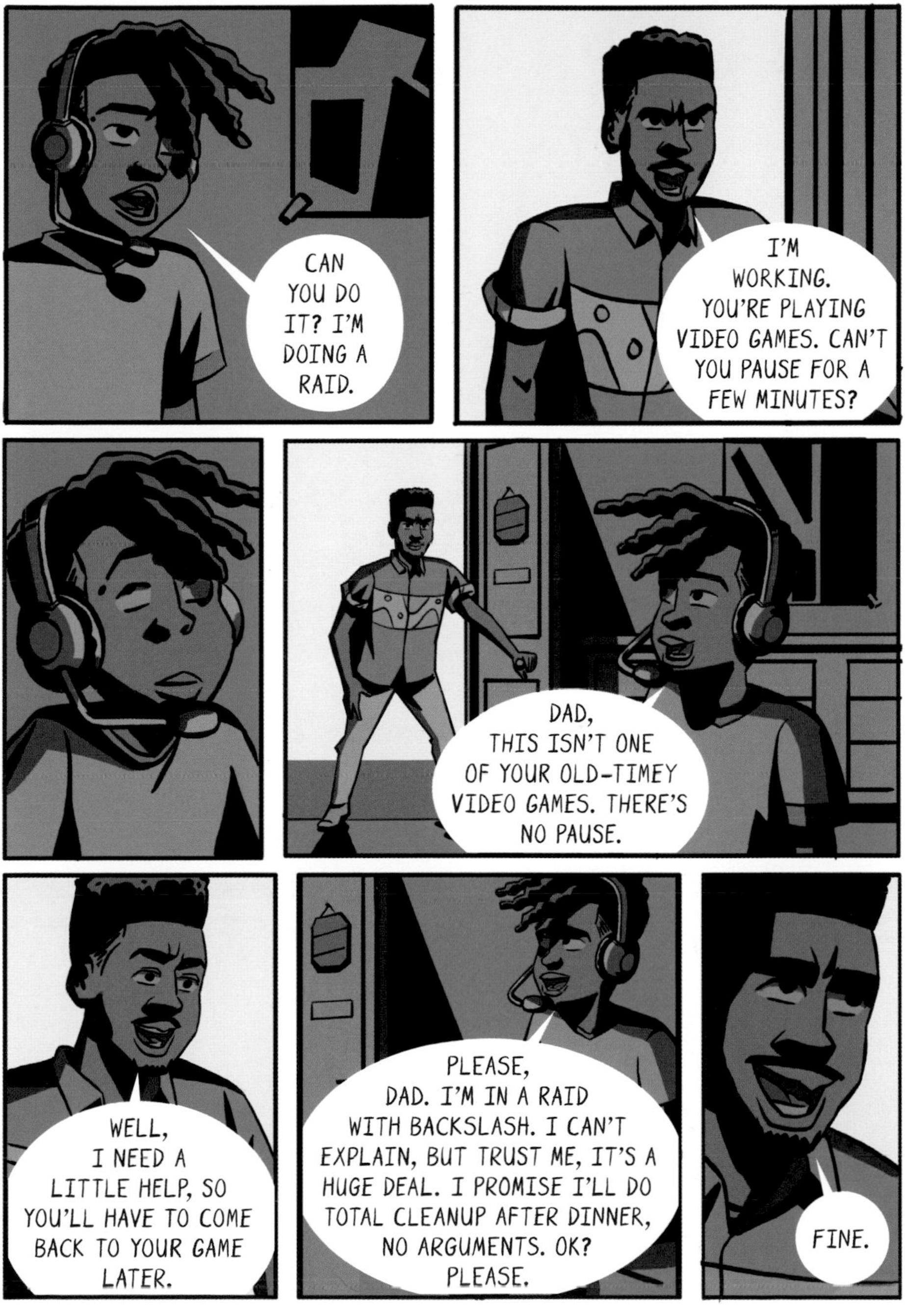
CAN YOU DO IT? I'M DOING A RAID.
I'M WORKING. YOU'RE PLAYING VIDEO GAMES. CAN'T YOU PAUSE FOR A FEW MINUTES?
DAD, THIS ISN'T ONE OF YOUR OLD-TIMEY VIDEO GAMES. THERE'S NO PAUSE.
WELL, I NEED A LITTLE HELP, SO YOU'LL HAVE TO COME BACK TO YOUR GAME LATER.
PLEASE, DAD. I'M IN A RAID WITH BACKSLASH. I CAN'T EXPLAIN, BUT TRUST ME, IT'S A HUGE DEAL. I PROMISE I'LL DO TOTAL CLEANUP AFTER DINNER, NO ARGUMENTS. OK? PLEASE.
FINE.

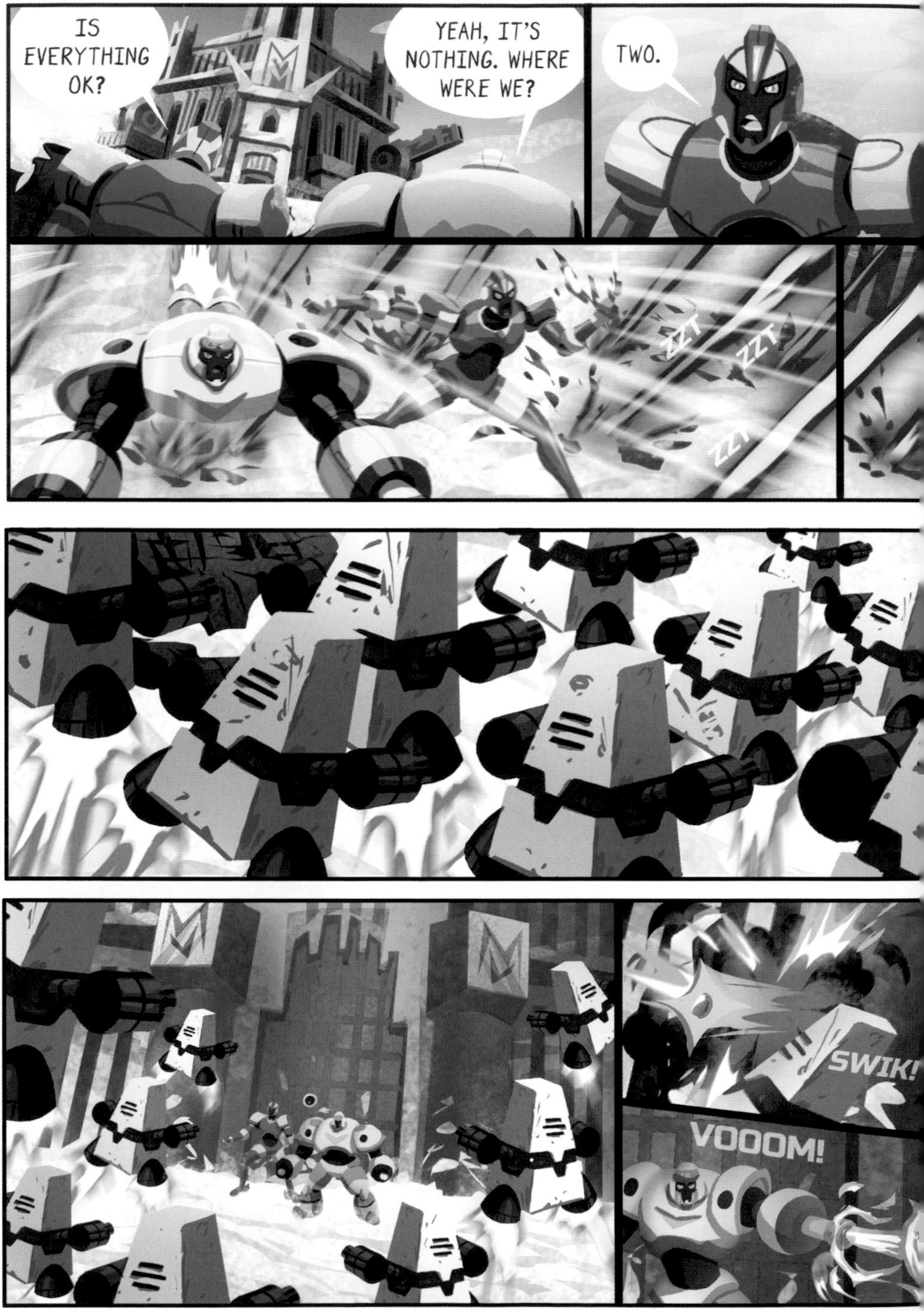
IS EVERYTHING OK?
YEAH, IT'S NOTHING. WHERE WERE WE?
TWO.
ZZT
ZZT
ZZT
SWIK!
VOOOM!

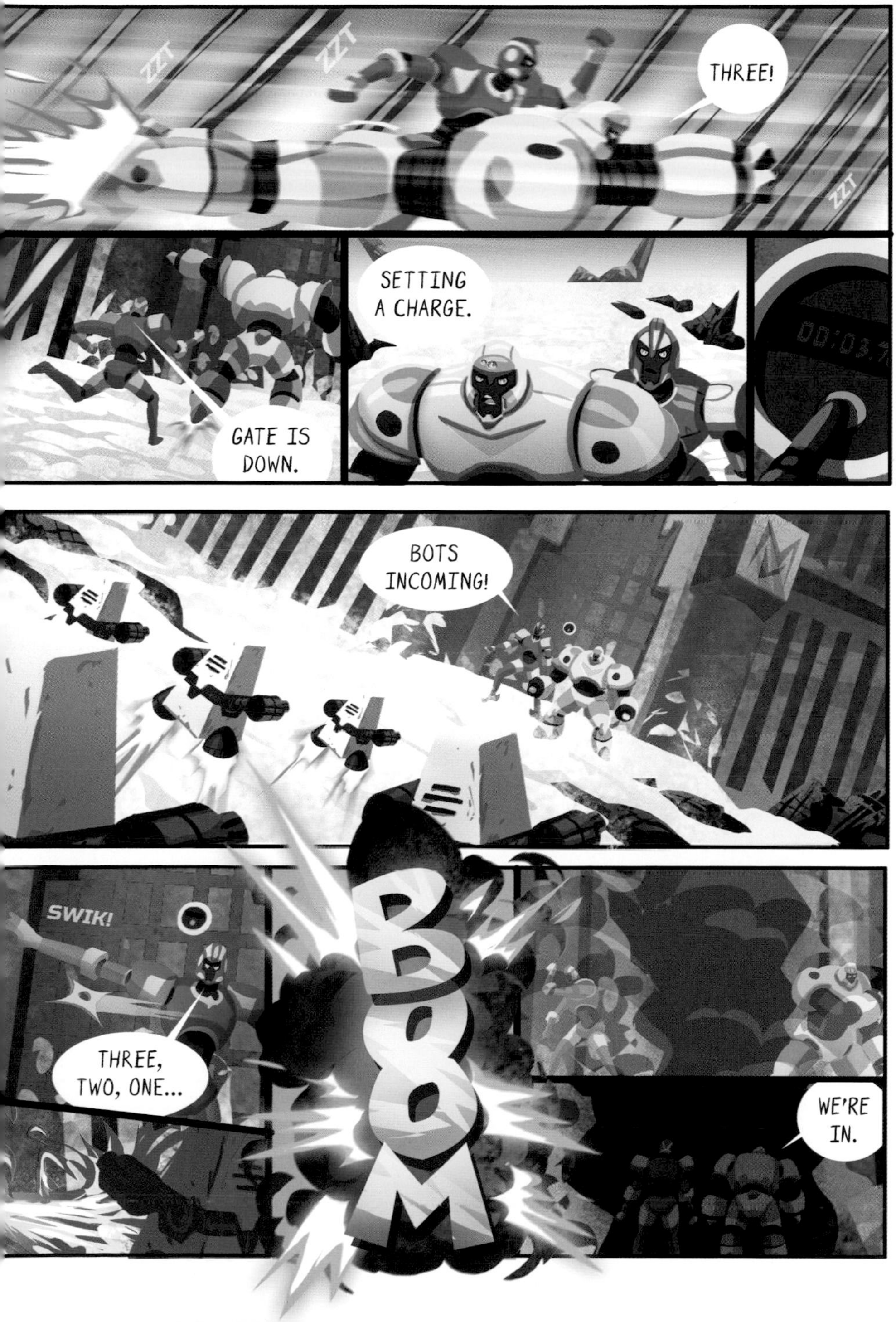
ZZT
ZZT
THREE!
ZZT
GATE IS DOWN.
SETTING A CHARGE.
BOTS INCOMING!
SWIK!
THREE, TWO, ONE...
BOOM
WE'RE IN.

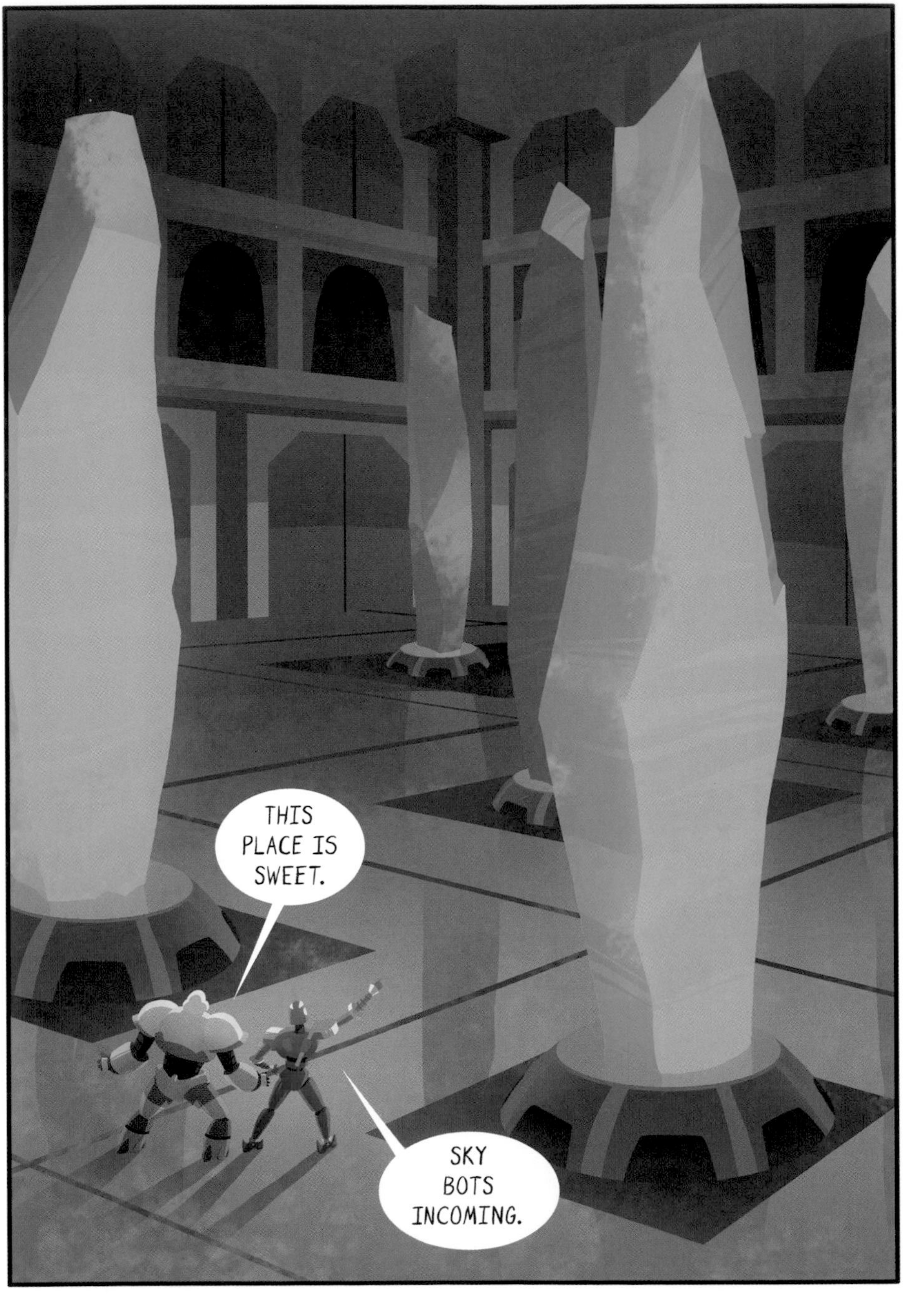
THIS PLACE IS SWEET.
SKY BOTS INCOMING.

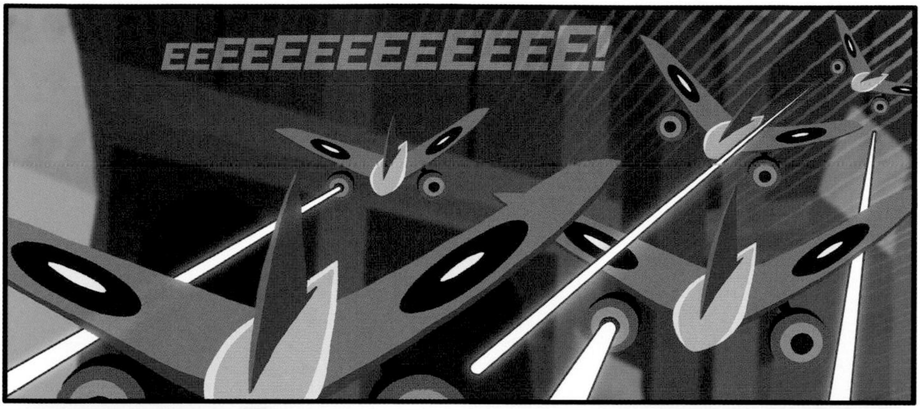
EEEEEEEEEEEEEE!

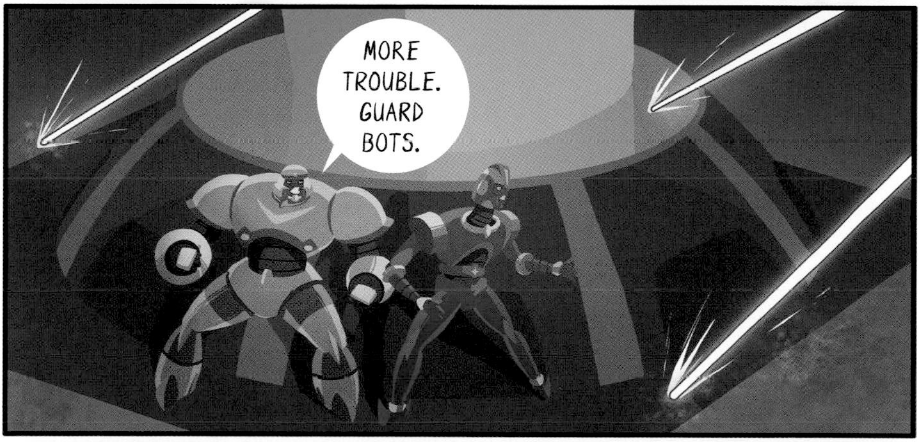
MORE TROUBLE. GUARD BOTS.

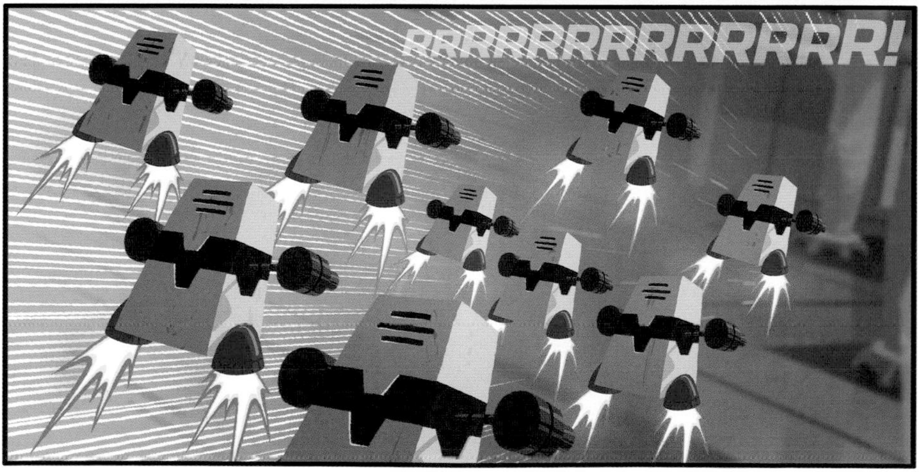
RRRRRRRRRRRRRR!

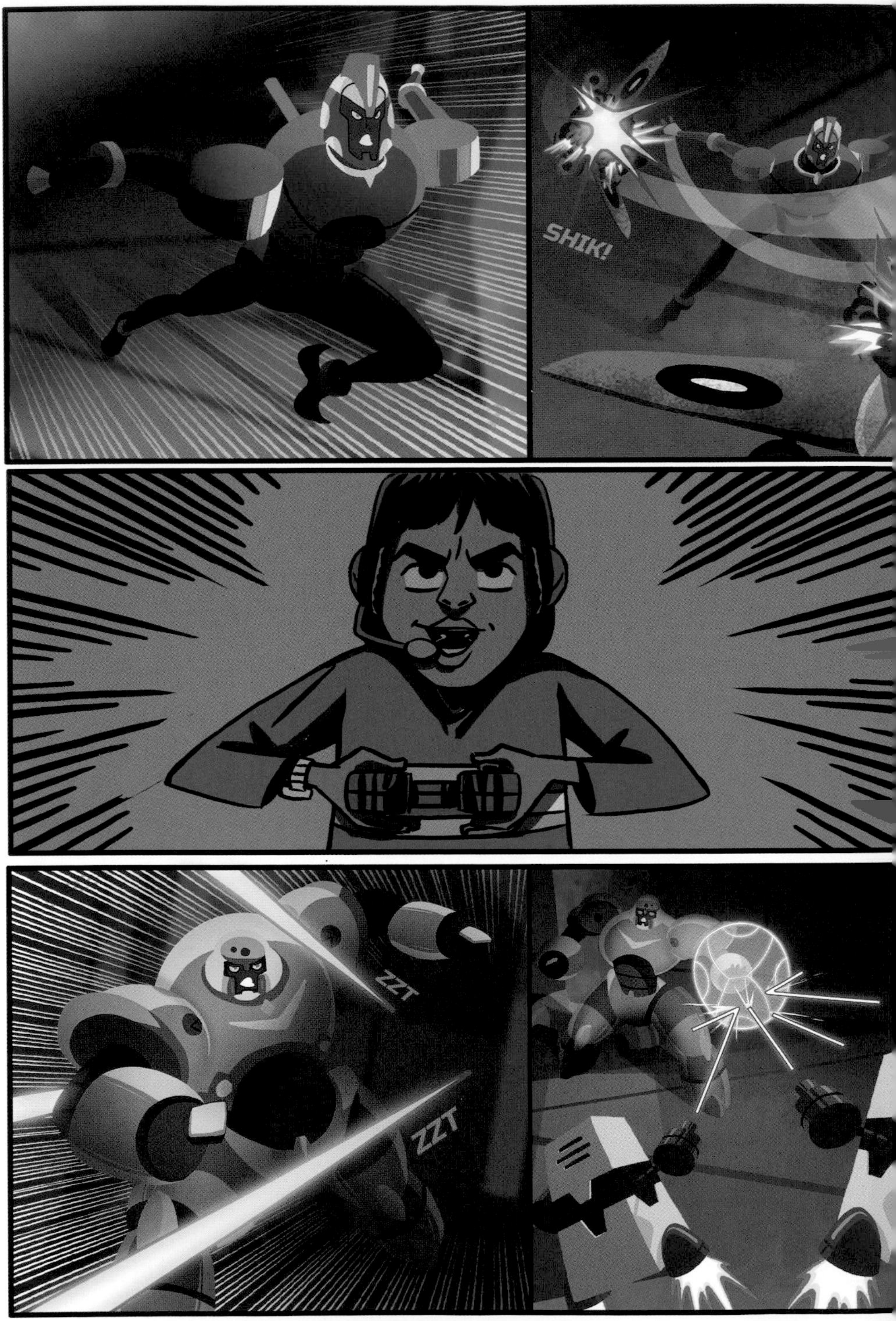
SHIK!
ZZT
ZZT

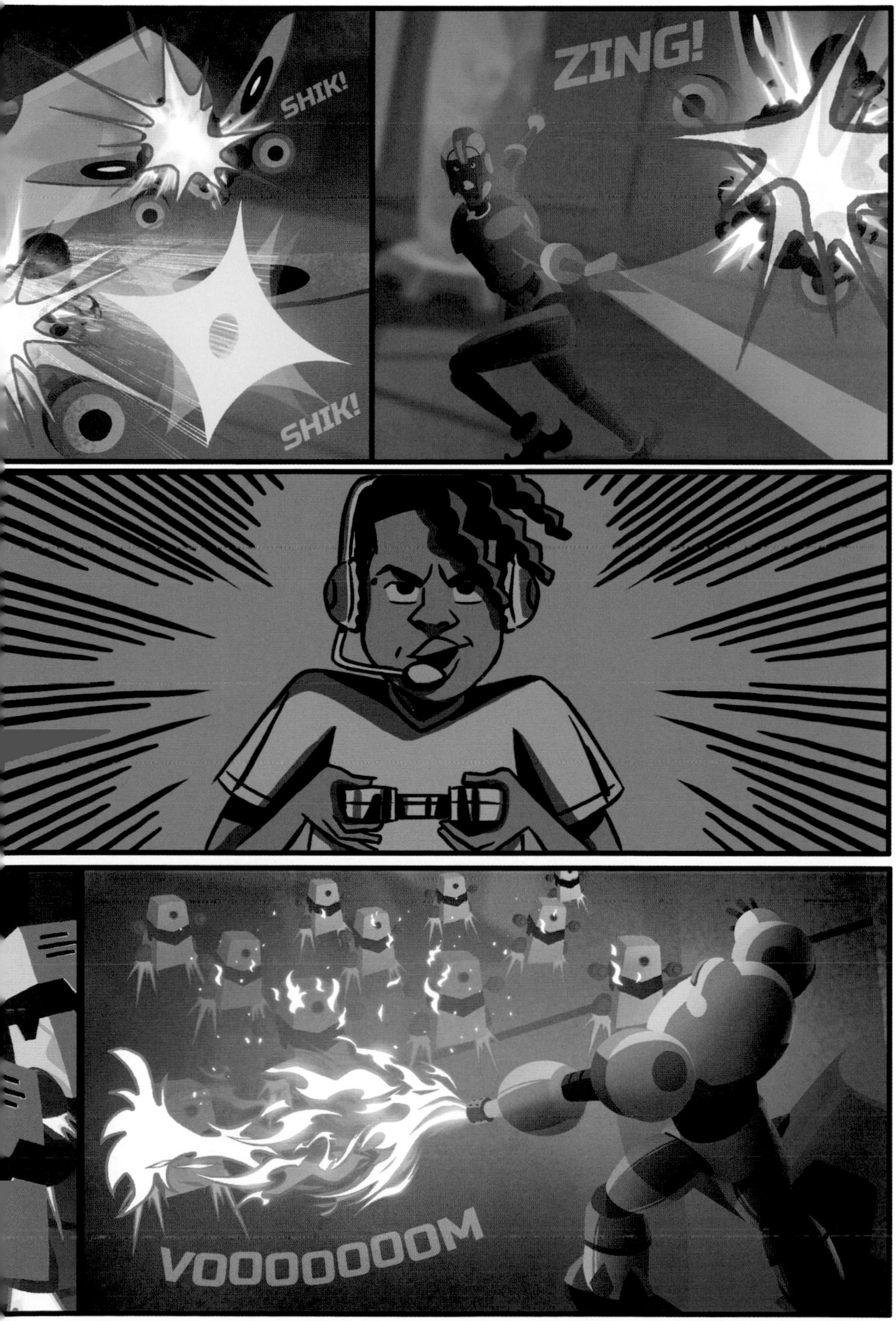
SHIK!
SHIK!
ZING!
VOOOOOOOM

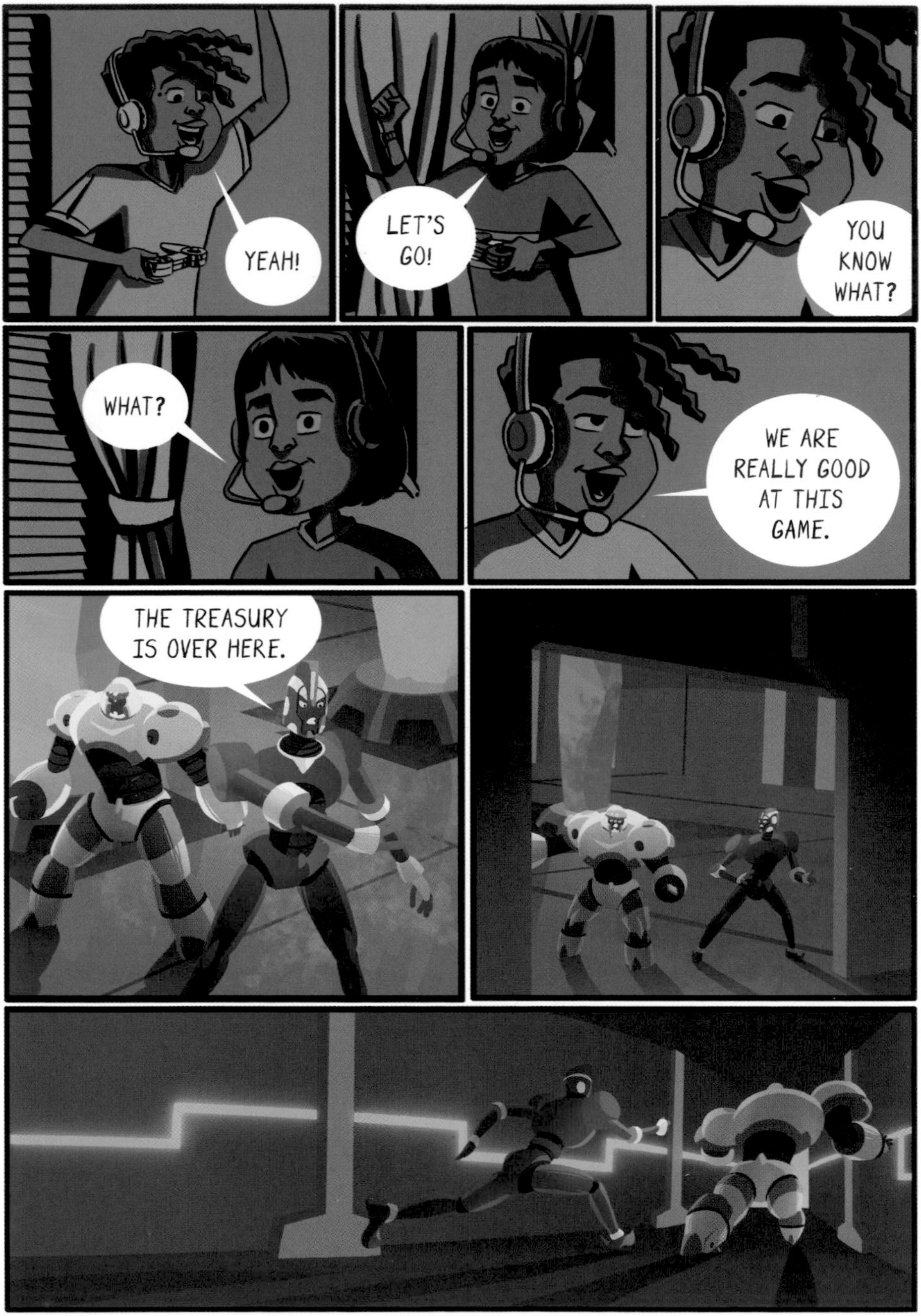
YEAH!
LET'S GO!
YOU KNOW WHAT?
WHAT?
WE ARE REALLY GOOD AT THIS GAME.
THE TREASURY IS OVER HERE.

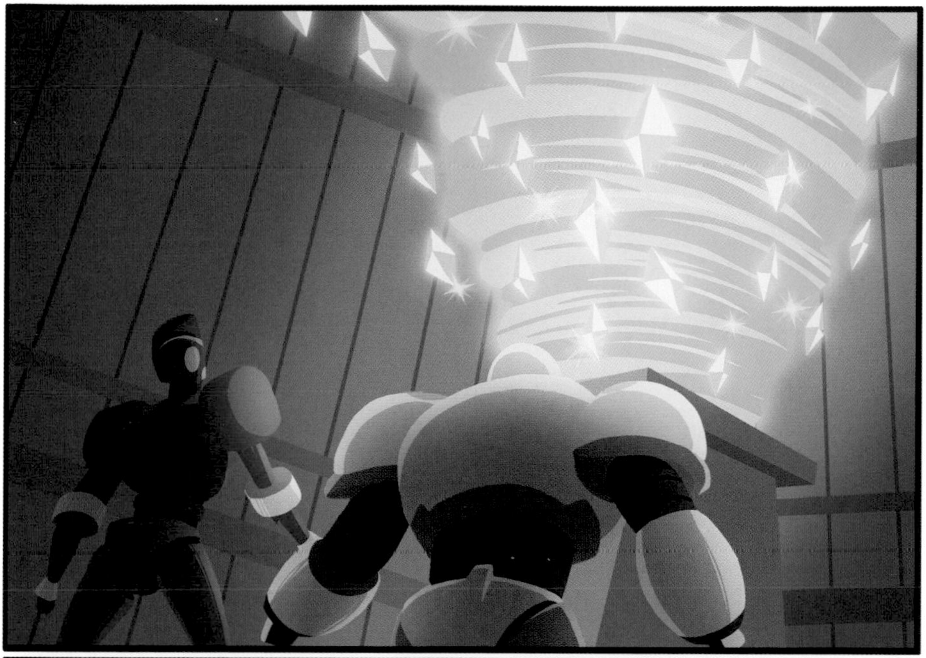

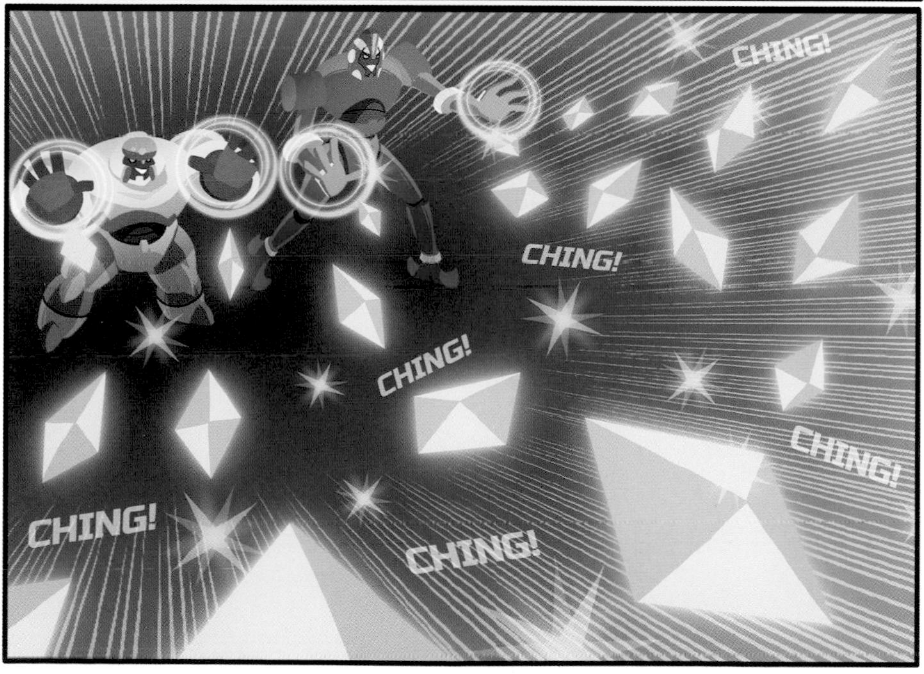
CHING!
CHING!
CHING!
CHING!
CHING!
CHING!

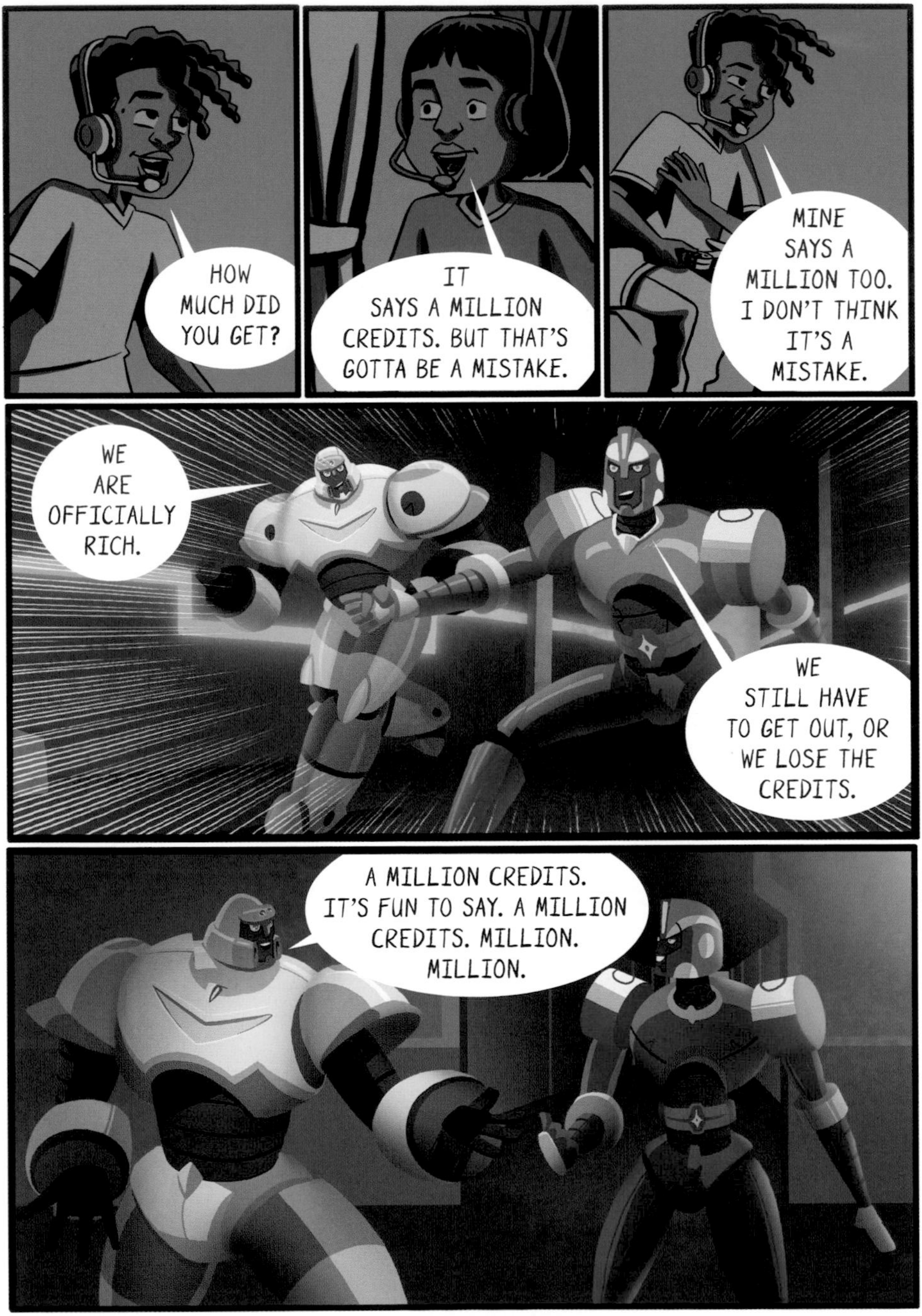
HOW MUCH DID YOU GET?
IT SAYS A MILLION CREDITS. BUT THAT'S GOTTA BE A MISTAKE.
MINE SAYS A MILLION TOO. I DON'T THINK IT'S A MISTAKE.
WE ARE OFFICIALLY RICH.
WE STILL HAVE TO GET OUT, OR WE LOSE THE CREDITS.
A MILLION CREDITS. IT'S FUN TO SAY. A MILLION CREDITS. MILLION. MILLION.

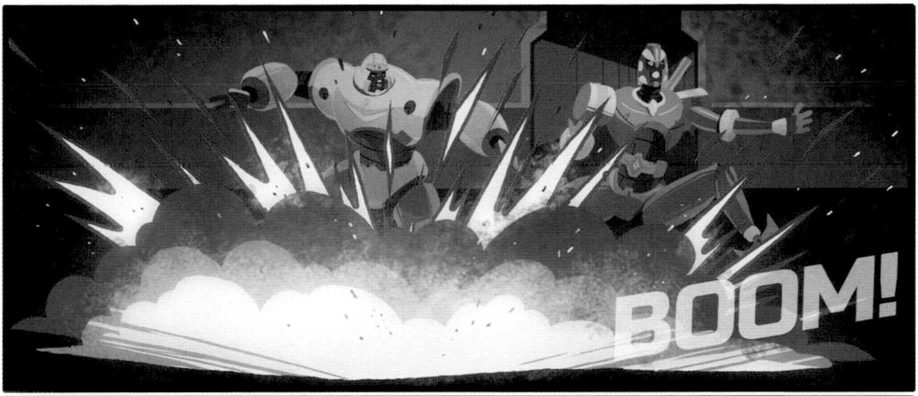
BOOM!

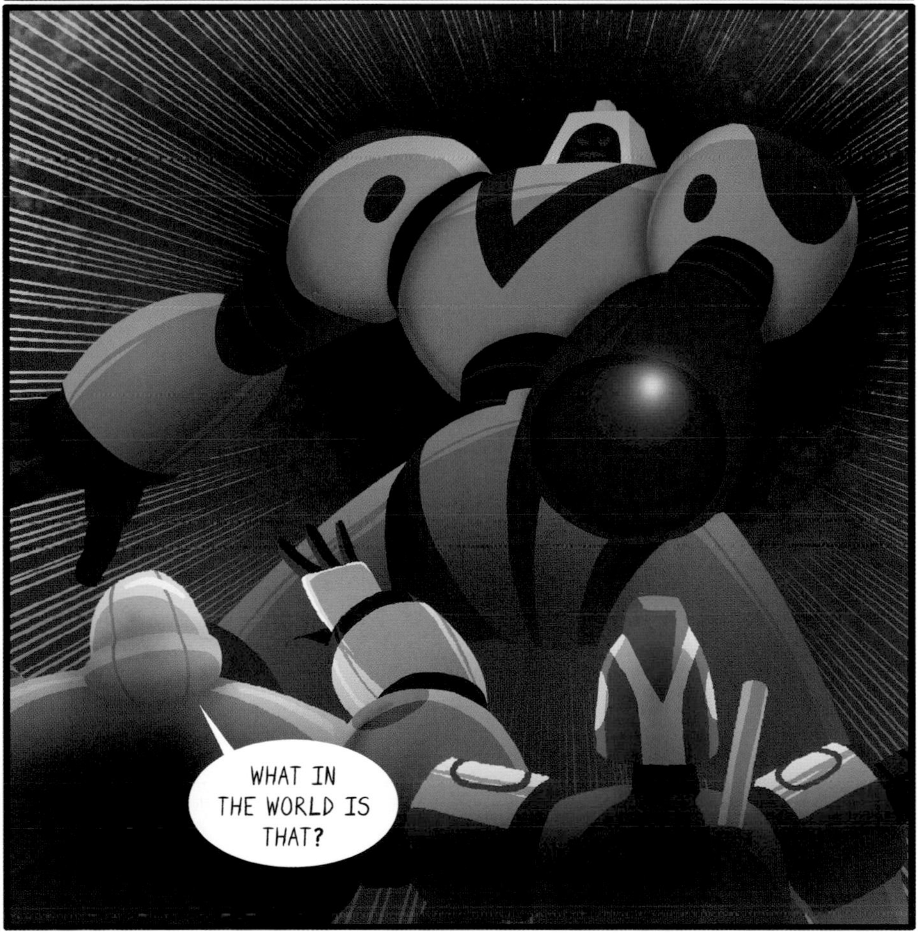
WHAT IN
THE WORLD IS
THAT?

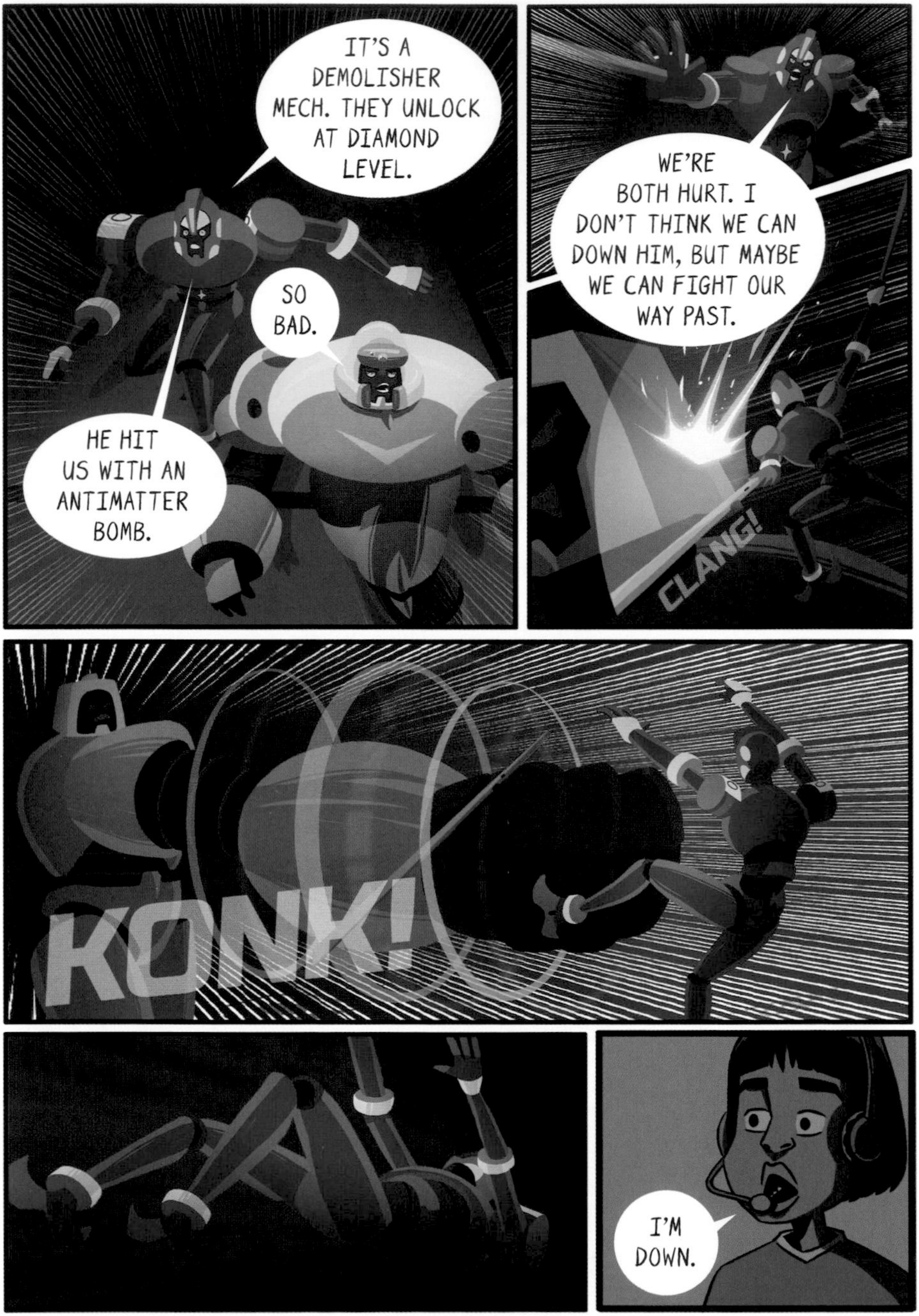
IT'S A DEMOLISHER MECH. THEY UNLOCK AT DIAMOND LEVEL.
SO BAD.
HE HIT US WITH AN ANTIMATTER BOMB.
WE'RE BOTH HURT. I DON'T THINK WE CAN DOWN HIM, BUT MAYBE WE CAN FIGHT OUR WAY PAST.
CLANG!
KONK!
I'M DOWN.

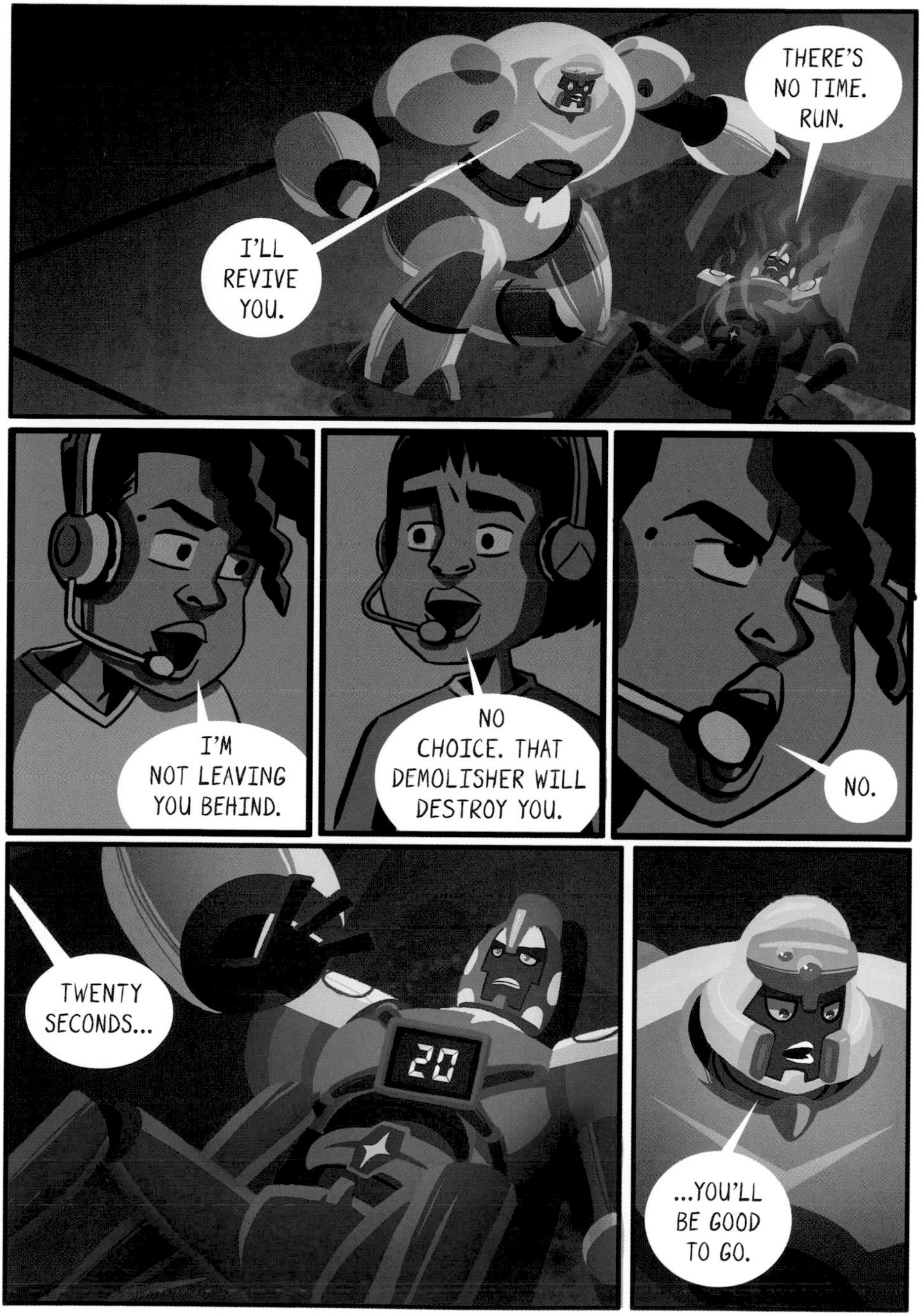
I'LL REVIVE YOU.
THERE'S NO TIME. RUN.
I'M NOT LEAVING YOU BEHIND.
NO CHOICE. THAT DEMOLISHER WILL DESTROY YOU.
NO.
TWENTY SECONDS...
20
...YOU'LL BE GOOD TO GO.

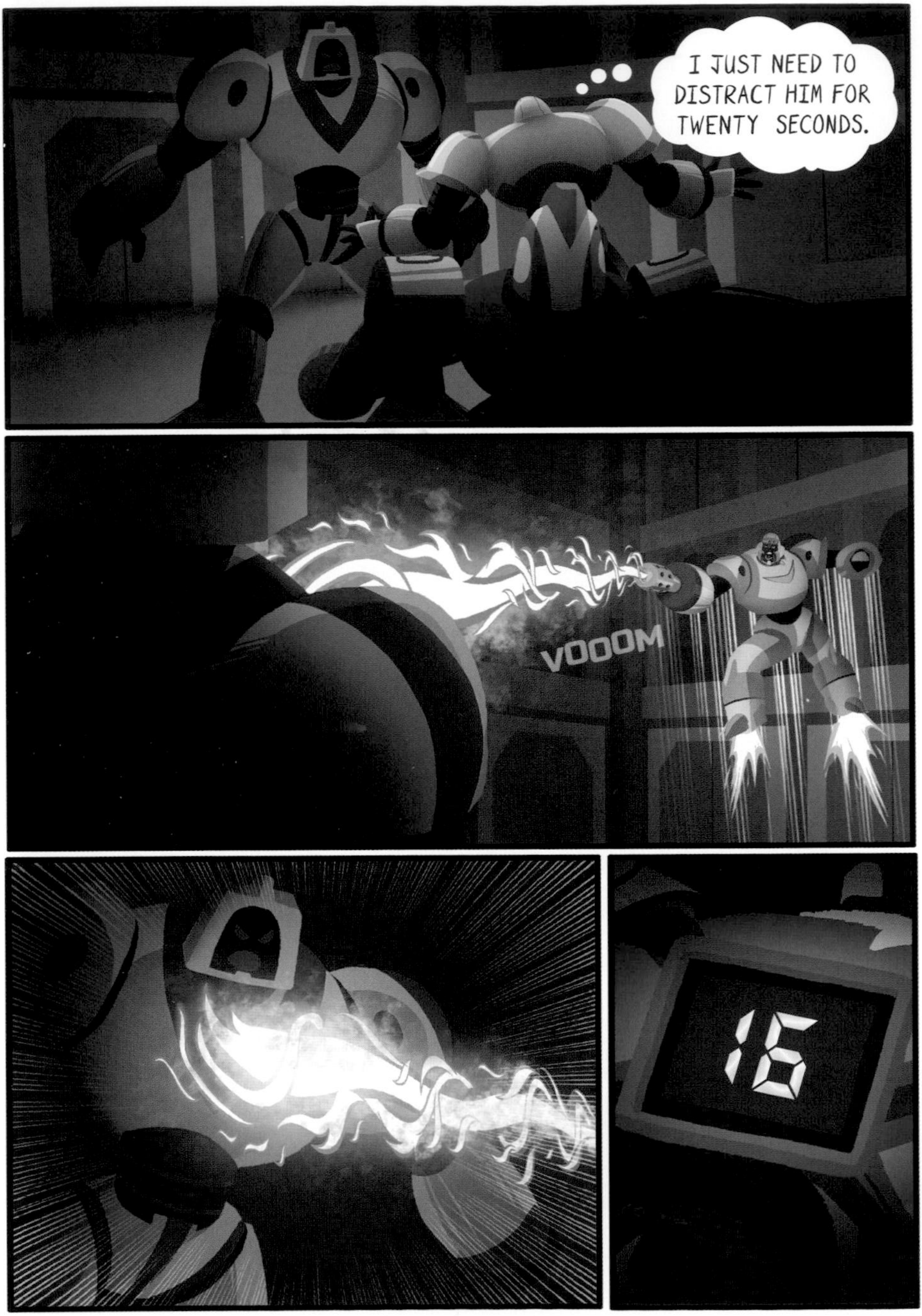
I JUST NEED TO DISTRACT HIM FOR TWENTY SECONDS.
VOOOM
16

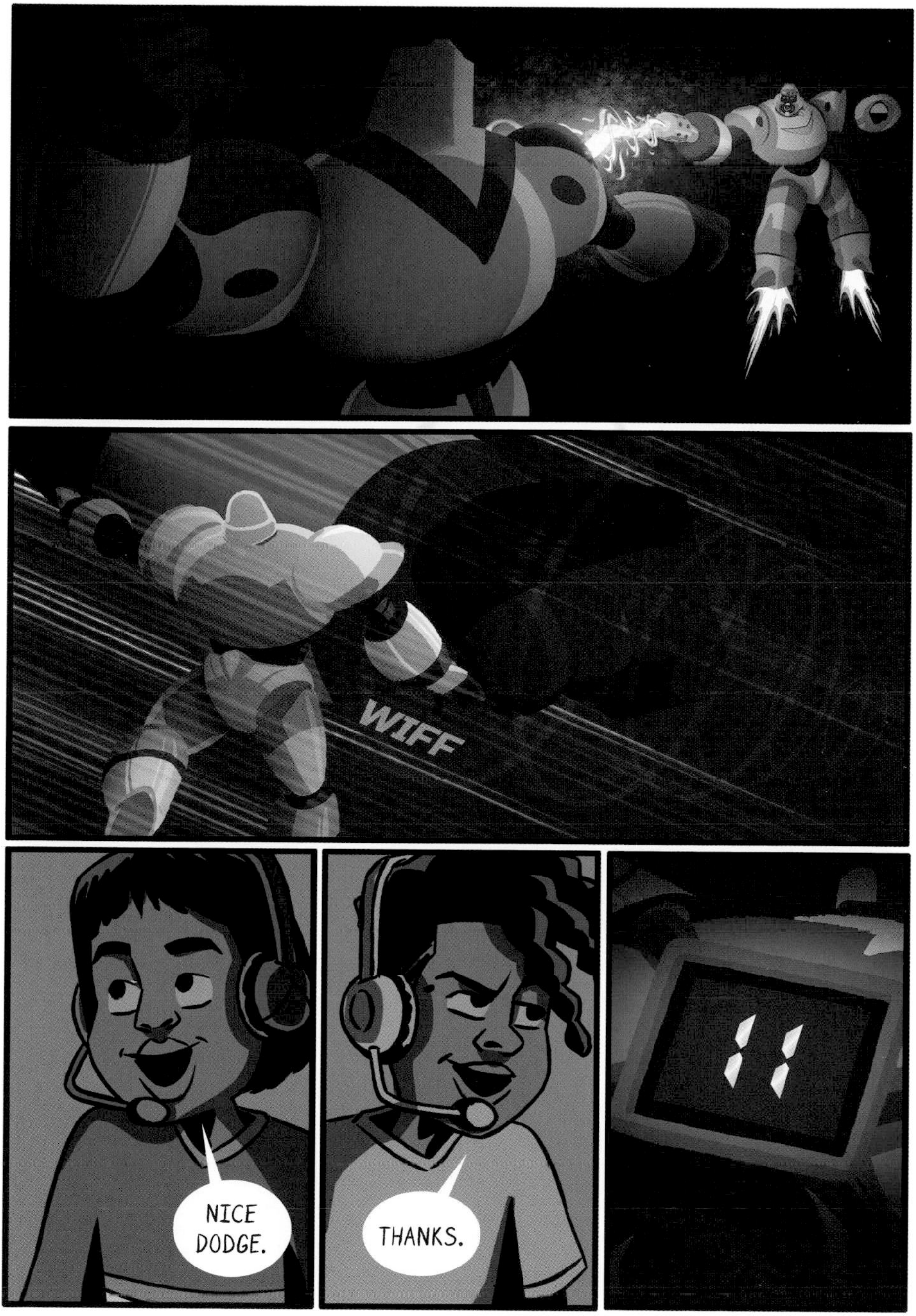
WIFF
NICE DODGE.
THANKS.

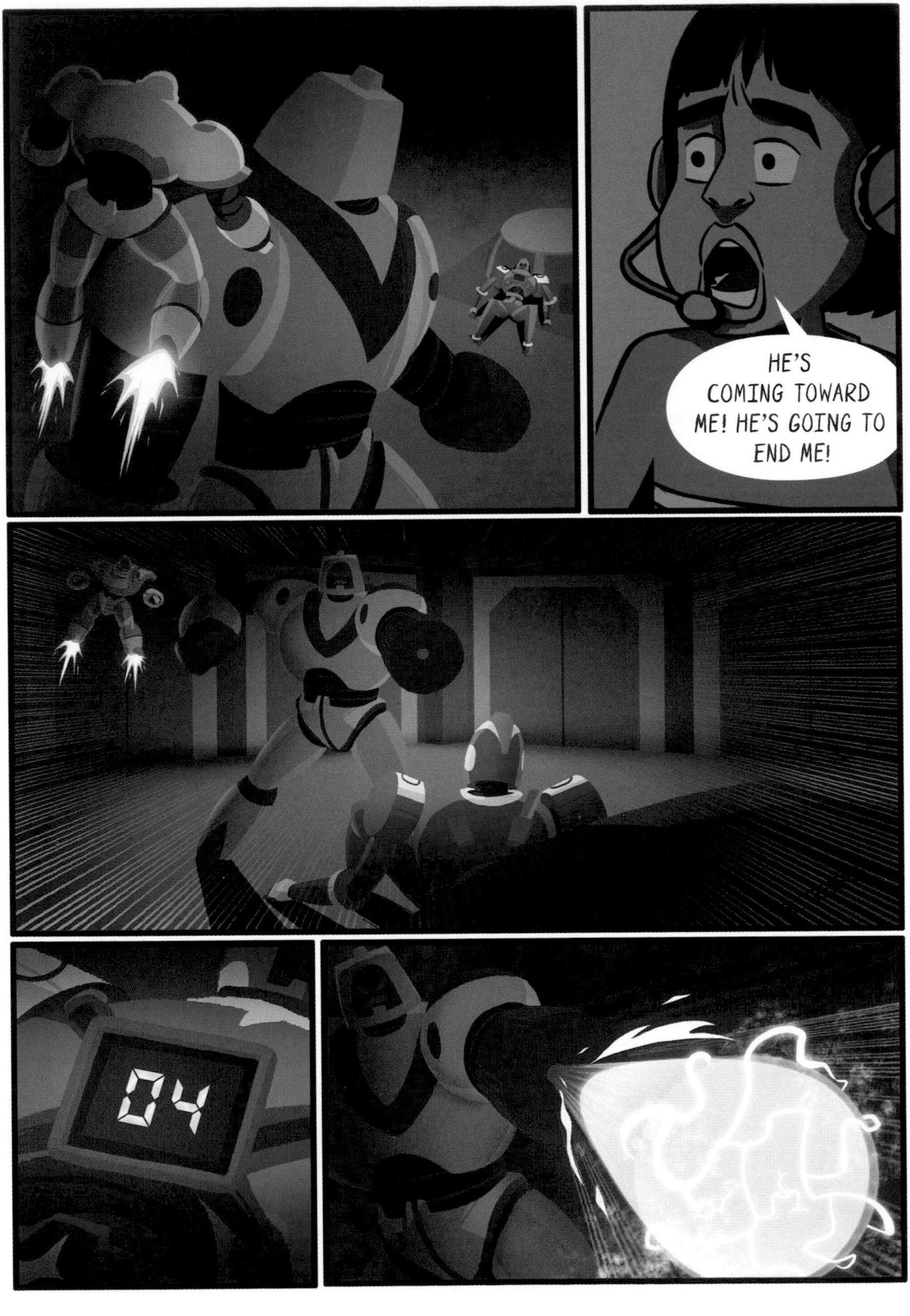
HE'S COMING TOWARD ME! HE'S GOING TO END ME!
04

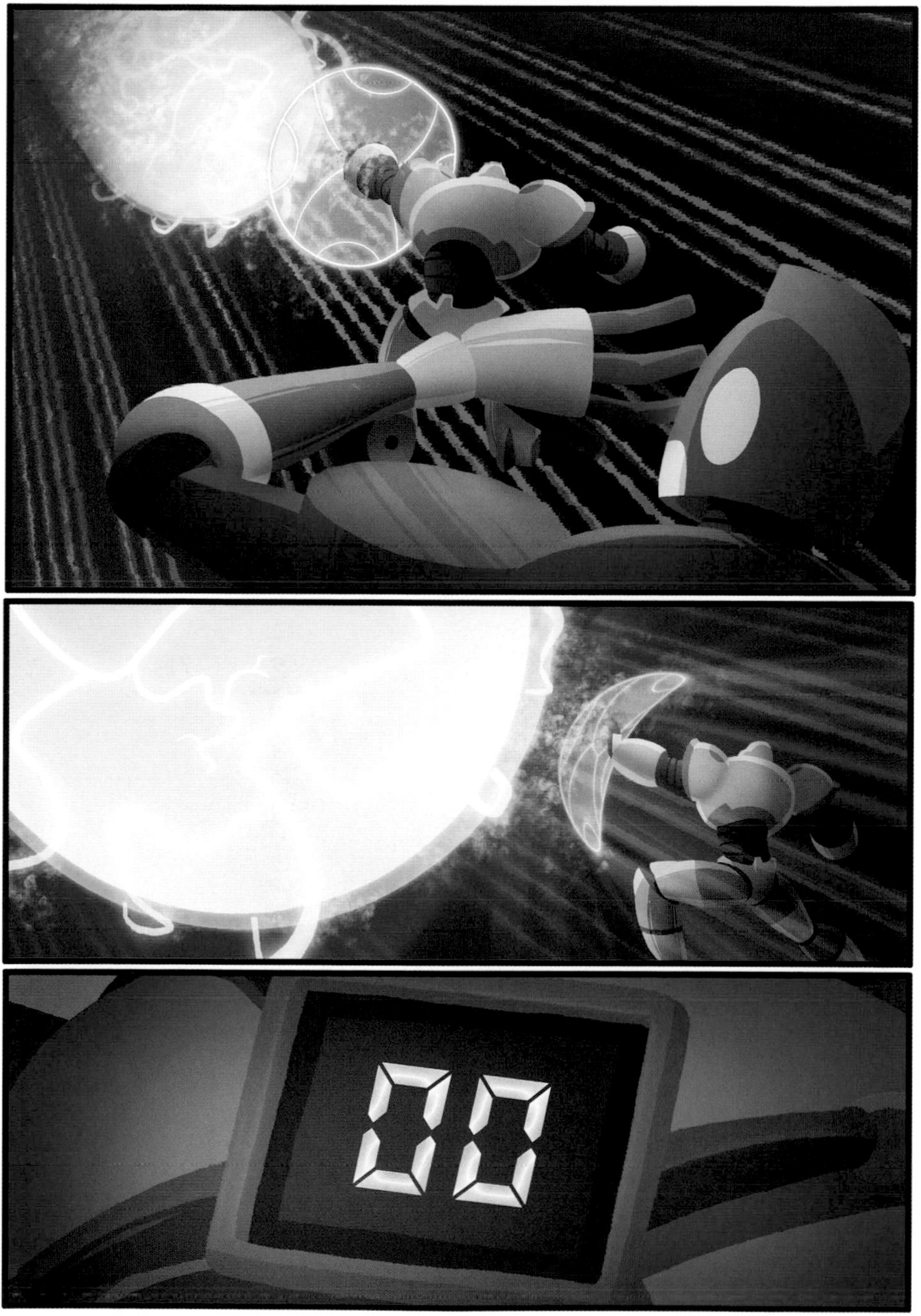
00

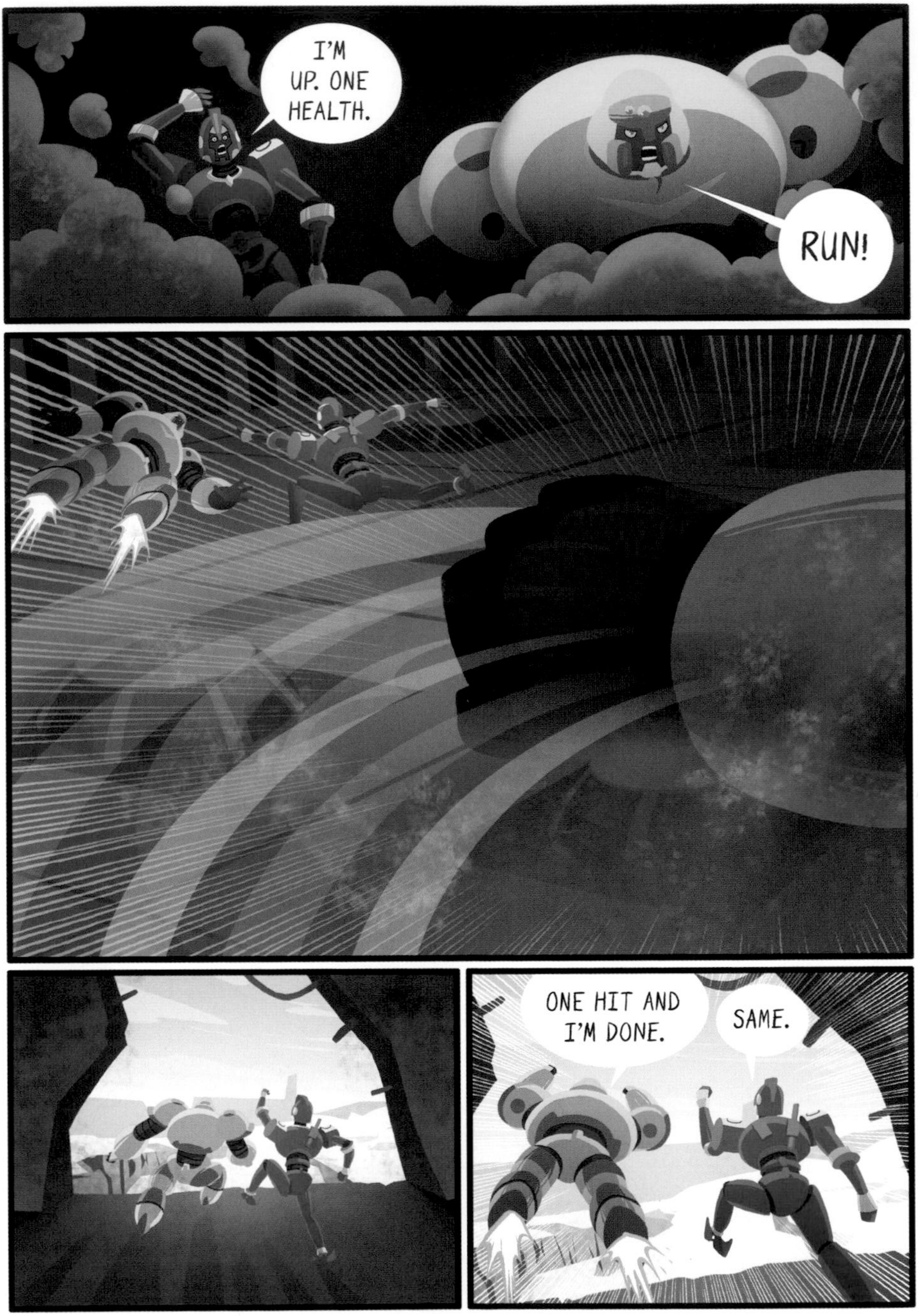
I'M UP. ONE HEALTH.
RUN!
ONE HIT AND I'M DONE.
SAME.

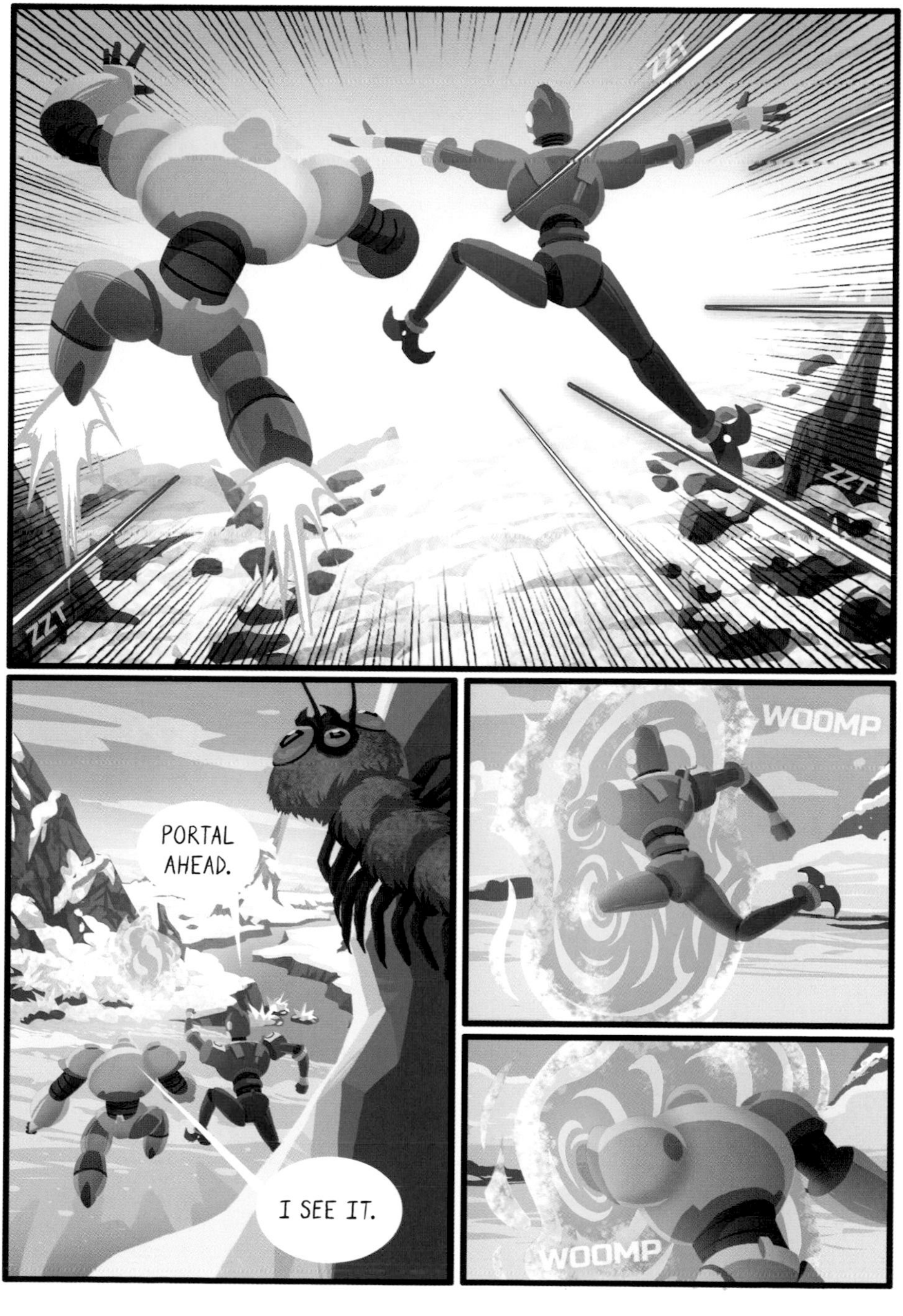
ZZT
ZZT
ZZT
ZZT
PORTAL AHEAD.
I SEE IT.
WOOMP
WOOMP

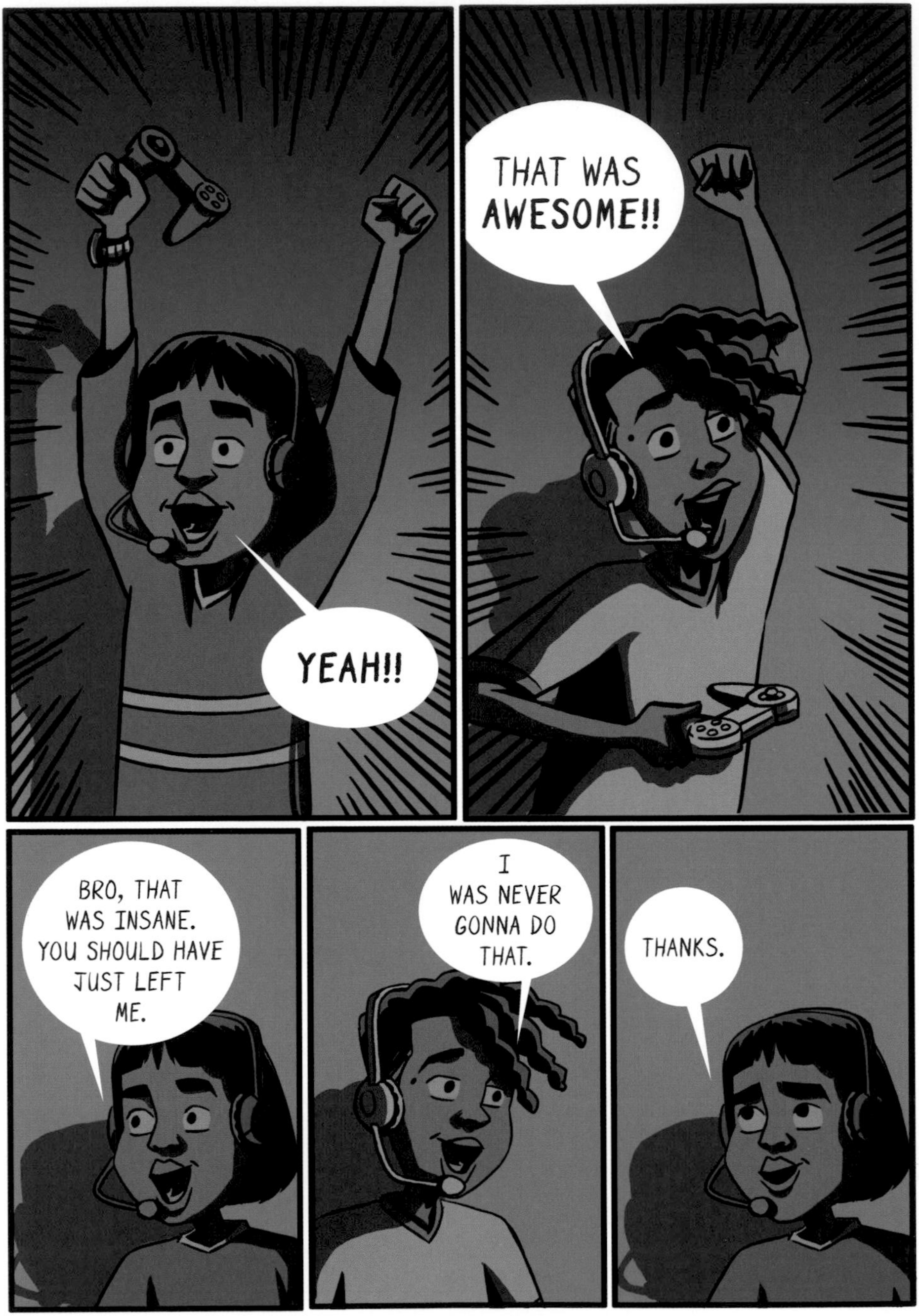
YEAH!!
THAT WAS AWESOME!!
BRO, THAT WAS INSANE. YOU SHOULD HAVE JUST LEFT ME.
I WAS NEVER GONNA DO THAT.
THANKS.

CHAPTER 4
BALANCE

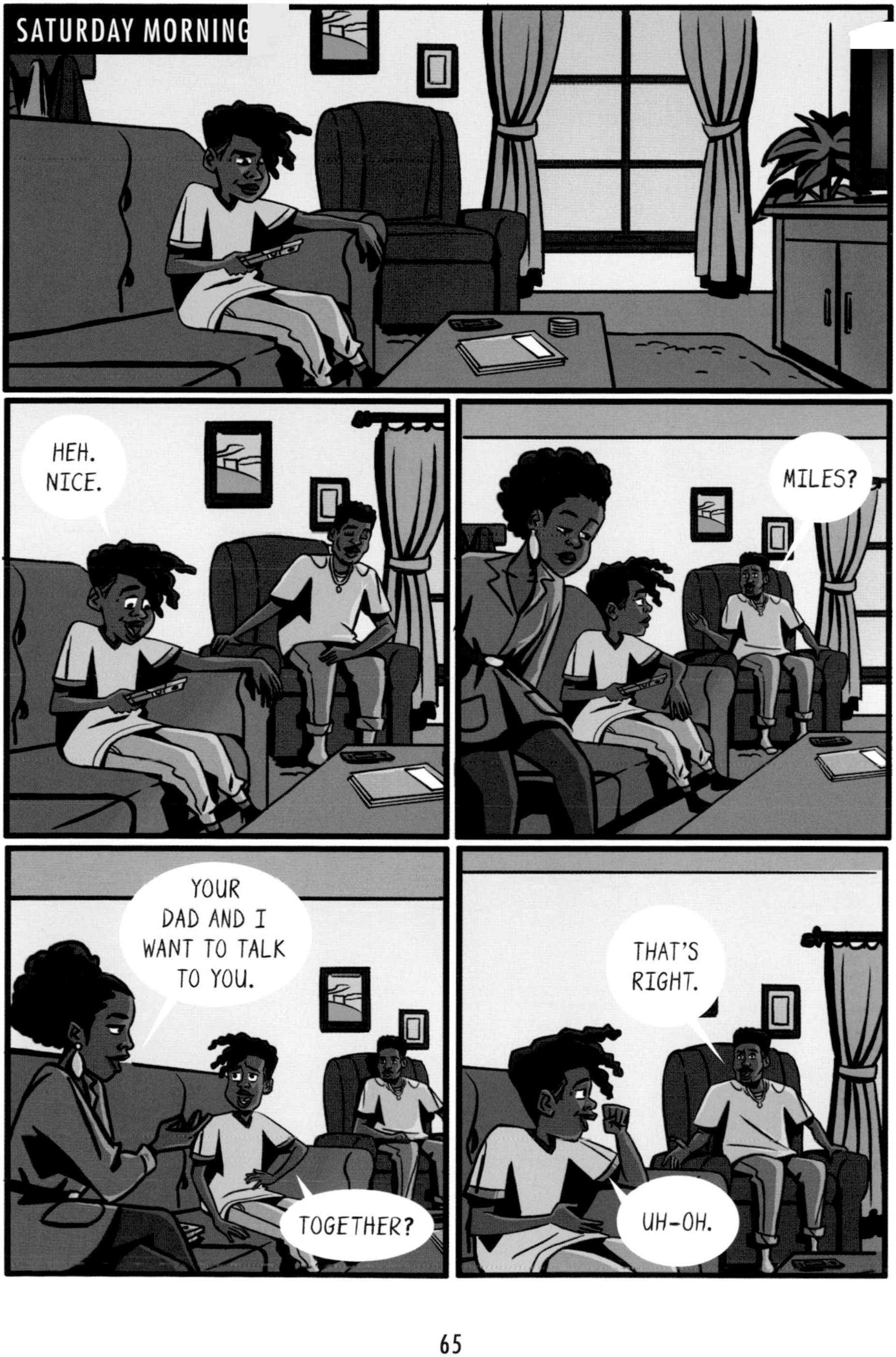
SATURDAY MORNING
HEH. NICE.
MILES?
YOUR DAD AND I WANT TO TALK TO YOU.
TOGETHER?
THAT'S RIGHT.
UH-OH.

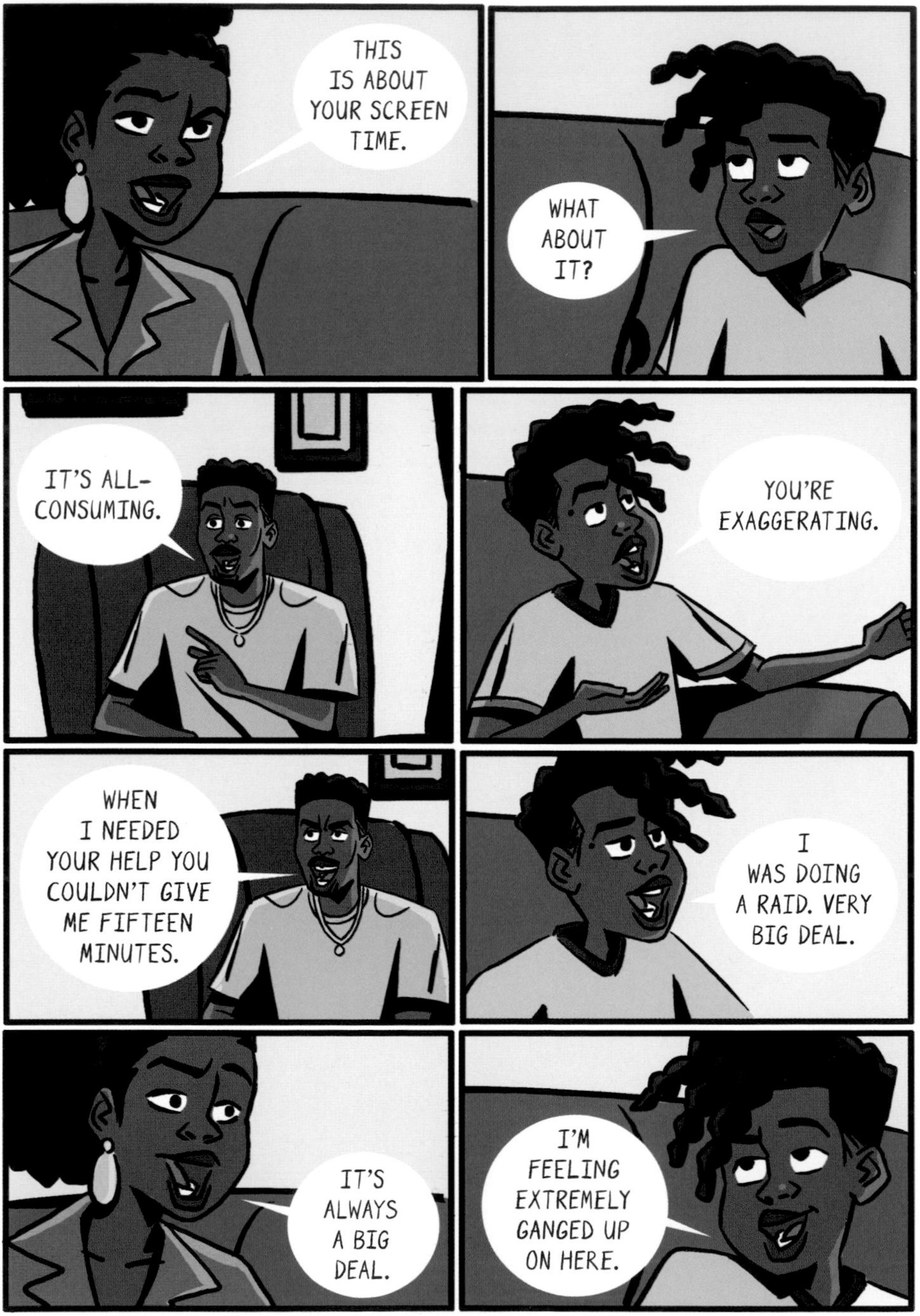
THIS IS ABOUT YOUR SCREEN TIME.
WHAT ABOUT IT?
IT'S ALL-CONSUMING.
YOU'RE EXAGGERATING.
WHEN I NEEDED YOUR HELP YOU COULDN'T GIVE ME FIFTEEN MINUTES.
I WAS DOING A RAID. VERY BIG DEAL.
IT'S ALWAYS A BIG DEAL.
I'M FEELING EXTREMELY GANGED UP ON HERE.

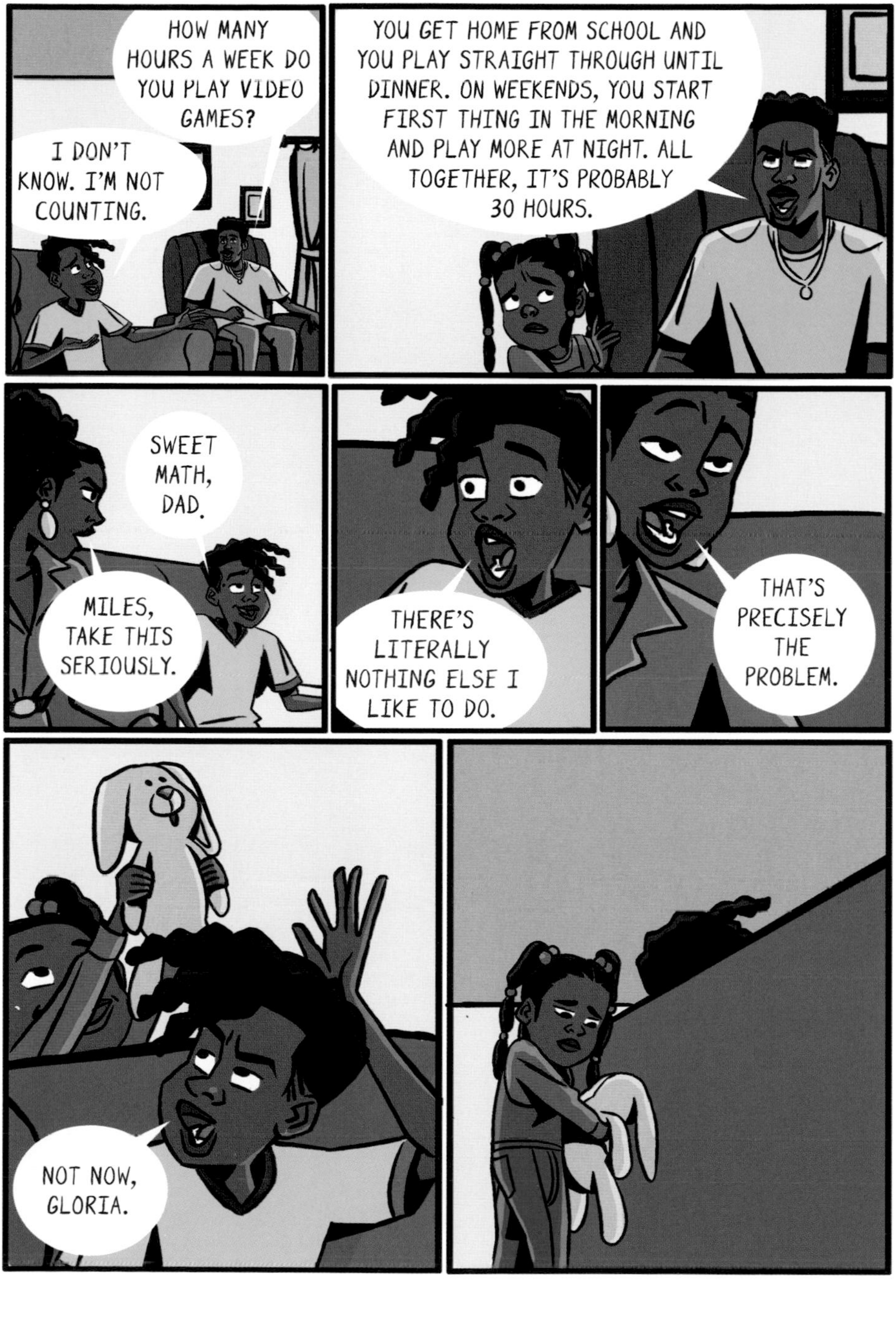
HOW MANY HOURS A WEEK DO YOU PLAY VIDEO GAMES?
I DON'T KNOW. I'M NOT COUNTING.
YOU GET HOME FROM SCHOOL AND YOU PLAY STRAIGHT THROUGH UNTIL DINNER. ON WEEKENDS, YOU START FIRST THING IN THE MORNING AND PLAY MORE AT NIGHT. ALL TOGETHER, IT'S PROBABLY 30 HOURS.
SWEET MATH, DAD.
MILES, TAKE THIS SERIOUSLY.
THERE'S LITERALLY NOTHING ELSE I LIKE TO DO.
THAT'S PRECISELY THE PROBLEM.
NOT NOW, GLORIA.

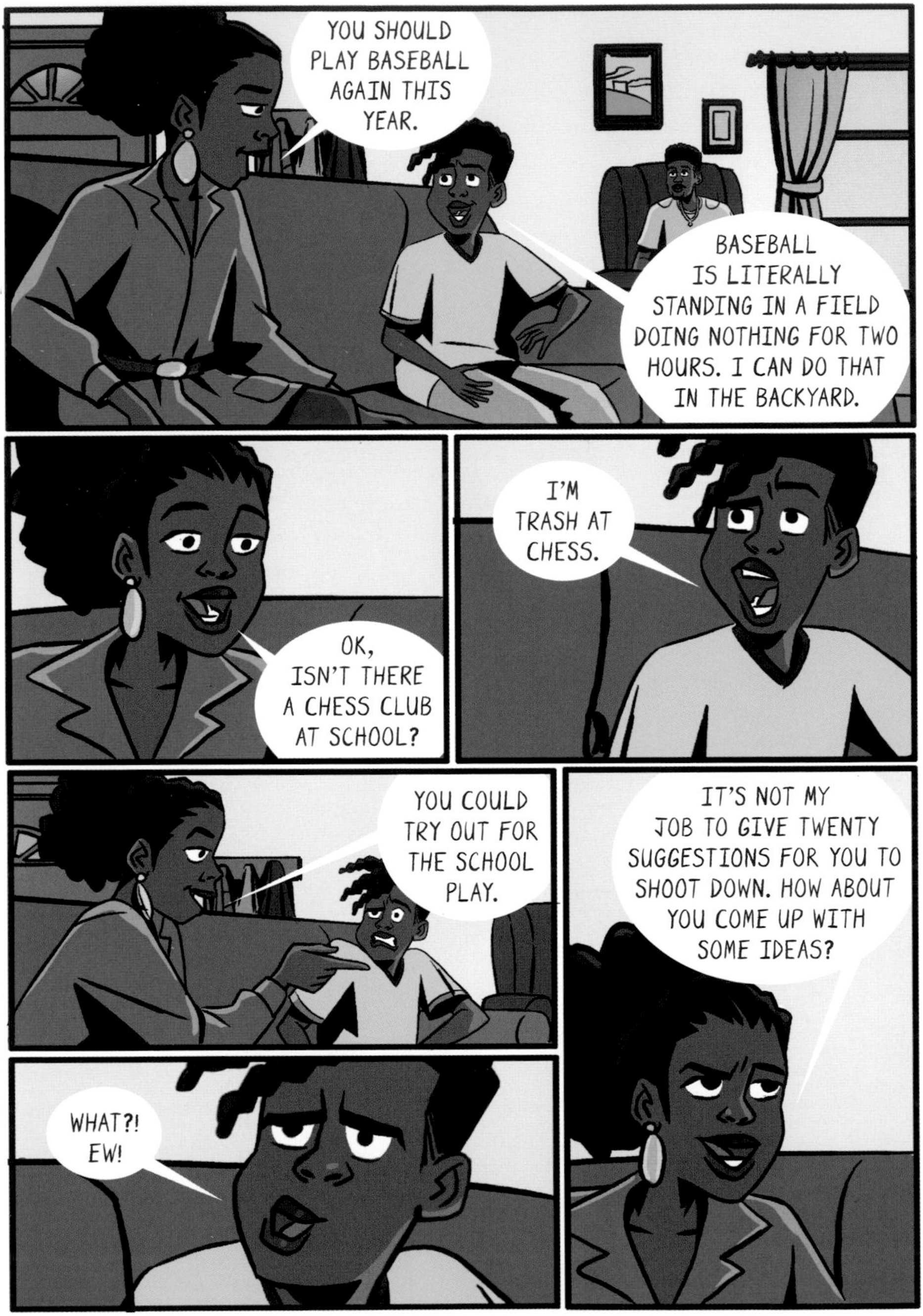
YOU SHOULD PLAY BASEBALL AGAIN THIS YEAR.
BASEBALL IS LITERALLY STANDING IN A FIELD DOING NOTHING FOR TWO HOURS. I CAN DO THAT IN THE BACKYARD.
OK, ISN'T THERE A CHESS CLUB AT SCHOOL?
I'M TRASH AT CHESS.
YOU COULD TRY OUT FOR THE SCHOOL PLAY.
WHAT?! EW!
IT'S NOT MY JOB TO GIVE TWENTY SUGGESTIONS FOR YOU TO SHOOT DOWN. HOW ABOUT YOU COME UP WITH SOME IDEAS?

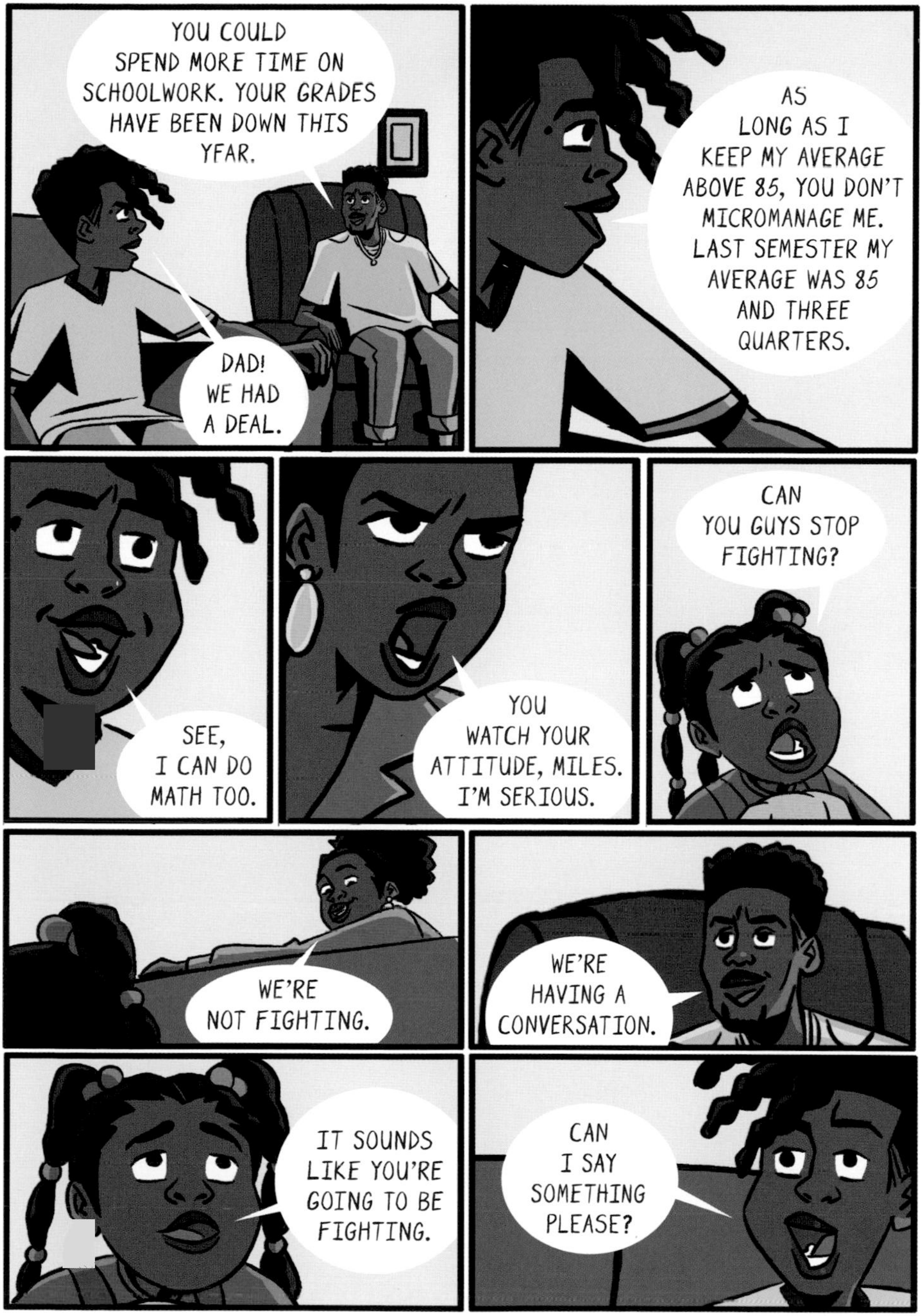
YOU COULD SPEND MORE TIME ON SCHOOLWORK. YOUR GRADES HAVE BEEN DOWN THIS YEAR.
DAD! WE HAD A DEAL.
AS LONG AS I KEEP MY AVERAGE ABOVE 85, YOU DON'T MICROMANAGE ME. LAST SEMESTER MY AVERAGE WAS 85 AND THREE QUARTERS.
SEE, I CAN DO MATH TOO.
YOU WATCH YOUR ATTITUDE, MILES. I'M SERIOUS.
CAN YOU GUYS STOP FIGHTING?
WE'RE NOT FIGHTING.
WE'RE HAVING A CONVERSATION.
IT SOUNDS LIKE YOU'RE GOING TO BE FIGHTING.
CAN I SAY SOMETHING PLEASE?

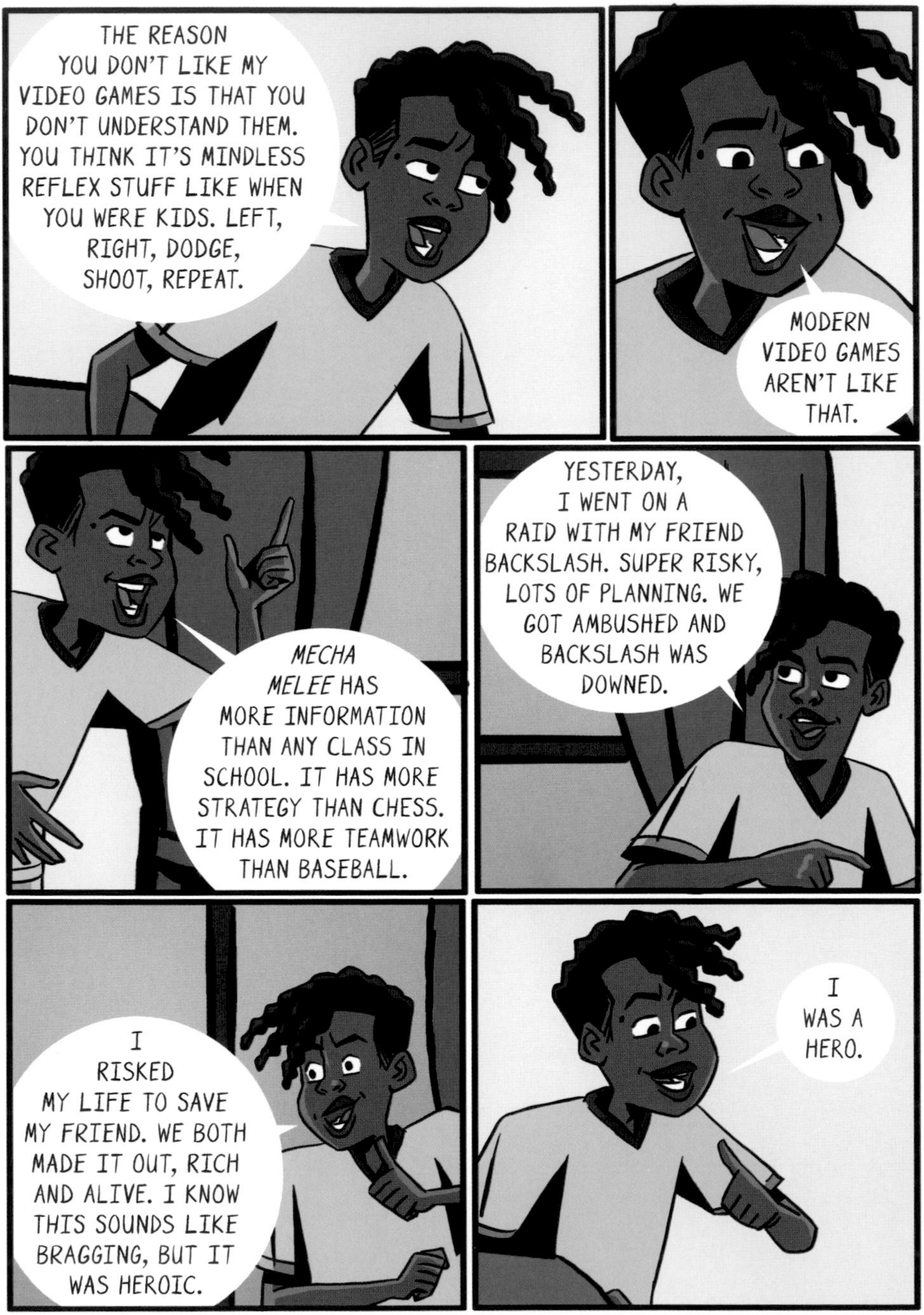
THE REASON YOU DON'T LIKE MY VIDEO GAMES IS THAT YOU DON'T UNDERSTAND THEM. YOU THINK IT'S MINDLESS REFLEX STUFF LIKE WHEN YOU WERE KIDS. LEFT, RIGHT, DODGE, SHOOT, REPEAT.
MODERN VIDEO GAMES AREN'T LIKE THAT.
MECHA MELEE HAS MORE INFORMATION THAN ANY CLASS IN SCHOOL. IT HAS MORE STRATEGY THAN CHESS. IT HAS MORE TEAMWORK THAN BASEBALL.
YESTERDAY, I WENT ON A RAID WITH MY FRIEND BACKSLASH. SUPER RISKY, LOTS OF PLANNING. WE GOT AMBUSHED AND BACKSLASH WAS DOWNED.
I RISKED MY LIFE TO SAVE MY FRIEND. WE BOTH MADE IT OUT, RICH AND ALIVE. I KNOW THIS SOUNDS LIKE BRAGGING, BUT IT WAS HEROIC.
I WAS A HERO.

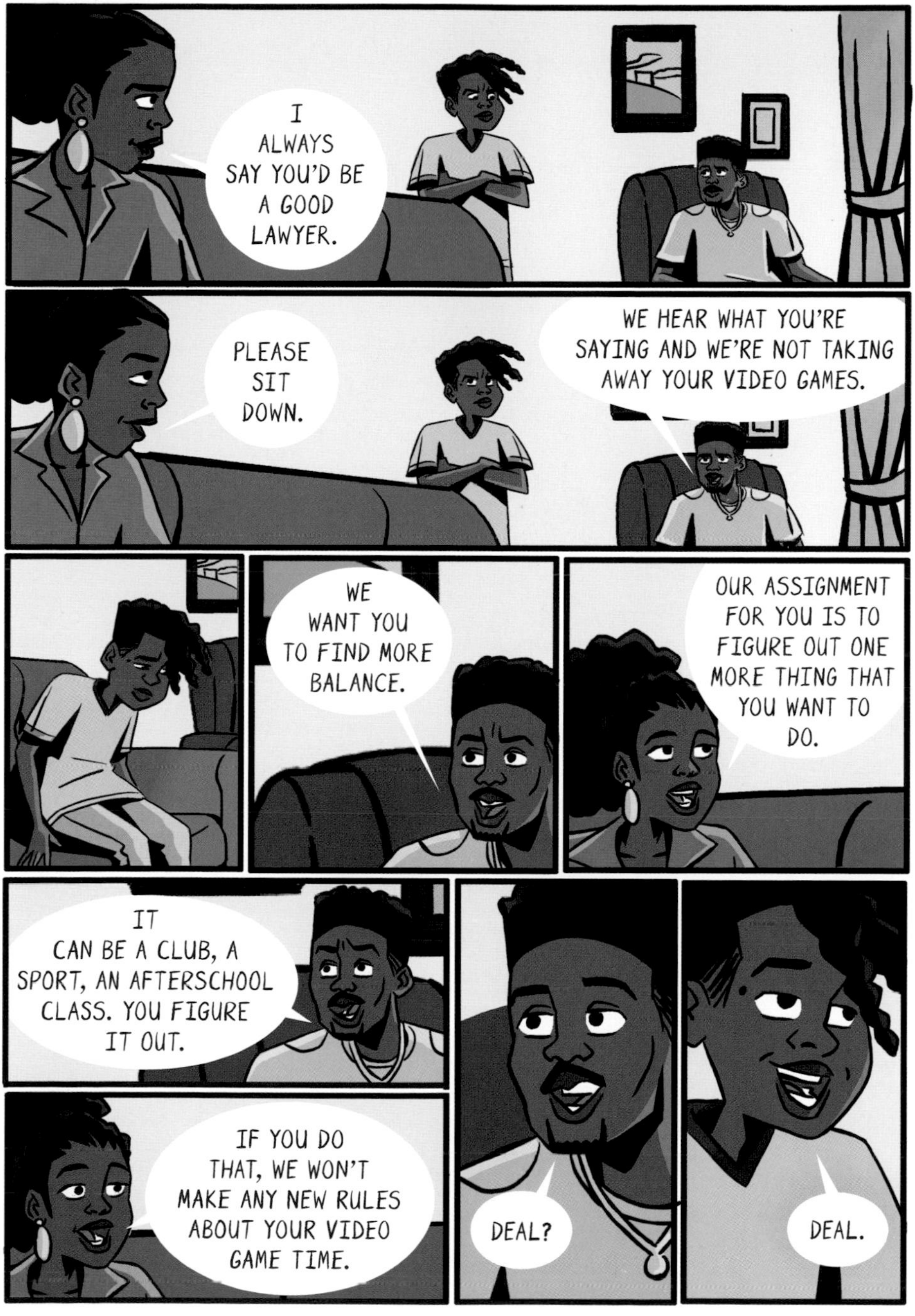

I ALWAYS SAY YOU'D BE A GOOD LAWYER.
PLEASE SIT DOWN.
WE HEAR WHAT YOU'RE SAYING AND WE'RE NOT TAKING AWAY YOUR VIDEO GAMES.
WE WANT YOU TO FIND MORE BALANCE.
OUR ASSIGNMENT FOR YOU IS TO FIGURE OUT ONE MORE THING THAT YOU WANT TO DO.
IT CAN BE A CLUB, A SPORT, AN AFTERSCHOOL CLASS. YOU FIGURE IT OUT.
IF YOU DO THAT, WE WON'T MAKE ANY NEW RULES ABOUT YOUR VIDEO GAME TIME.
DEAL?
DEAL.

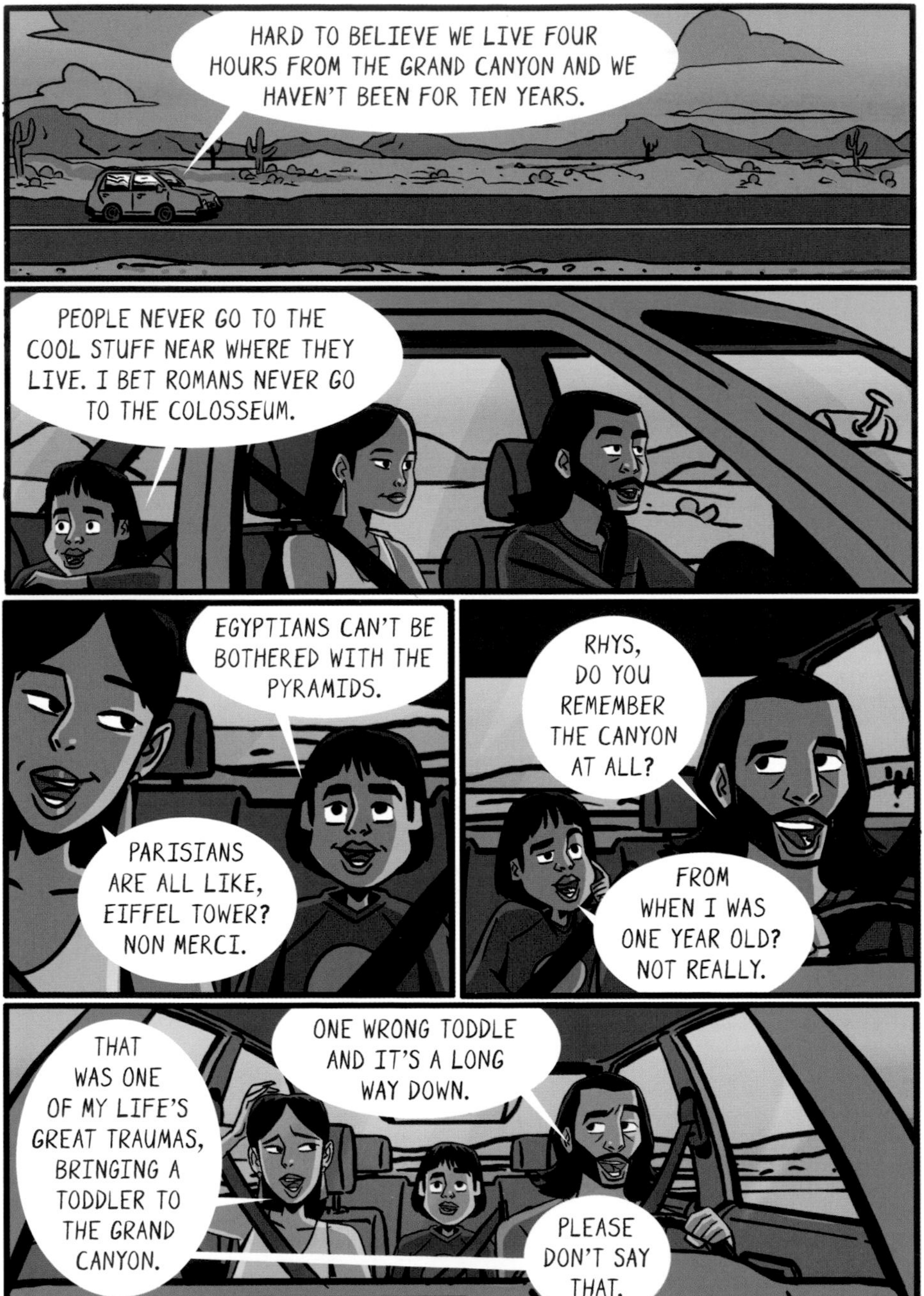
HARD TO BELIEVE WE LIVE FOUR HOURS FROM THE GRAND CANYON AND WE HAVEN'T BEEN FOR TEN YEARS.
PEOPLE NEVER GO TO THE COOL STUFF NEAR WHERE THEY LIVE. I BET ROMANS NEVER GO TO THE COLOSSEUM.
EGYPTIANS CAN'T BE BOTHERED WITH THE PYRAMIDS.
PARISIANS ARE ALL LIKE, EIFFEL TOWER? NON MERCI.
RHYS, DO YOU REMEMBER THE CANYON AT ALL?
FROM WHEN I WAS ONE YEAR OLD? NOT REALLY.
THAT WAS ONE OF MY LIFE'S GREAT TRAUMAS, BRINGING A TODDLER TO THE GRAND CANYON.
ONE WRONG TODDLE AND IT'S A LONG WAY DOWN.
PLEASE DON'T SAY THAT.

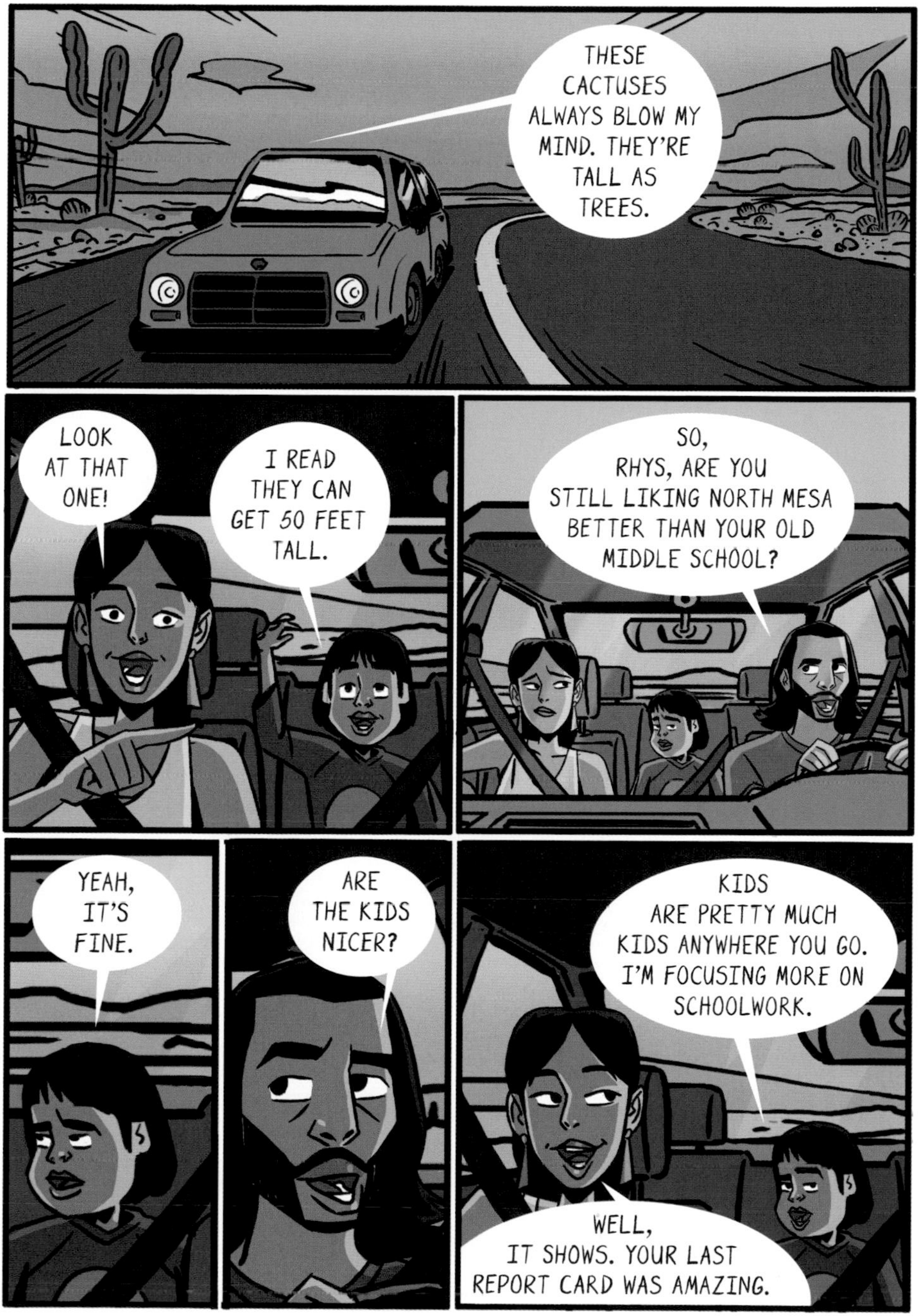
THESE CACTUSES ALWAYS BLOW MY MIND. THEY'RE TALL AS TREES.
LOOK AT THAT ONE!
I READ THEY CAN GET 50 FEET TALL.
SO, RHYS, ARE YOU STILL LIKING NORTH MESA BETTER THAN YOUR OLD MIDDLE SCHOOL?
YEAH, IT'S FINE.
ARE THE KIDS NICER?
KIDS ARE PRETTY MUCH KIDS ANYWHERE YOU GO. I'M FOCUSING MORE ON SCHOOLWORK.
WELL, IT SHOWS. YOUR LAST REPORT CARD WAS AMAZING.

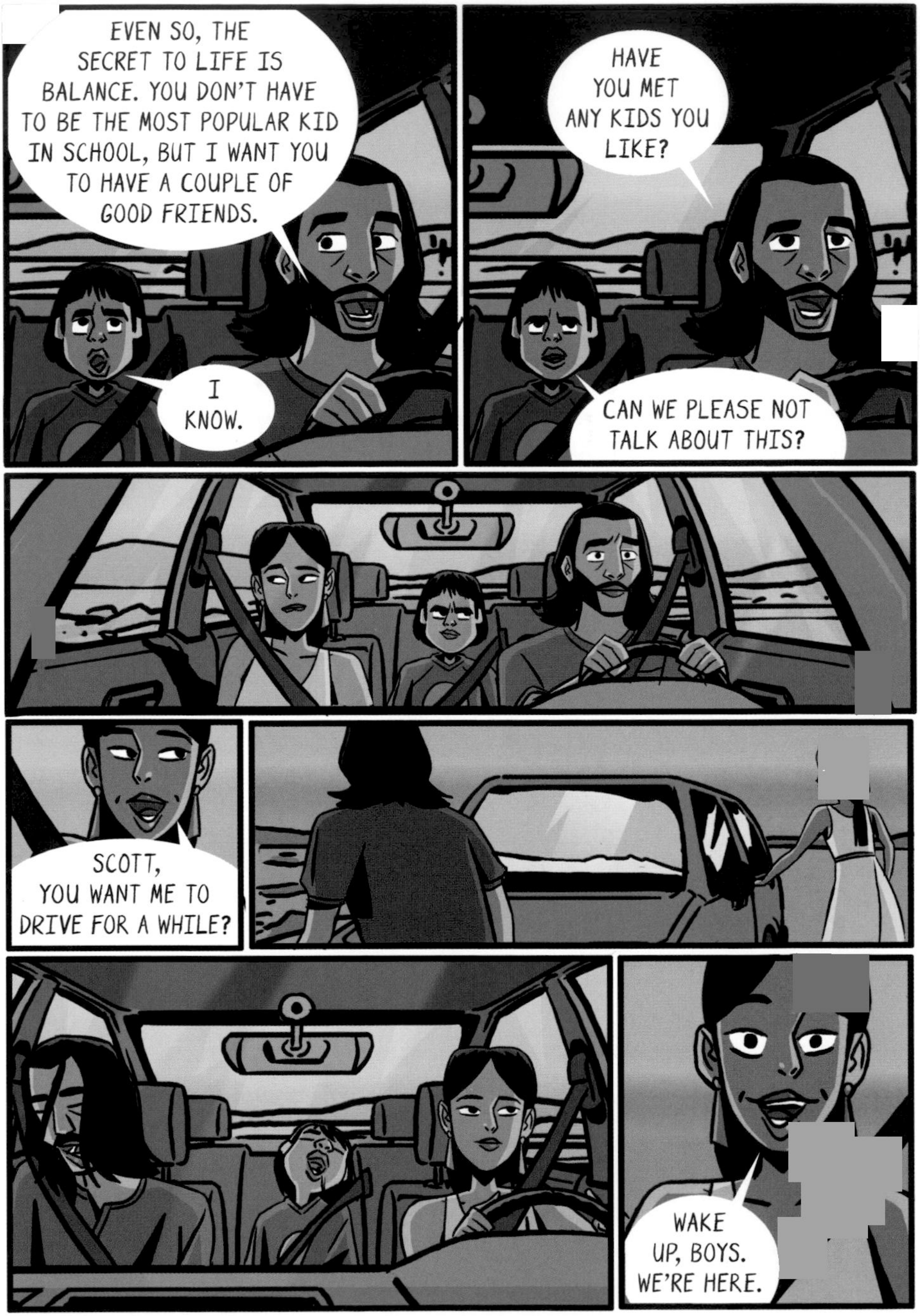
EVEN SO, THE SECRET TO LIFE IS BALANCE. YOU DON'T HAVE TO BE THE MOST POPULAR KID IN SCHOOL, BUT I WANT YOU TO HAVE A COUPLE OF GOOD FRIENDS.
I KNOW.
HAVE YOU MET ANY KIDS YOU LIKE?
CAN WE PLEASE NOT TALK ABOUT THIS?
SCOTT, YOU WANT ME TO DRIVE FOR A WHILE?
WAKE UP, BOYS. WE'RE HERE.

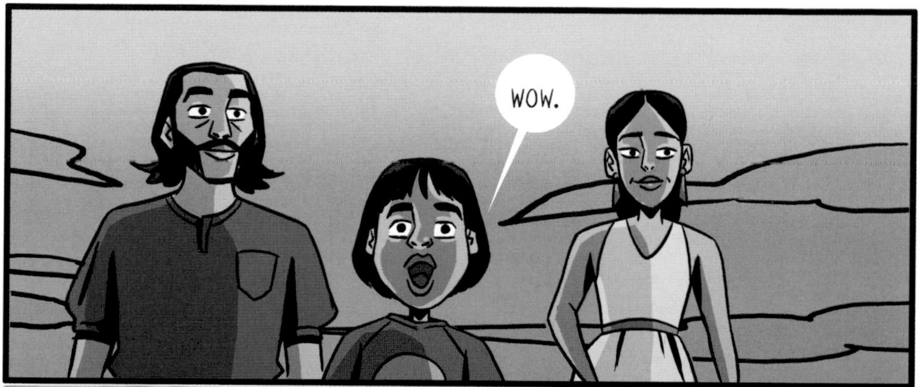
WOW.

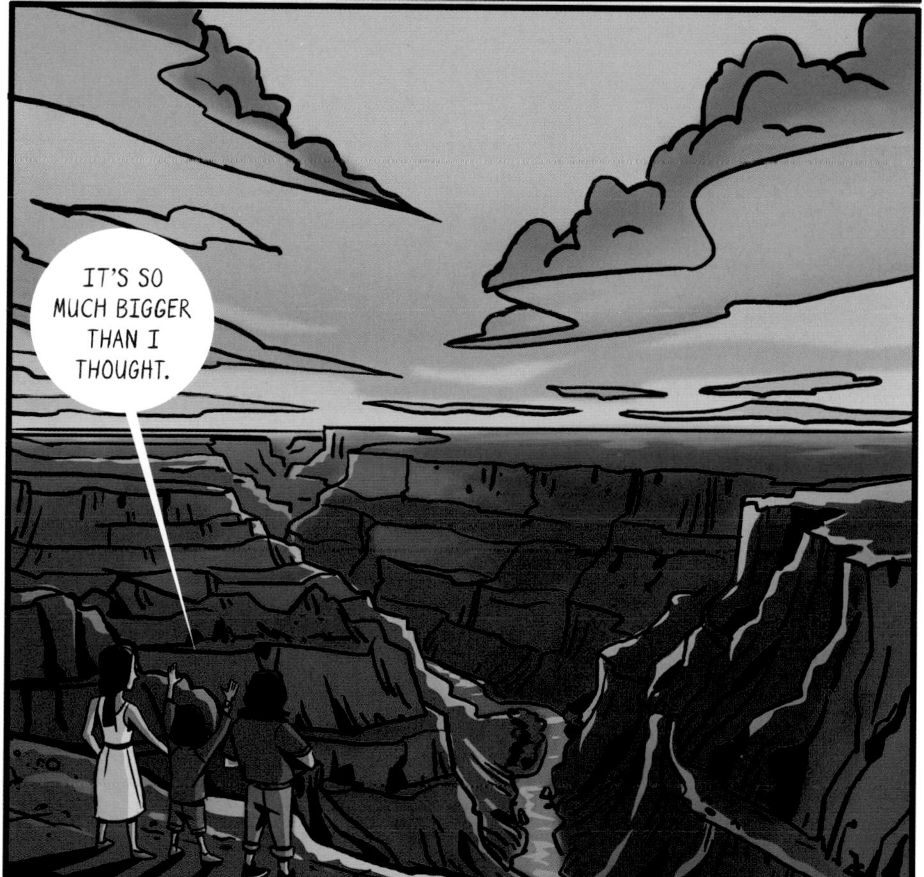
IT'S SO MUCH BIGGER THAN I THOUGHT.

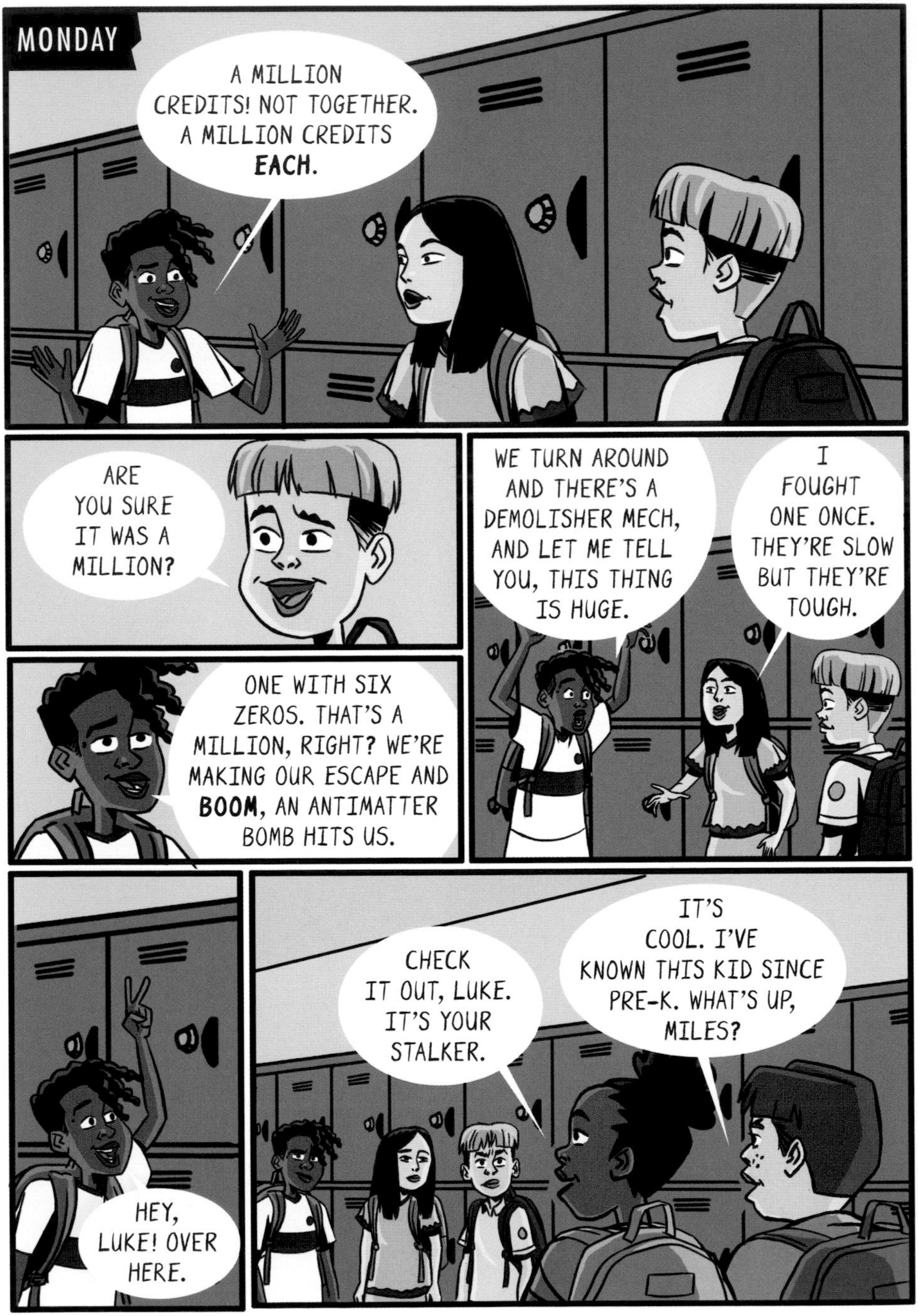
MONDAY
A MILLION CREDITS! NOT TOGETHER. A MILLION CREDITS **EACH**.
ARE YOU SURE IT WAS A MILLION?
ONE WITH SIX ZEROS. THAT'S A MILLION, RIGHT? WE'RE MAKING OUR ESCAPE AND **BOOM**, AN ANTIMATTER BOMB HITS US.
WE TURN AROUND AND THERE'S A DEMOLISHER MECH, AND LET ME TELL YOU, THIS THING IS HUGE.
I FOUGHT ONE ONCE. THEY'RE SLOW BUT THEY'RE TOUGH.
HEY, LUKE! OVER HERE.
CHECK IT OUT, LUKE. IT'S YOUR STALKER.
IT'S COOL. I'VE KNOWN THIS KID SINCE PRE-K. WHAT'S UP, MILES?

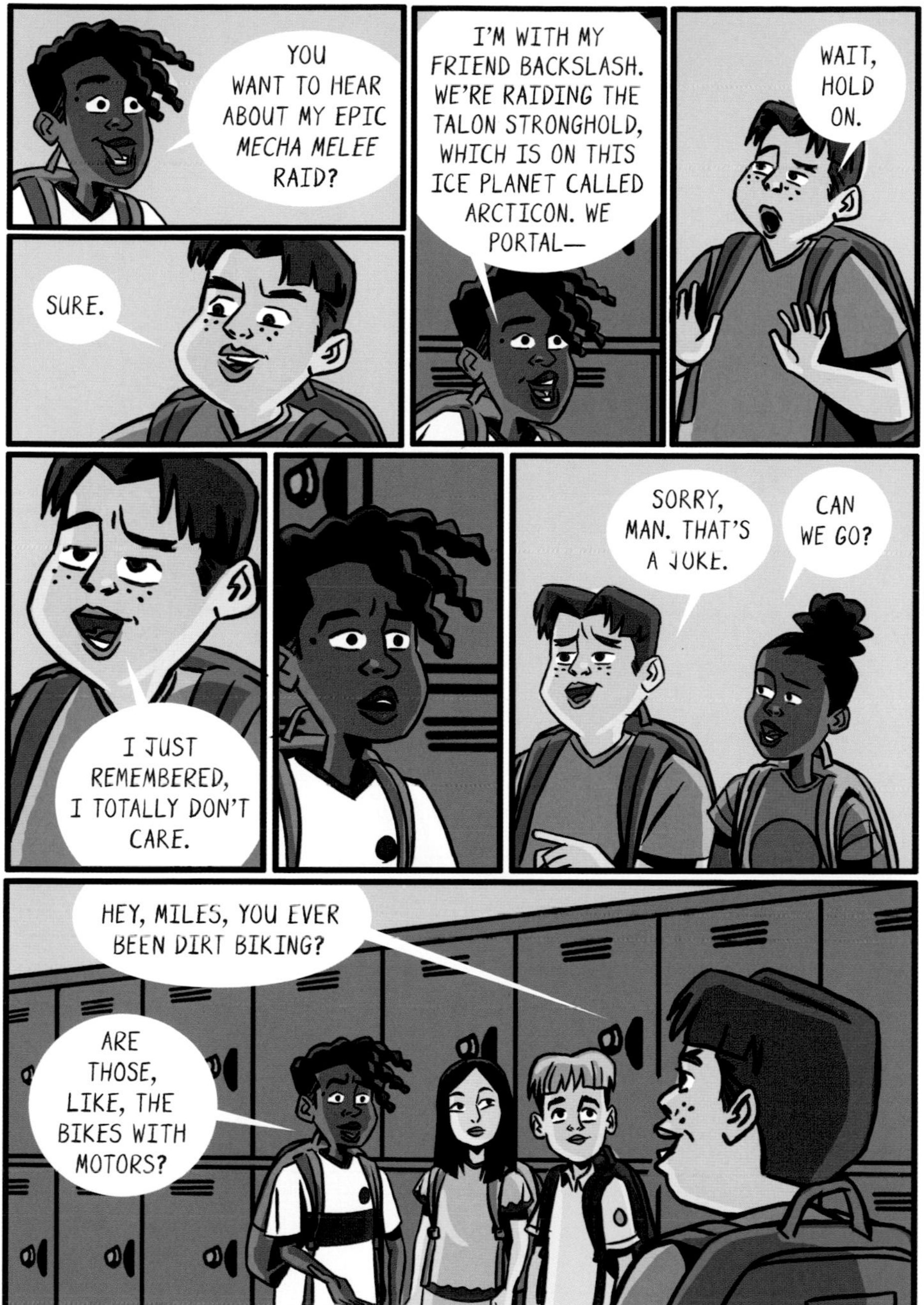
YOU WANT TO HEAR ABOUT MY EPIC *MECHA MELEE* RAID?
SURE.
I'M WITH MY FRIEND BACKSLASH. WE'RE RAIDING THE TALON STRONGHOLD, WHICH IS ON THIS ICE PLANET CALLED ARCTICON. WE PORTAL—
WAIT, HOLD ON.
I JUST REMEMBERED, I TOTALLY DON'T CARE.
SORRY, MAN. THAT'S A JOKE.
CAN WE GO?
HEY, MILES, YOU EVER BEEN DIRT BIKING?
ARE THOSE, LIKE, THE BIKES WITH MOTORS?

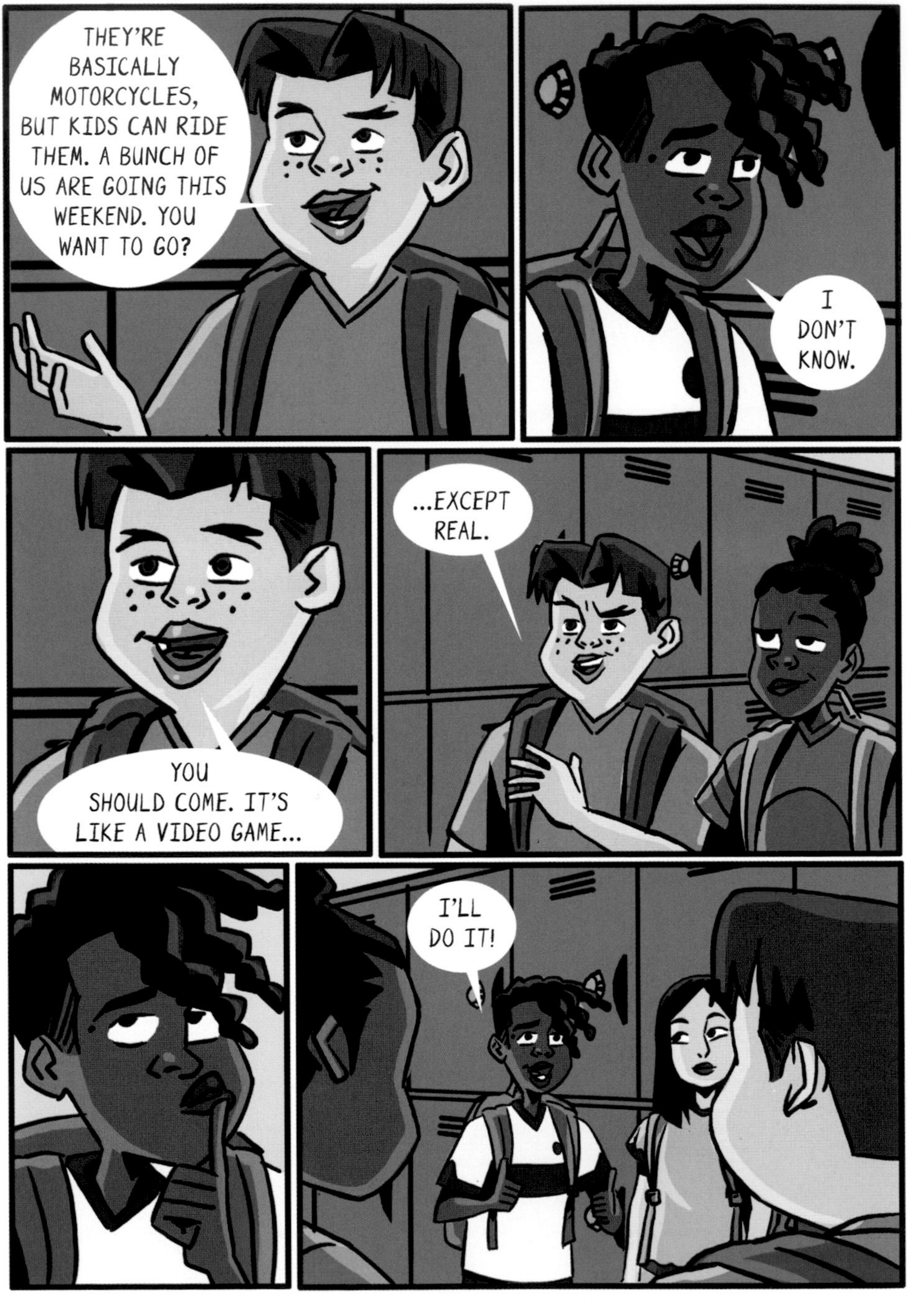
THEY'RE BASICALLY MOTORCYCLES, BUT KIDS CAN RIDE THEM. A BUNCH OF US ARE GOING THIS WEEKEND. YOU WANT TO GO?
I DON'T KNOW.
YOU SHOULD COME. IT'S LIKE A VIDEO GAME...
...EXCEPT REAL.
I'LL DO IT!

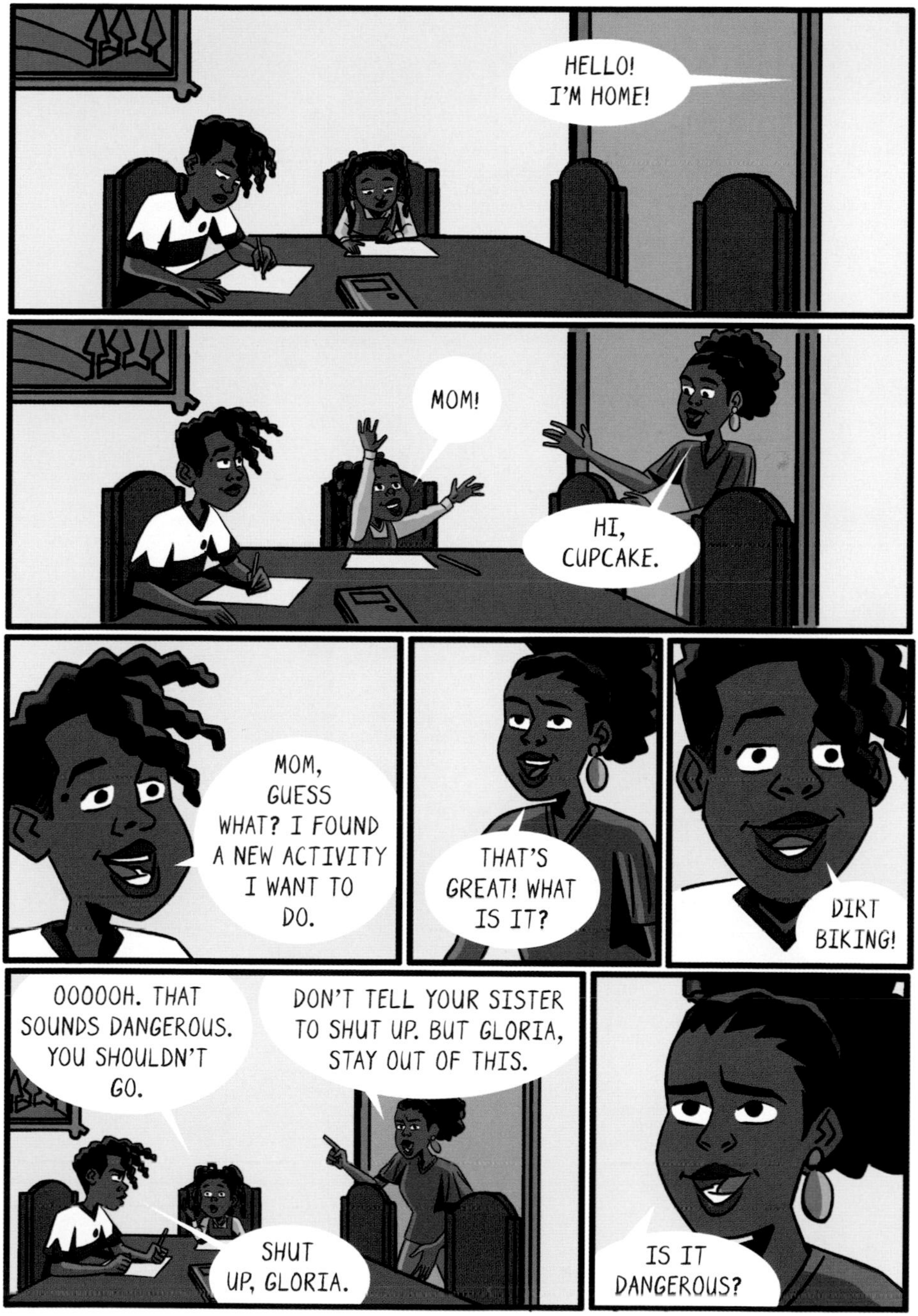
HELLO! I'M HOME!
MOM!
HI, CUPCAKE.
MOM, GUESS WHAT? I FOUND A NEW ACTIVITY I WANT TO DO.
THAT'S GREAT! WHAT IS IT?
DIRT BIKING!
OOOOOH. THAT SOUNDS DANGEROUS. YOU SHOULDN'T GO.
SHUT UP, GLORIA.
DON'T TELL YOUR SISTER TO SHUT UP. BUT GLORIA, STAY OUT OF THIS.
IS IT DANGEROUS?

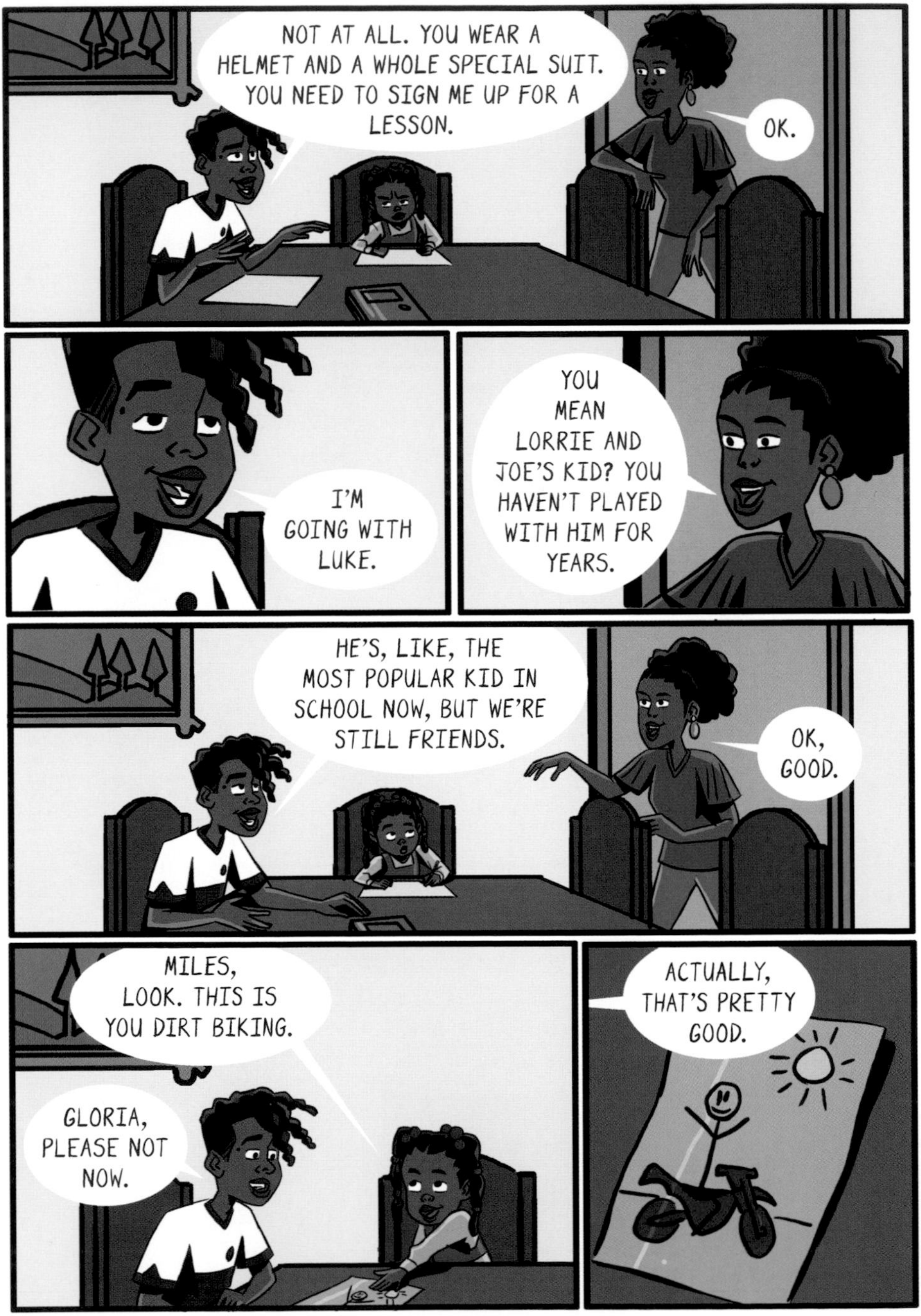
NOT AT ALL. YOU WEAR A HELMET AND A WHOLE SPECIAL SUIT. YOU NEED TO SIGN ME UP FOR A LESSON.
OK.
I'M GOING WITH LUKE.
YOU MEAN LORRIE AND JOE'S KID? YOU HAVEN'T PLAYED WITH HIM FOR YEARS.
HE'S, LIKE, THE MOST POPULAR KID IN SCHOOL NOW, BUT WE'RE STILL FRIENDS.
OK, GOOD.
MILES, LOOK. THIS IS YOU DIRT BIKING.
GLORIA, PLEASE NOT NOW.
ACTUALLY, THAT'S PRETTY GOOD.

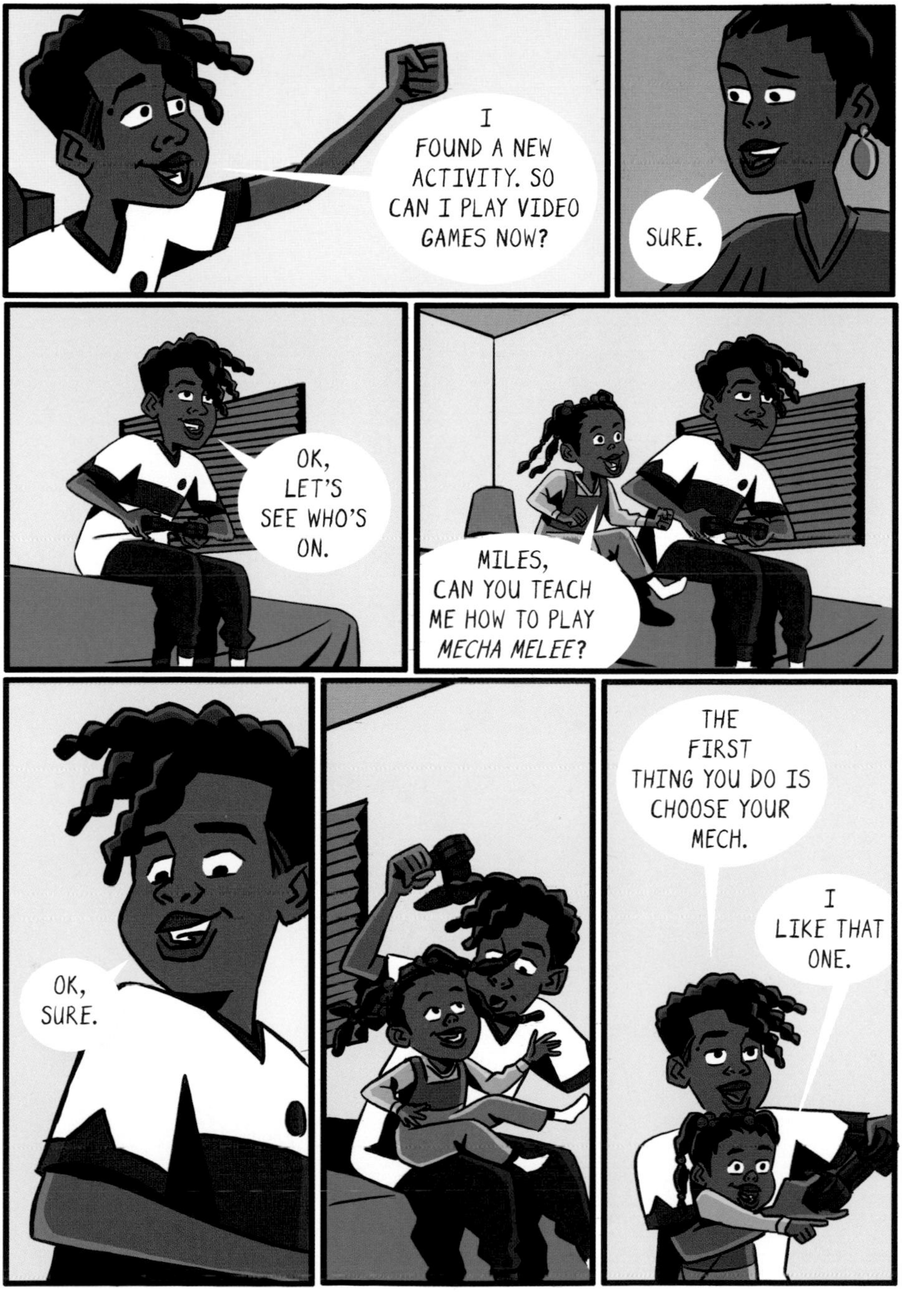

I FOUND A NEW ACTIVITY. SO CAN I PLAY VIDEO GAMES NOW?
SURE.
OK, LET'S SEE WHO'S ON.
MILES, CAN YOU TEACH ME HOW TO PLAY *MECHA MELEE*?
OK, SURE.
THE FIRST THING YOU DO IS CHOOSE YOUR MECH.
I LIKE THAT ONE.

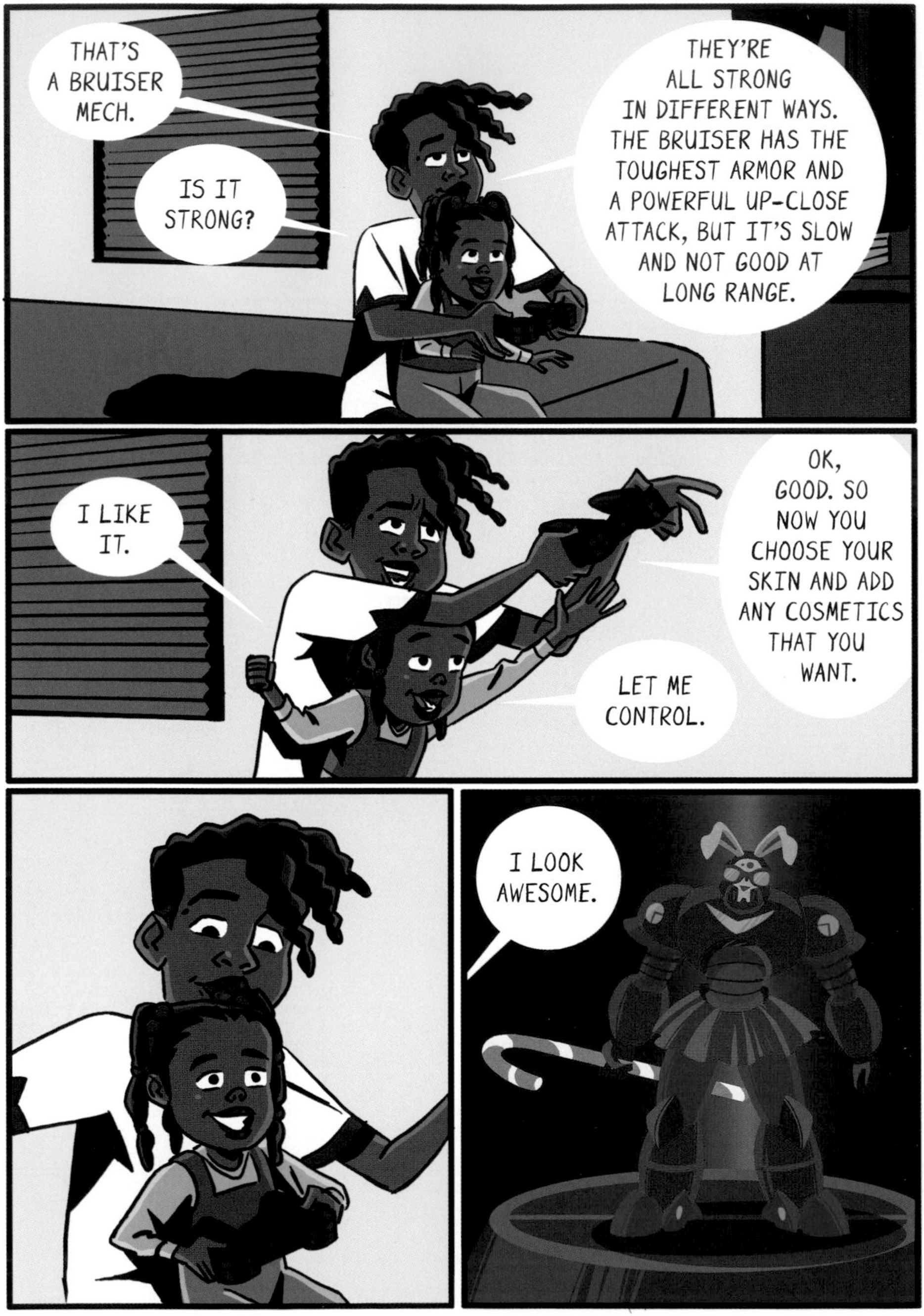
THAT'S A BRUISER MECH.
IS IT STRONG?
THEY'RE ALL STRONG IN DIFFERENT WAYS. THE BRUISER HAS THE TOUGHEST ARMOR AND A POWERFUL UP-CLOSE ATTACK, BUT IT'S SLOW AND NOT GOOD AT LONG RANGE.
I LIKE IT.
OK, GOOD. SO NOW YOU CHOOSE YOUR SKIN AND ADD ANY COSMETICS THAT YOU WANT.
LET ME CONTROL.
I LOOK AWESOME.

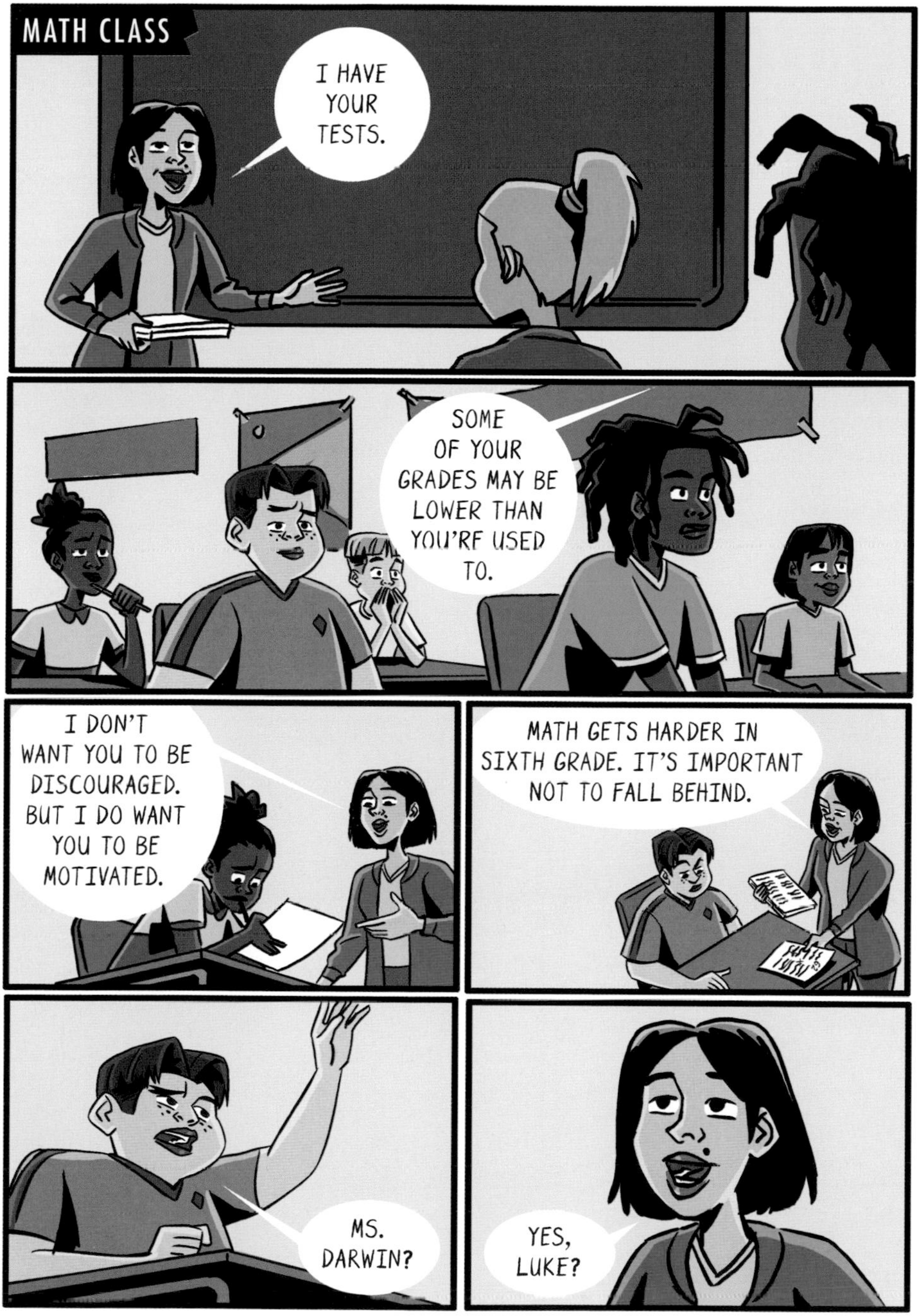
MATH CLASS
I HAVE YOUR TESTS.
SOME OF YOUR GRADES MAY BE LOWER THAN YOU'RE USED TO.
I DON'T WANT YOU TO BE DISCOURAGED. BUT I DO WANT YOU TO BE MOTIVATED.
MATH GETS HARDER IN SIXTH GRADE. IT'S IMPORTANT NOT TO FALL BEHIND.
MS. DARWIN?
YES, LUKE?

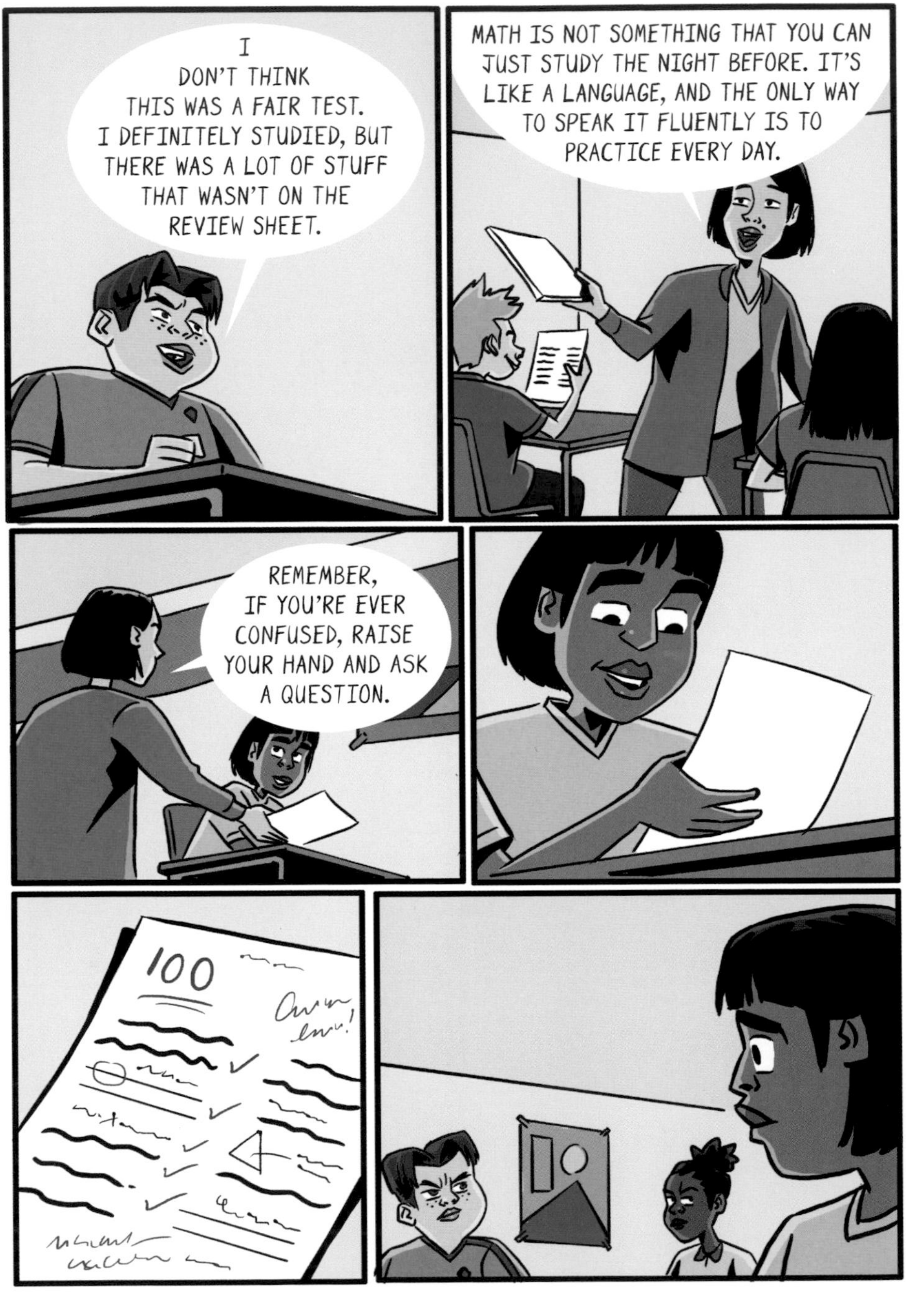
I DON'T THINK THIS WAS A FAIR TEST. I DEFINITELY STUDIED, BUT THERE WAS A LOT OF STUFF THAT WASN'T ON THE REVIEW SHEET.
MATH IS NOT SOMETHING THAT YOU CAN JUST STUDY THE NIGHT BEFORE. IT'S LIKE A LANGUAGE, AND THE ONLY WAY TO SPEAK IT FLUENTLY IS TO PRACTICE EVERY DAY.
REMEMBER, IF YOU'RE EVER CONFUSED, RAISE YOUR HAND AND ASK A QUESTION.
100

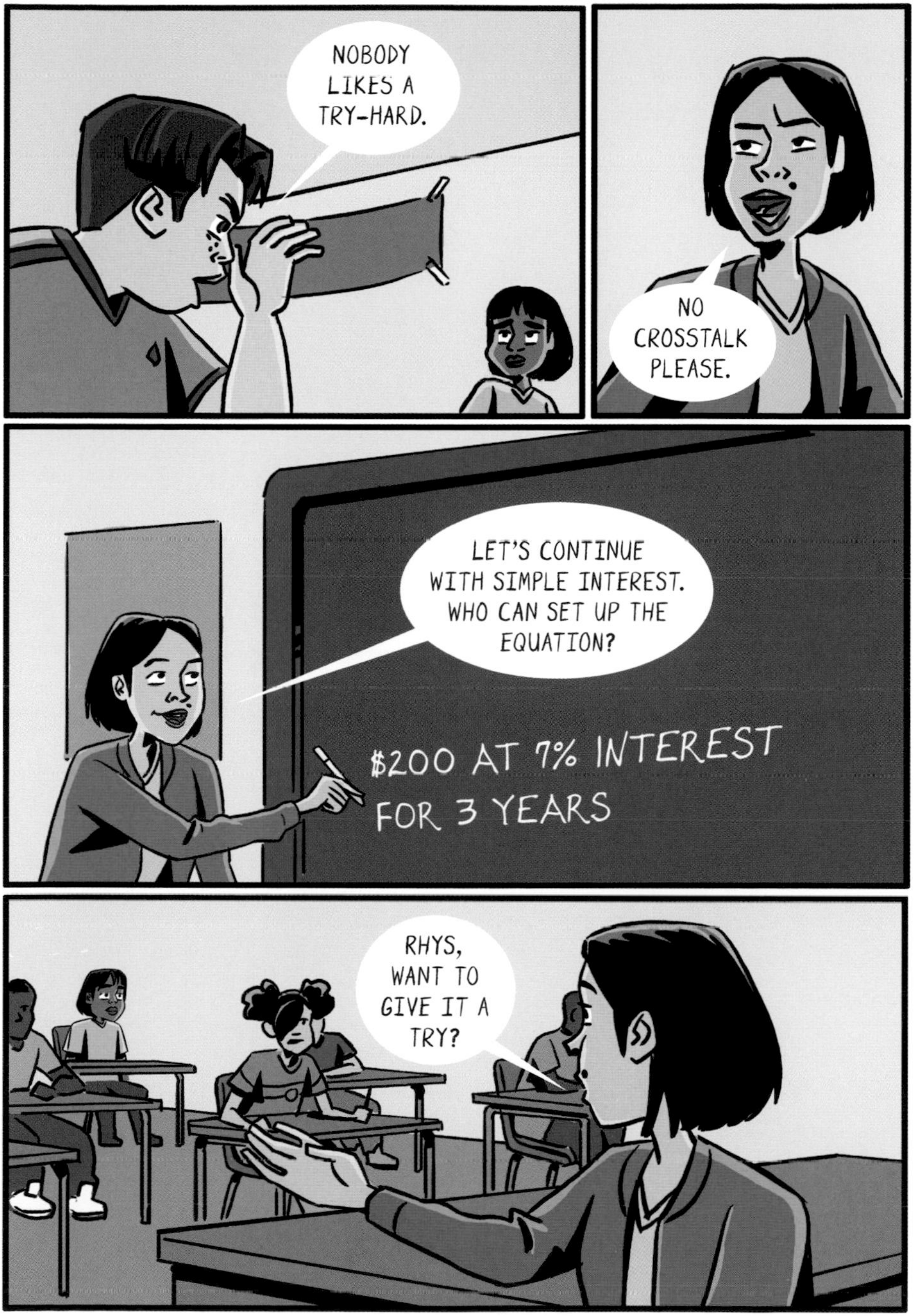
NOBODY LIKES A TRY-HARD.
NO CROSSTALK PLEASE.
LET'S CONTINUE WITH SIMPLE INTEREST. WHO CAN SET UP THE EQUATION?
$200 AT 7% INTEREST FOR 3 YEARS
RHYS, WANT TO GIVE IT A TRY?

CHAPTER 5
STRONGHOLD

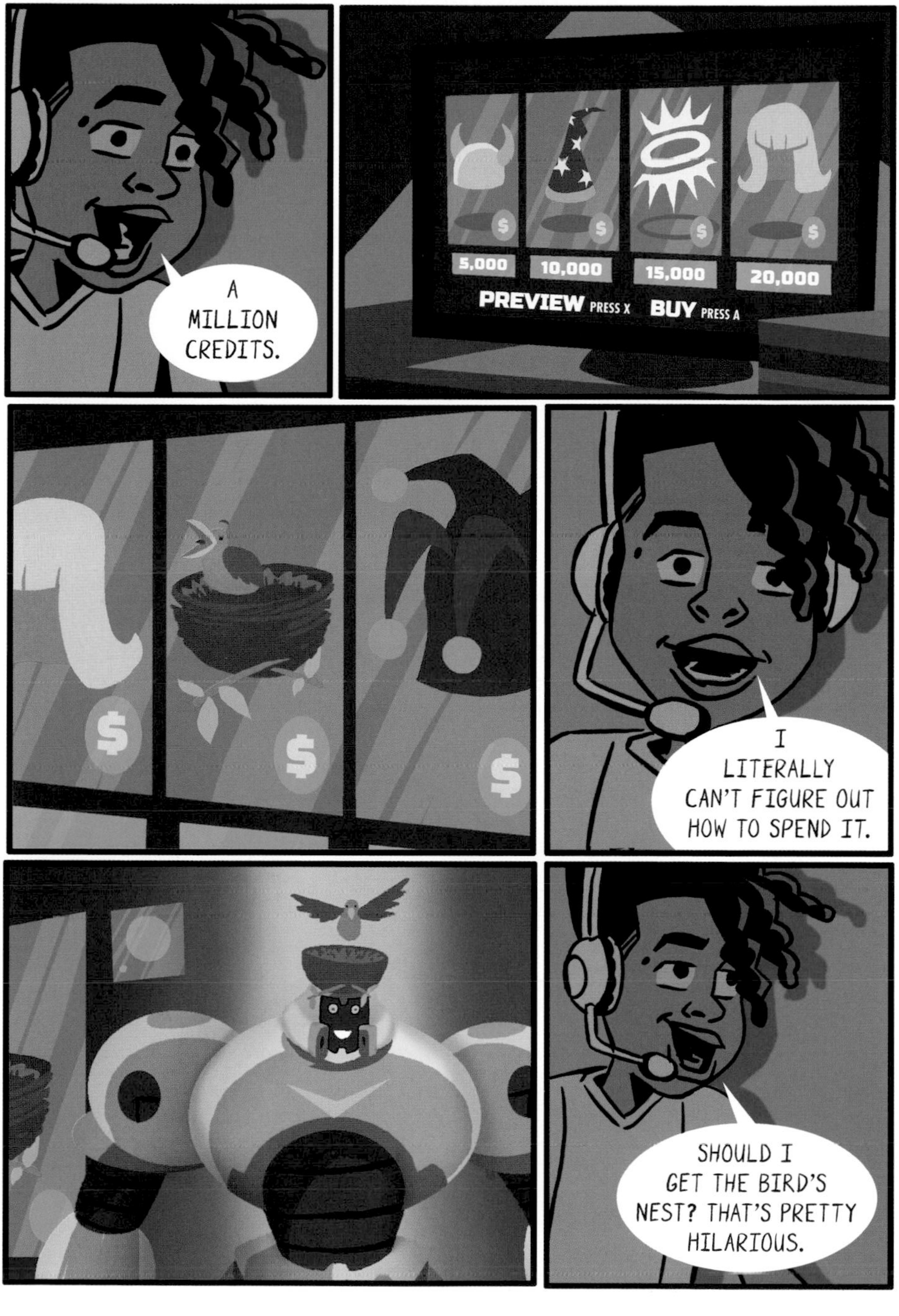
A MILLION CREDITS.
5,000
10,000
15,000
20,000
PREVIEW PRESS X BUY PRESS A
I LITERALLY CAN'T FIGURE OUT HOW TO SPEND IT.
SHOULD I GET THE BIRD'S NEST? THAT'S PRETTY HILARIOUS.

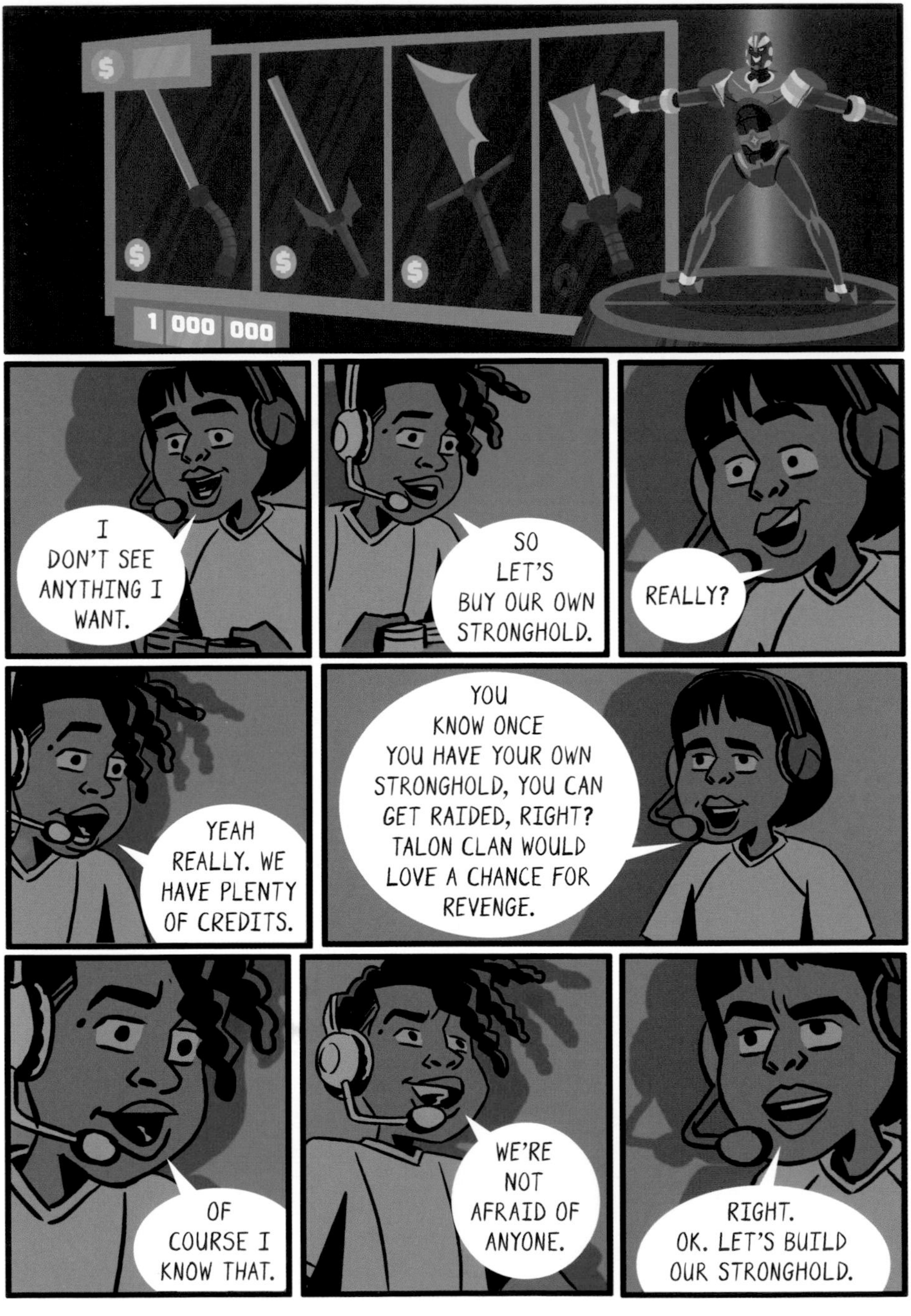
1 000 000
I DON'T SEE ANYTHING I WANT.
SO LET'S BUY OUR OWN STRONGHOLD.
REALLY?
YEAH REALLY. WE HAVE PLENTY OF CREDITS.
YOU KNOW ONCE YOU HAVE YOUR OWN STRONGHOLD, YOU CAN GET RAIDED, RIGHT? TALON CLAN WOULD LOVE A CHANCE FOR REVENGE.
OF COURSE I KNOW THAT.
WE'RE NOT AFRAID OF ANYONE.
RIGHT. OK. LET'S BUILD OUR STRONGHOLD.

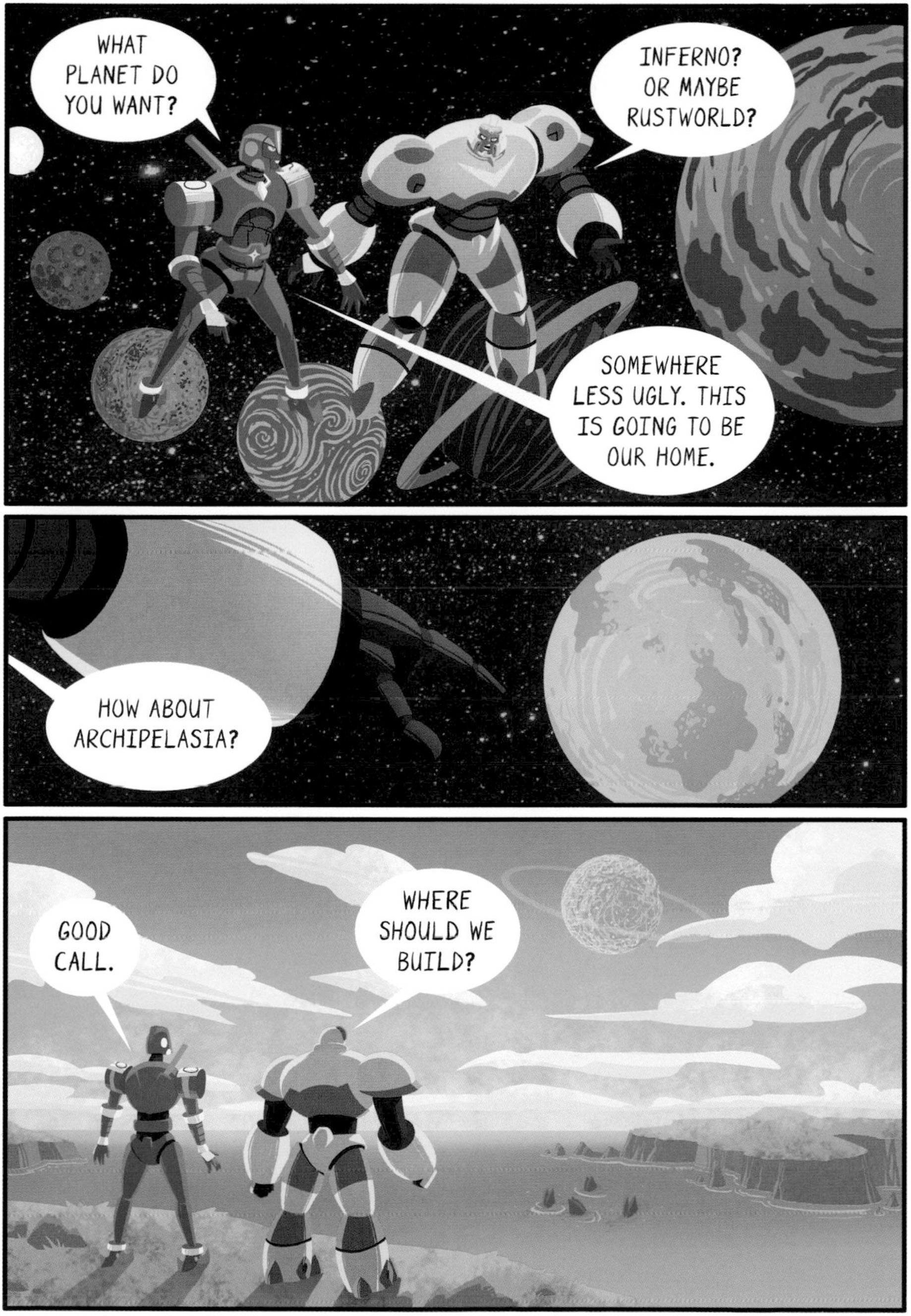
WHAT PLANET DO YOU WANT?
INFERNO? OR MAYBE RUSTWORLD?
SOMEWHERE LESS UGLY. THIS IS GOING TO BE OUR HOME.
HOW ABOUT ARCHIPELASIA?
GOOD CALL.
WHERE SHOULD WE BUILD?

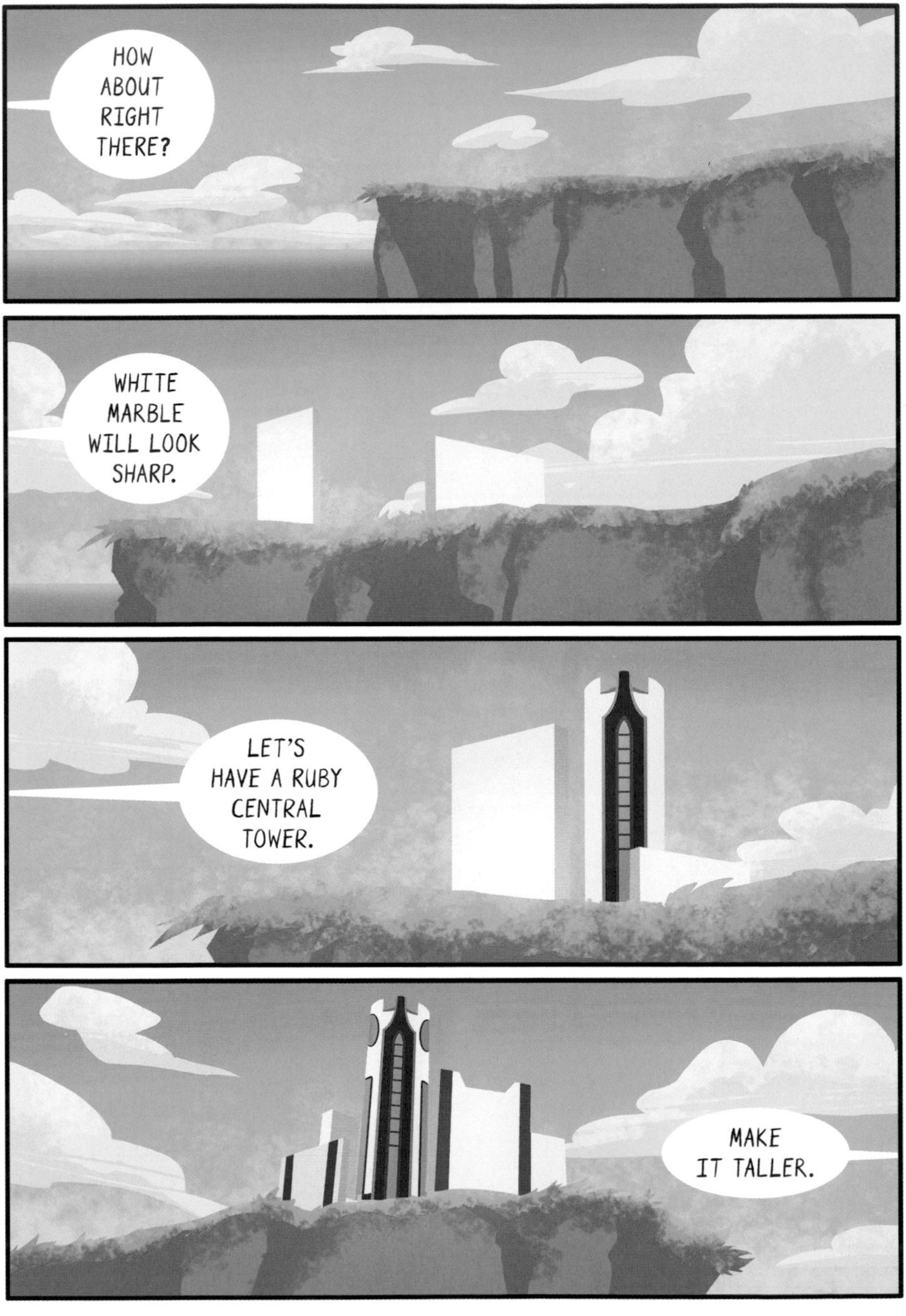
HOW ABOUT RIGHT THERE?
WHITE MARBLE WILL LOOK SHARP.
LET'S HAVE A RUBY CENTRAL TOWER.
MAKE IT TALLER.

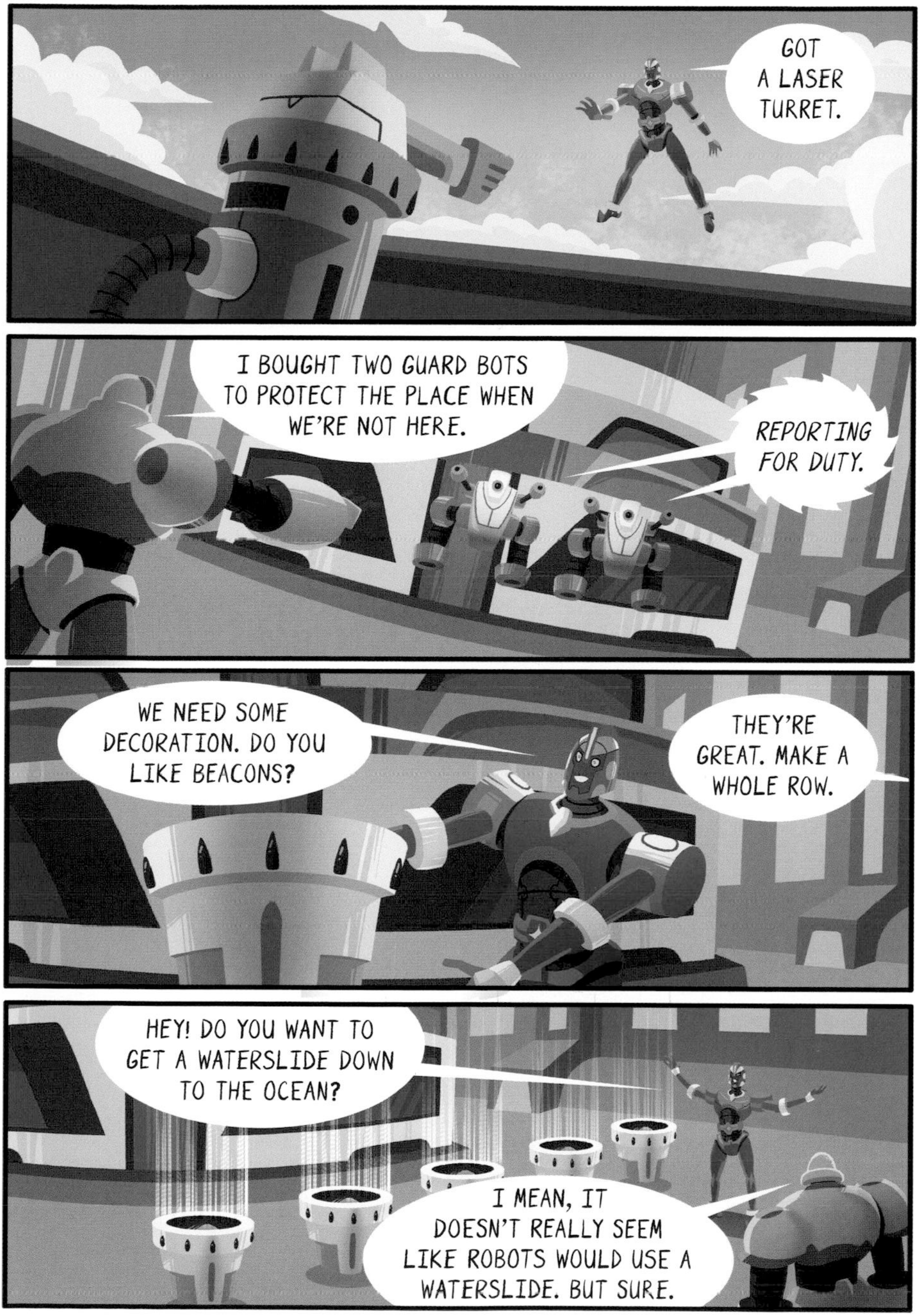
GOT A LASER TURRET.
I BOUGHT TWO GUARD BOTS TO PROTECT THE PLACE WHEN WE'RE NOT HERE.
REPORTING FOR DUTY.
WE NEED SOME DECORATION. DO YOU LIKE BEACONS?
THEY'RE GREAT. MAKE A WHOLE ROW.
HEY! DO YOU WANT TO GET A WATERSLIDE DOWN TO THE OCEAN?
I MEAN, IT DOESN'T REALLY SEEM LIKE ROBOTS WOULD USE A WATERSLIDE. BUT SURE.

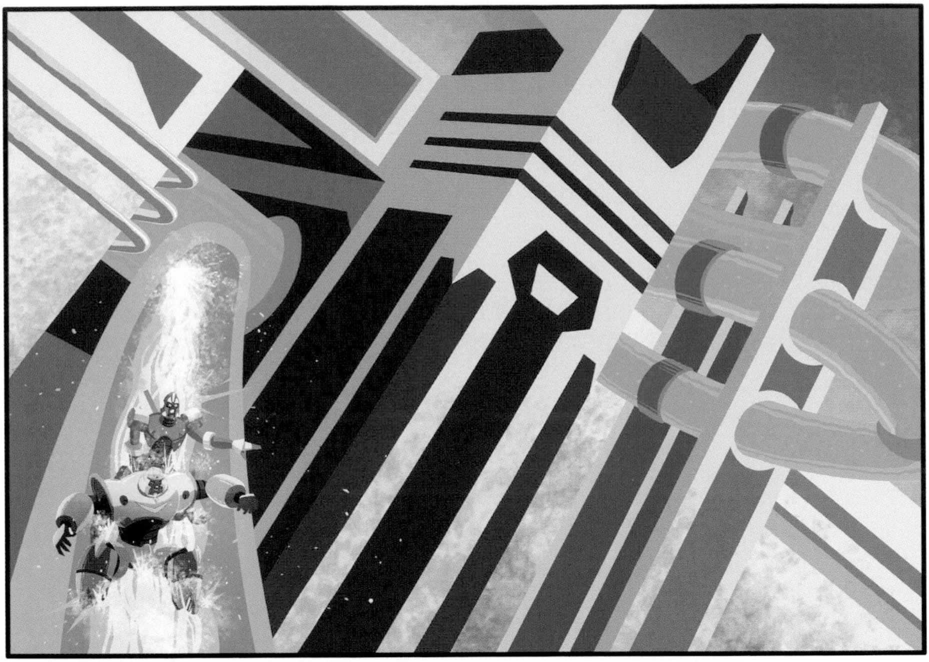

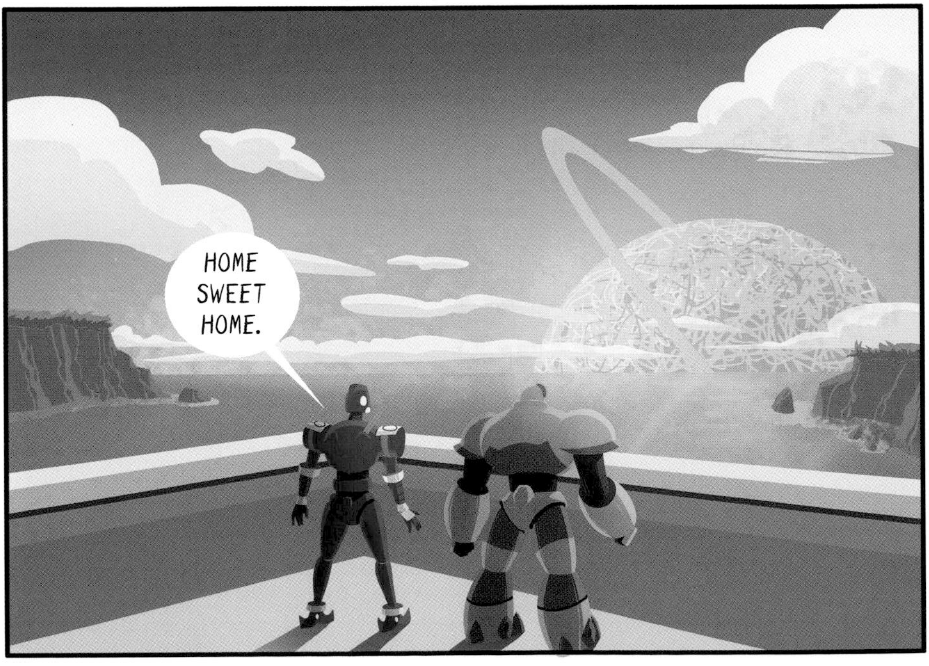
HOME SWEET HOME.

CHAPTER 6
OFF ROAD

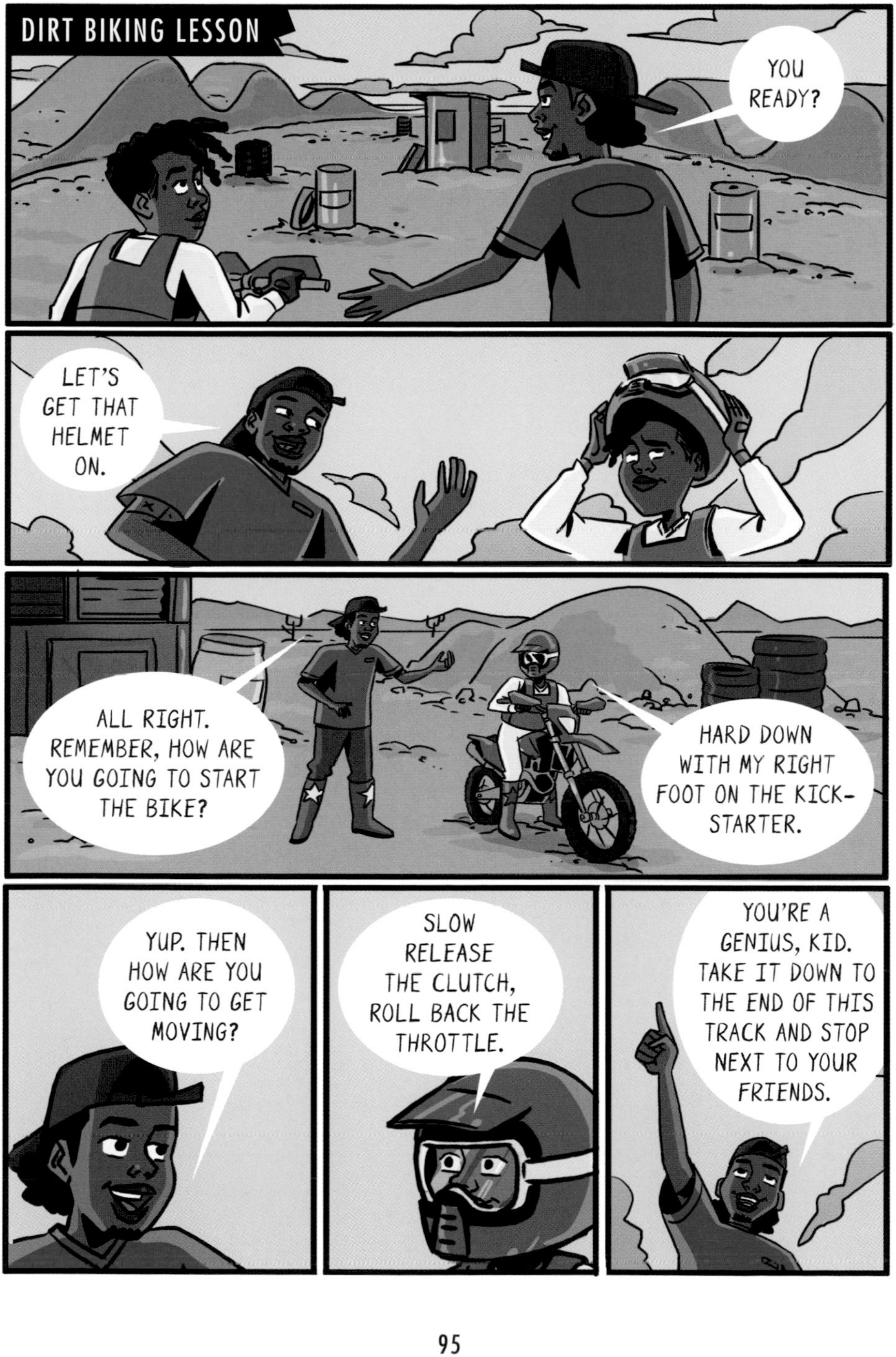
DIRT BIKING LESSON
YOU READY?
LET'S GET THAT HELMET ON.
ALL RIGHT. REMEMBER, HOW ARE YOU GOING TO START THE BIKE?
HARD DOWN WITH MY RIGHT FOOT ON THE KICK-STARTER.
YUP. THEN HOW ARE YOU GOING TO GET MOVING?
SLOW RELEASE THE CLUTCH, ROLL BACK THE THROTTLE.
YOU'RE A GENIUS, KID. TAKE IT DOWN TO THE END OF THIS TRACK AND STOP NEXT TO YOUR FRIENDS.

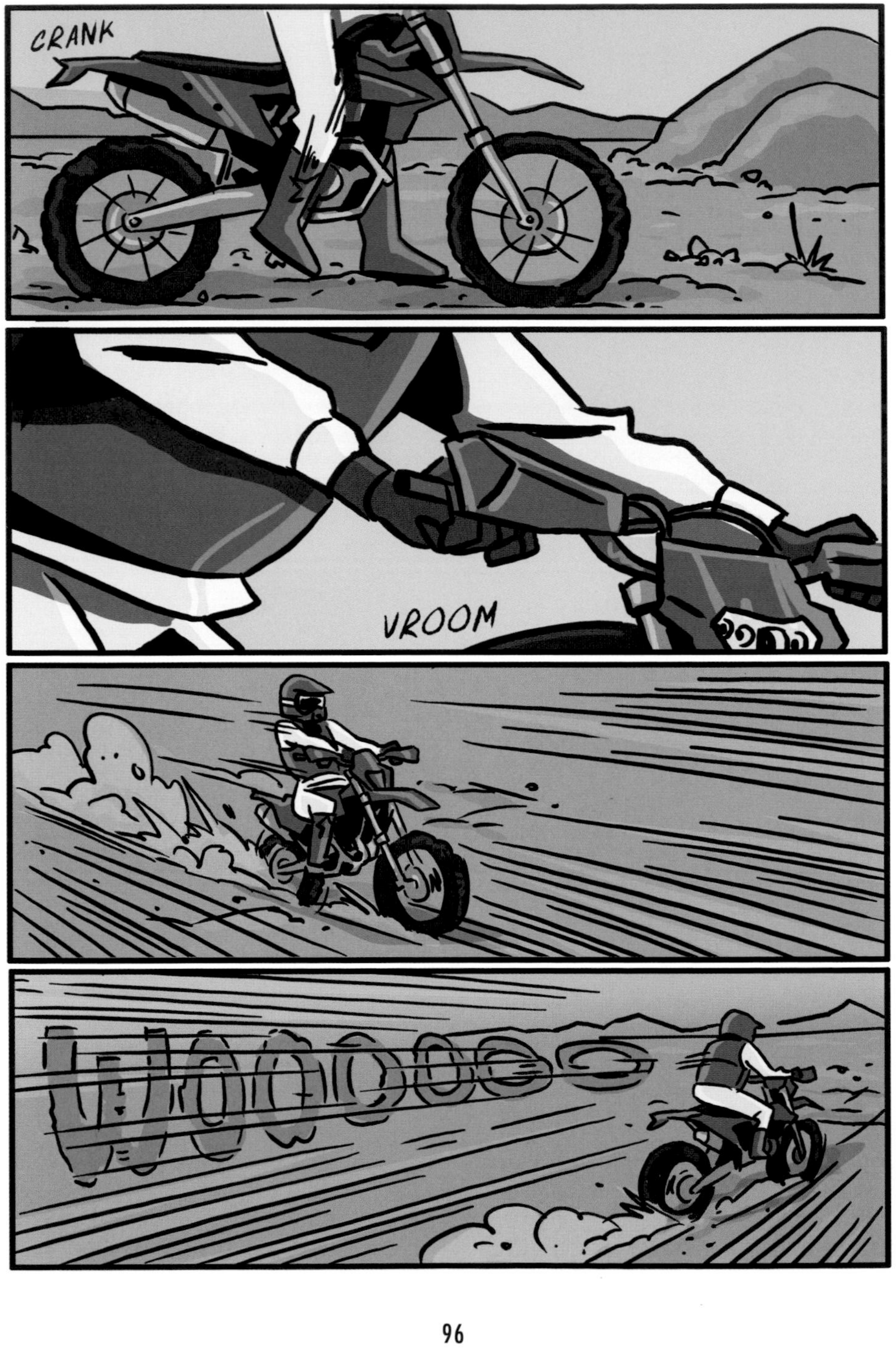
CRANK
VROOM
WOOOOOO

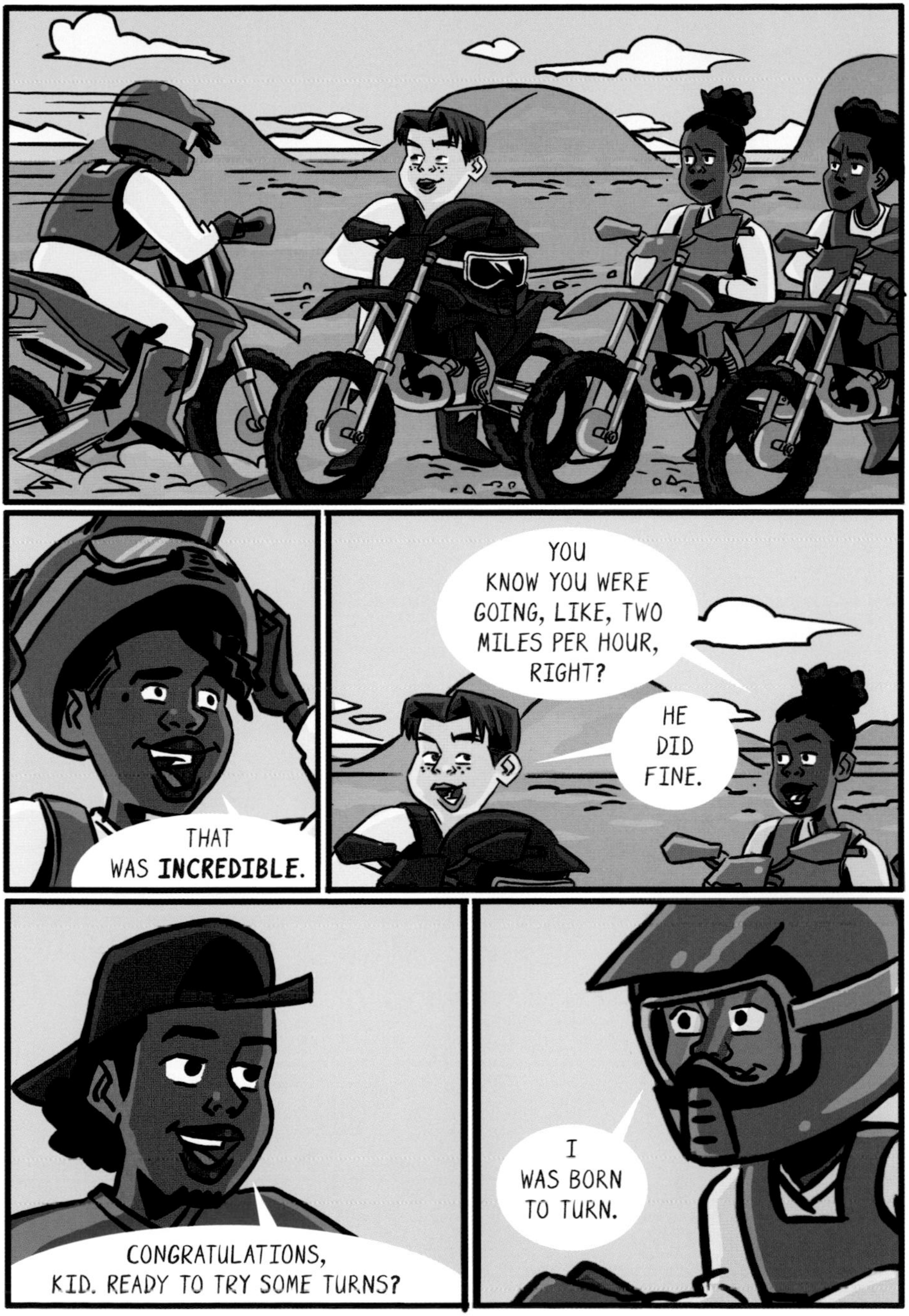
THAT WAS **INCREDIBLE**.
YOU KNOW YOU WERE GOING, LIKE, TWO MILES PER HOUR, RIGHT?
HE DID FINE.
CONGRATULATIONS, KID. READY TO TRY SOME TURNS?
I WAS BORN TO TURN.

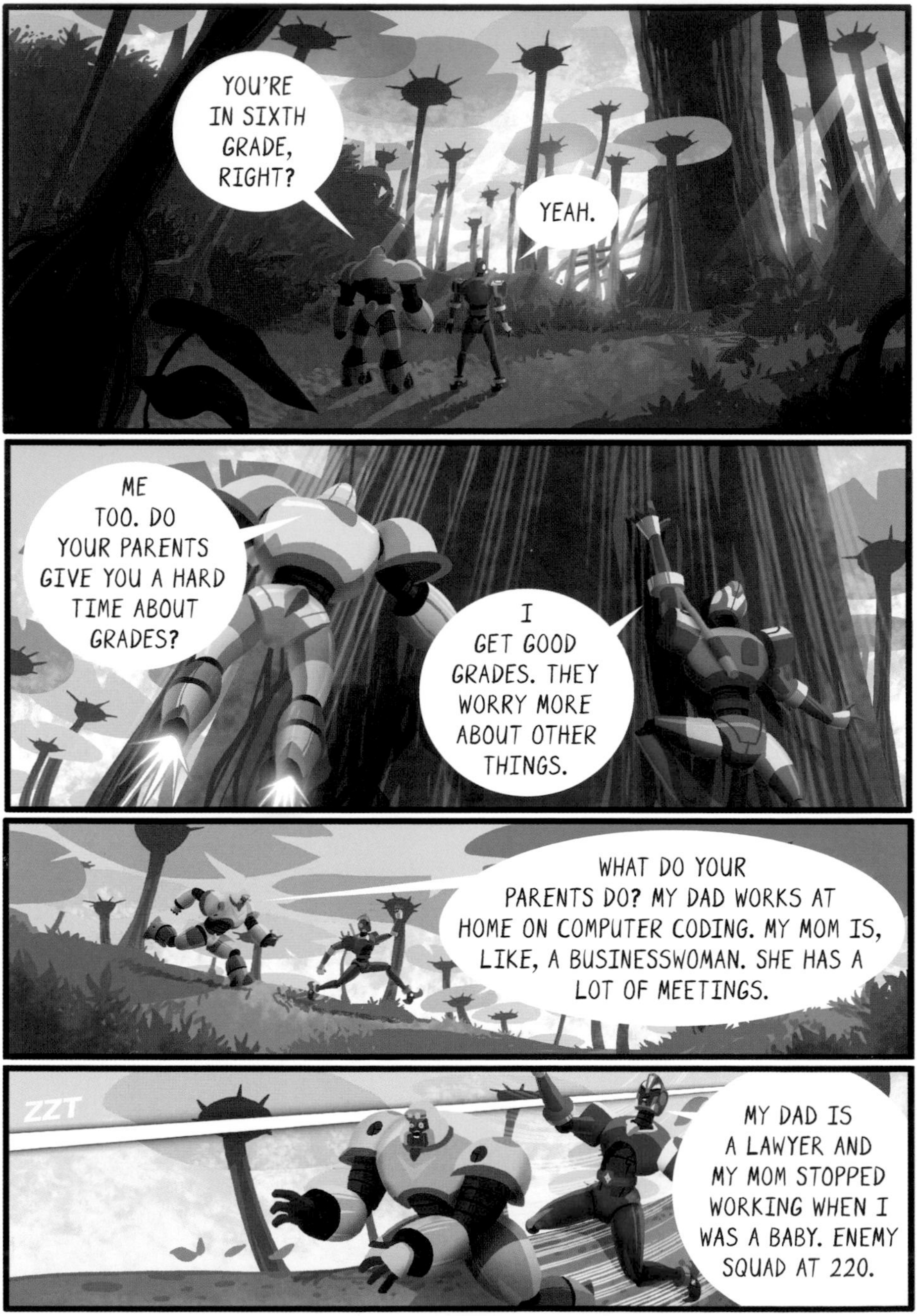
YOU'RE IN SIXTH GRADE, RIGHT?
YEAH.
ME TOO. DO YOUR PARENTS GIVE YOU A HARD TIME ABOUT GRADES?
I GET GOOD GRADES. THEY WORRY MORE ABOUT OTHER THINGS.
WHAT DO YOUR PARENTS DO? MY DAD WORKS AT HOME ON COMPUTER CODING. MY MOM IS, LIKE, A BUSINESSWOMAN. SHE HAS A LOT OF MEETINGS.
ZZT
MY DAD IS A LAWYER AND MY MOM STOPPED WORKING WHEN I WAS A BABY. ENEMY SQUAD AT 220.

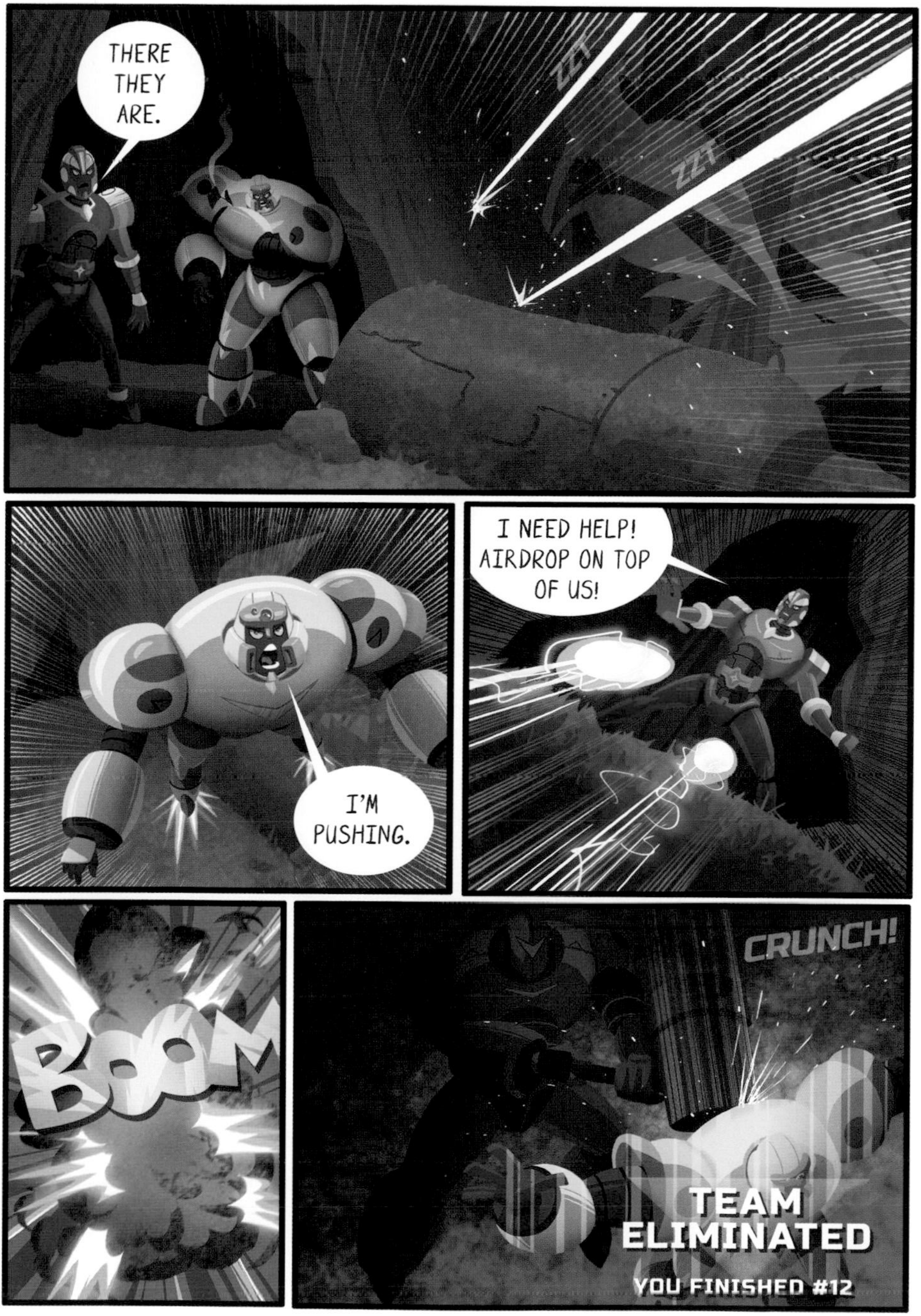
THERE THEY ARE.
ZZT
ZZT
I'M PUSHING.
I NEED HELP! AIRDROP ON TOP OF US!
BOOM
CRUNCH!
TEAM ELIMINATED
YOU FINISHED #12

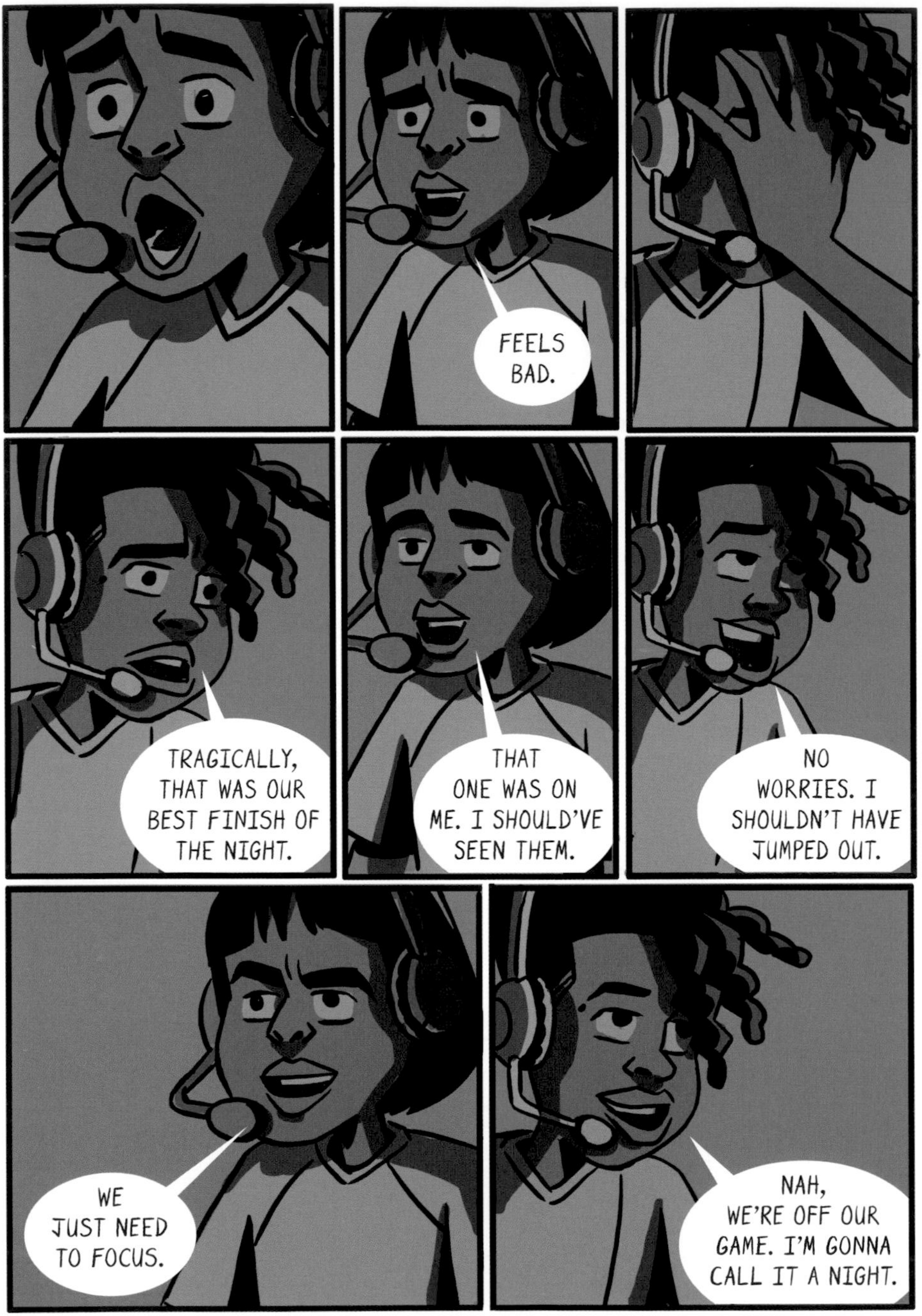
FEELS BAD.
TRAGICALLY, THAT WAS OUR BEST FINISH OF THE NIGHT.
THAT ONE WAS ON ME. I SHOULD'VE SEEN THEM.
NO WORRIES. I SHOULDN'T HAVE JUMPED OUT.
WE JUST NEED TO FOCUS.
NAH, WE'RE OFF OUR GAME. I'M GONNA CALL IT A NIGHT.

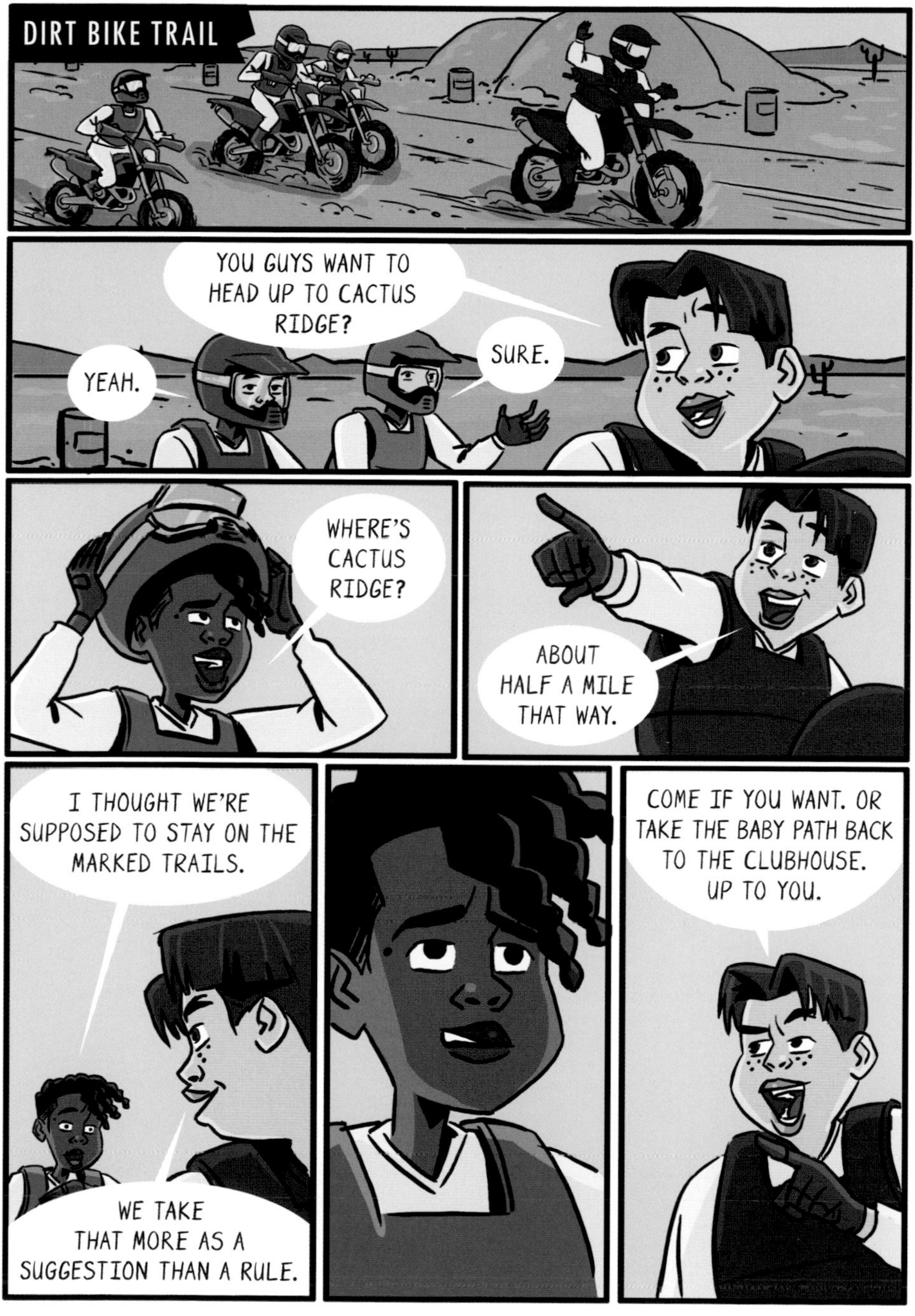
DIRT BIKE TRAIL
YOU GUYS WANT TO HEAD UP TO CACTUS RIDGE?
YEAH.
SURE.
WHERE'S CACTUS RIDGE?
ABOUT HALF A MILE THAT WAY.
I THOUGHT WE'RE SUPPOSED TO STAY ON THE MARKED TRAILS.
WE TAKE THAT MORE AS A SUGGESTION THAN A RULE.
COME IF YOU WANT. OR TAKE THE BABY PATH BACK TO THE CLUBHOUSE. UP TO YOU.

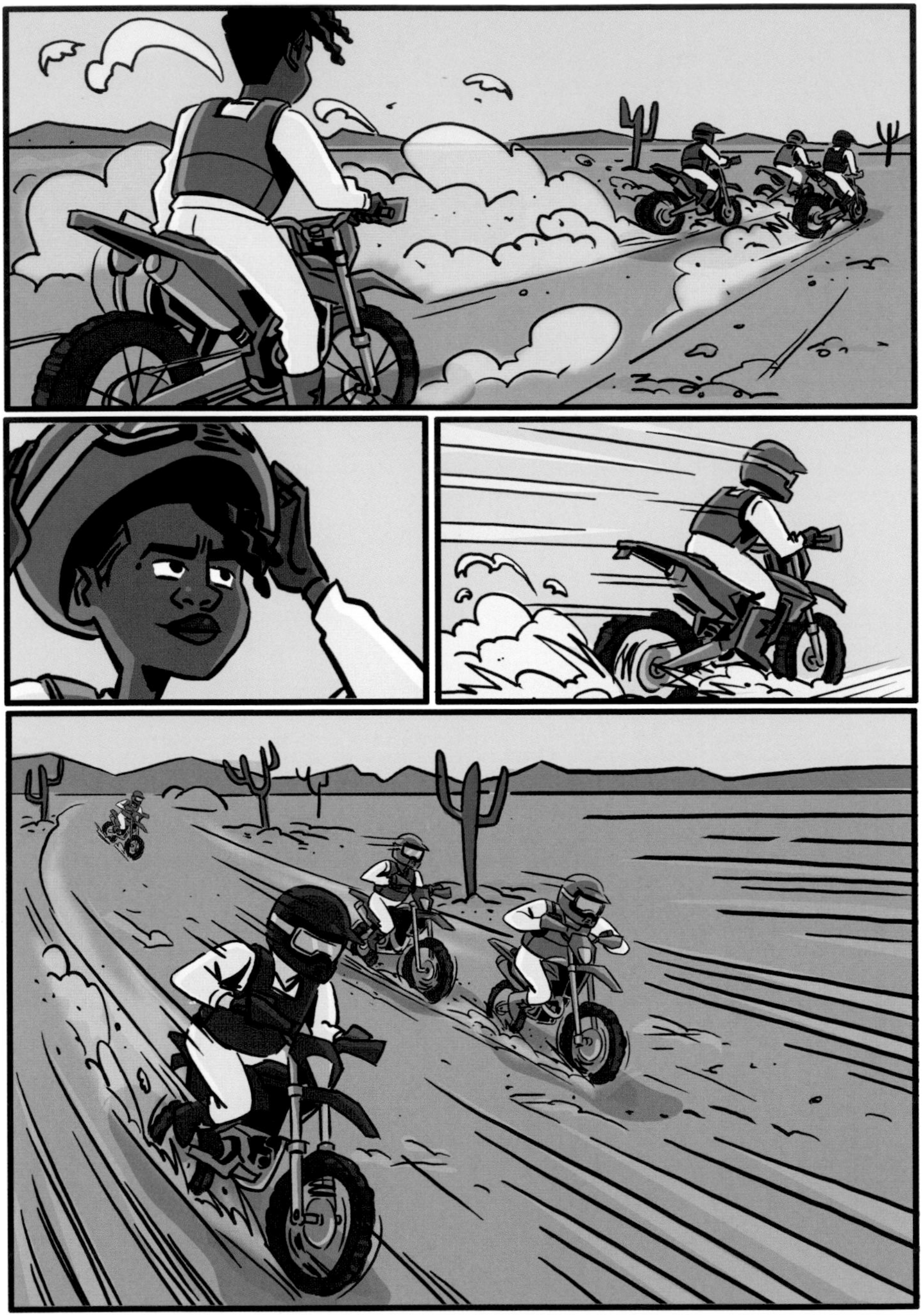

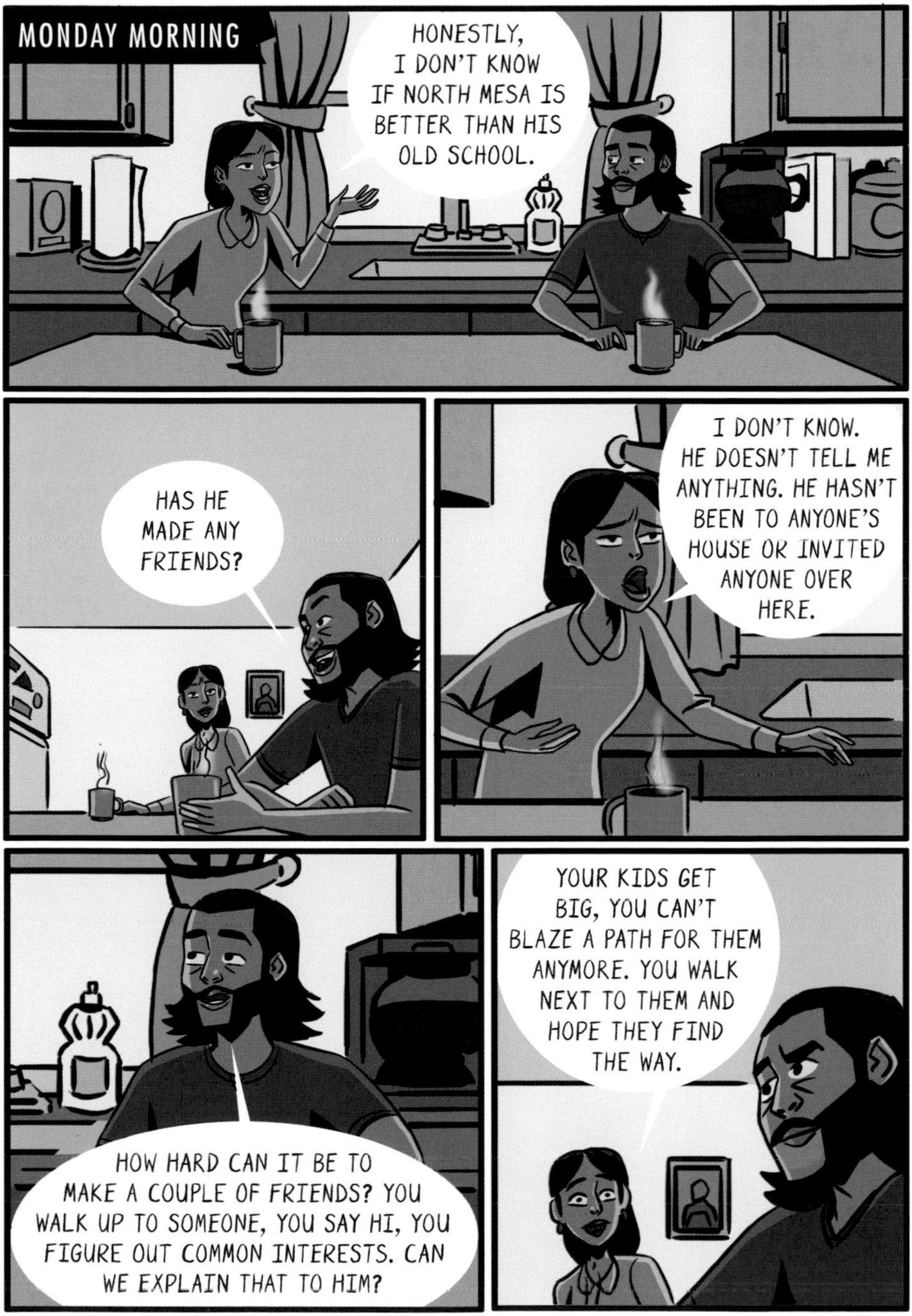
MONDAY MORNING
HONESTLY, I DON'T KNOW IF NORTH MESA IS BETTER THAN HIS OLD SCHOOL.
HAS HE MADE ANY FRIENDS?
I DON'T KNOW. HE DOESN'T TELL ME ANYTHING. HE HASN'T BEEN TO ANYONE'S HOUSE OR INVITED ANYONE OVER HERE.
HOW HARD CAN IT BE TO MAKE A COUPLE OF FRIENDS? YOU WALK UP TO SOMEONE, YOU SAY HI, YOU FIGURE OUT COMMON INTERESTS. CAN WE EXPLAIN THAT TO HIM?
YOUR KIDS GET BIG, YOU CAN'T BLAZE A PATH FOR THEM ANYMORE. YOU WALK NEXT TO THEM AND HOPE THEY FIND THE WAY.

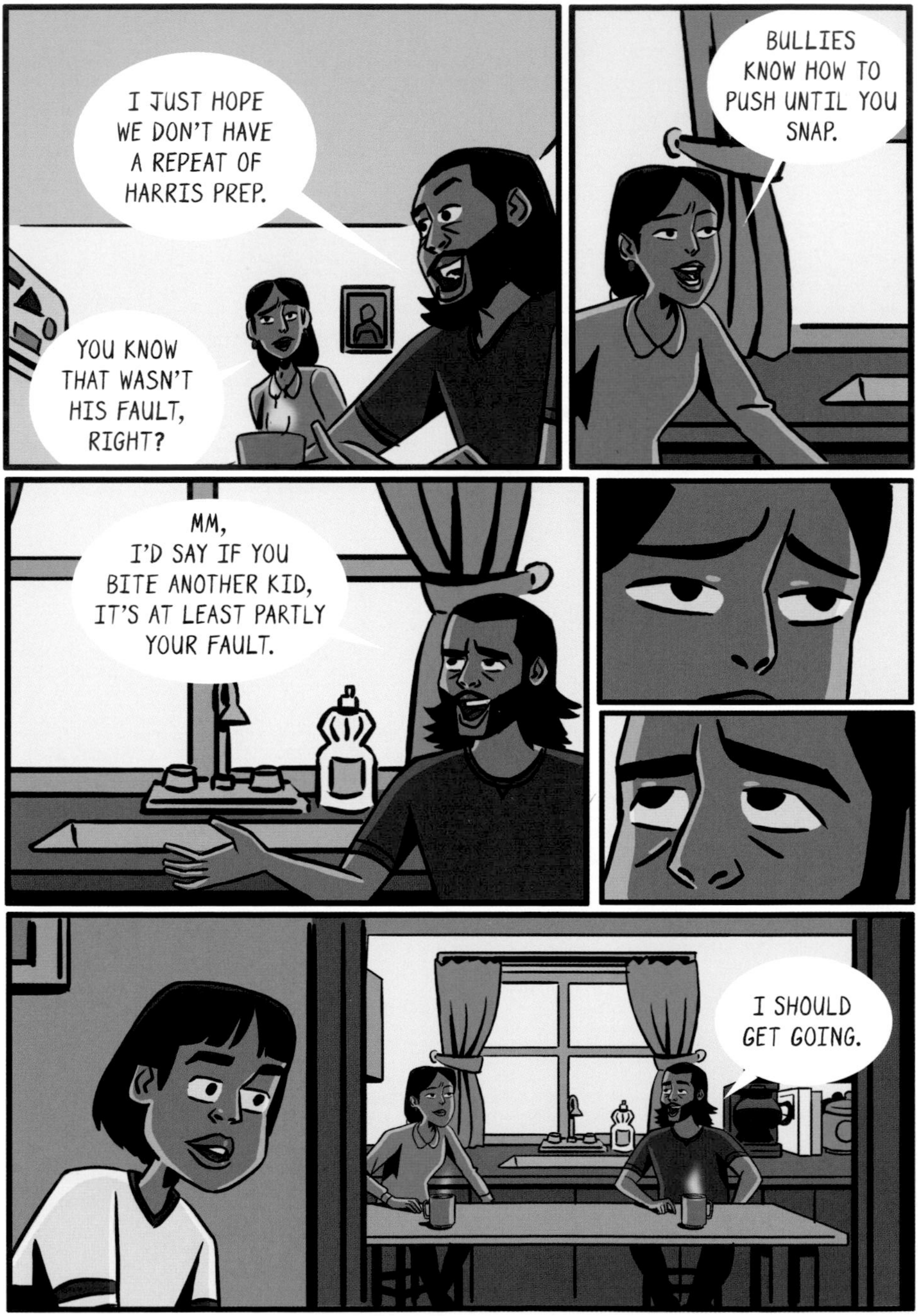
I JUST HOPE WE DON'T HAVE A REPEAT OF HARRIS PREP.
YOU KNOW THAT WASN'T HIS FAULT, RIGHT?
BULLIES KNOW HOW TO PUSH UNTIL YOU SNAP.
MM, I'D SAY IF YOU BITE ANOTHER KID, IT'S AT LEAST PARTLY YOUR FAULT.
I SHOULD GET GOING.

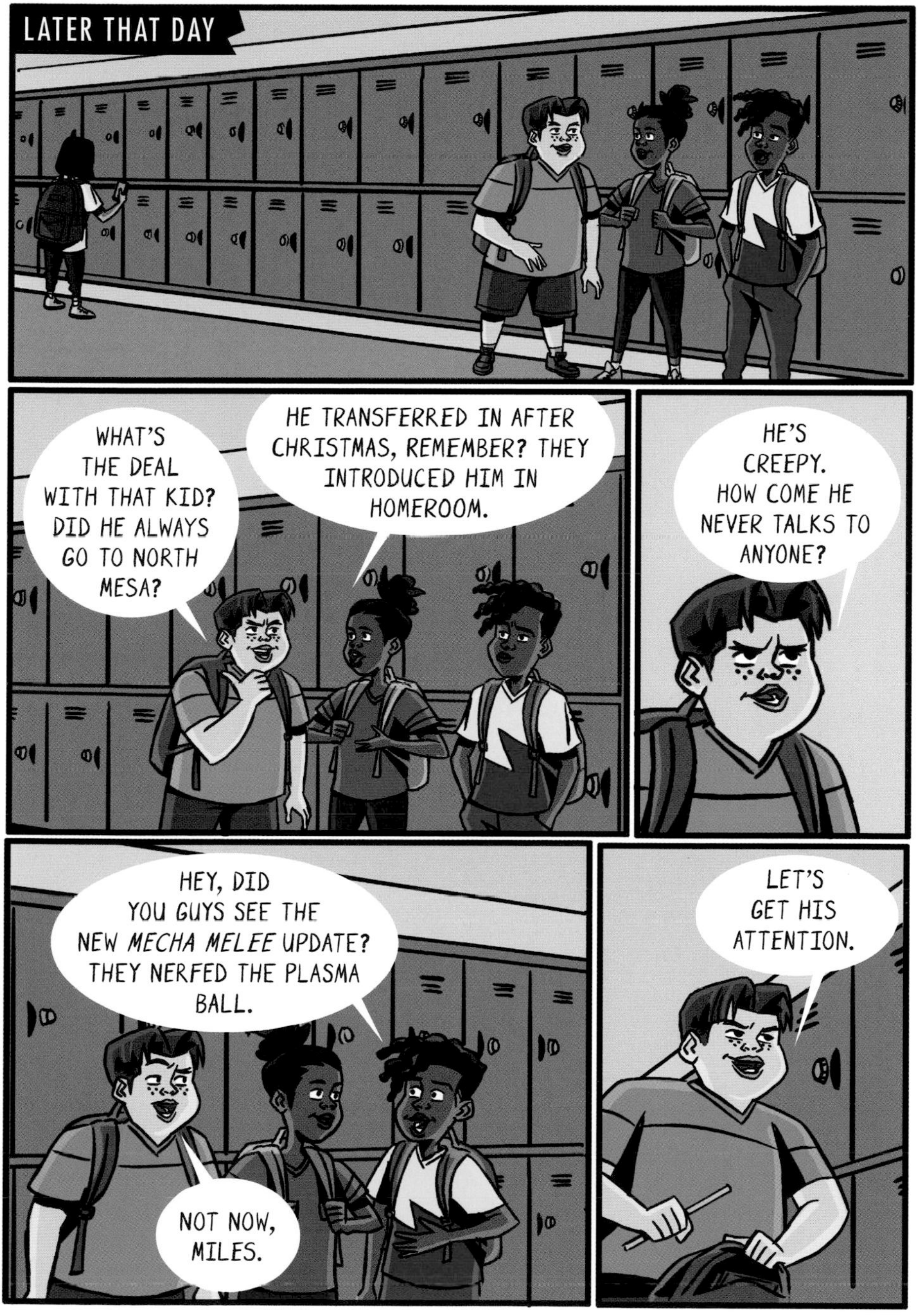
LATER THAT DAY
WHAT'S THE DEAL WITH THAT KID? DID HE ALWAYS GO TO NORTH MESA?
HE TRANSFERRED IN AFTER CHRISTMAS, REMEMBER? THEY INTRODUCED HIM IN HOMEROOM.
HE'S CREEPY. HOW COME HE NEVER TALKS TO ANYONE?
HEY, DID YOU GUYS SEE THE NEW *MECHA MELEE* UPDATE? THEY NERFED THE PLASMA BALL.
NOT NOW, MILES.
LET'S GET HIS ATTENTION.

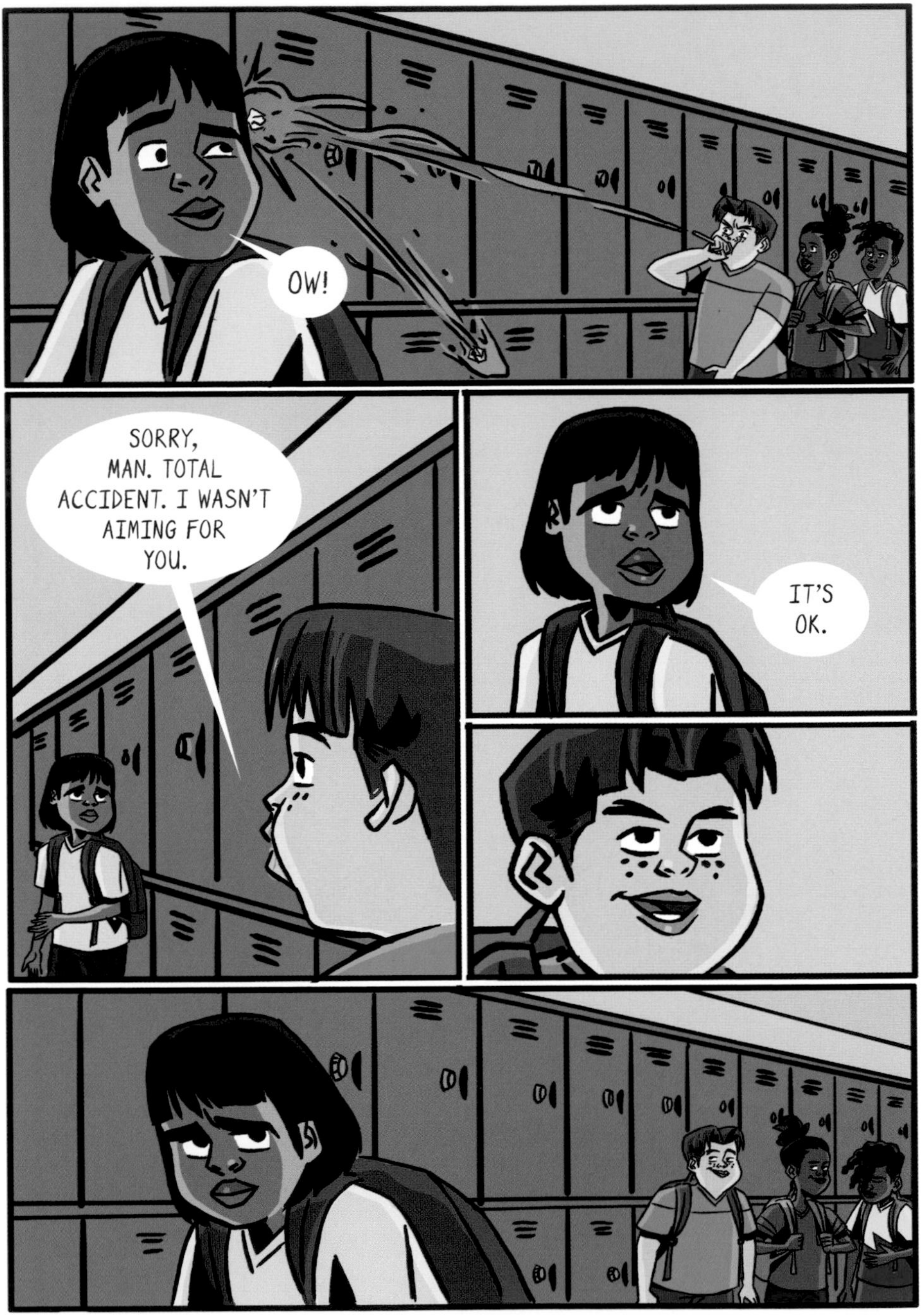
OW!
SORRY, MAN. TOTAL ACCIDENT. I WASN'T AIMING FOR YOU.
IT'S OK.

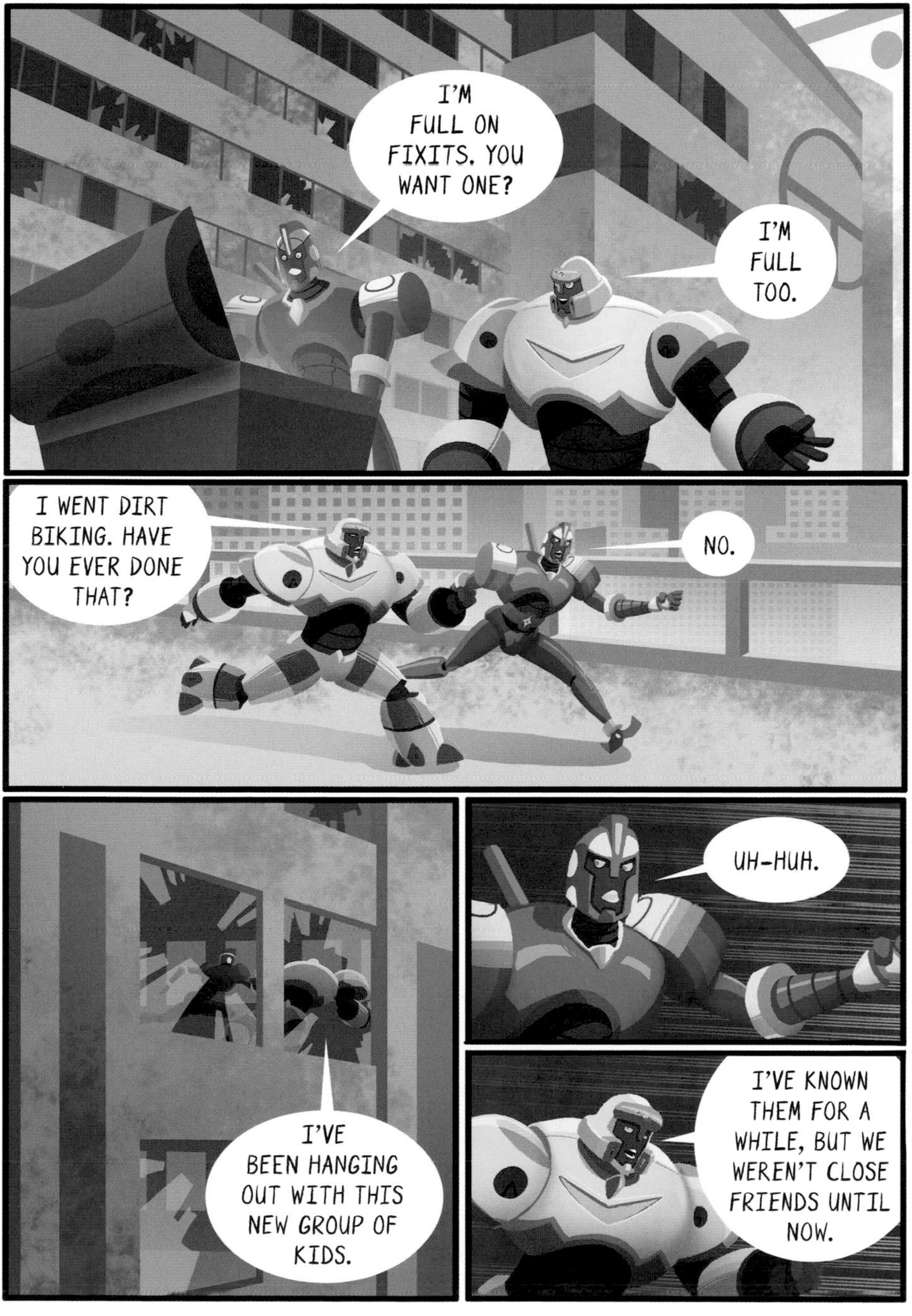
I'M FULL ON FIXITS. YOU WANT ONE?
I'M FULL TOO.
I WENT DIRT BIKING. HAVE YOU EVER DONE THAT?
NO.
I'VE BEEN HANGING OUT WITH THIS NEW GROUP OF KIDS.
UH-HUH.
I'VE KNOWN THEM FOR A WHILE, BUT WE WEREN'T CLOSE FRIENDS UNTIL NOW.

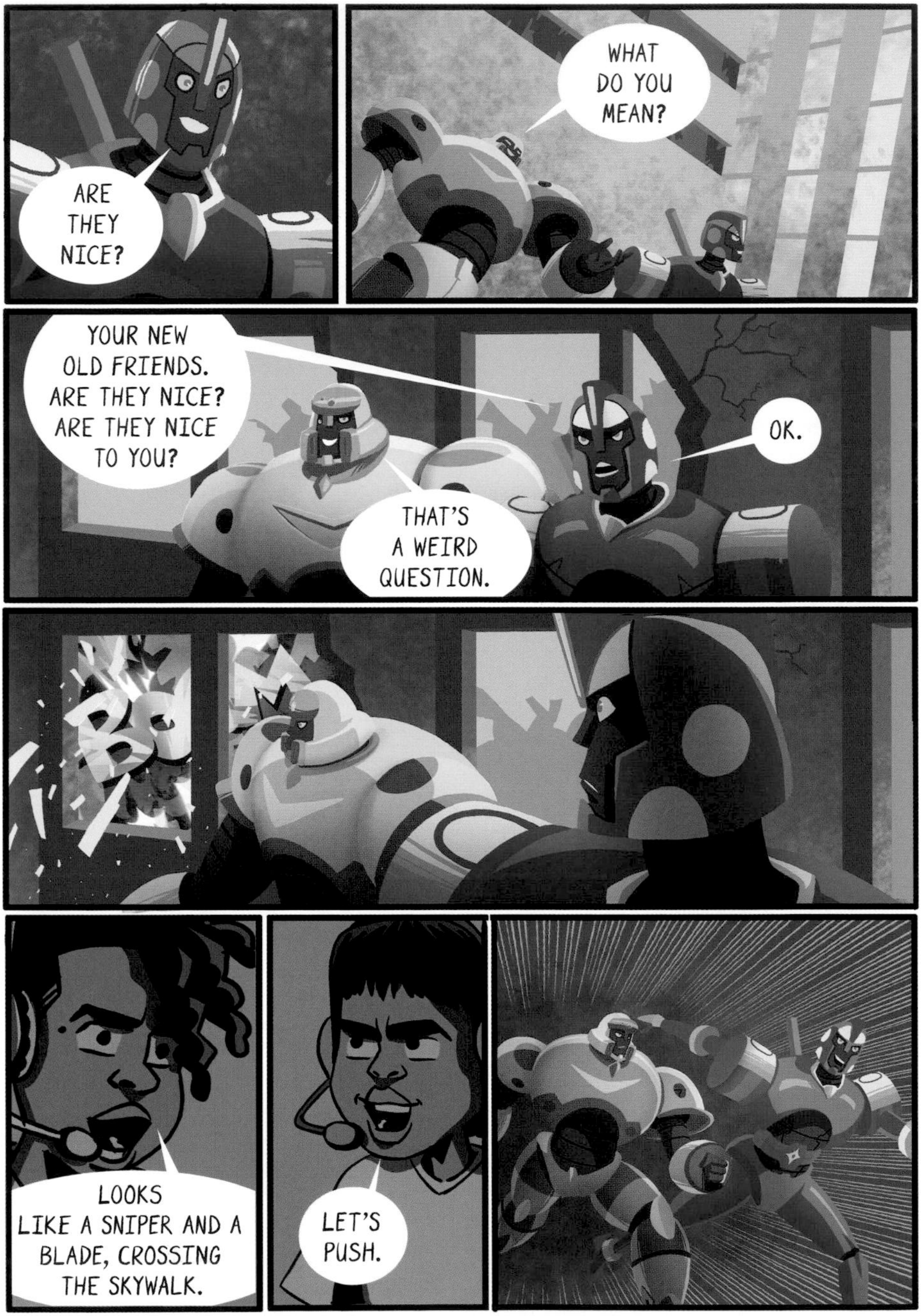
ARE THEY NICE?
WHAT DO YOU MEAN?
YOUR NEW OLD FRIENDS. ARE THEY NICE? ARE THEY NICE TO YOU?
THAT'S A WEIRD QUESTION.
OK.
LOOKS LIKE A SNIPER AND A BLADE, CROSSING THE SKYWALK.
LET'S PUSH.

CHAPTER 7
KEEP-AWAY

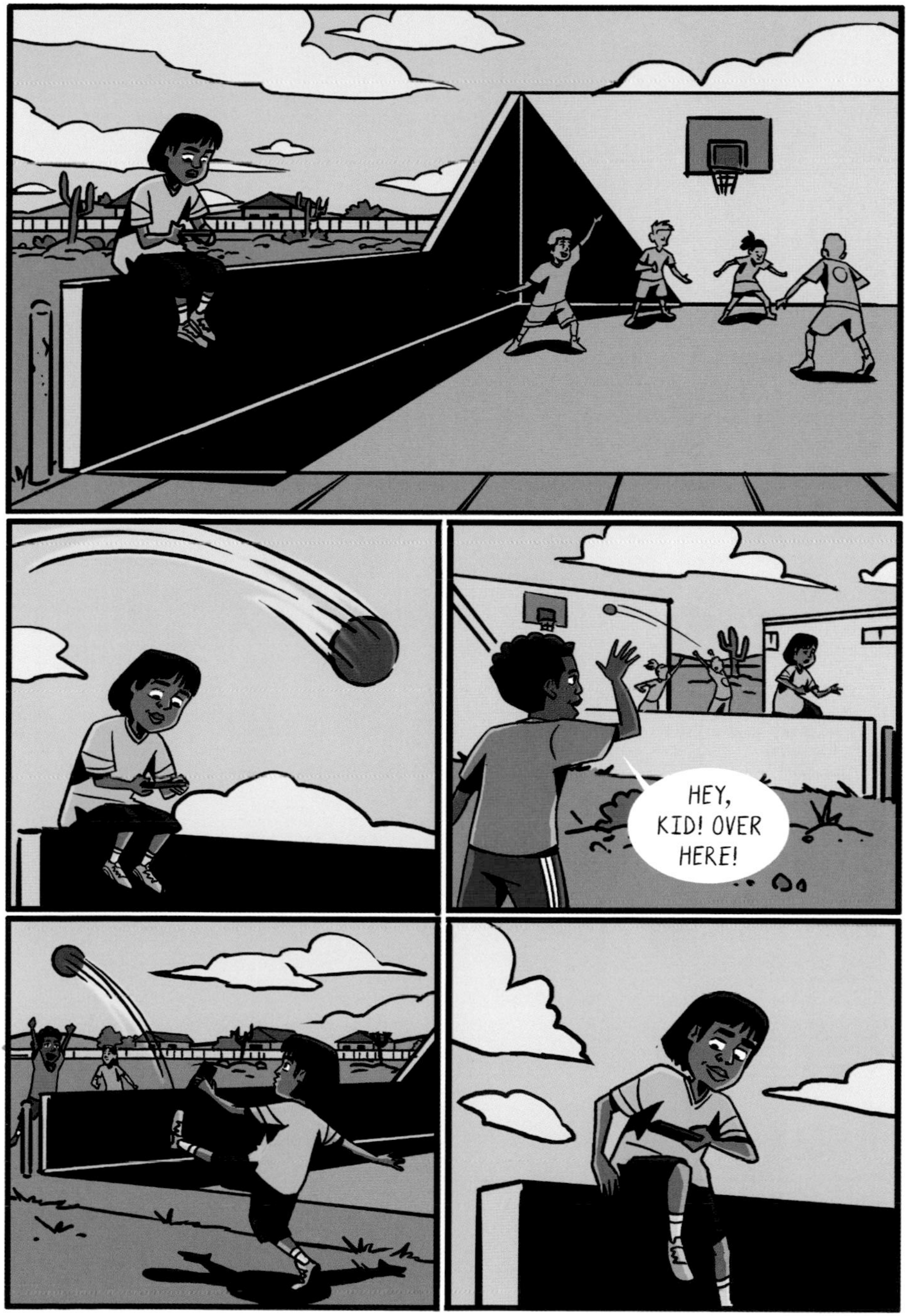
HEY, KID! OVER HERE!

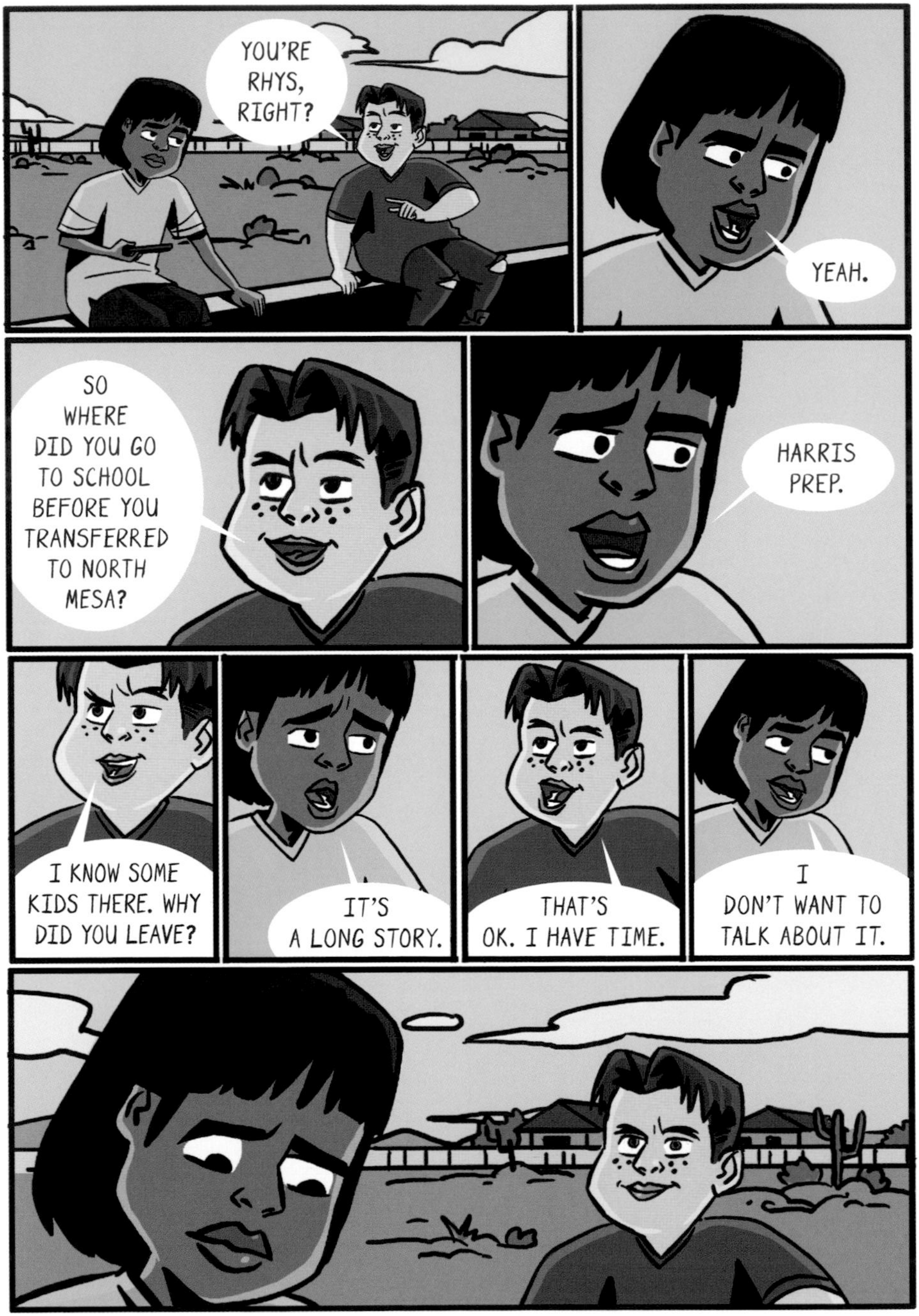
YOU'RE RHYS, RIGHT?
YEAH.
SO WHERE DID YOU GO TO SCHOOL BEFORE YOU TRANSFERRED TO NORTH MESA?
HARRIS PREP.
I KNOW SOME KIDS THERE. WHY DID YOU LEAVE?
IT'S A LONG STORY.
THAT'S OK. I HAVE TIME.
I DON'T WANT TO TALK ABOUT IT.

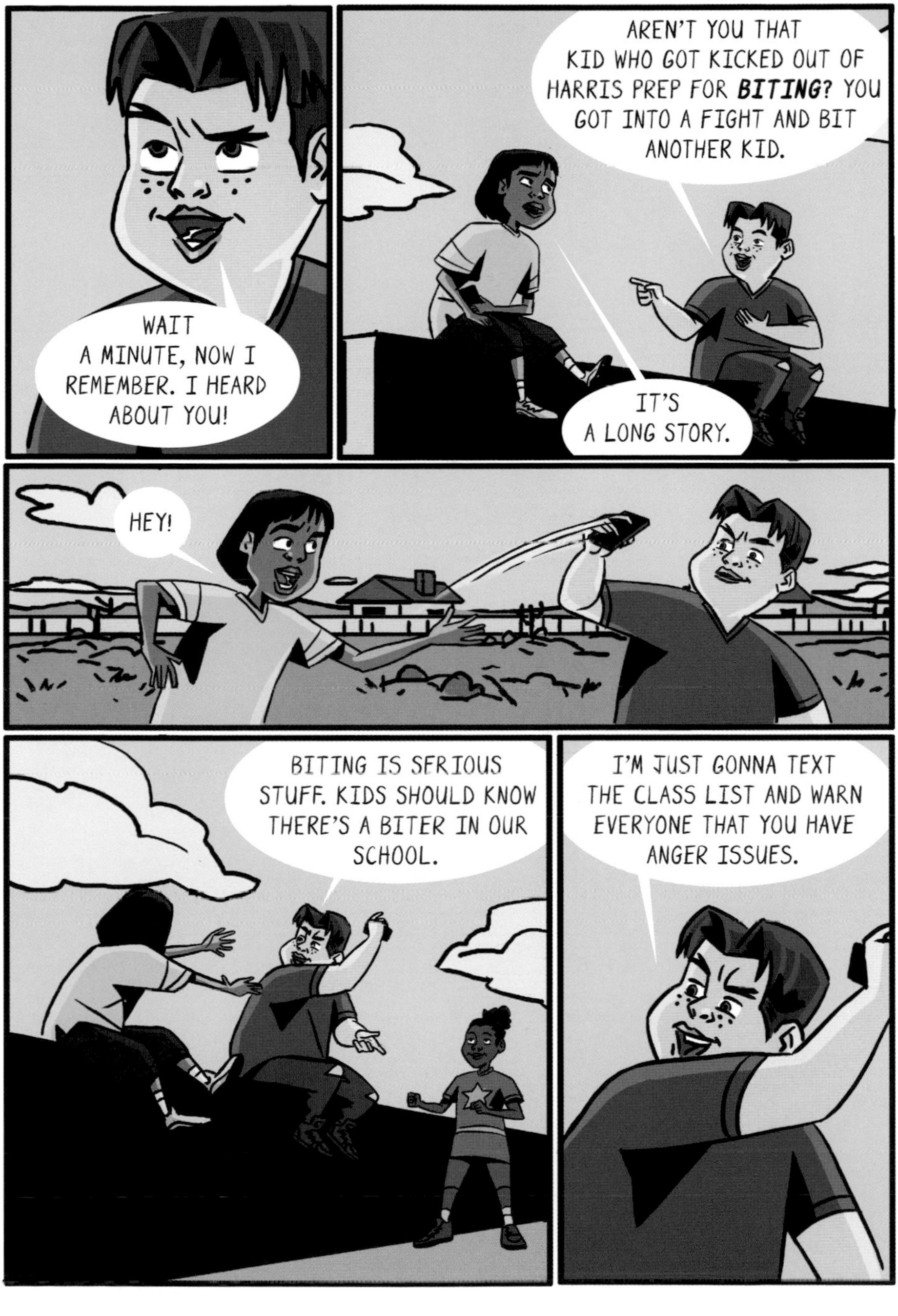
WAIT A MINUTE, NOW I REMEMBER. I HEARD ABOUT YOU!
AREN'T YOU THAT KID WHO GOT KICKED OUT OF HARRIS PREP FOR BITING? YOU GOT INTO A FIGHT AND BIT ANOTHER KID.
IT'S A LONG STORY.
HEY!
BITING IS SERIOUS STUFF. KIDS SHOULD KNOW THERE'S A BITER IN OUR SCHOOL.
I'M JUST GONNA TEXT THE CLASS LIST AND WARN EVERYONE THAT YOU HAVE ANGER ISSUES.

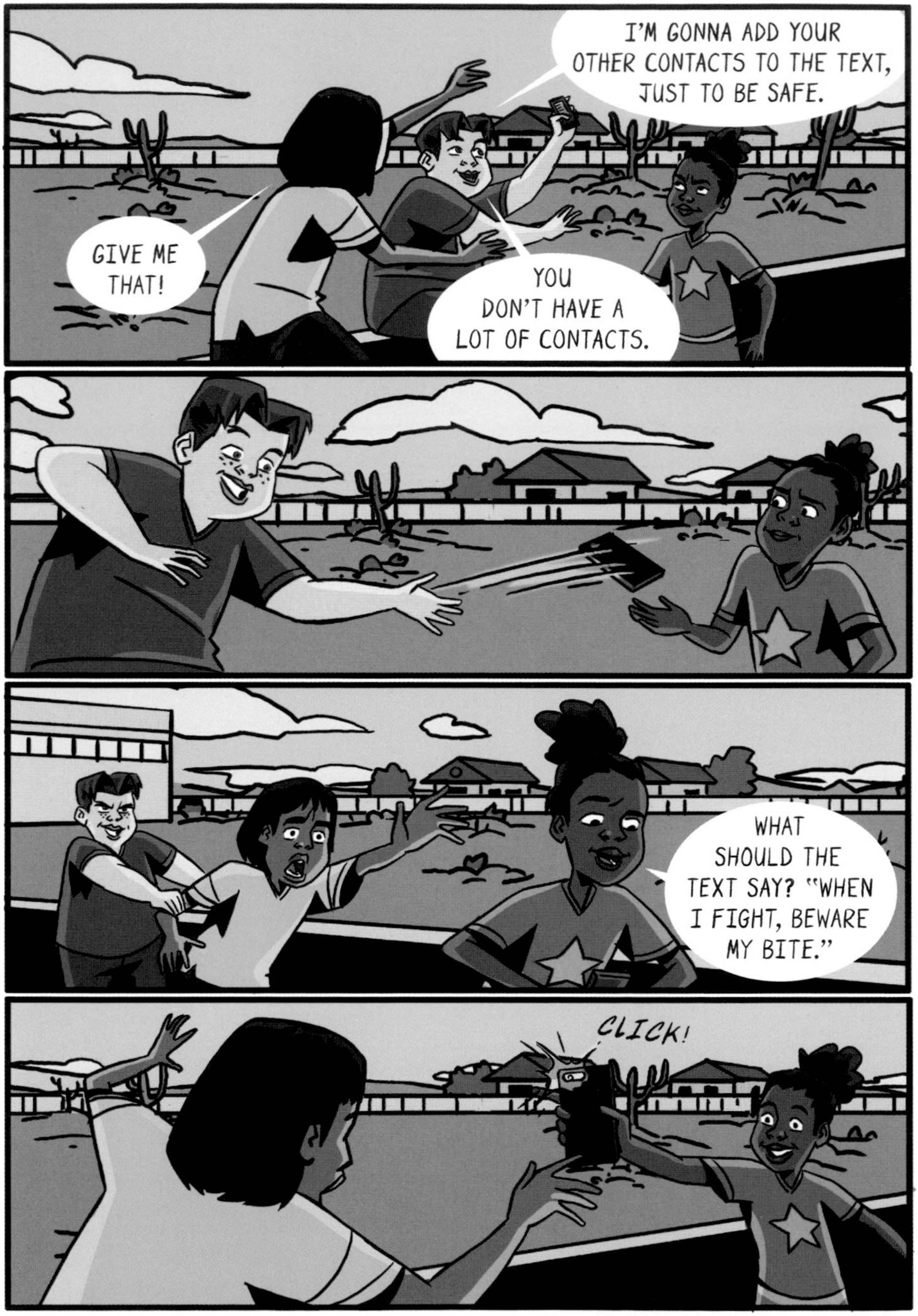
I'M GONNA ADD YOUR OTHER CONTACTS TO THE TEXT, JUST TO BE SAFE.
GIVE ME THAT!
YOU DON'T HAVE A LOT OF CONTACTS.
WHAT SHOULD THE TEXT SAY? "WHEN I FIGHT, BEWARE MY BITE."
CLICK!

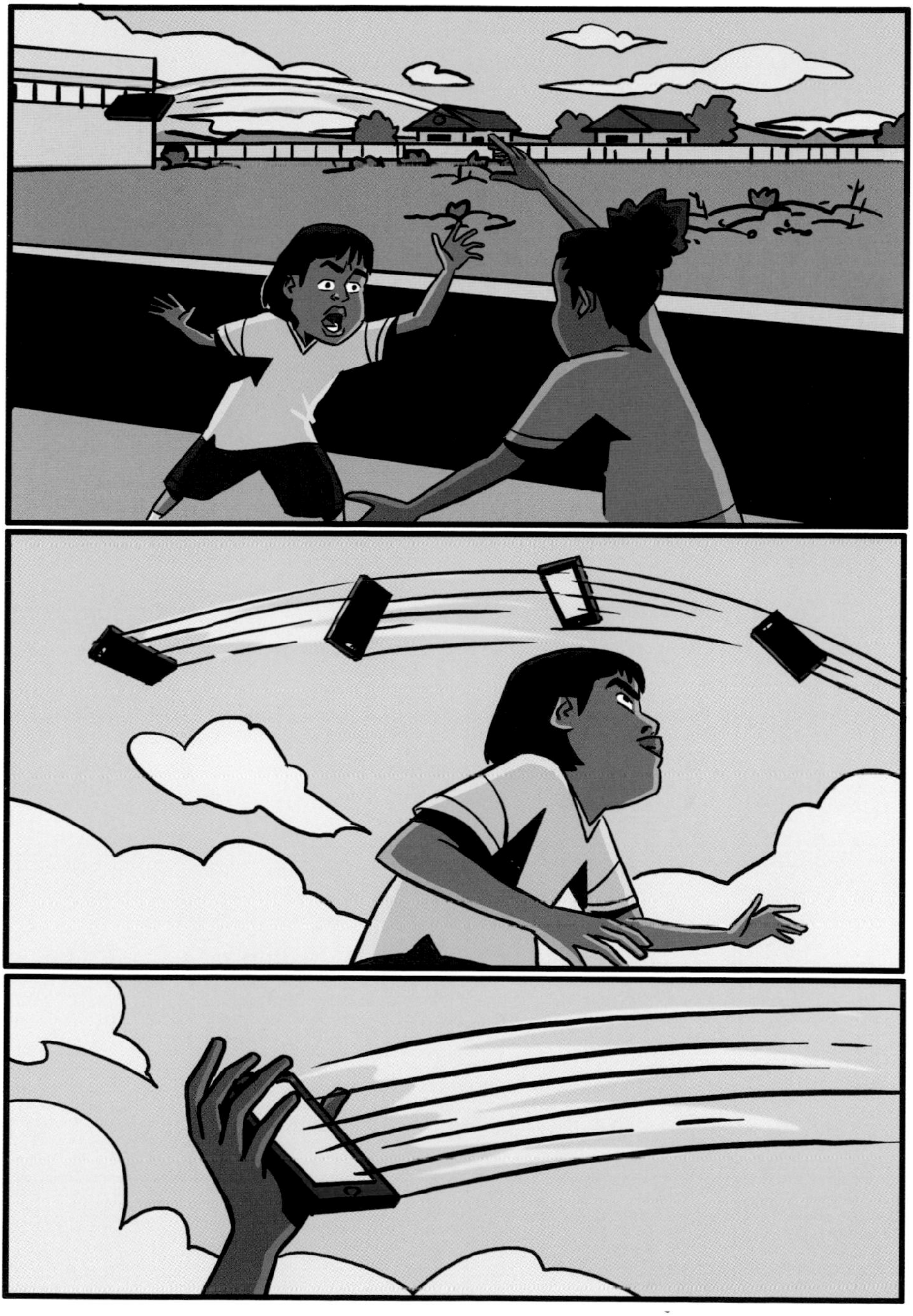

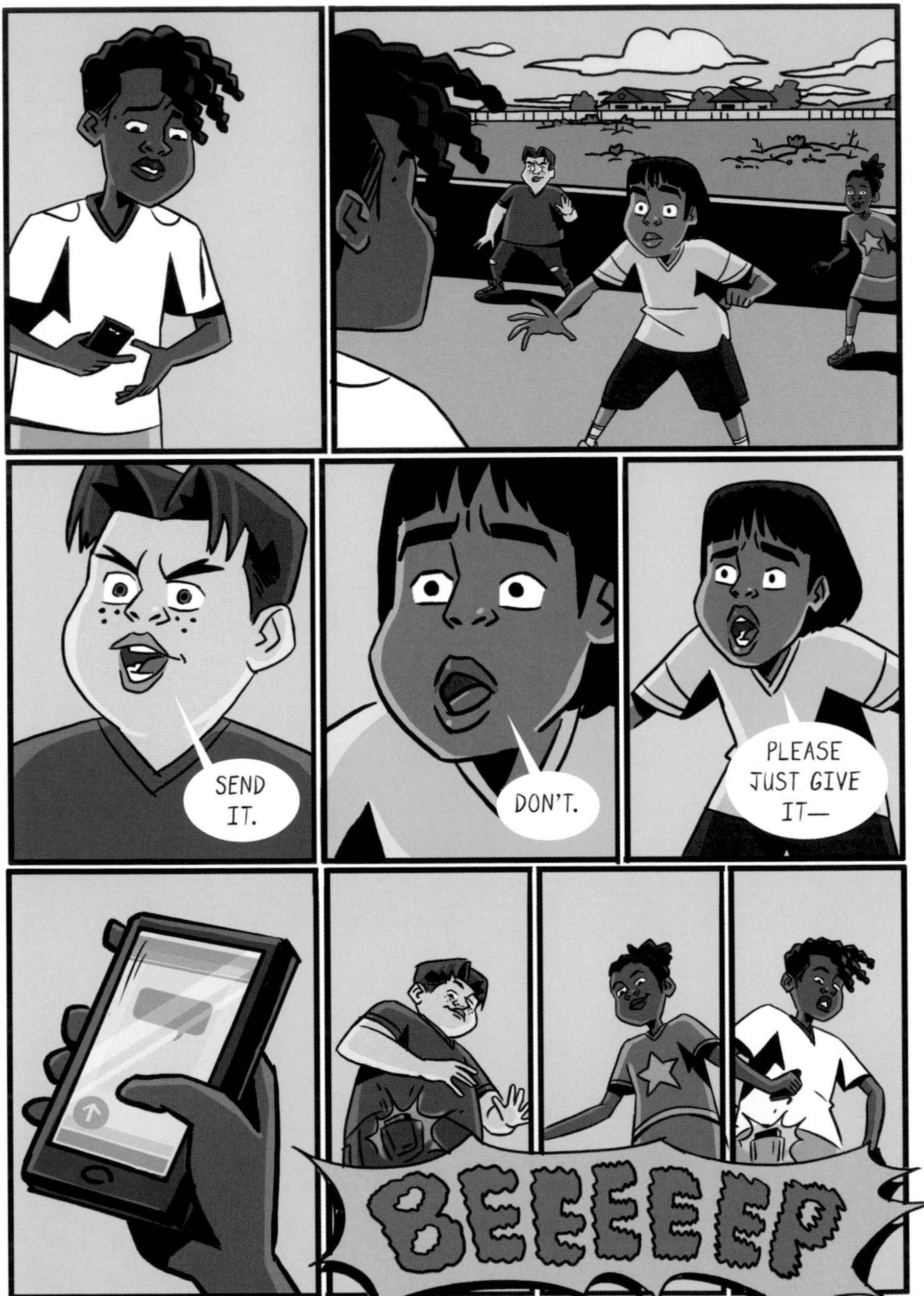
SEND IT.
DON'T.
PLEASE JUST GIVE IT—
BEEEEEP

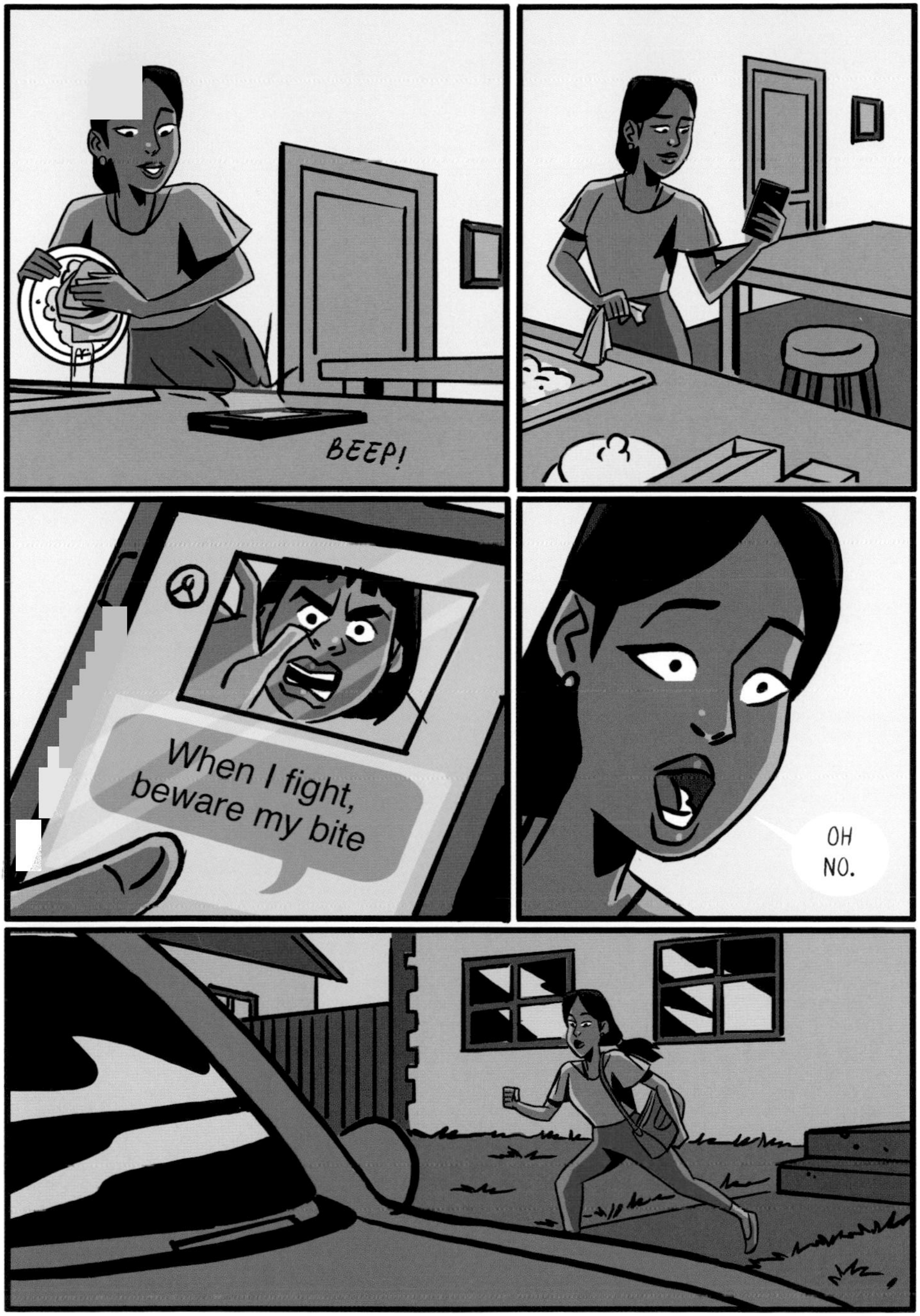
BEEP!
When I fight, beware my bite
OH NO.

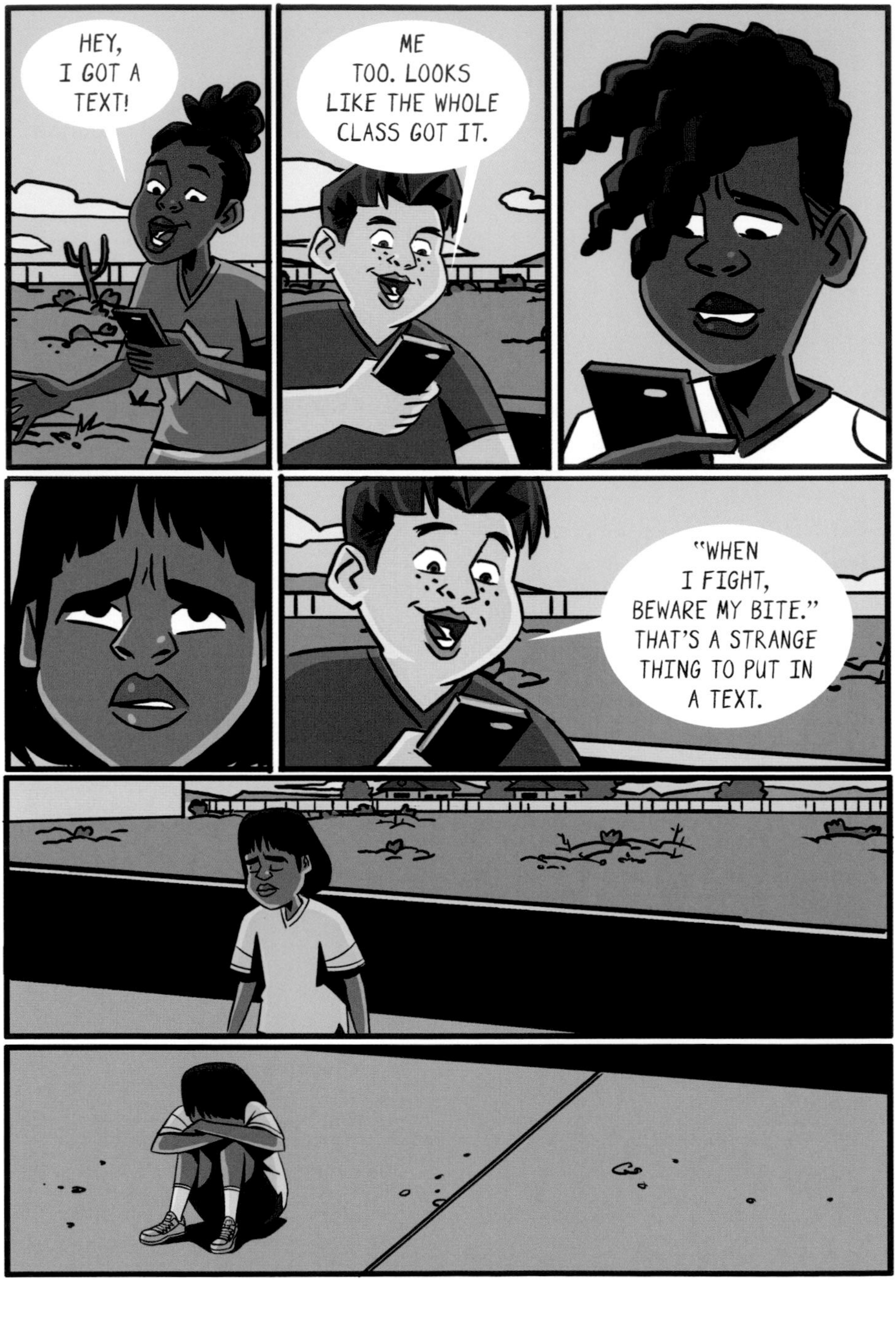
HEY, I GOT A TEXT!
ME TOO. LOOKS LIKE THE WHOLE CLASS GOT IT.
"WHEN I FIGHT, BEWARE MY BITE." THAT'S A STRANGE THING TO PUT IN A TEXT.

CHAPTER 8
ANGER ISSUES

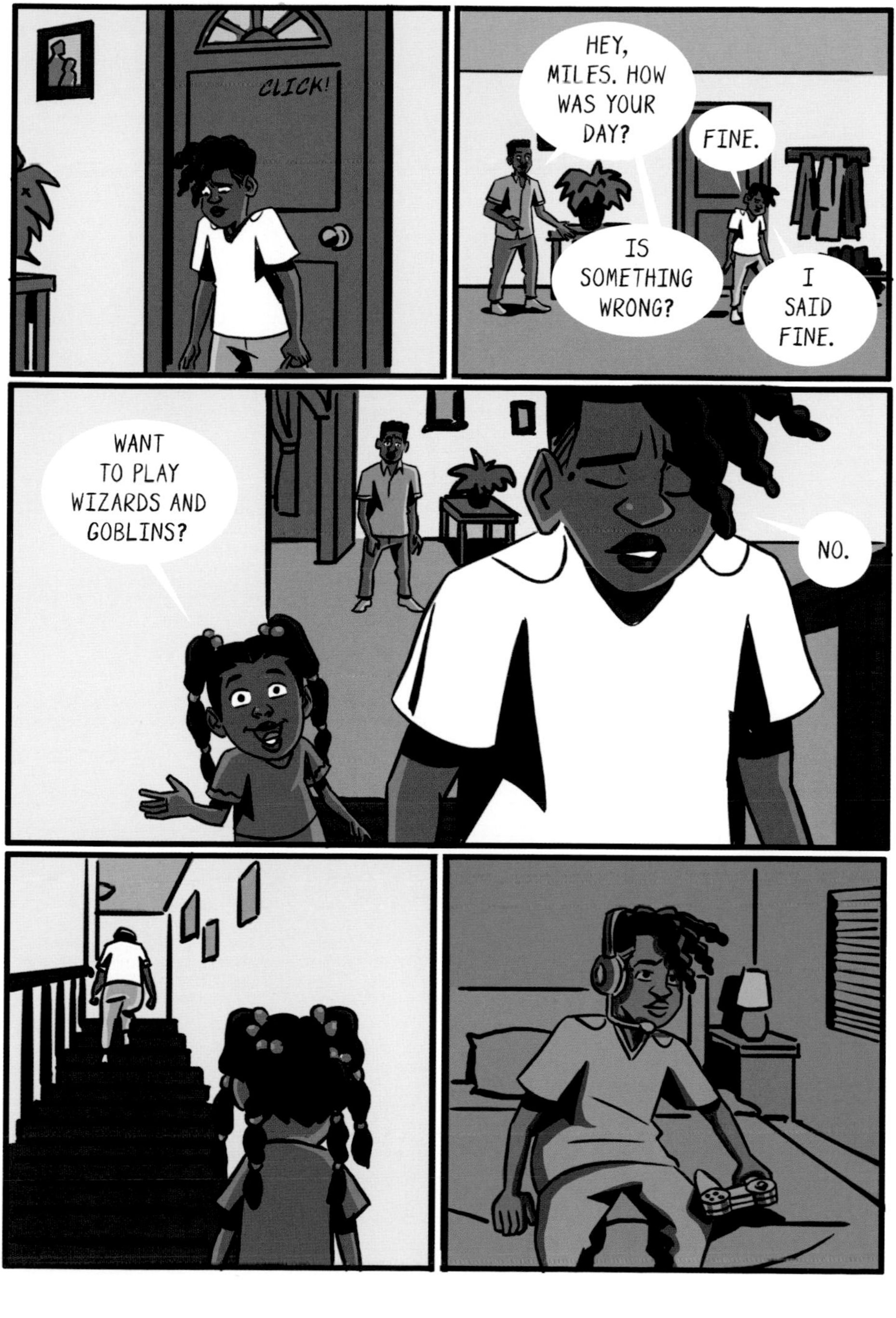
CLICK!
HEY, MILES. HOW WAS YOUR DAY?
FINE.
IS SOMETHING WRONG?
I SAID FINE.
WANT TO PLAY WIZARDS AND GOBLINS?
NO.

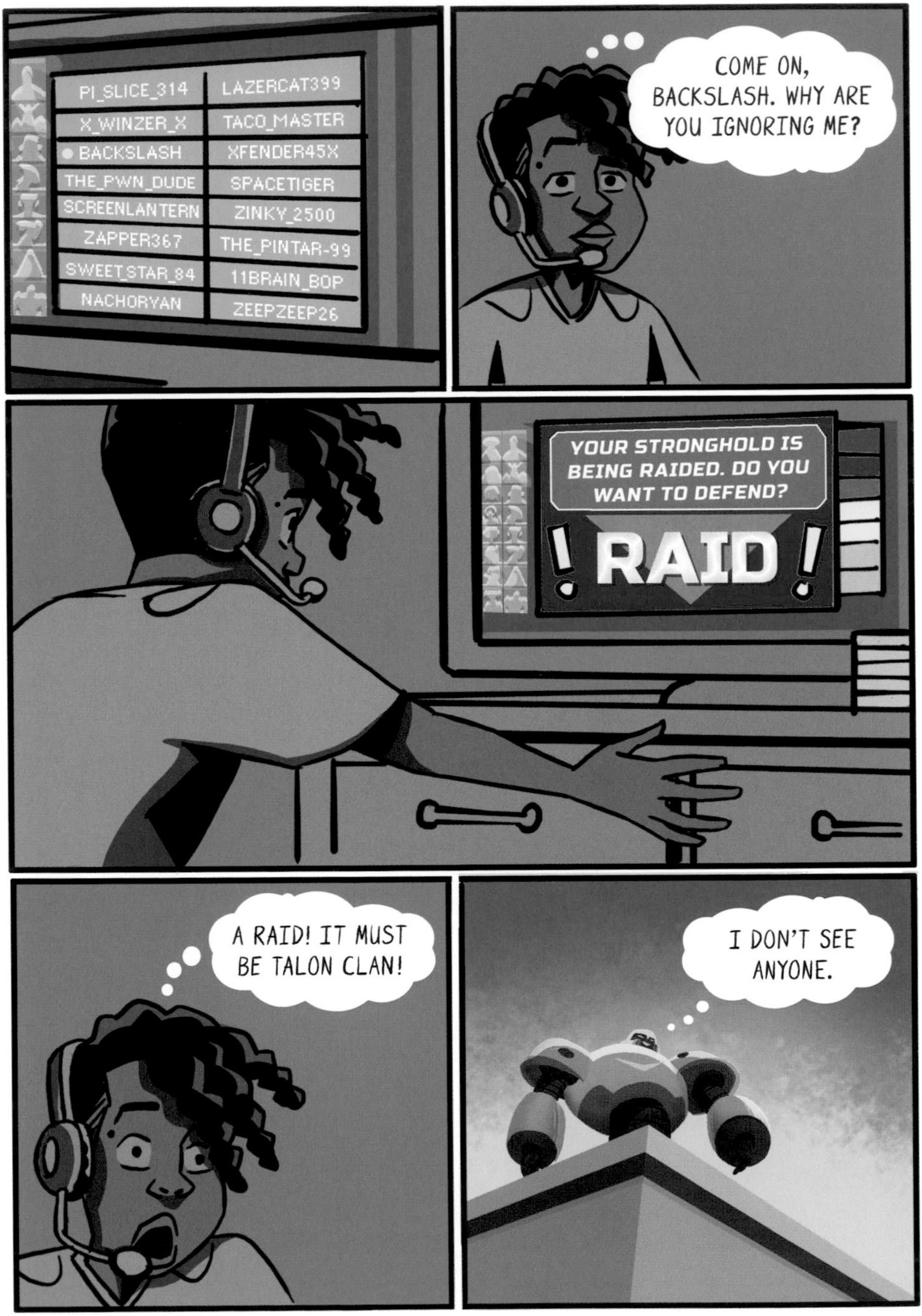
PI_SLICE_314
X_WINZER_X
BACKSLASH
THE_PWN_DUDE
SCREENLANTERN
ZAPPER367
SWEET_STAR_84
NACHORYAN
LAZERCAT399
TACO_MASTER
XFENDER45X
SPACETIGER
ZINKY_2500
THE_PINTAR-99
11BRAIN_BOP
ZEEPZEEP26
COME ON, BACKSLASH. WHY ARE YOU IGNORING ME?
YOUR STRONGHOLD IS BEING RAIDED. DO YOU WANT TO DEFEND?
! RAID !
A RAID! IT MUST BE TALON CLAN!
I DON'T SEE ANYONE.

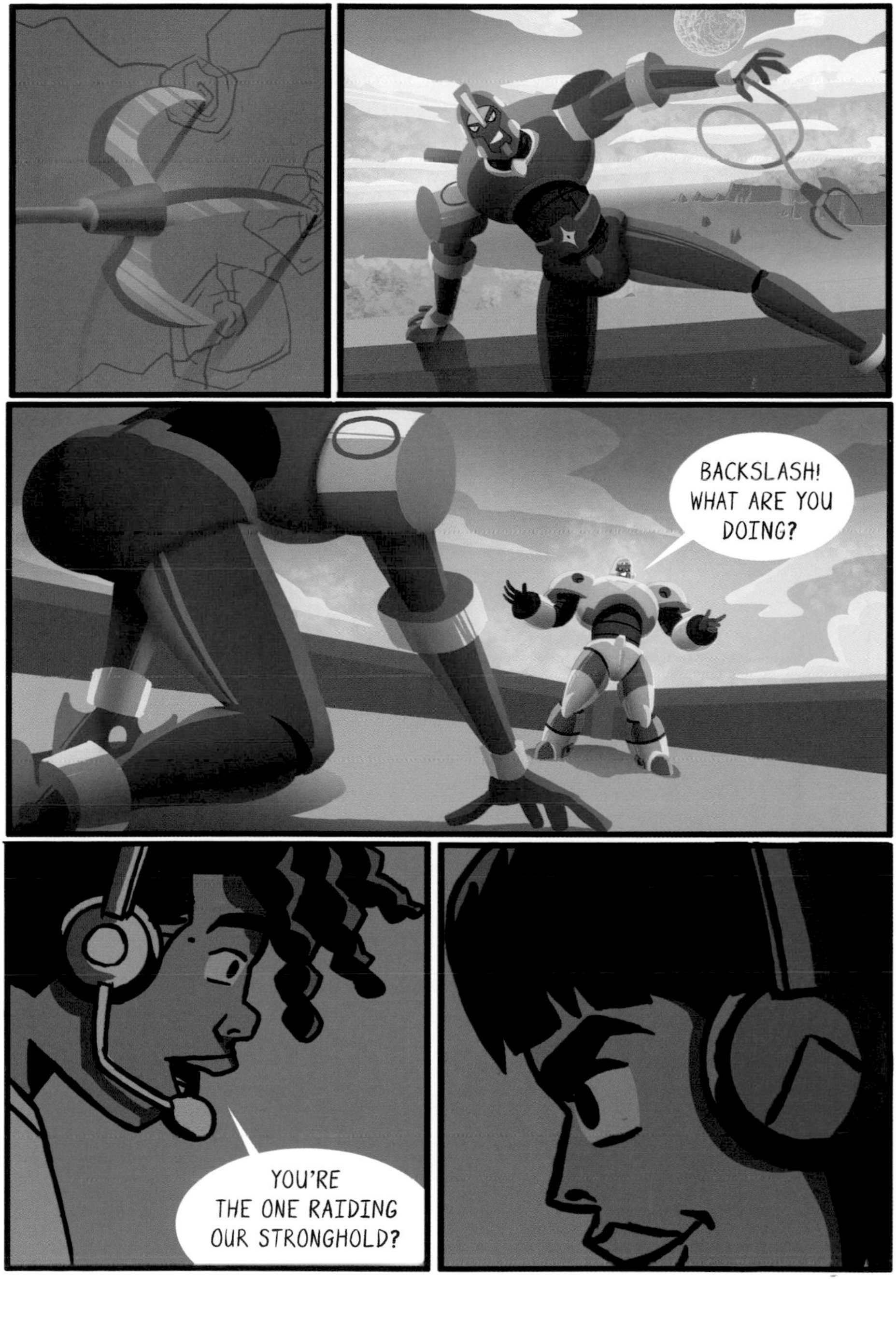
BACKSLASH! WHAT ARE YOU DOING?
YOU'RE THE ONE RAIDING OUR STRONGHOLD?

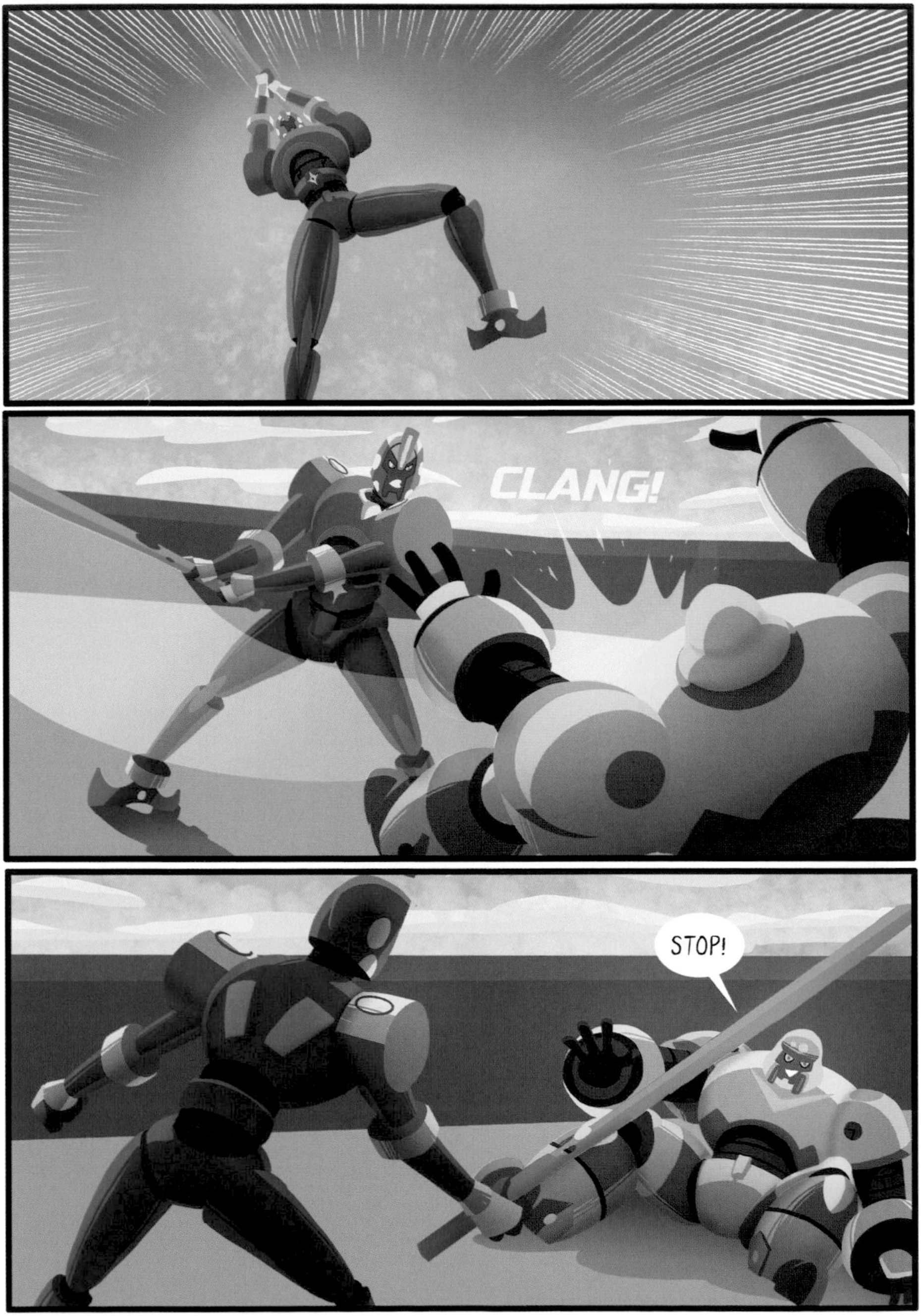
CLANG!
STOP!

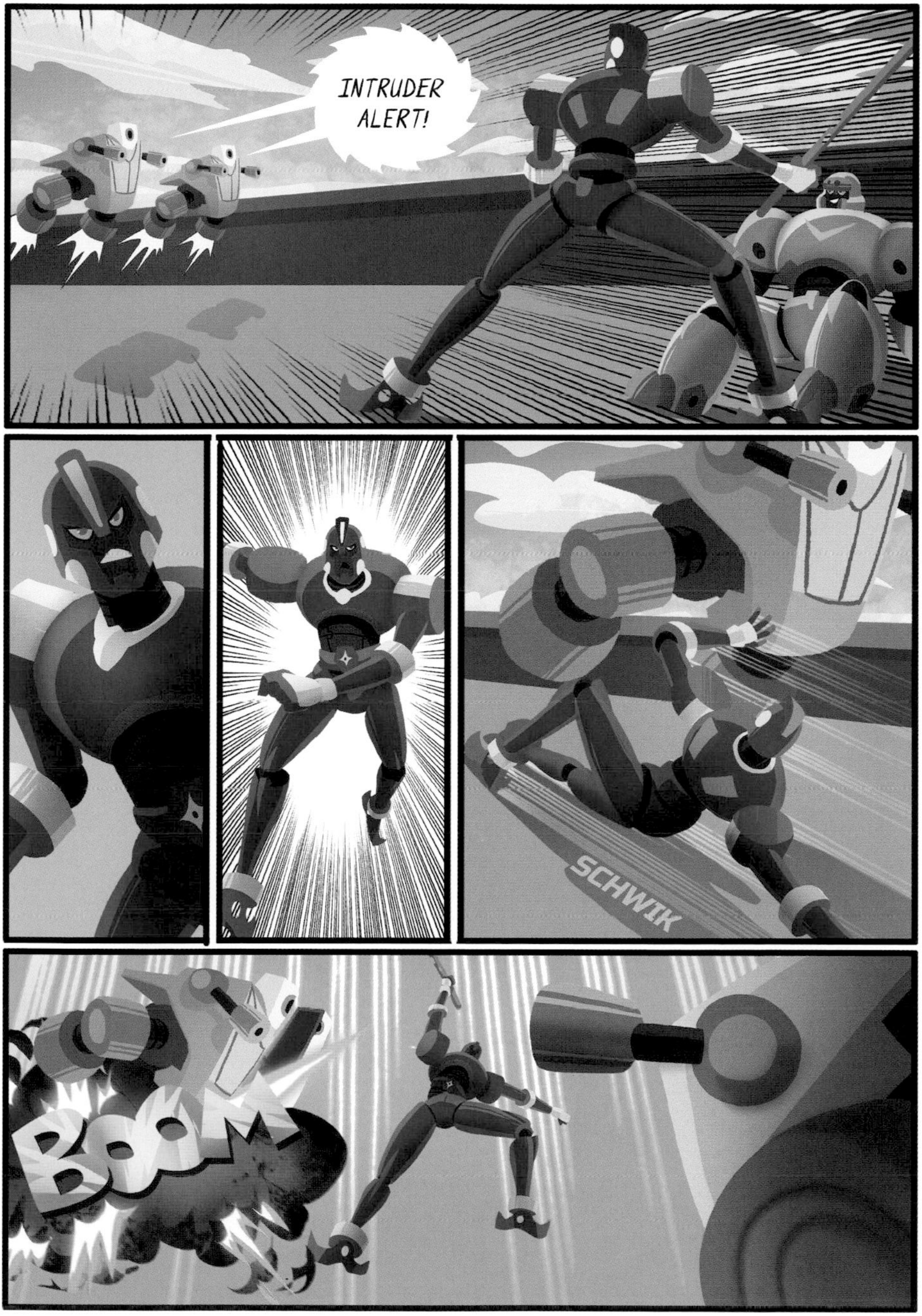
INTRUDER ALERT!
SCHWIK
BOOM

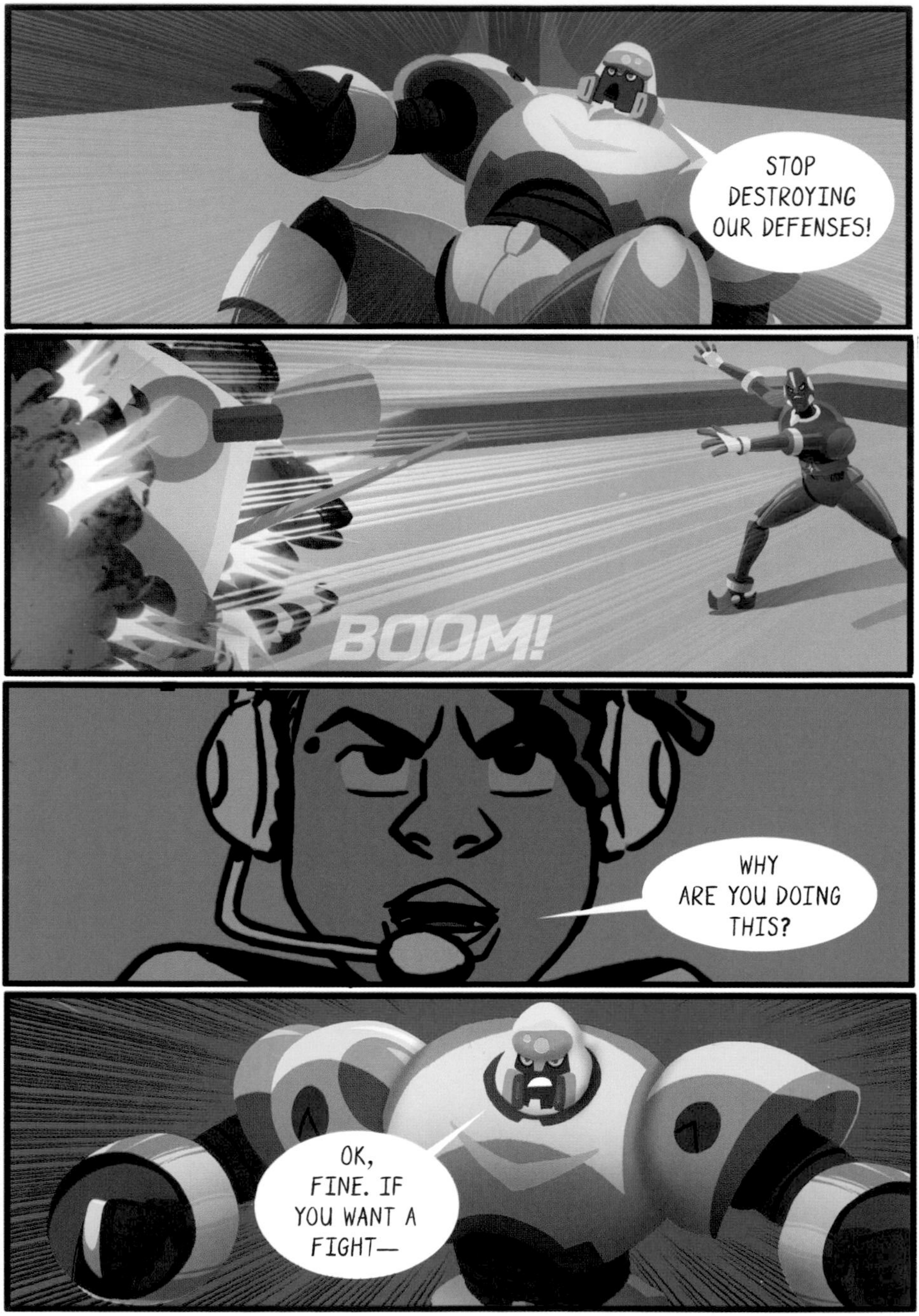
STOP DESTROYING OUR DEFENSES!
BOOM!
WHY ARE YOU DOING THIS?
OK, FINE. IF YOU WANT A FIGHT—

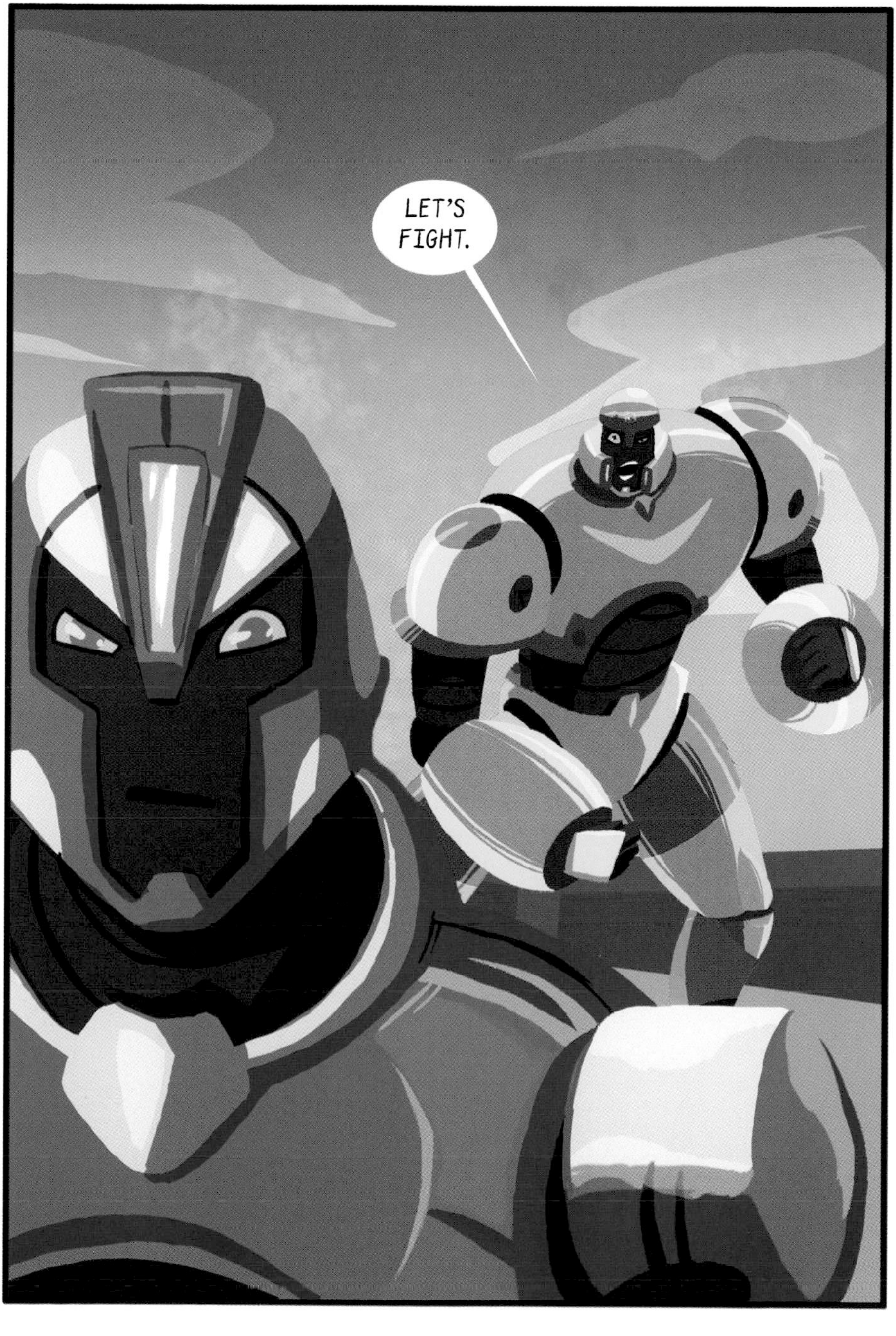
LET'S FIGHT.

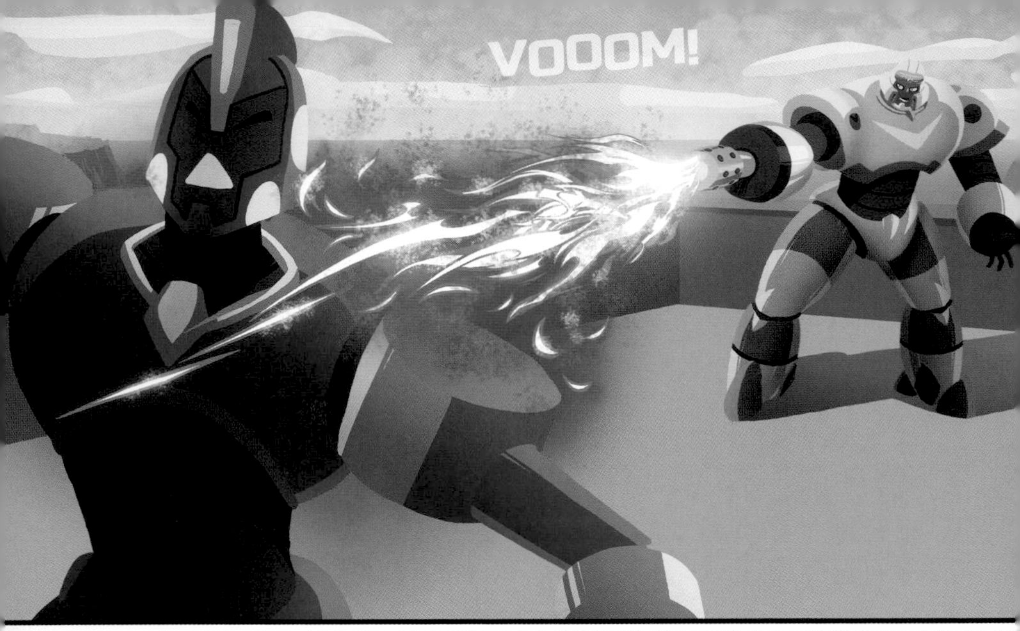
VOOOM!

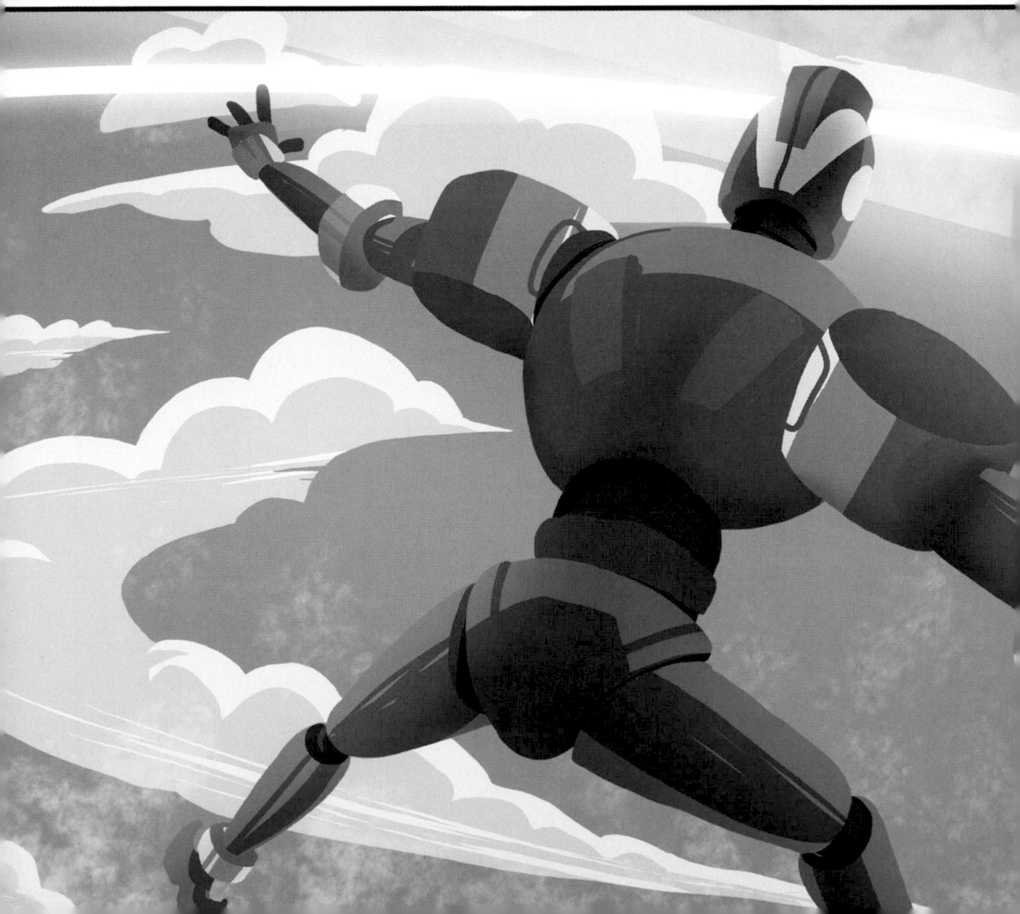

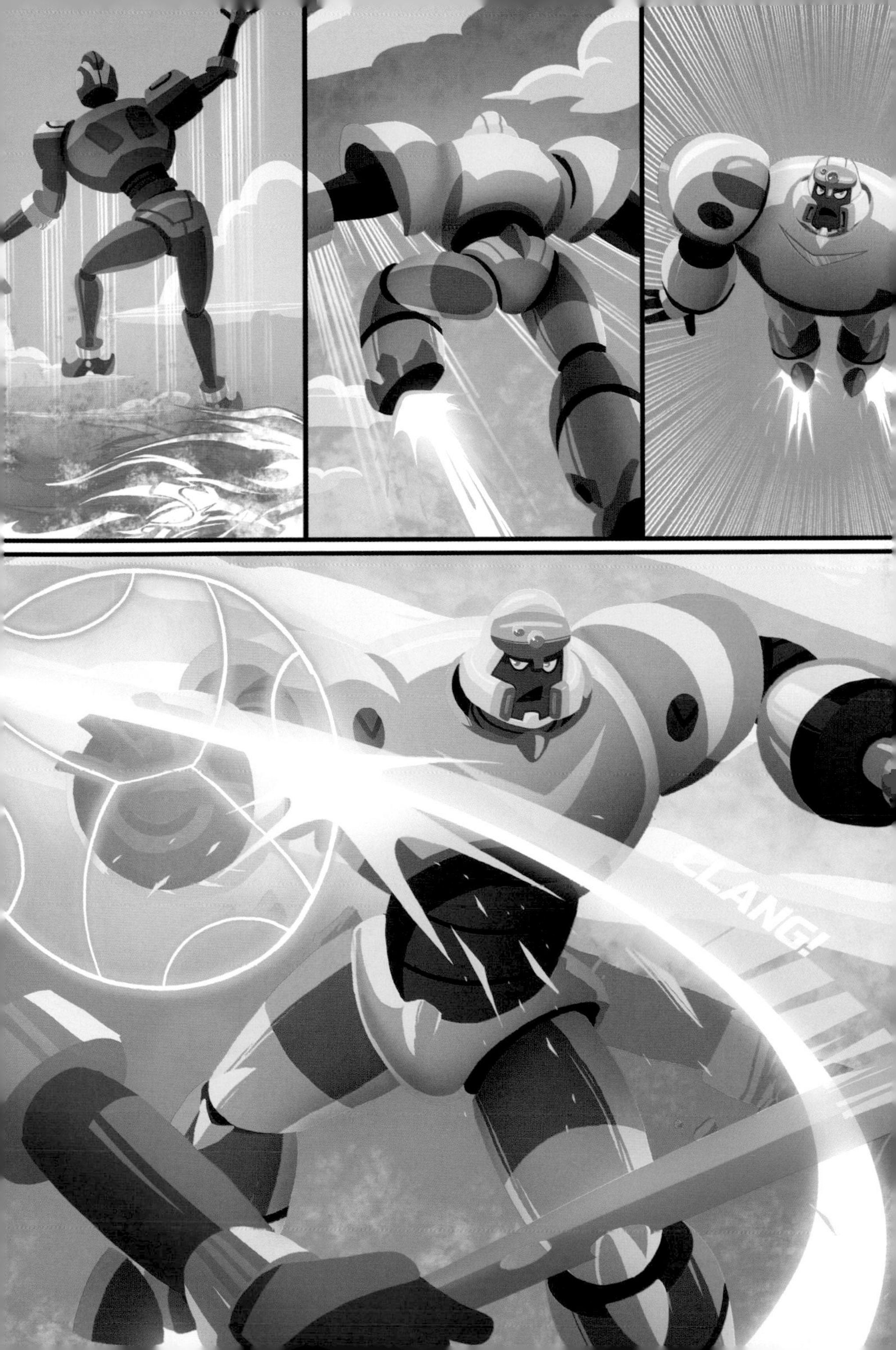
CLANG!

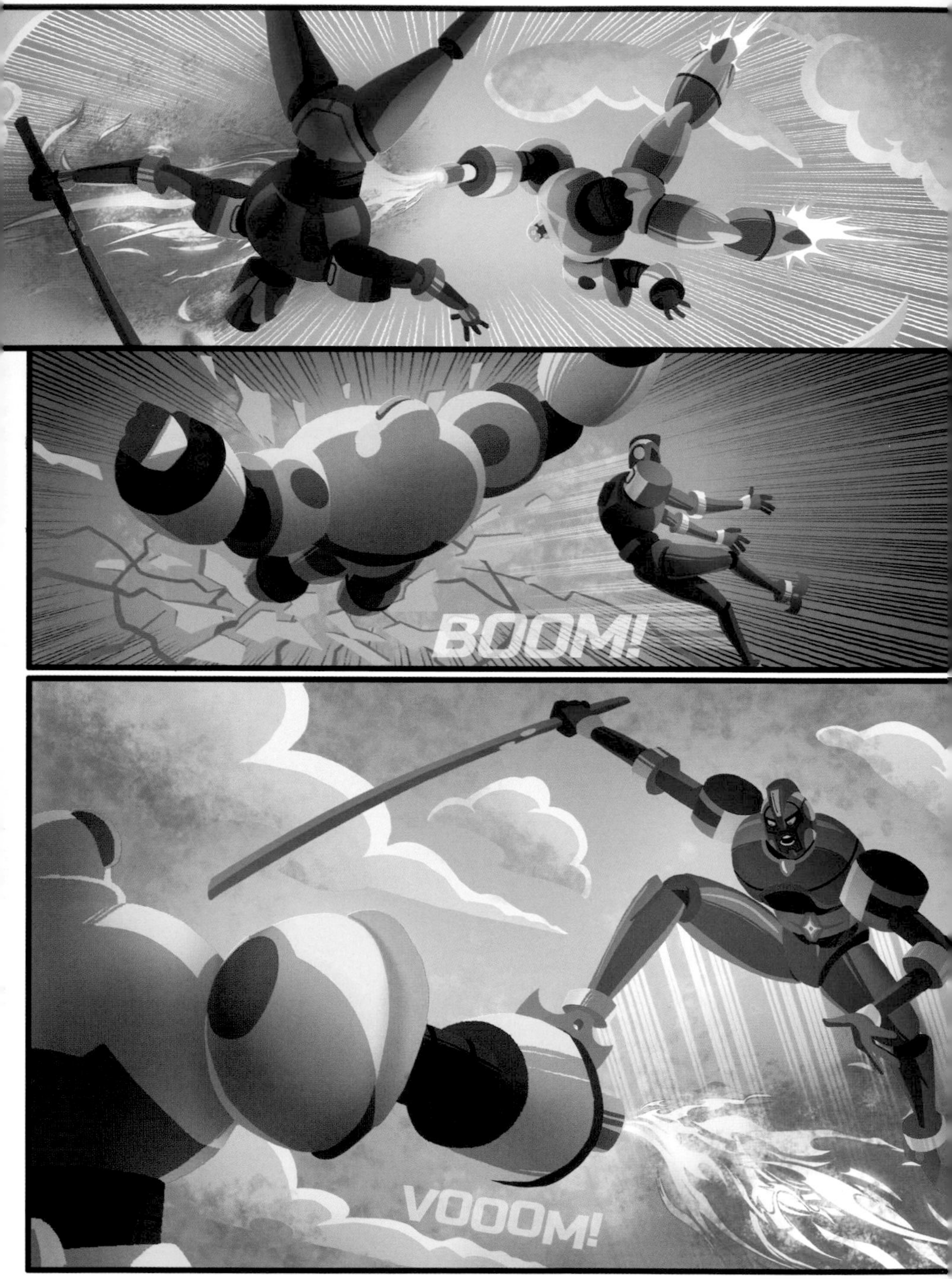
BOOM!
VOOOM!

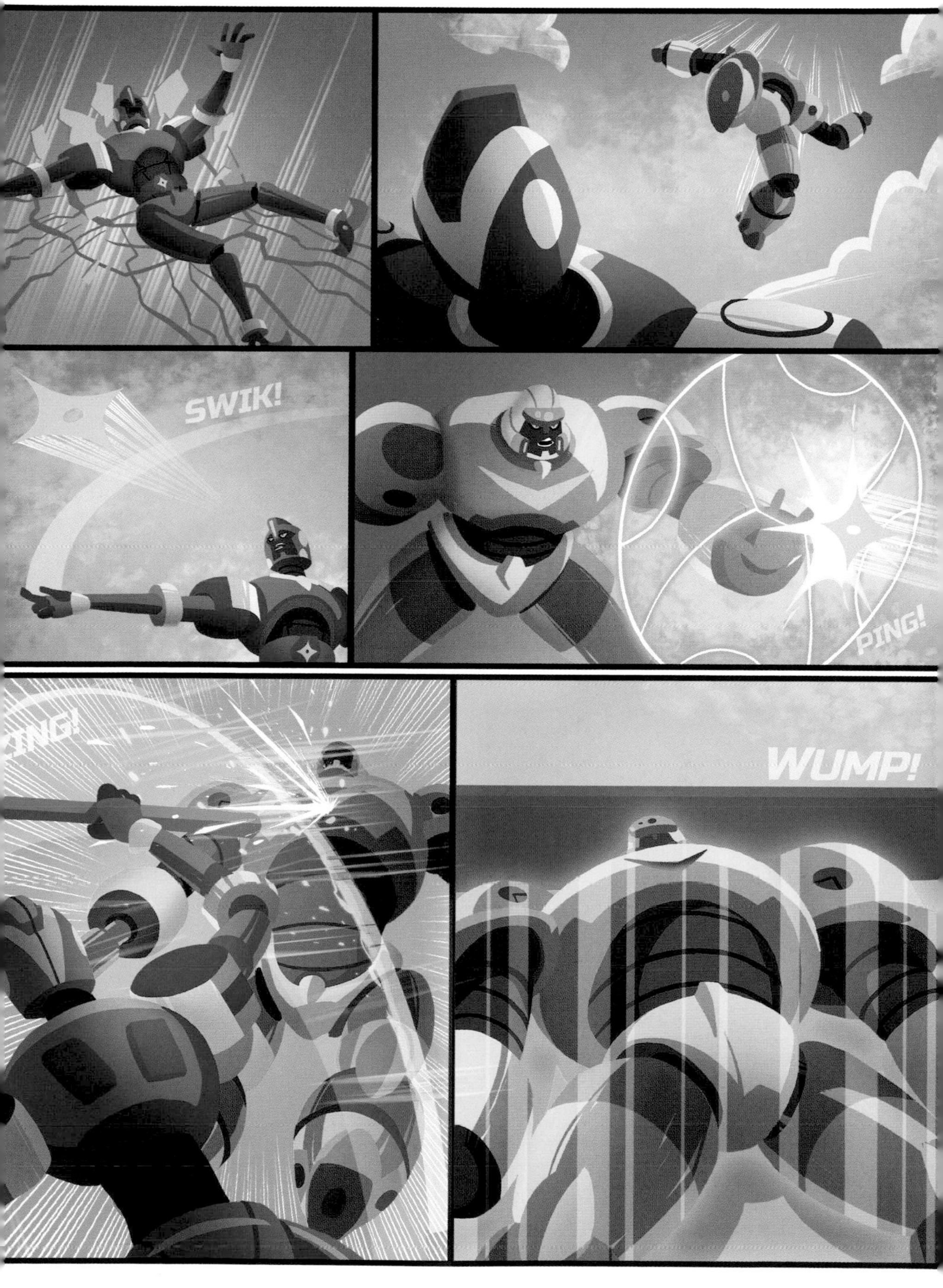
SWIK!
PING!
ING!
WUMP!

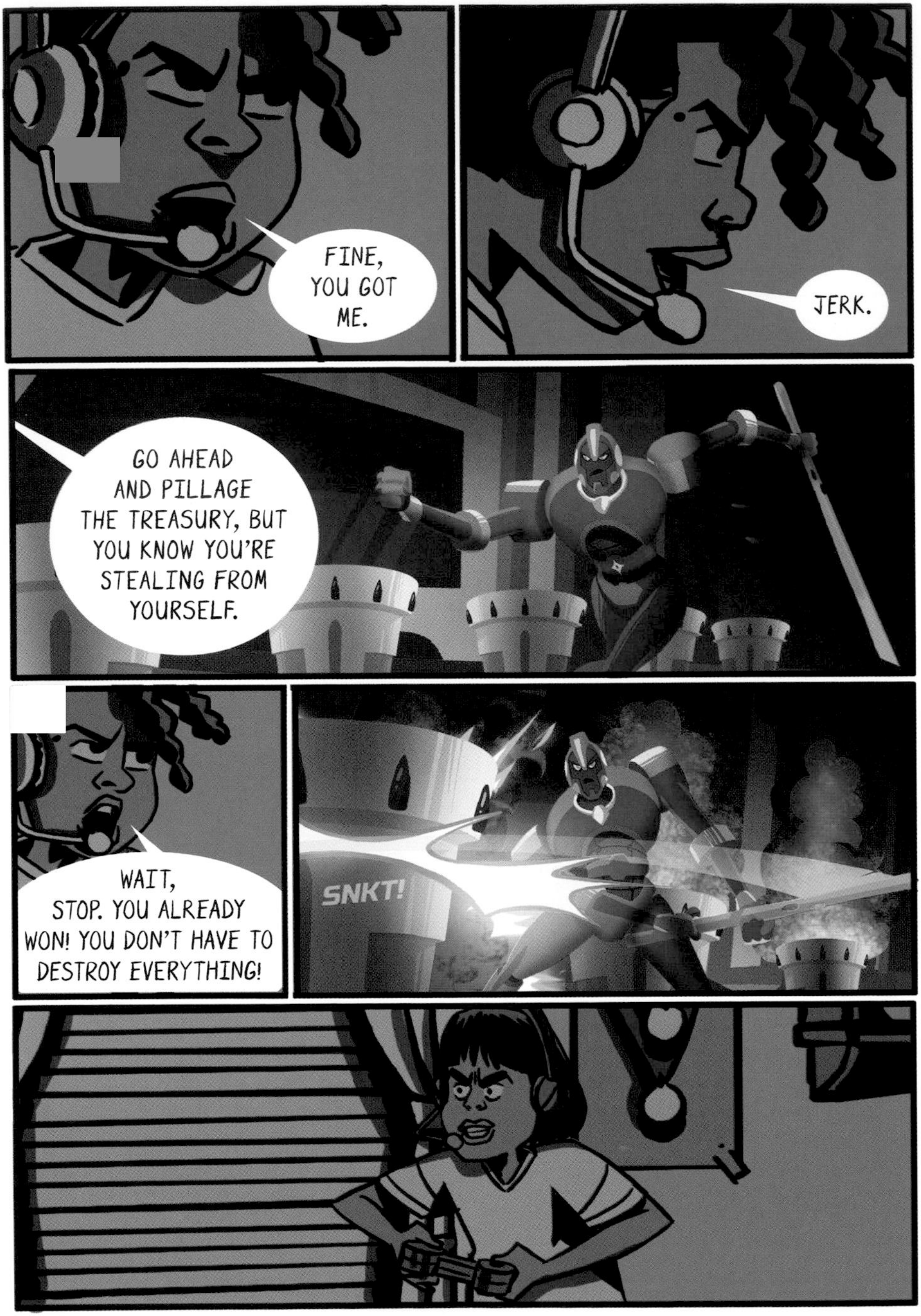
FINE, YOU GOT ME.
JERK.
GO AHEAD AND PILLAGE THE TREASURY, BUT YOU KNOW YOU'RE STEALING FROM YOURSELF.
WAIT, STOP. YOU ALREADY WON! YOU DON'T HAVE TO DESTROY EVERYTHING!
SNKT!

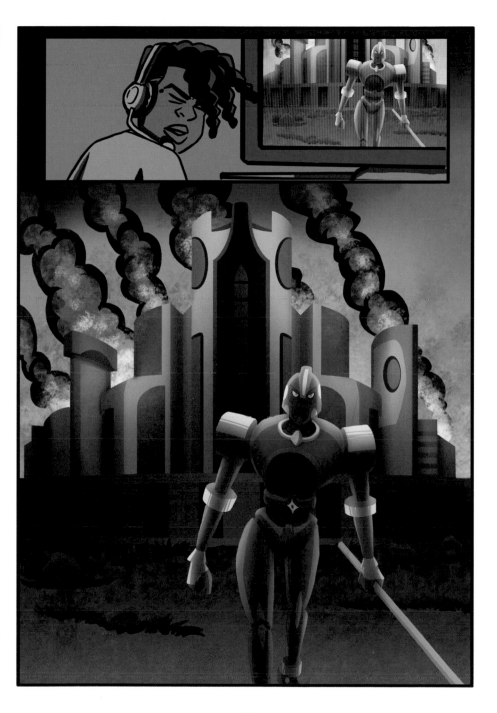

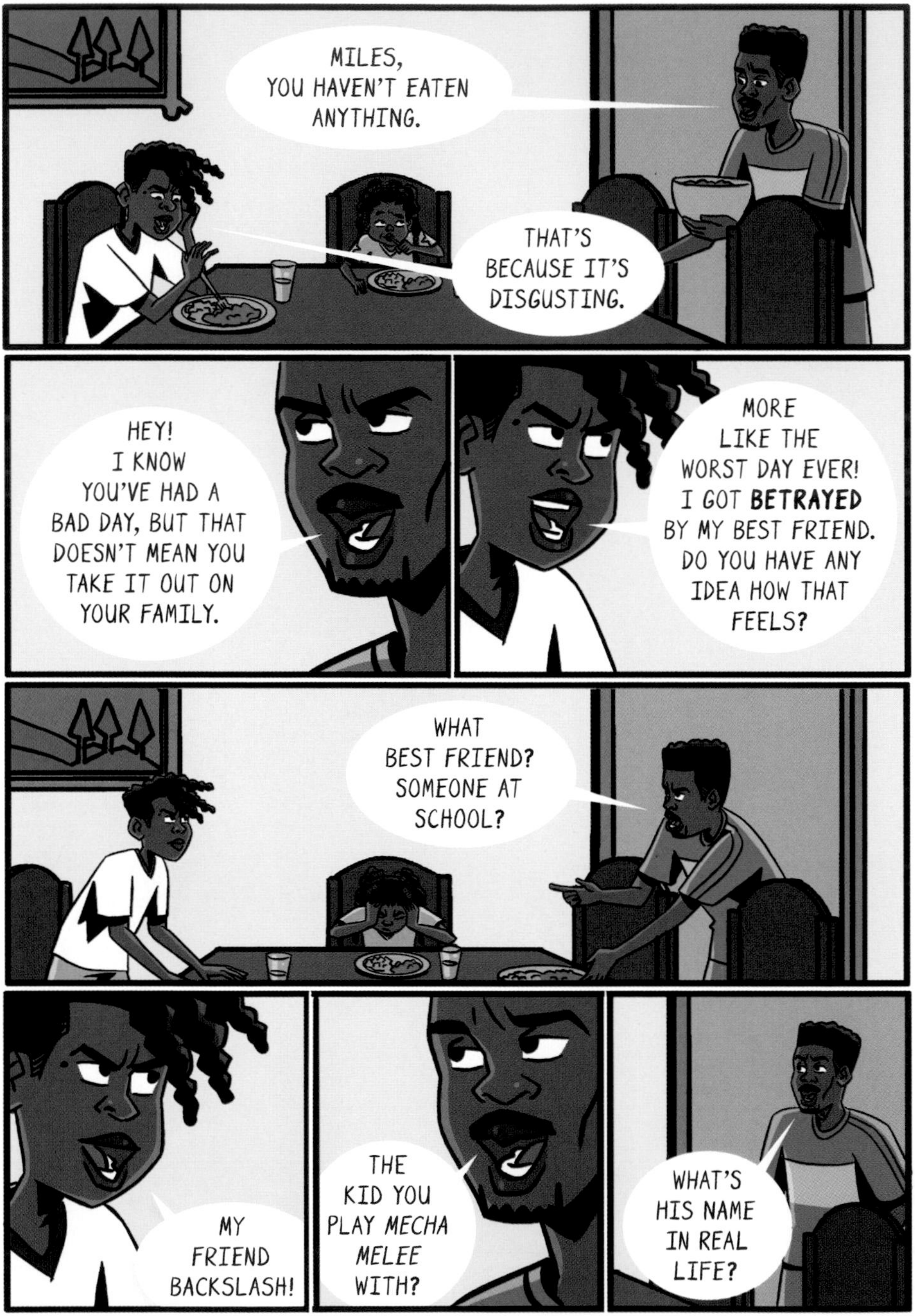
MILES, YOU HAVEN'T EATEN ANYTHING.
THAT'S BECAUSE IT'S DISGUSTING.
HEY! I KNOW YOU'VE HAD A BAD DAY, BUT THAT DOESN'T MEAN YOU TAKE IT OUT ON YOUR FAMILY.
MORE LIKE THE WORST DAY EVER! I GOT **BETRAYED** BY MY BEST FRIEND. DO YOU HAVE ANY IDEA HOW THAT FEELS?
WHAT BEST FRIEND? SOMEONE AT SCHOOL?
MY FRIEND BACKSLASH!
THE KID YOU PLAY *MECHA MELEE* WITH?
WHAT'S HIS NAME IN REAL LIFE?

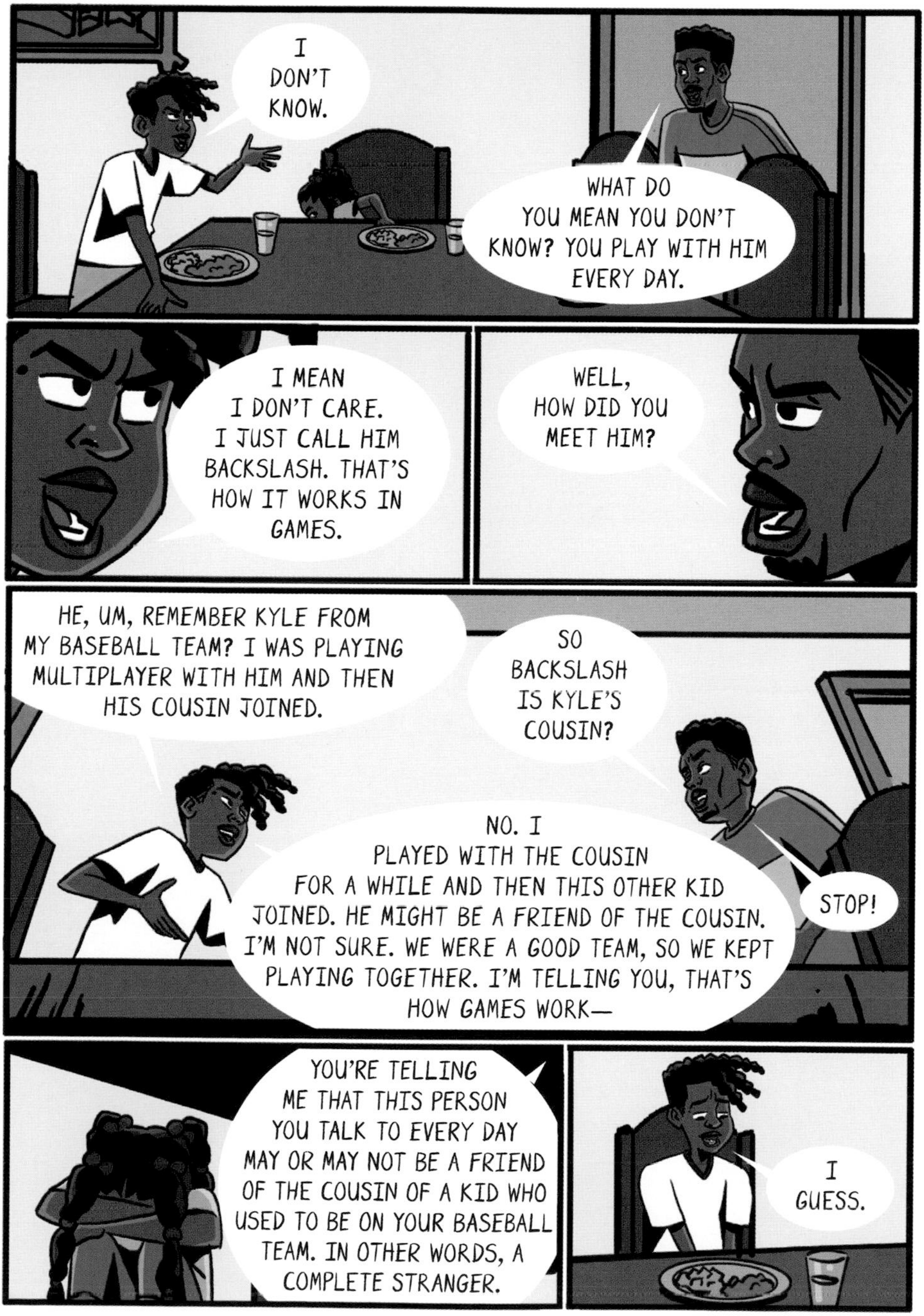
I DON'T KNOW.
WHAT DO YOU MEAN YOU DON'T KNOW? YOU PLAY WITH HIM EVERY DAY.
I MEAN I DON'T CARE. I JUST CALL HIM BACKSLASH. THAT'S HOW IT WORKS IN GAMES.
WELL, HOW DID YOU MEET HIM?
HE, UM, REMEMBER KYLE FROM MY BASEBALL TEAM? I WAS PLAYING MULTIPLAYER WITH HIM AND THEN HIS COUSIN JOINED.
SO BACKSLASH IS KYLE'S COUSIN?
NO. I PLAYED WITH THE COUSIN FOR A WHILE AND THEN THIS OTHER KID JOINED. HE MIGHT BE A FRIEND OF THE COUSIN. I'M NOT SURE. WE WERE A GOOD TEAM, SO WE KEPT PLAYING TOGETHER. I'M TELLING YOU, THAT'S HOW GAMES WORK—
STOP!
YOU'RE TELLING ME THAT THIS PERSON YOU TALK TO EVERY DAY MAY OR MAY NOT BE A FRIEND OF THE COUSIN OF A KID WHO USED TO BE ON YOUR BASEBALL TEAM. IN OTHER WORDS, A COMPLETE STRANGER.
I GUESS.

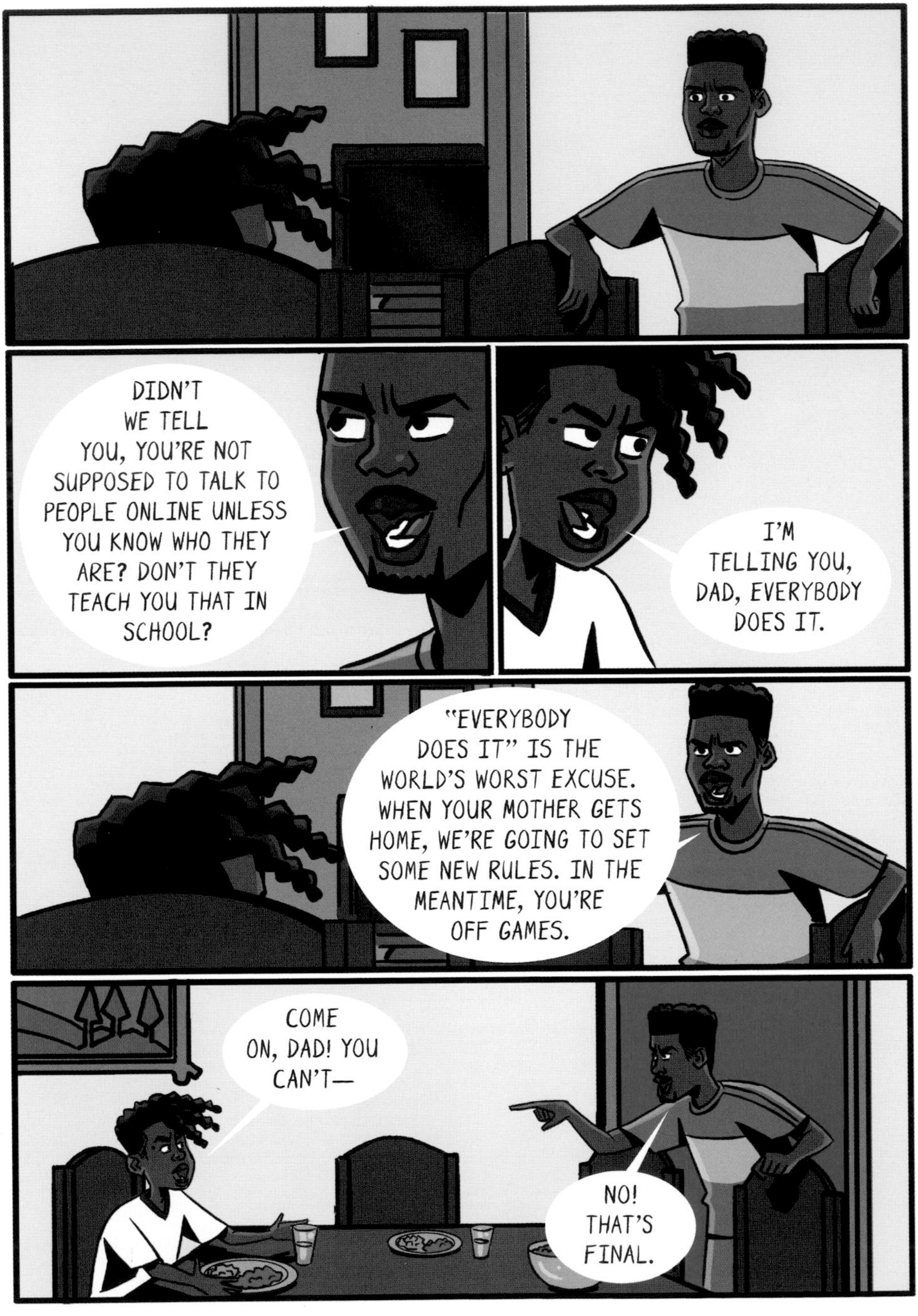
DIDN'T WE TELL YOU, YOU'RE NOT SUPPOSED TO TALK TO PEOPLE ONLINE UNLESS YOU KNOW WHO THEY ARE? DON'T THEY TEACH YOU THAT IN SCHOOL?
I'M TELLING YOU, DAD, EVERYBODY DOES IT.
"EVERYBODY DOES IT" IS THE WORLD'S WORST EXCUSE. WHEN YOUR MOTHER GETS HOME, WE'RE GOING TO SET SOME NEW RULES. IN THE MEANTIME, YOU'RE OFF GAMES.
COME ON, DAD! YOU CAN'T—
NO! THAT'S FINAL.

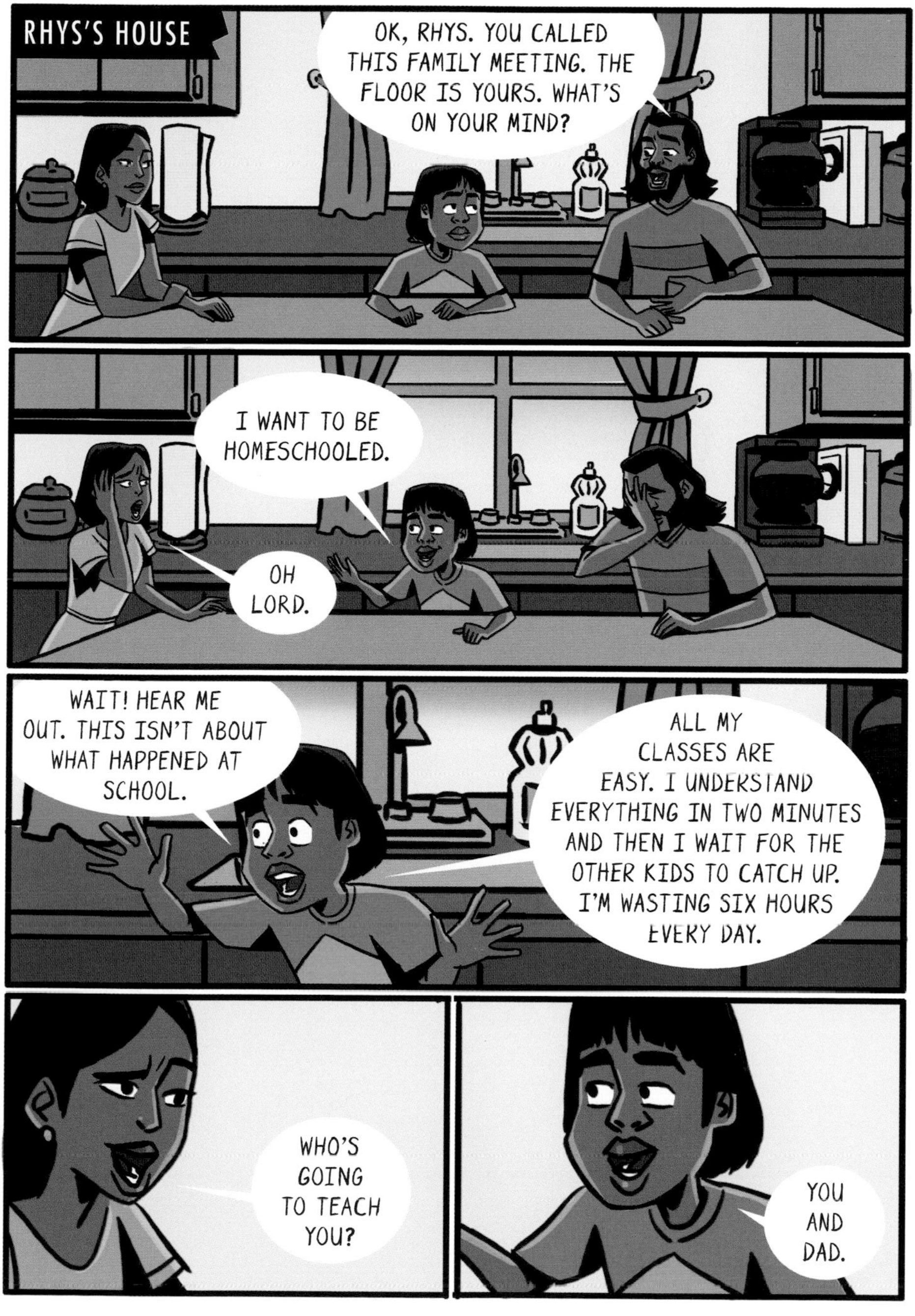
RHYS'S HOUSE
OK, RHYS. YOU CALLED THIS FAMILY MEETING. THE FLOOR IS YOURS. WHAT'S ON YOUR MIND?
I WANT TO BE HOMESCHOOLED.
OH LORD.
WAIT! HEAR ME OUT. THIS ISN'T ABOUT WHAT HAPPENED AT SCHOOL.
ALL MY CLASSES ARE EASY. I UNDERSTAND EVERYTHING IN TWO MINUTES AND THEN I WAIT FOR THE OTHER KIDS TO CATCH UP. I'M WASTING SIX HOURS EVERY DAY.
WHO'S GOING TO TEACH YOU?
YOU AND DAD.

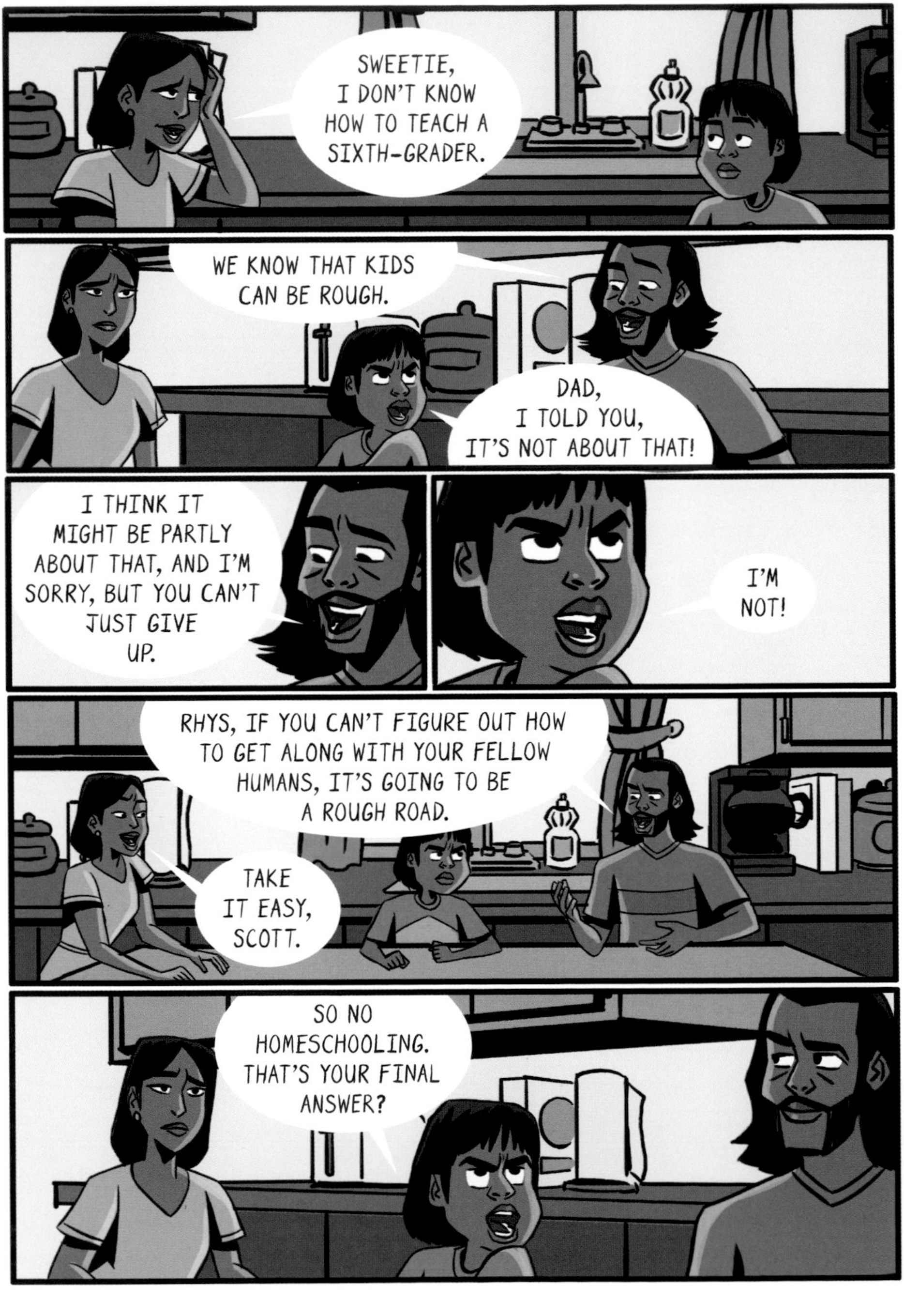
SWEETIE, I DON'T KNOW HOW TO TEACH A SIXTH-GRADER.
WE KNOW THAT KIDS CAN BE ROUGH.
DAD, I TOLD YOU, IT'S NOT ABOUT THAT!
I THINK IT MIGHT BE PARTLY ABOUT THAT, AND I'M SORRY, BUT YOU CAN'T JUST GIVE UP.
I'M NOT!
RHYS, IF YOU CAN'T FIGURE OUT HOW TO GET ALONG WITH YOUR FELLOW HUMANS, IT'S GOING TO BE A ROUGH ROAD.
TAKE IT EASY, SCOTT.
SO NO HOMESCHOOLING. THAT'S YOUR FINAL ANSWER?

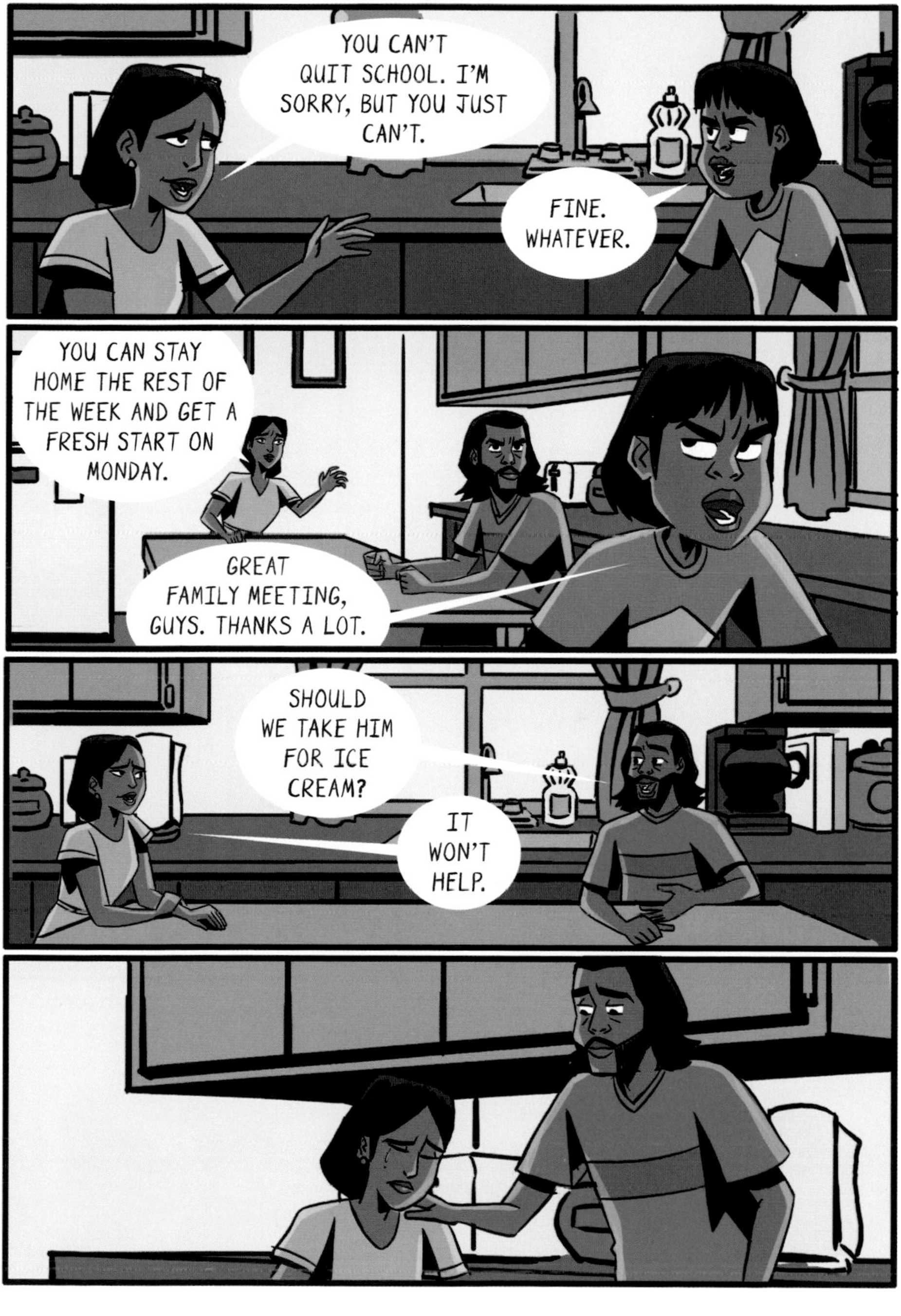
YOU CAN'T QUIT SCHOOL. I'M SORRY, BUT YOU JUST CAN'T.
FINE. WHATEVER.
YOU CAN STAY HOME THE REST OF THE WEEK AND GET A FRESH START ON MONDAY.
GREAT FAMILY MEETING, GUYS. THANKS A LOT.
SHOULD WE TAKE HIM FOR ICE CREAM?
IT WON'T HELP.

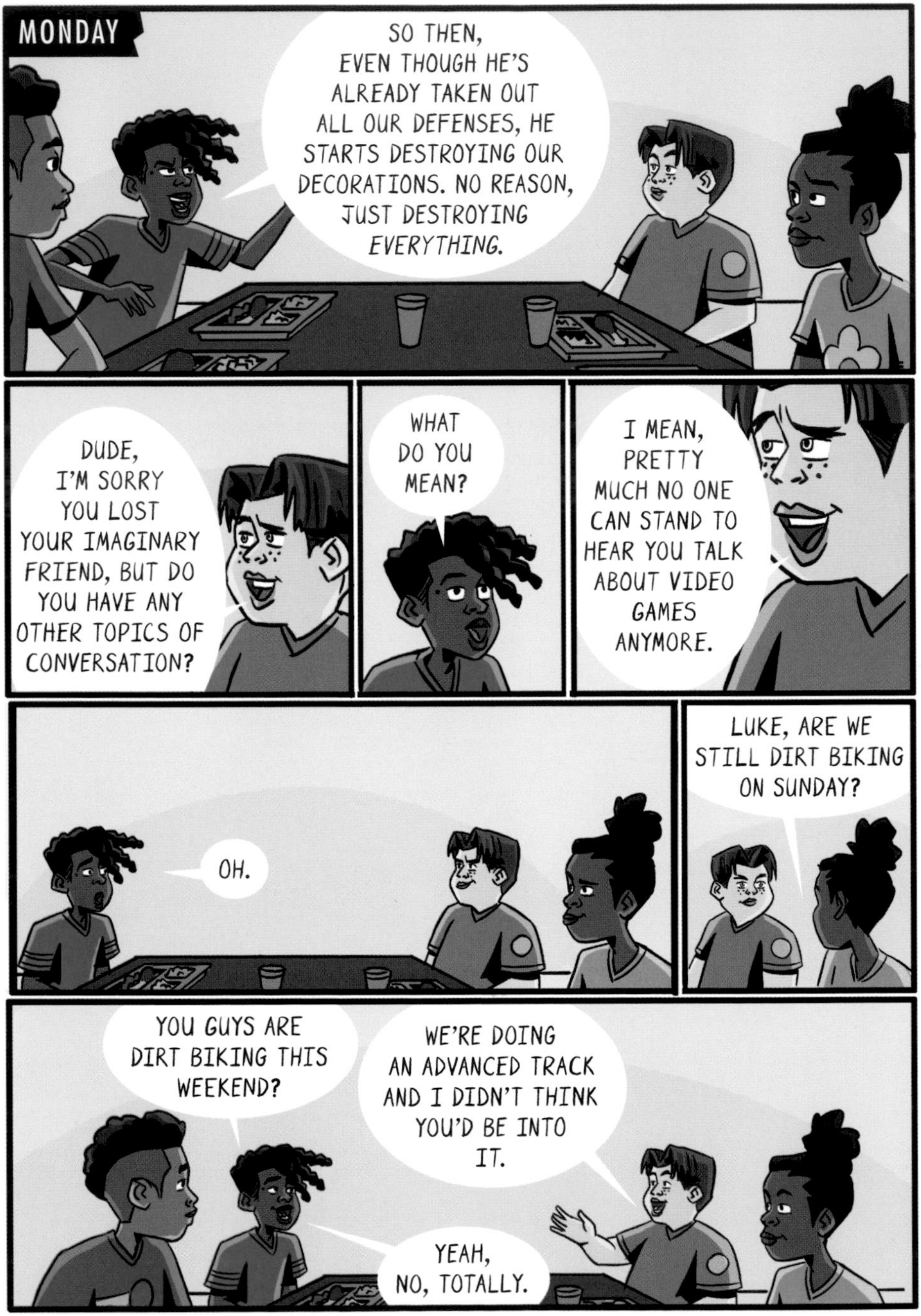
MONDAY
SO THEN, EVEN THOUGH HE'S ALREADY TAKEN OUT ALL OUR DEFENSES, HE STARTS DESTROYING OUR DECORATIONS. NO REASON, JUST DESTROYING *EVERYTHING.*
DUDE, I'M SORRY YOU LOST YOUR IMAGINARY FRIEND, BUT DO YOU HAVE ANY OTHER TOPICS OF CONVERSATION?
WHAT DO YOU MEAN?
I MEAN, PRETTY MUCH NO ONE CAN STAND TO HEAR YOU TALK ABOUT VIDEO GAMES ANYMORE.
OH.
LUKE, ARE WE STILL DIRT BIKING ON SUNDAY?
YOU GUYS ARE DIRT BIKING THIS WEEKEND?
WE'RE DOING AN ADVANCED TRACK AND I DIDN'T THINK YOU'D BE INTO IT.
YEAH, NO, TOTALLY.

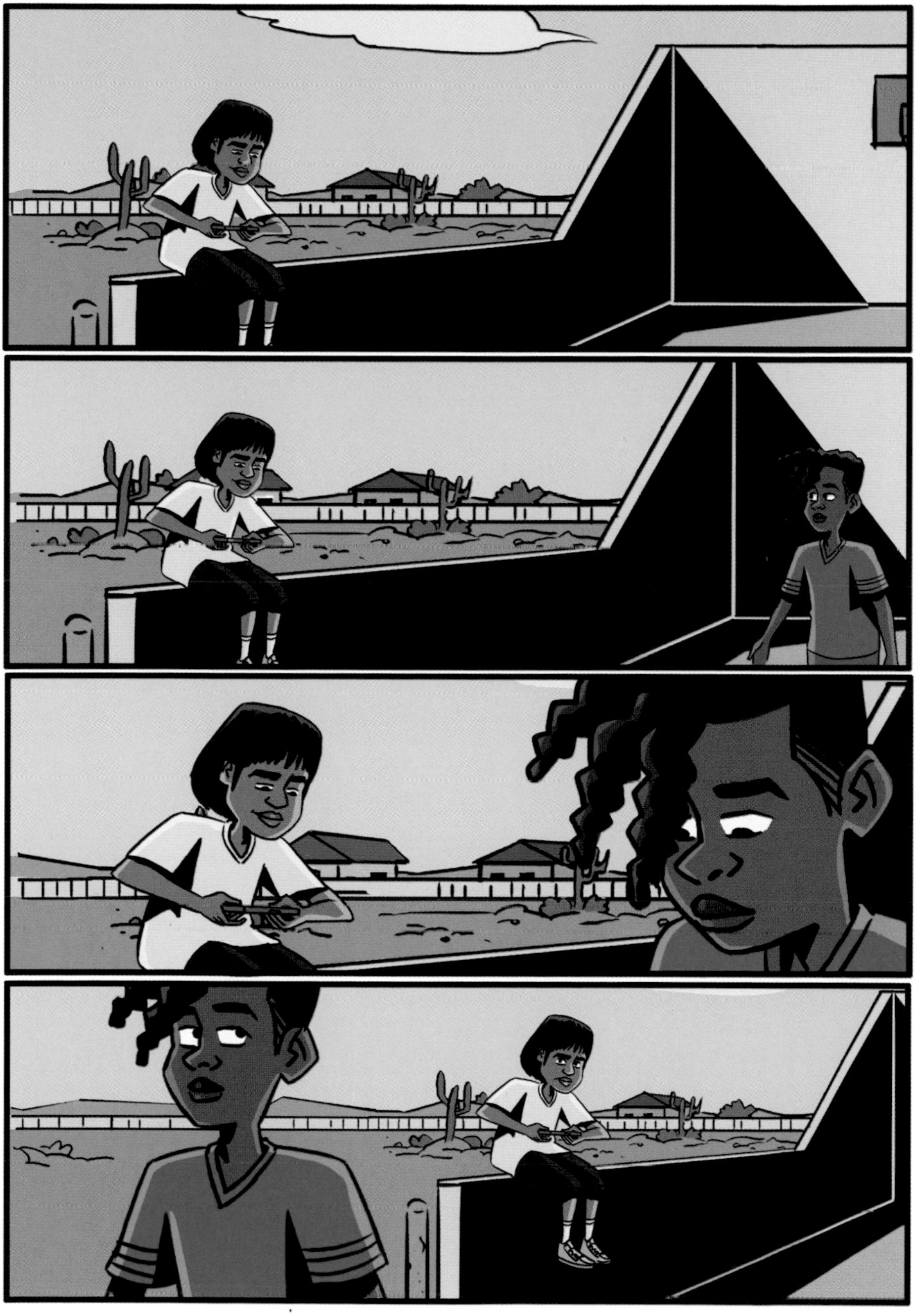

CHAPTER 9
EVERY GAME EVER

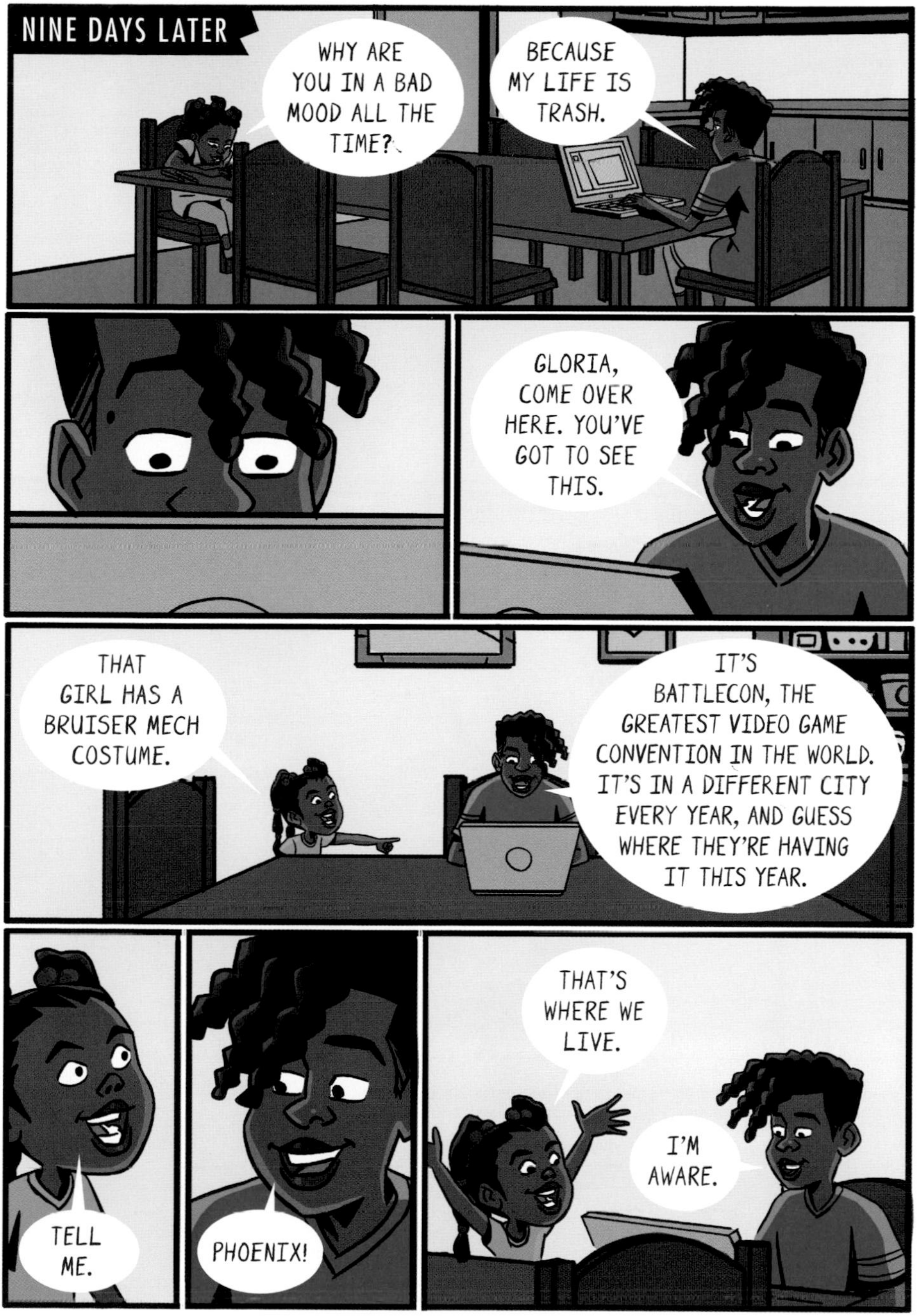
NINE DAYS LATER
WHY ARE YOU IN A BAD MOOD ALL THE TIME?
BECAUSE MY LIFE IS TRASH.
GLORIA, COME OVER HERE. YOU'VE GOT TO SEE THIS.
THAT GIRL HAS A BRUISER MECH COSTUME.
IT'S BATTLECON, THE GREATEST VIDEO GAME CONVENTION IN THE WORLD. IT'S IN A DIFFERENT CITY EVERY YEAR, AND GUESS WHERE THEY'RE HAVING IT THIS YEAR.
TELL ME.
PHOENIX!
THAT'S WHERE WE LIVE.
I'M AWARE.

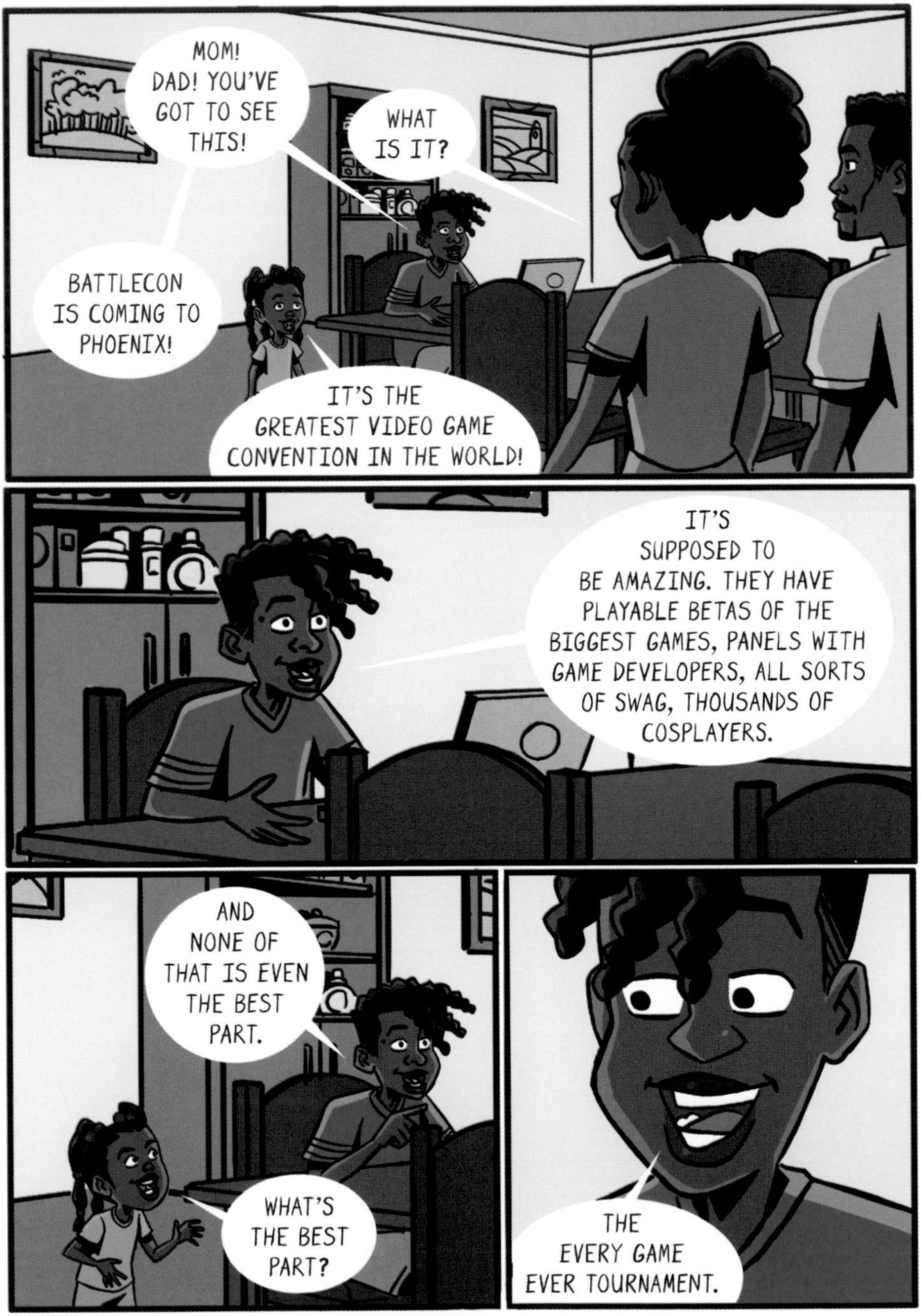
MOM! DAD! YOU'VE GOT TO SEE THIS!
WHAT IS IT?
BATTLECON IS COMING TO PHOENIX!
IT'S THE GREATEST VIDEO GAME CONVENTION IN THE WORLD!
IT'S SUPPOSED TO BE AMAZING. THEY HAVE PLAYABLE BETAS OF THE BIGGEST GAMES, PANELS WITH GAME DEVELOPERS, ALL SORTS OF SWAG, THOUSANDS OF COSPLAYERS.
AND NONE OF THAT IS EVEN THE BEST PART.
WHAT'S THE BEST PART?
THE EVERY GAME EVER TOURNAMENT.

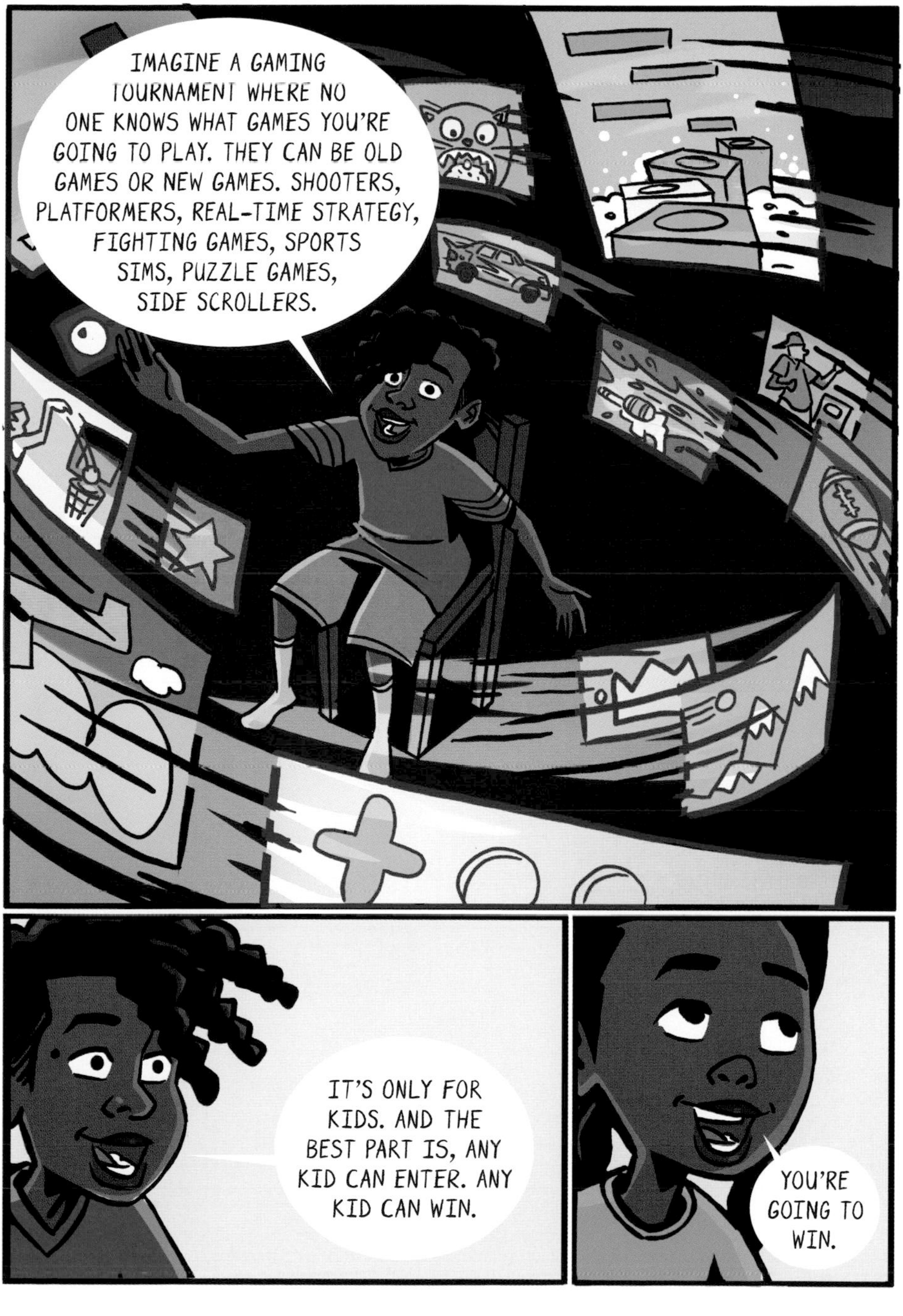
IMAGINE A GAMING TOURNAMENT WHERE NO ONE KNOWS WHAT GAMES YOU'RE GOING TO PLAY. THEY CAN BE OLD GAMES OR NEW GAMES. SHOOTERS, PLATFORMERS, REAL-TIME STRATEGY, FIGHTING GAMES, SPORTS SIMS, PUZZLE GAMES, SIDE SCROLLERS.
IT'S ONLY FOR KIDS. AND THE BEST PART IS, ANY KID CAN ENTER. ANY KID CAN WIN.
YOU'RE GOING TO WIN.

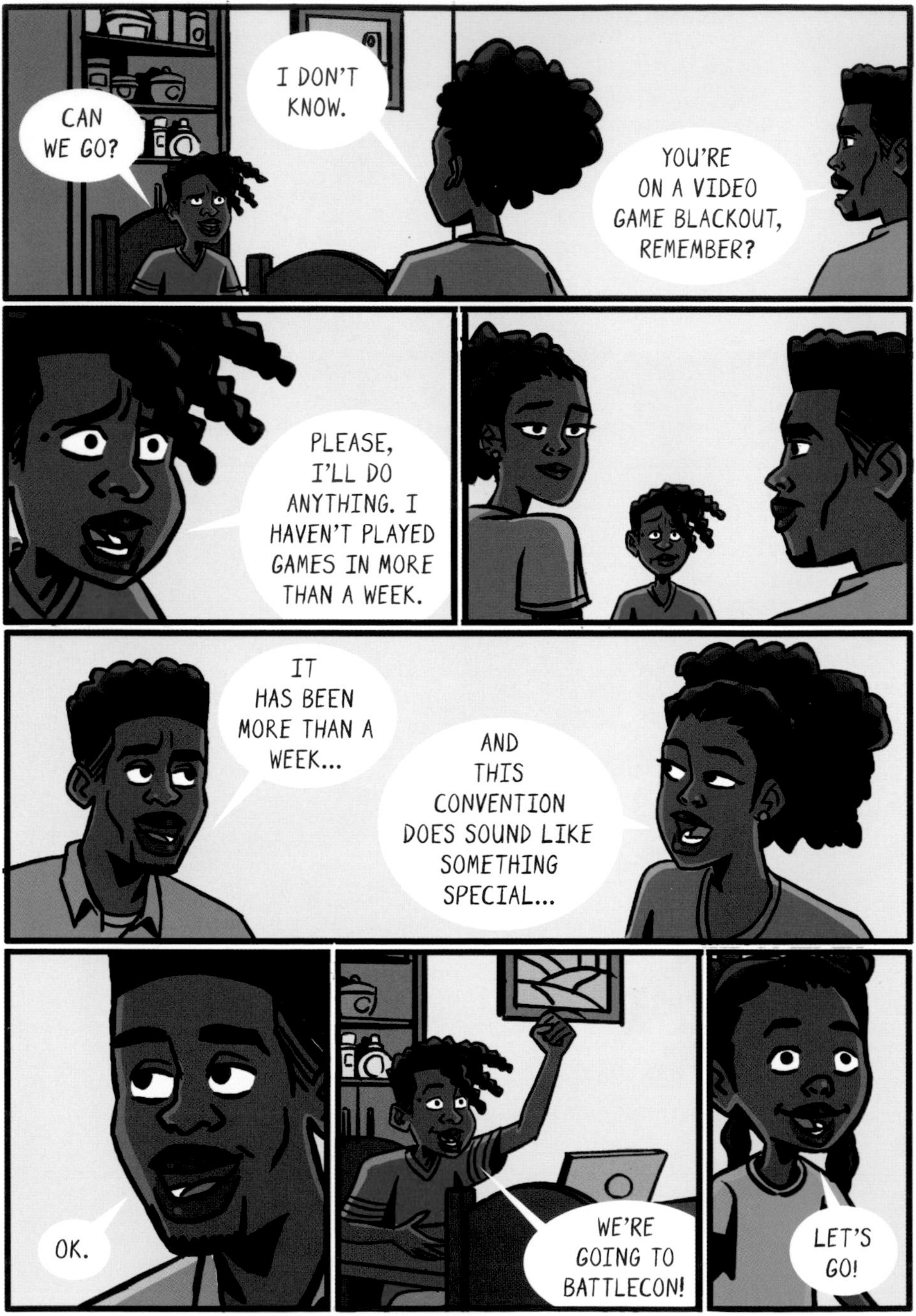
CAN WE GO?
I DON'T KNOW.
YOU'RE ON A VIDEO GAME BLACKOUT, REMEMBER?
PLEASE, I'LL DO ANYTHING. I HAVEN'T PLAYED GAMES IN MORE THAN A WEEK.
IT HAS BEEN MORE THAN A WEEK...
AND THIS CONVENTION DOES SOUND LIKE SOMETHING SPECIAL...
OK.
WE'RE GOING TO BATTLECON!
LET'S GO!

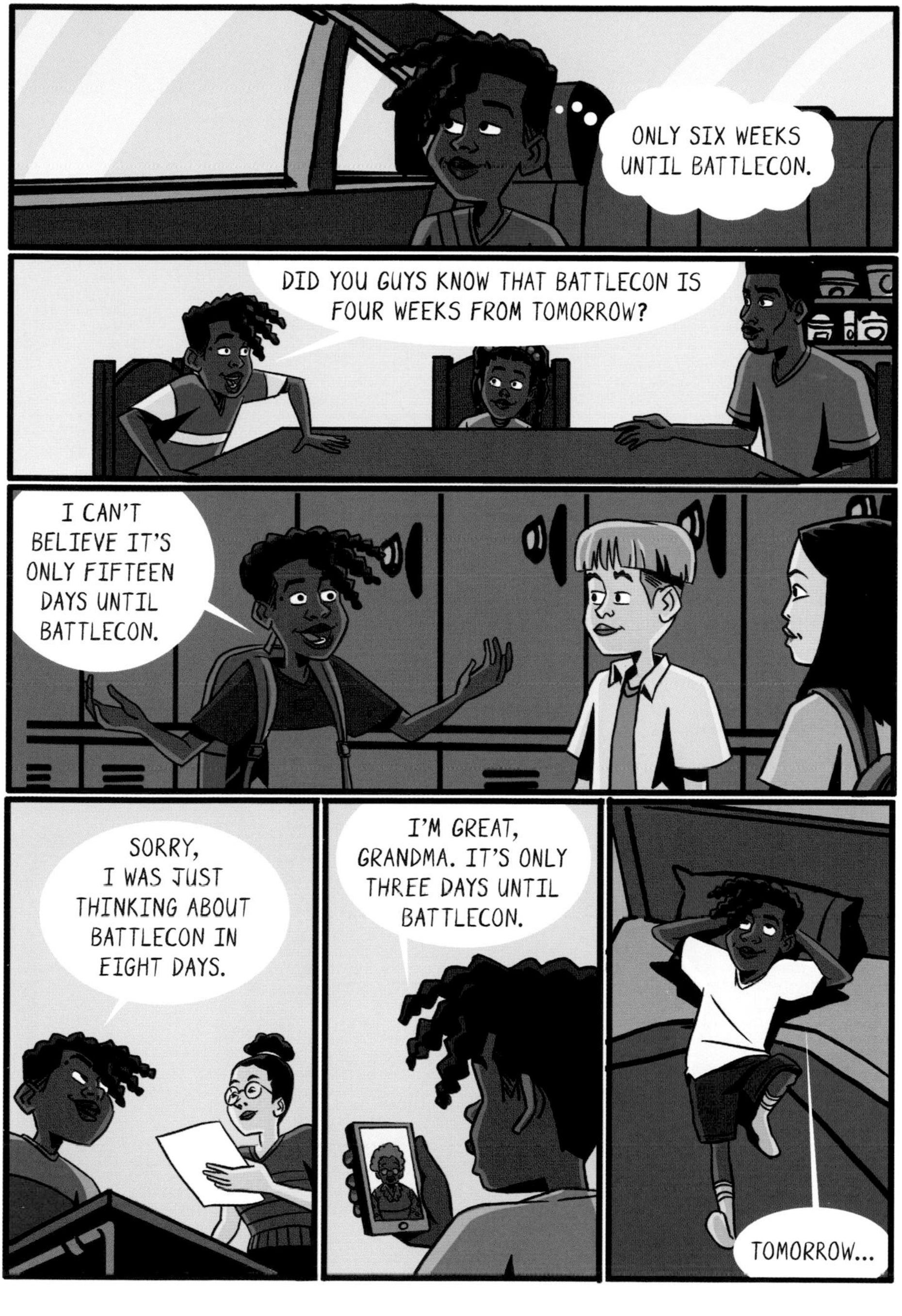
ONLY SIX WEEKS UNTIL BATTLECON.
DID YOU GUYS KNOW THAT BATTLECON IS FOUR WEEKS FROM TOMORROW?
I CAN'T BELIEVE IT'S ONLY FIFTEEN DAYS UNTIL BATTLECON.
SORRY, I WAS JUST THINKING ABOUT BATTLECON IN EIGHT DAYS.
I'M GREAT, GRANDMA. IT'S ONLY THREE DAYS UNTIL BATTLECON.
TOMORROW...

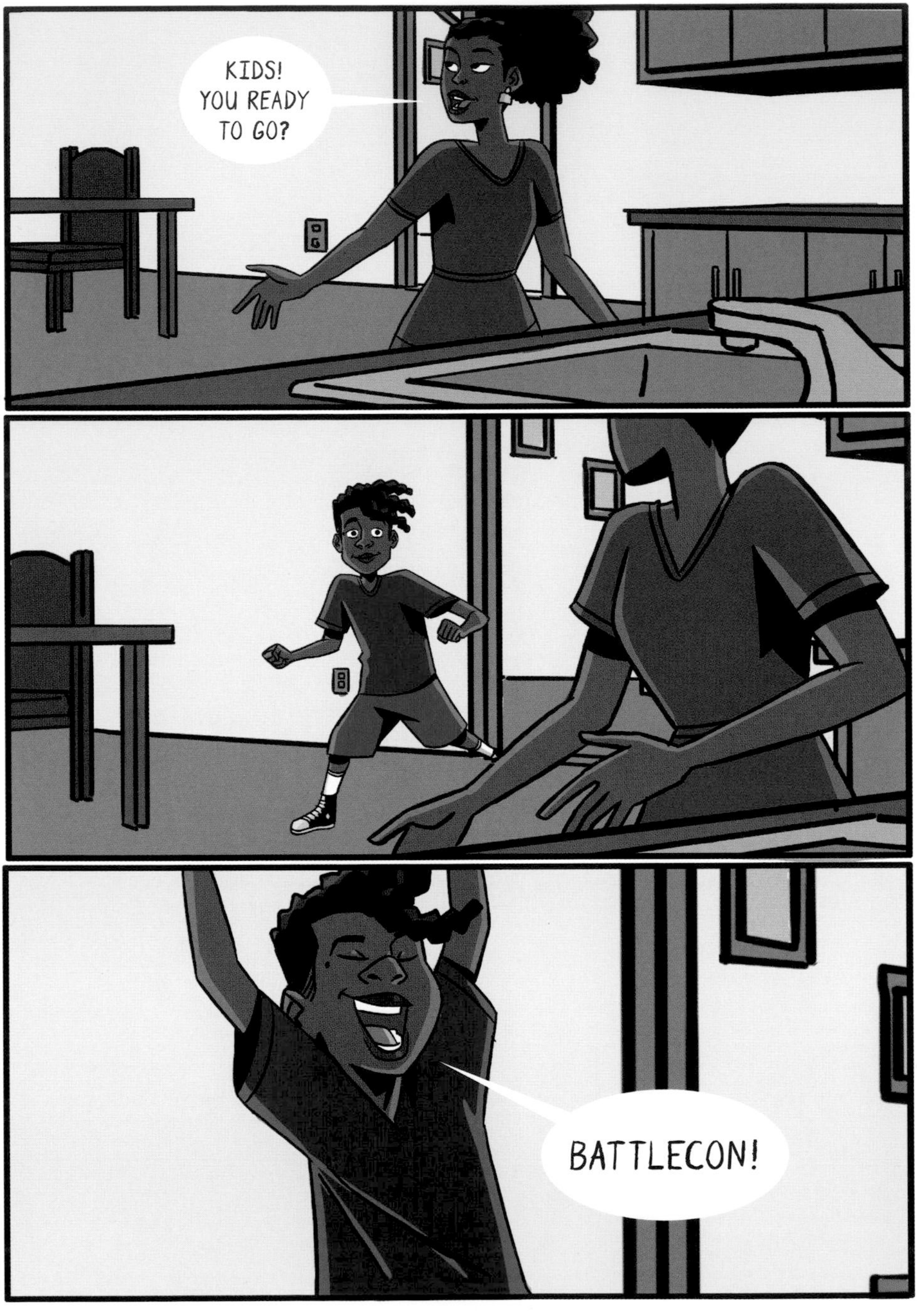
KIDS! YOU READY TO GO?
BATTLECON!

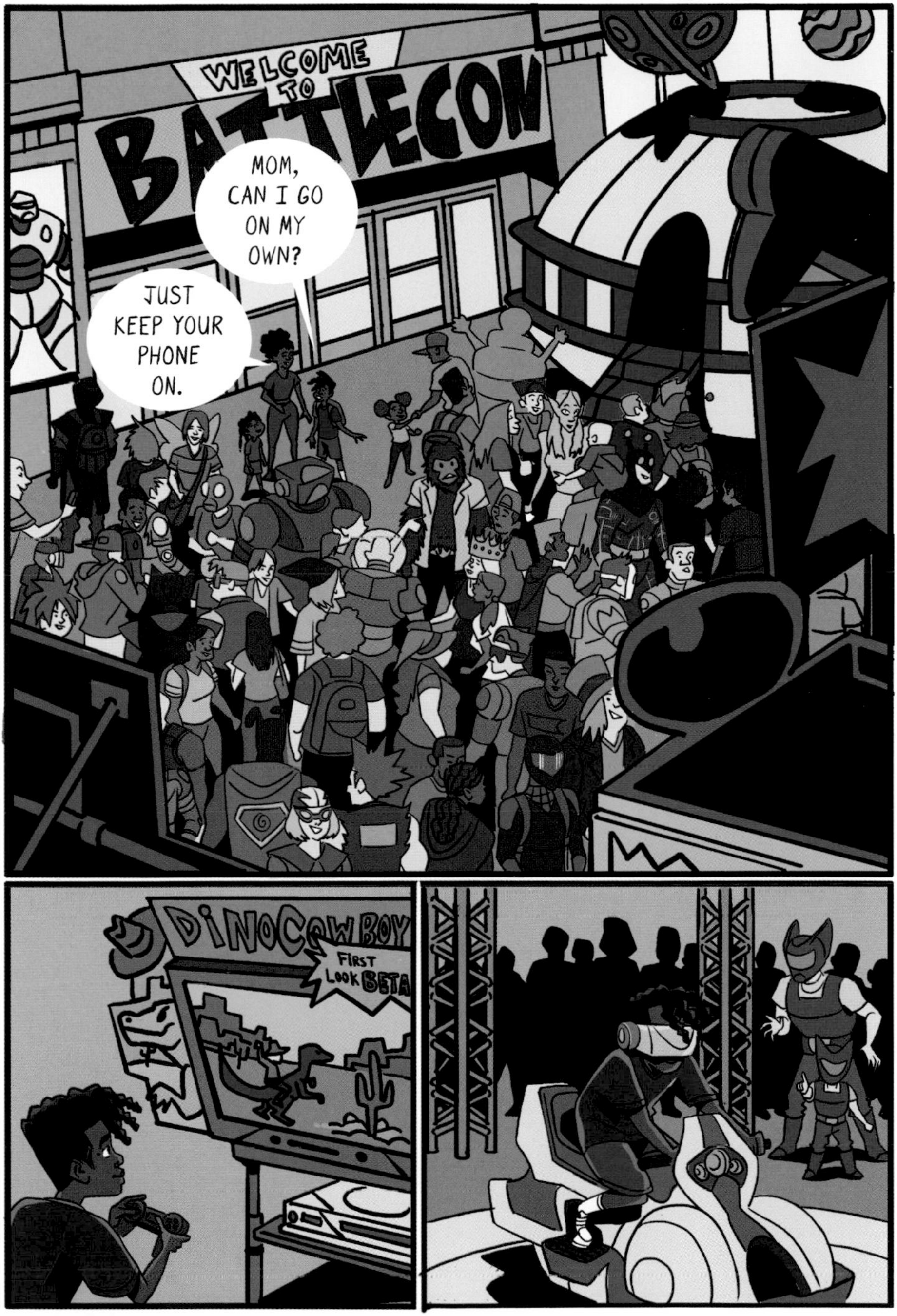
WELCOME TO BATTLECON
MOM, CAN I GO ON MY OWN?
JUST KEEP YOUR PHONE ON.
DINOCOWBOY
FIRST LOOK BETA

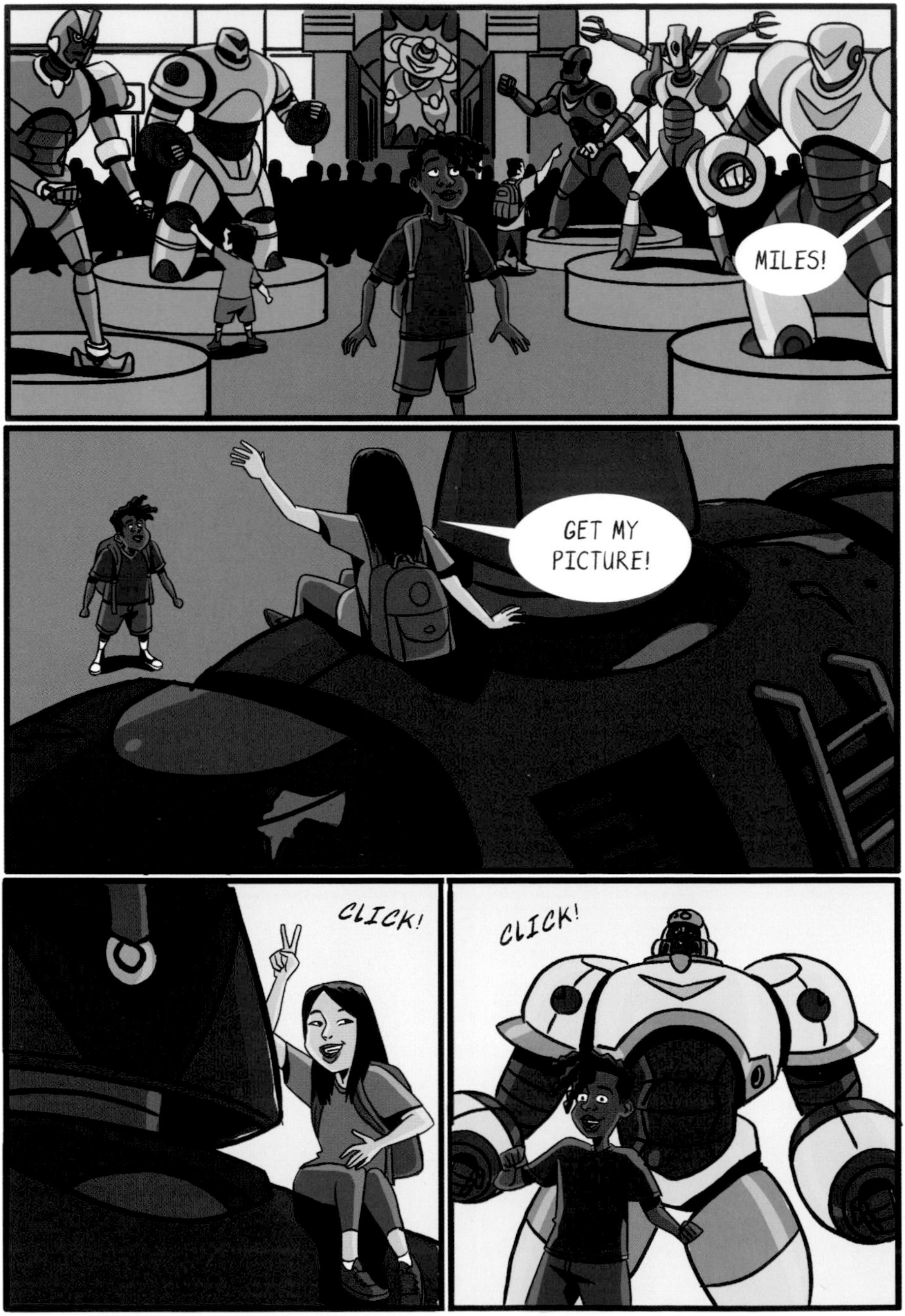
MILES!
GET MY PICTURE!
CLICK!
CLICK!

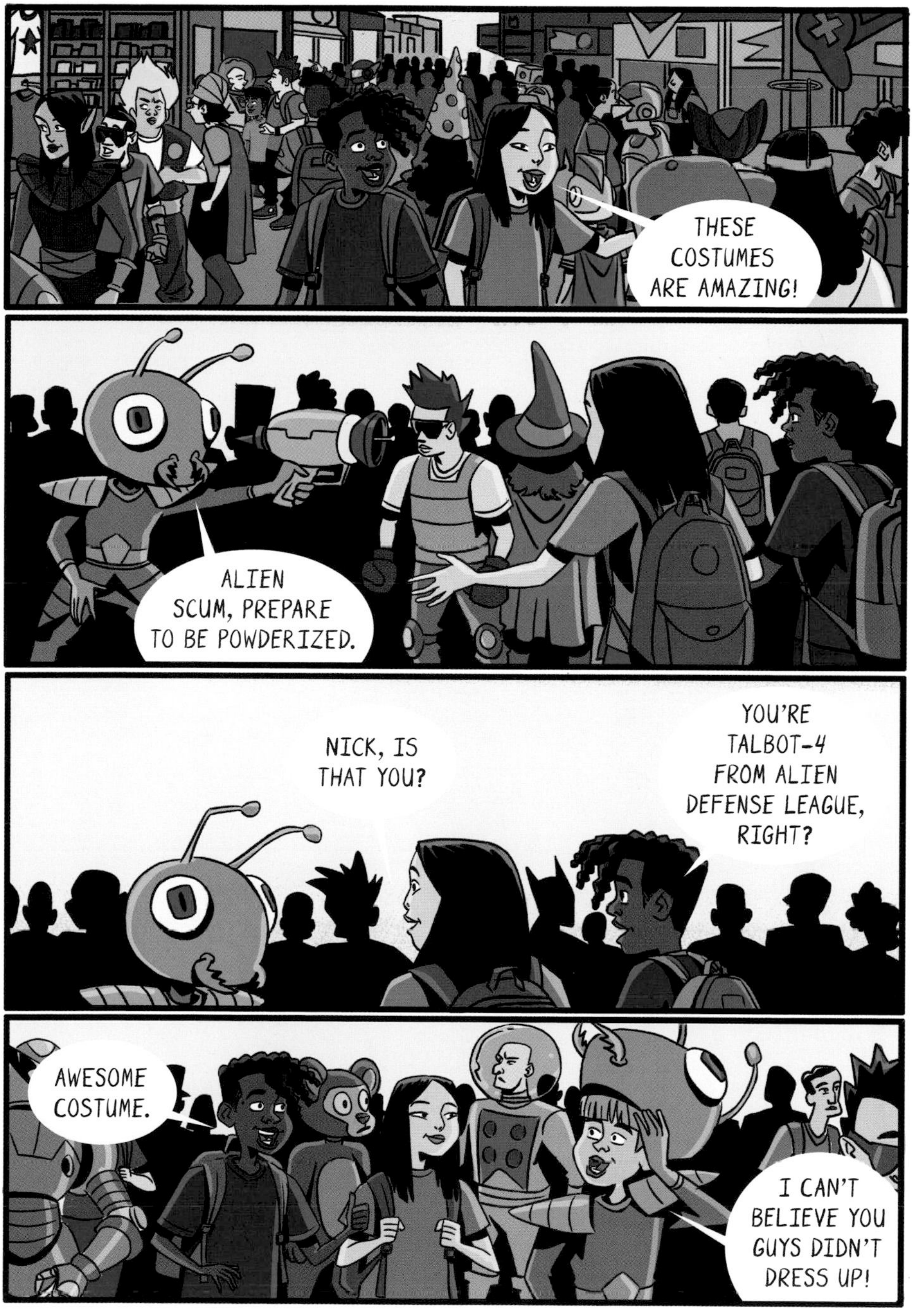
THESE COSTUMES ARE AMAZING!
ALIEN SCUM, PREPARE TO BE POWDERIZED.
NICK, IS THAT YOU?
YOU'RE TALBOT-4 FROM ALIEN DEFENSE LEAGUE, RIGHT?
AWESOME COSTUME.
I CAN'T BELIEVE YOU GUYS DIDN'T DRESS UP!

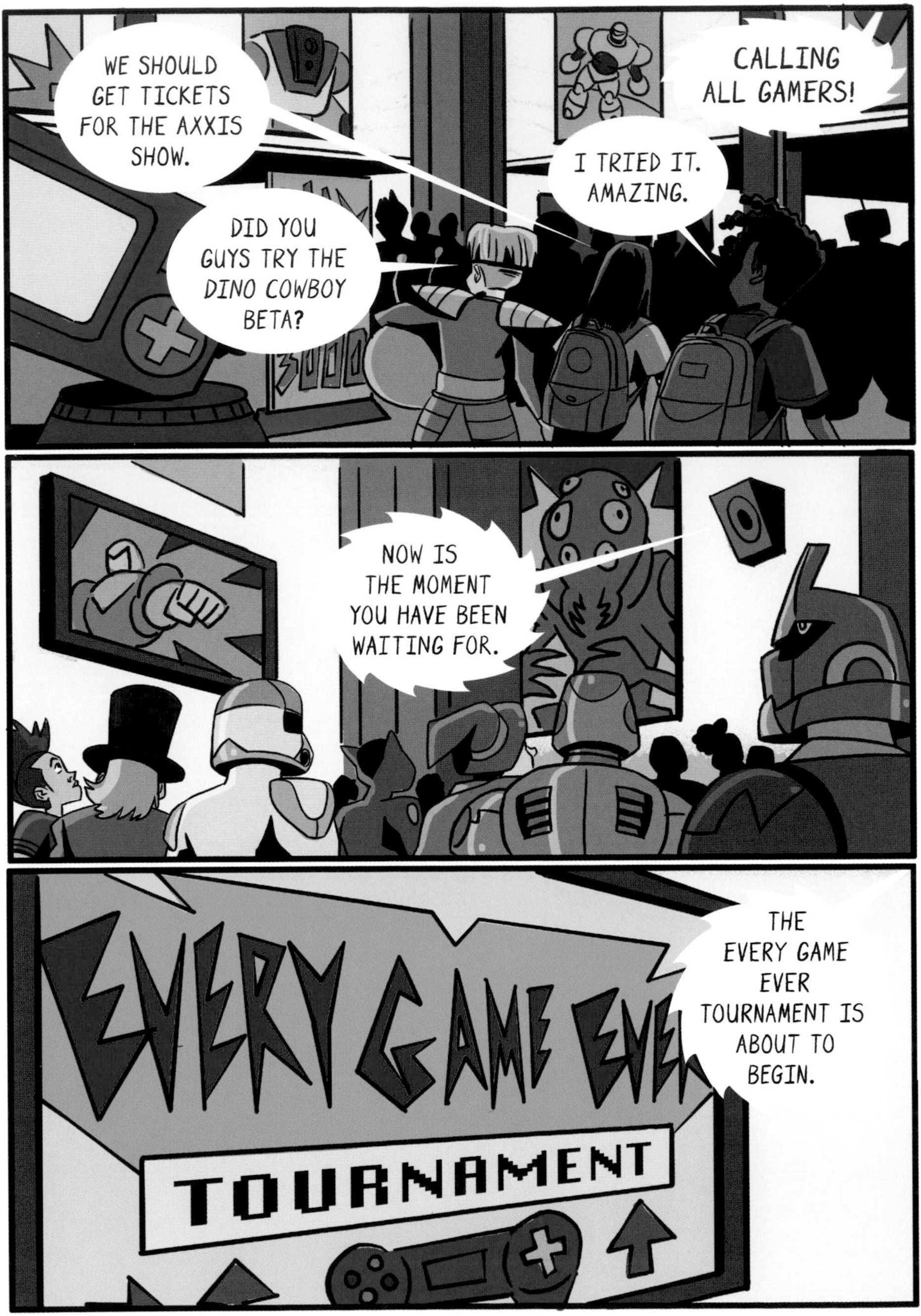
WE SHOULD GET TICKETS FOR THE AXXIS SHOW.
DID YOU GUYS TRY THE *DINO COWBOY* BETA?
I TRIED IT. AMAZING.
CALLING ALL GAMERS!
NOW IS THE MOMENT YOU HAVE BEEN WAITING FOR.
EVERY GAME EVE
TOURNAMENT
THE EVERY GAME EVER TOURNAMENT IS ABOUT TO BEGIN.

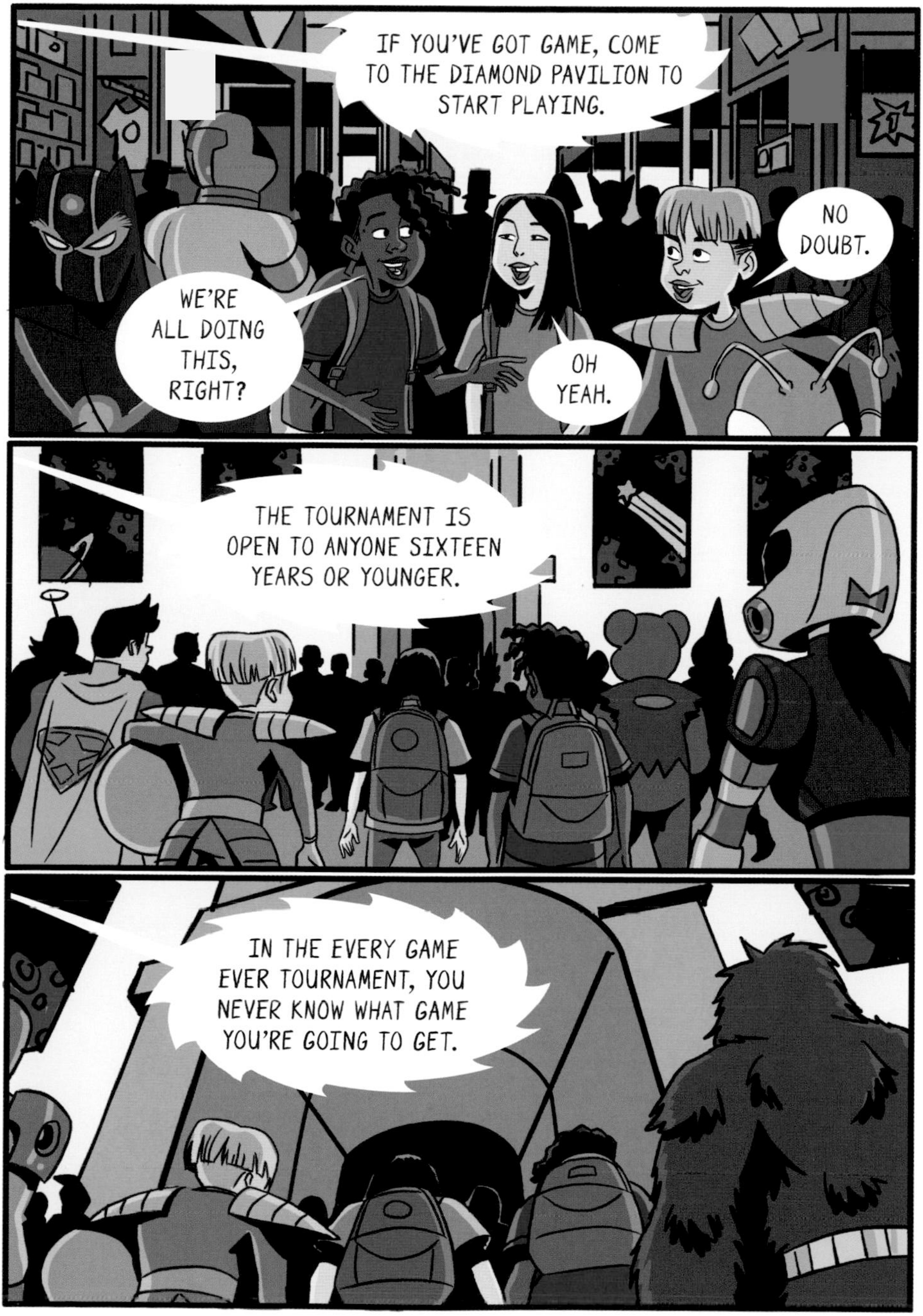
IF YOU'VE GOT GAME, COME TO THE DIAMOND PAVILION TO START PLAYING.
WE'RE ALL DOING THIS, RIGHT?
OH YEAH.
NO DOUBT.
THE TOURNAMENT IS OPEN TO ANYONE SIXTEEN YEARS OR YOUNGER.
IN THE EVERY GAME EVER TOURNAMENT, YOU NEVER KNOW WHAT GAME YOU'RE GOING TO GET.

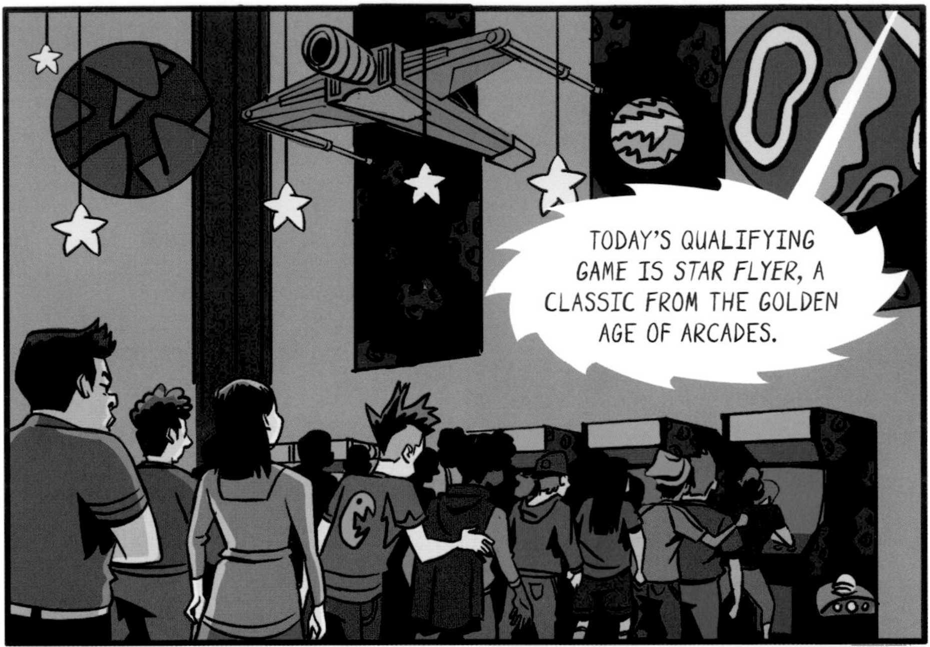
TODAY'S QUALIFYING GAME IS *STAR FLYER*, A CLASSIC FROM THE GOLDEN AGE OF ARCADES.

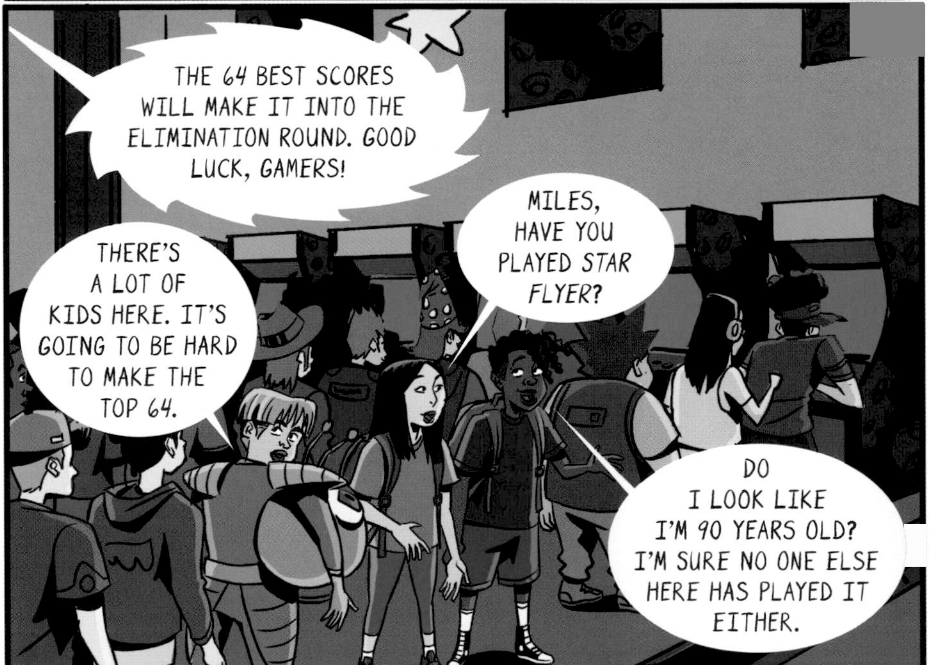
THE 64 BEST SCORES WILL MAKE IT INTO THE ELIMINATION ROUND. GOOD LUCK, GAMERS!
THERE'S A LOT OF KIDS HERE. IT'S GOING TO BE HARD TO MAKE THE TOP 64.
MILES, HAVE YOU PLAYED *STAR FLYER*?
DO I LOOK LIKE I'M 90 YEARS OLD? I'M SURE NO ONE ELSE HERE HAS PLAYED IT EITHER.

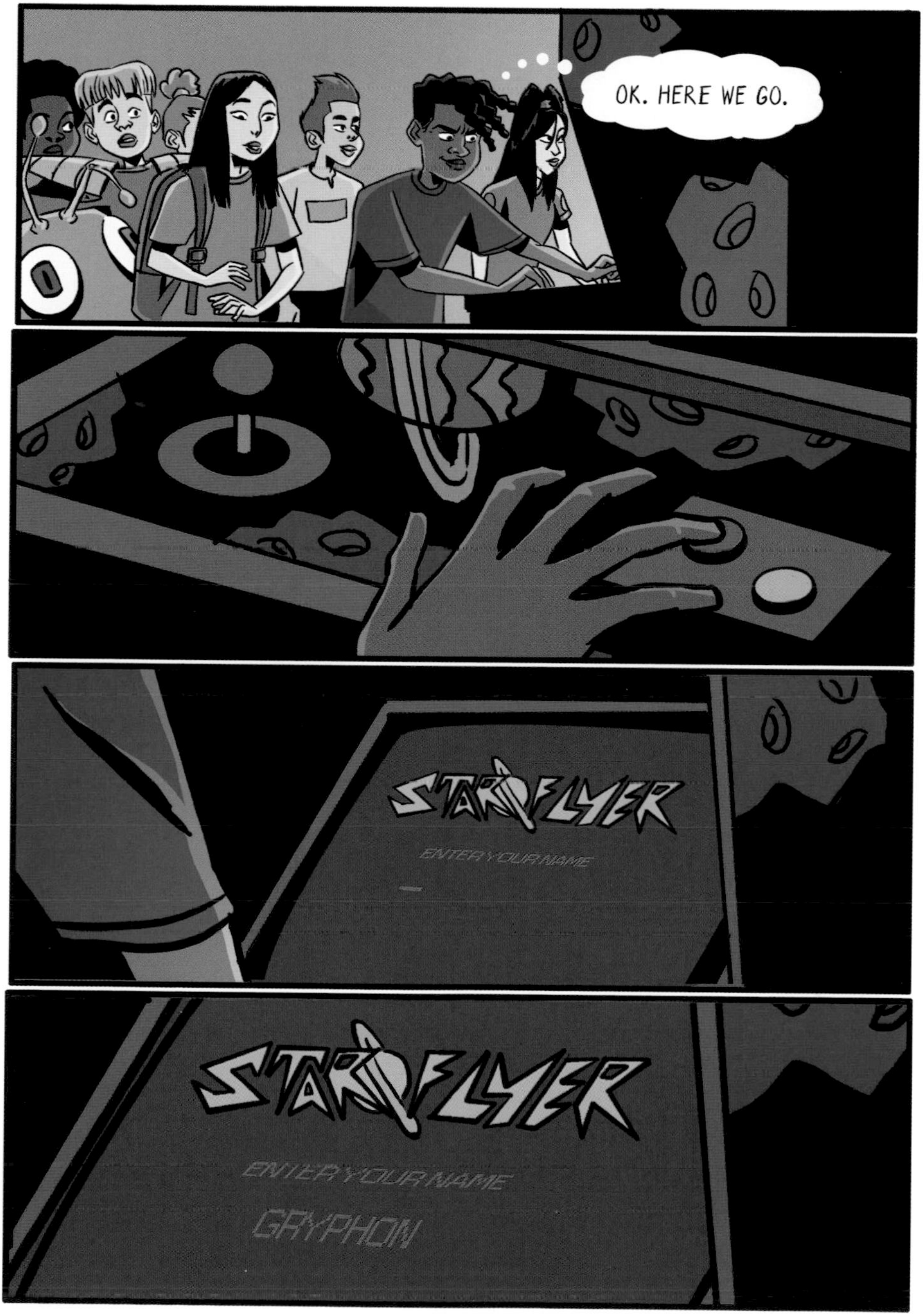
OK. HERE WE GO.
STARFLYER
ENTER YOUR NAME
STARFLYER
ENTER YOUR NAME
GRYPHON

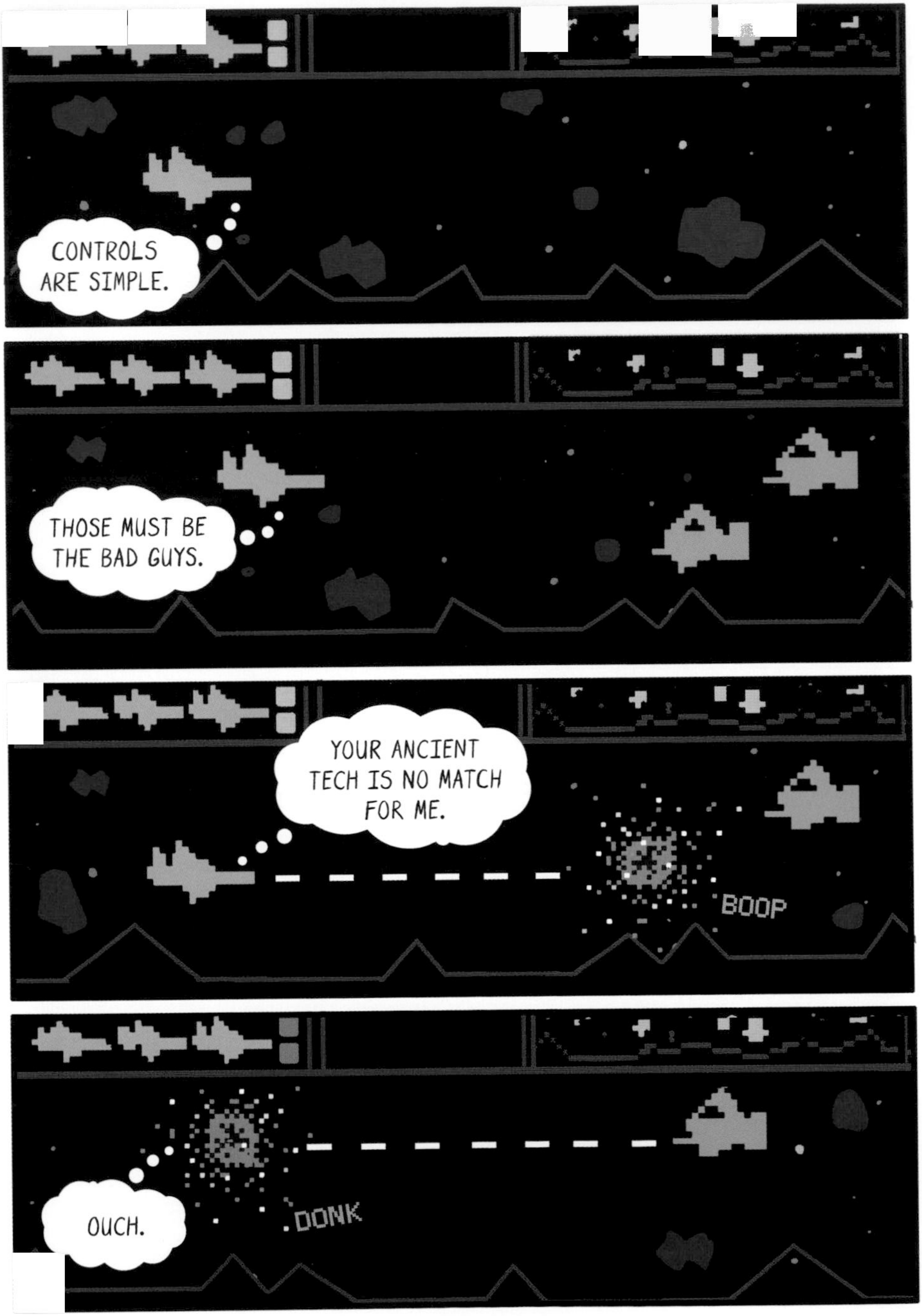
CONTROLS ARE SIMPLE.
THOSE MUST BE THE BAD GUYS.
YOUR ANCIENT TECH IS NO MATCH FOR ME.
BOOP
OUCH.
DONK

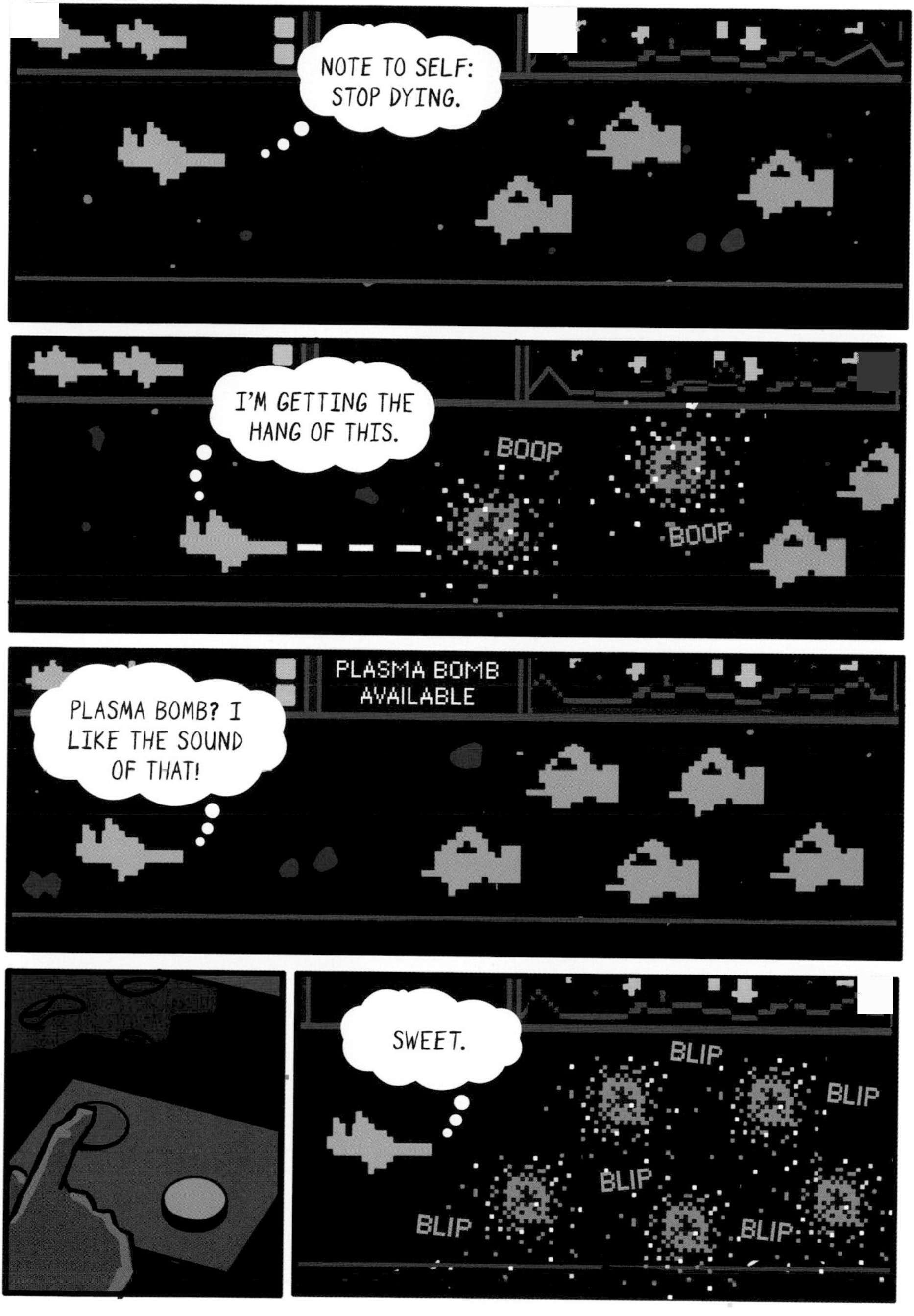
NOTE TO SELF: STOP DYING.
I'M GETTING THE HANG OF THIS.
BOOP
BOOP
PLASMA BOMB AVAILABLE
PLASMA BOMB? I LIKE THE SOUND OF THAT!
SWEET.
BLIP
BLIP
BLIP
BLIP
BLIP
BLIP

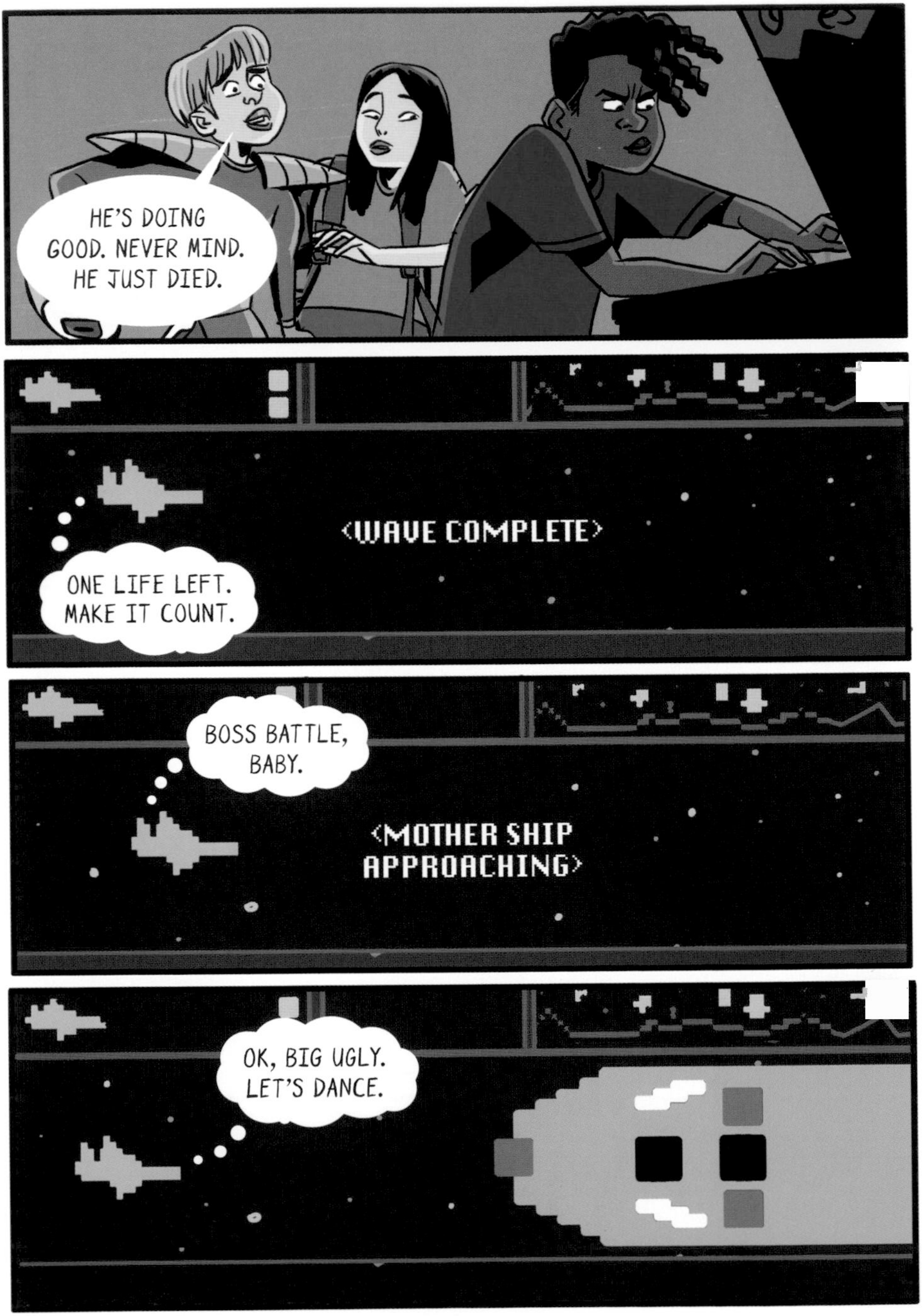
HE'S DOING GOOD. NEVER MIND. HE JUST DIED.
<WAVE COMPLETE>
ONE LIFE LEFT. MAKE IT COUNT.
BOSS BATTLE, BABY.
<MOTHER SHIP APPROACHING>
OK, BIG UGLY. LET'S DANCE.

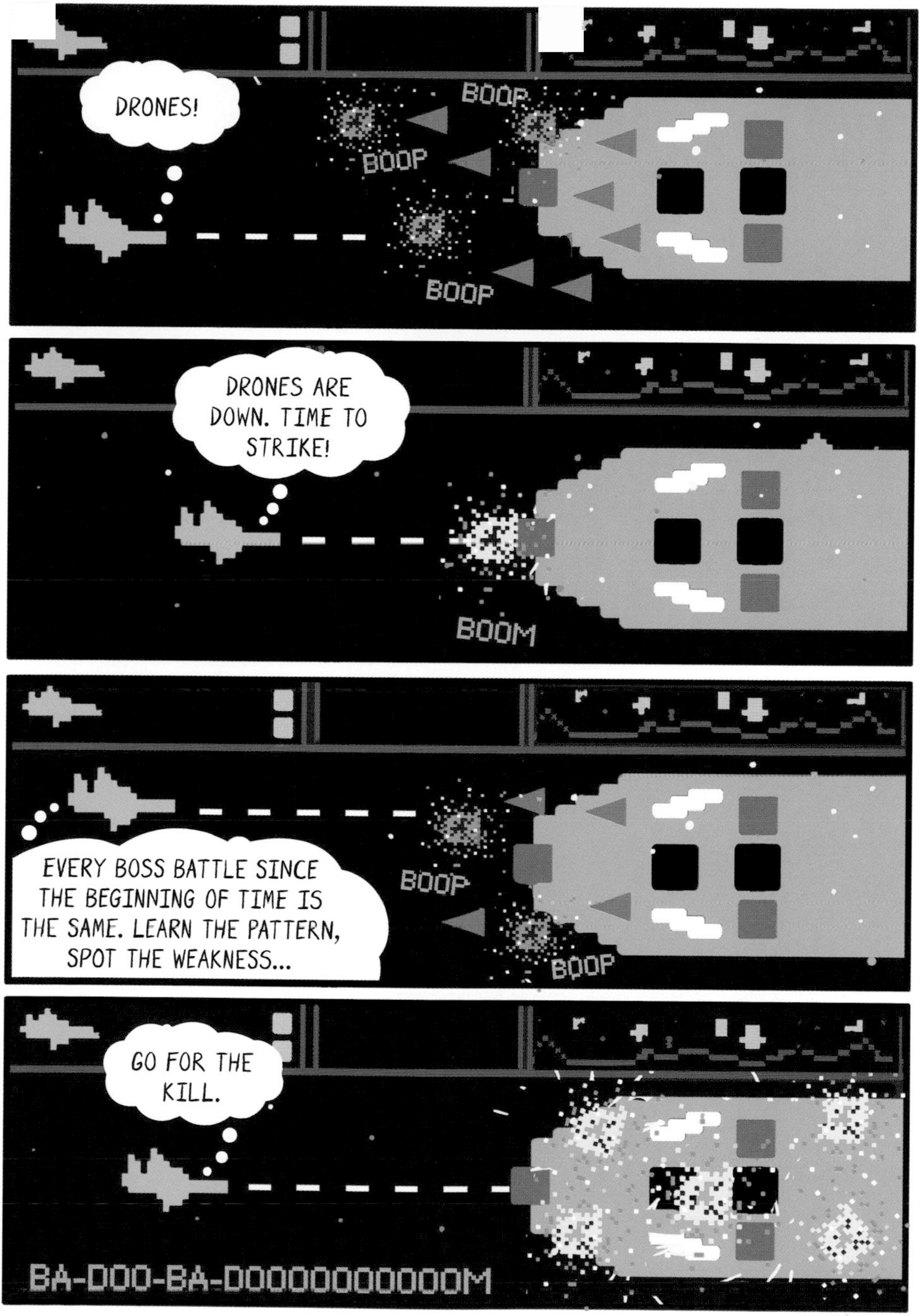
DRONES!
BOOP
BOOP
BOOP
DRONES ARE DOWN. TIME TO STRIKE!
BOOM
EVERY BOSS BATTLE SINCE THE BEGINNING OF TIME IS THE SAME. LEARN THE PATTERN, SPOT THE WEAKNESS...
BOOP
BOOP
GO FOR THE KILL.
BA-DOO-BA-DOOOOOOOOOOM

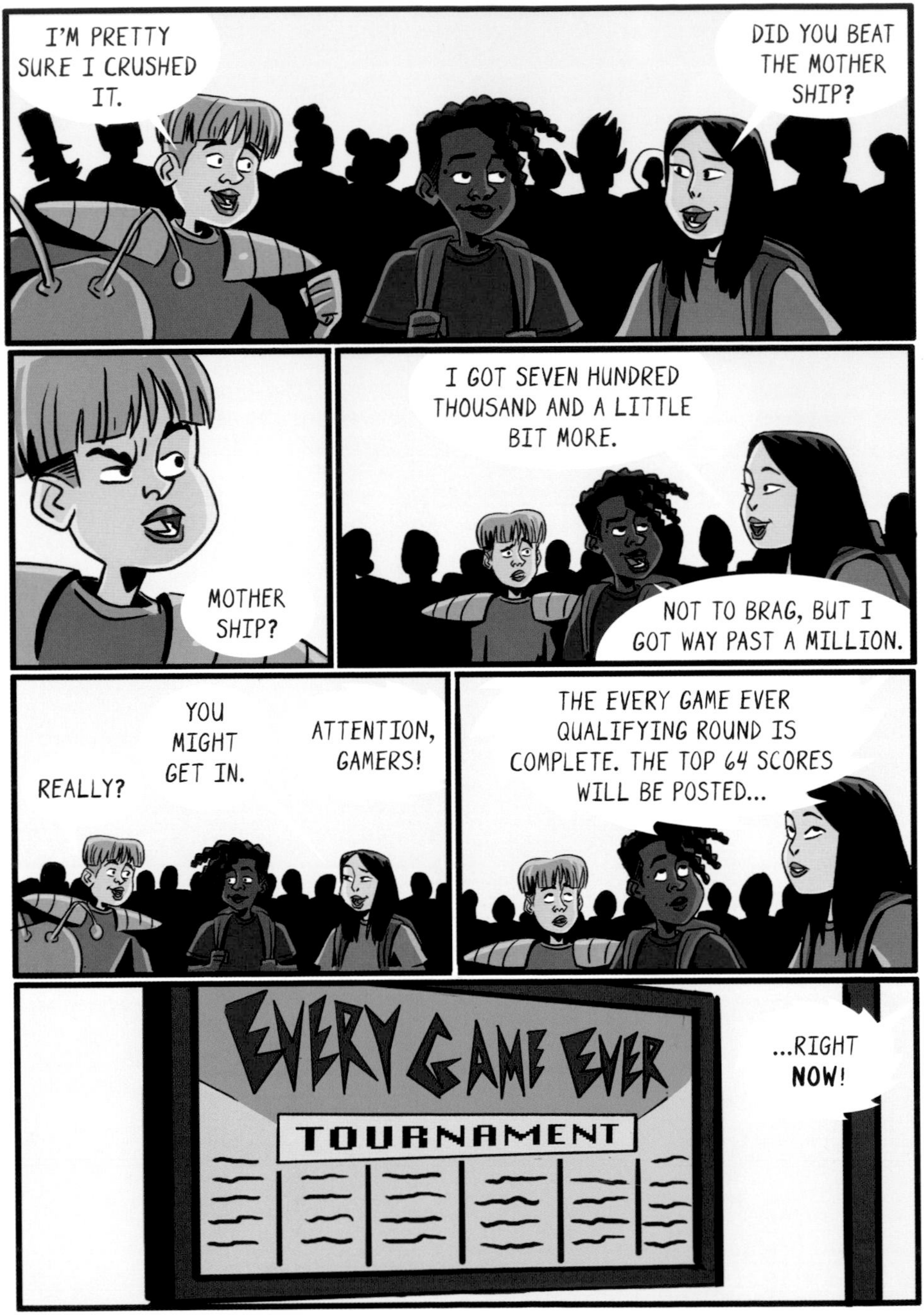
I'M PRETTY SURE I CRUSHED IT.
DID YOU BEAT THE MOTHER SHIP?
MOTHER SHIP?
I GOT SEVEN HUNDRED THOUSAND AND A LITTLE BIT MORE.
NOT TO BRAG, BUT I GOT WAY PAST A MILLION.
REALLY?
YOU MIGHT GET IN.
ATTENTION, GAMERS!
THE EVERY GAME EVER QUALIFYING ROUND IS COMPLETE. THE TOP 64 SCORES WILL BE POSTED...
EVERY GAME EVER
TOURNAMENT
...RIGHT **NOW**!

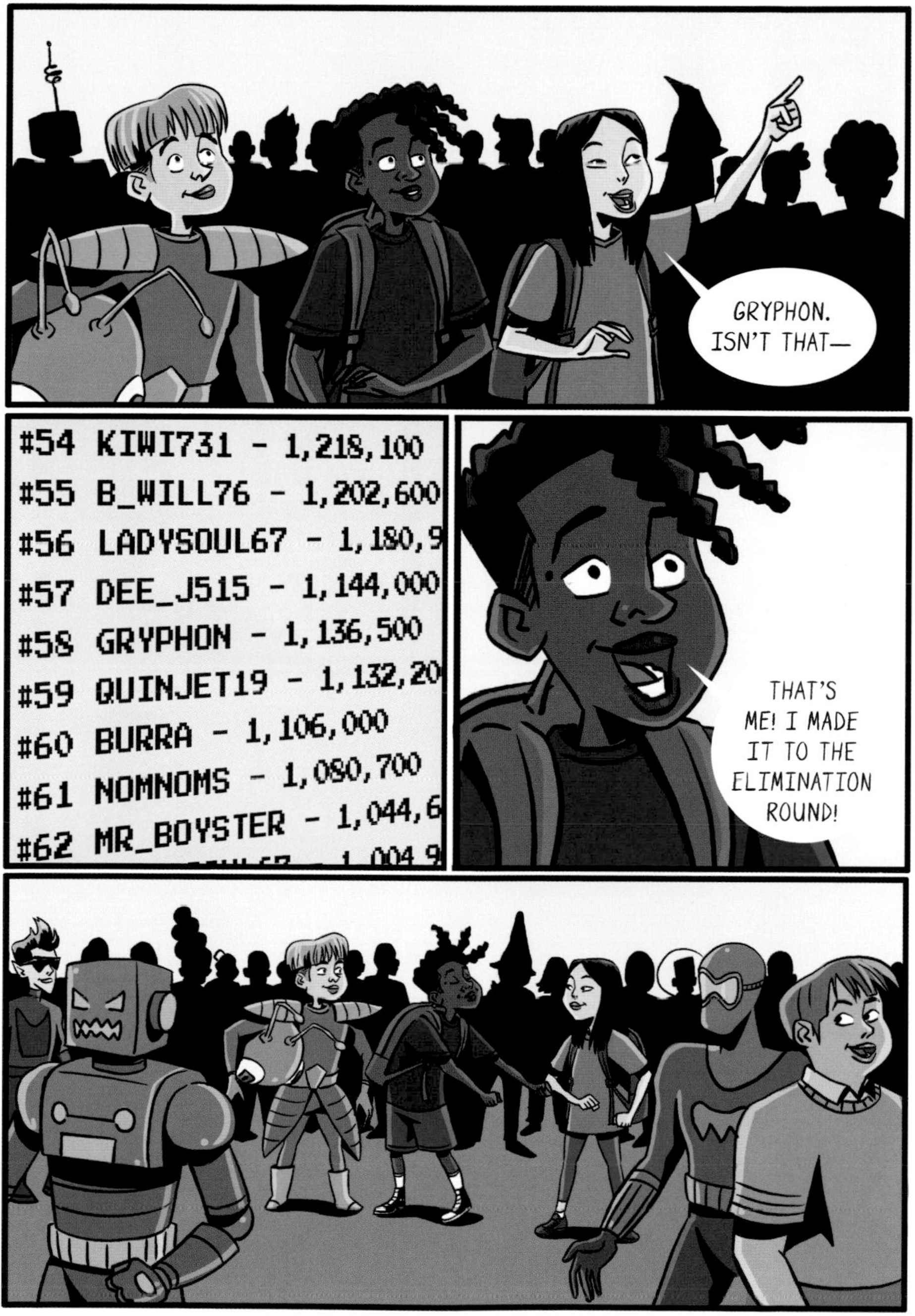
GRYPHON. ISN'T THAT—
#54 KIWI731 - 1,218,100
#55 B_WILL76 - 1,202,600
#56 LADYSOUL67 - 1,180,9
#57 DEE_J515 - 1,144,000
#58 GRYPHON - 1,136,500
#59 QUINJET19 - 1,132,20
#60 BURRA - 1,106,000
#61 NOMNOMS - 1,080,700
#62 MR_BOYSTER - 1,044,6
THAT'S ME! I MADE IT TO THE ELIMINATION ROUND!

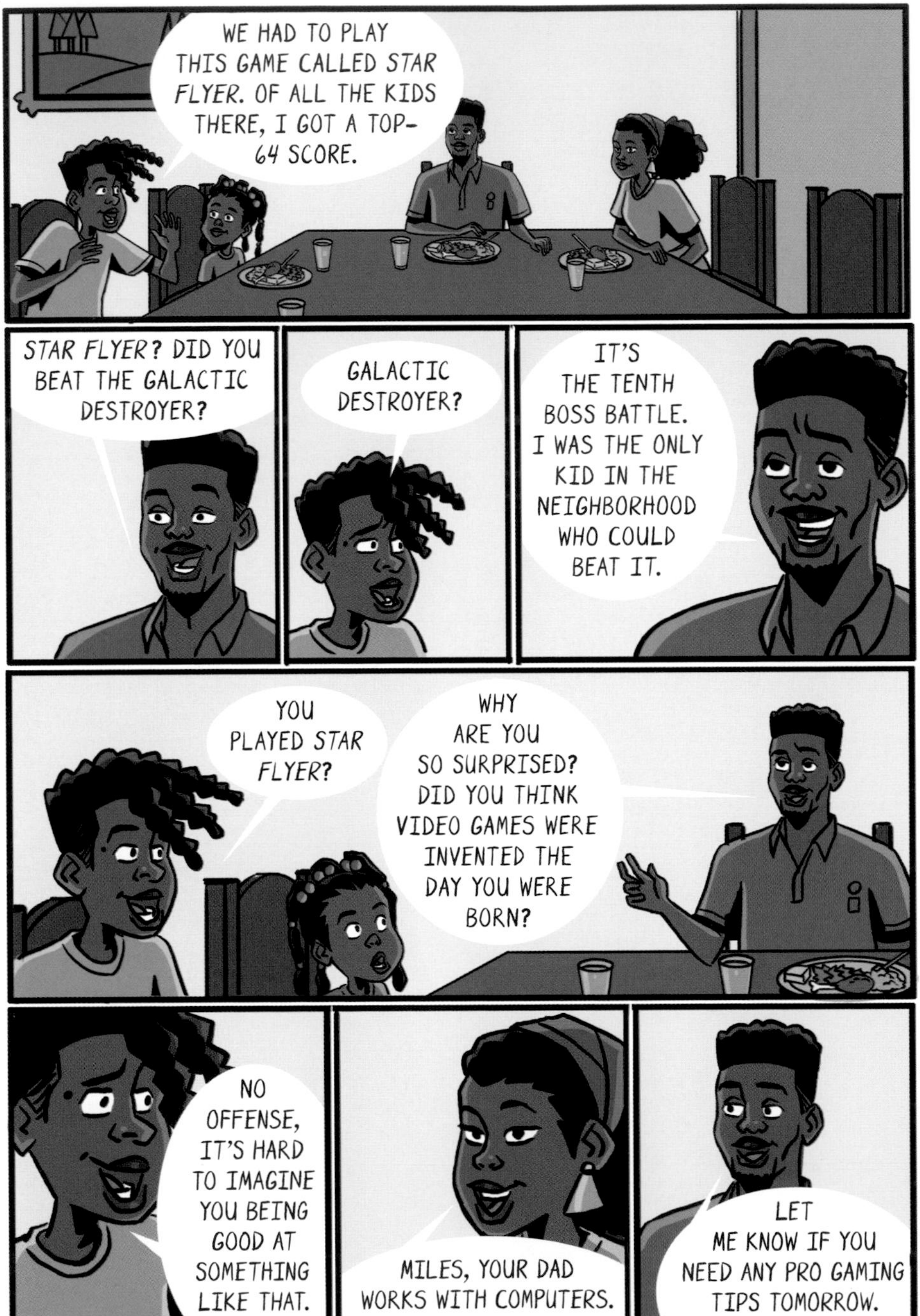
WE HAD TO PLAY THIS GAME CALLED *STAR FLYER*. OF ALL THE KIDS THERE, I GOT A TOP-64 SCORE.
STAR FLYER? DID YOU BEAT THE GALACTIC DESTROYER?
GALACTIC DESTROYER?
IT'S THE TENTH BOSS BATTLE. I WAS THE ONLY KID IN THE NEIGHBORHOOD WHO COULD BEAT IT.
YOU PLAYED *STAR FLYER*?
WHY ARE YOU SO SURPRISED? DID YOU THINK VIDEO GAMES WERE INVENTED THE DAY YOU WERE BORN?
NO OFFENSE, IT'S HARD TO IMAGINE YOU BEING GOOD AT SOMETHING LIKE THAT.
MILES, YOUR DAD WORKS WITH COMPUTERS.
LET ME KNOW IF YOU NEED ANY PRO GAMING TIPS TOMORROW.

CHAPTER 10
ELIMINATIONS

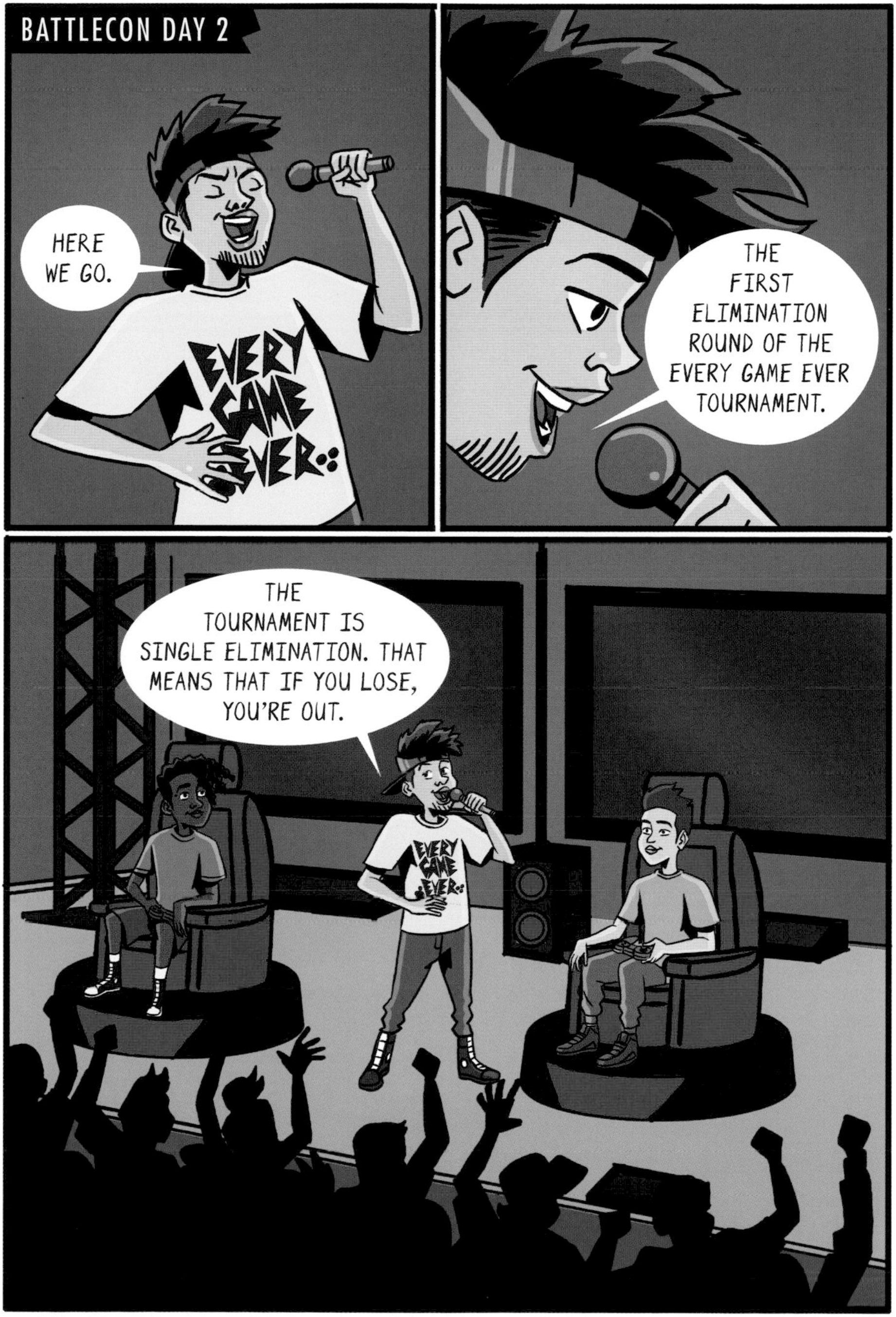
BATTLECON DAY 2
HERE WE GO.
EVERY GAME EVER
THE FIRST ELIMINATION ROUND OF THE EVERY GAME EVER TOURNAMENT.
THE TOURNAMENT IS SINGLE ELIMINATION. THAT MEANS THAT IF YOU LOSE, YOU'RE OUT.
EVERY GAME EVER

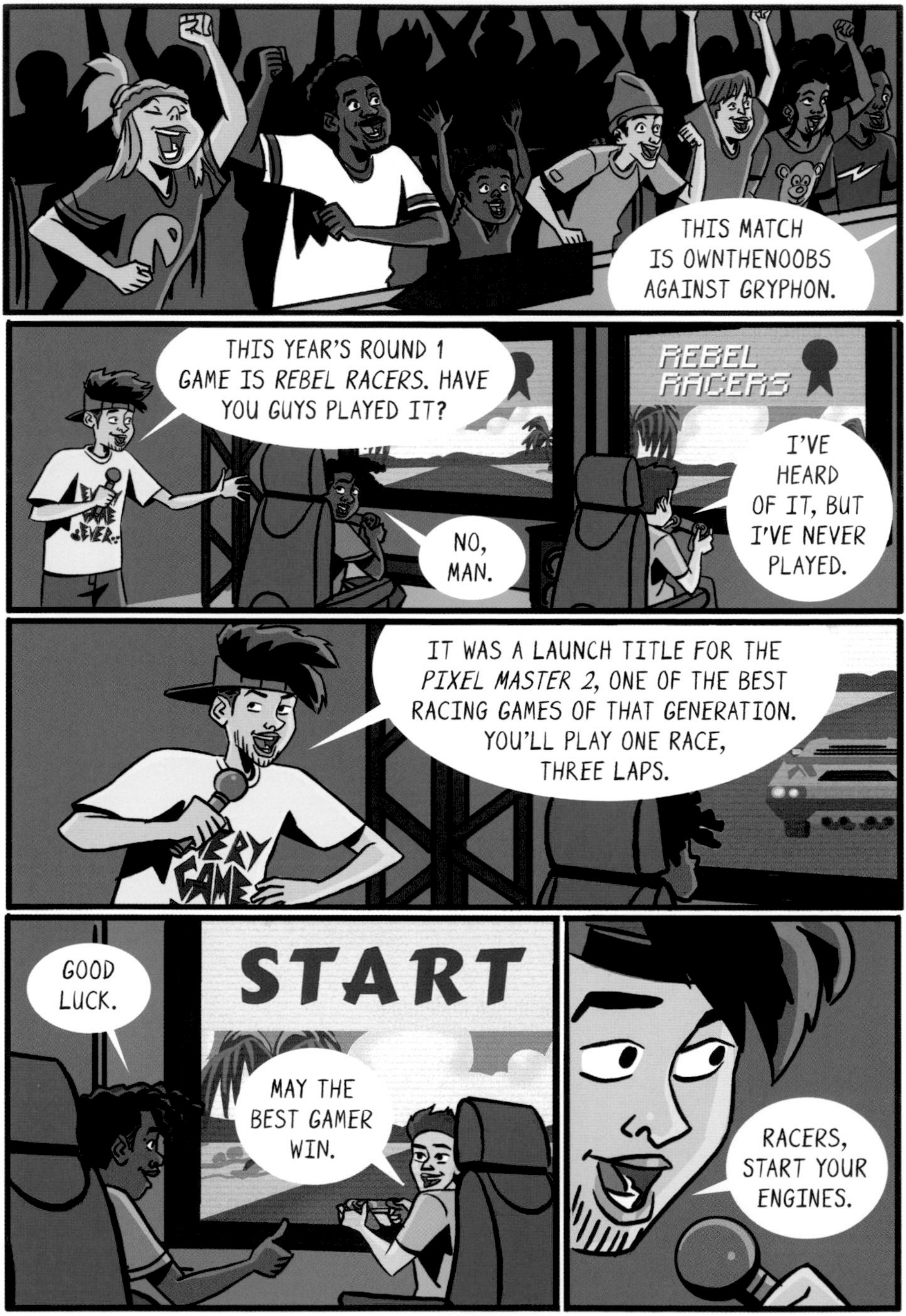
THIS MATCH IS OWNTHENOOBS AGAINST GRYPHON.
THIS YEAR'S ROUND 1 GAME IS *REBEL RACERS*. HAVE YOU GUYS PLAYED IT?
REBEL RACERS
NO, MAN.
I'VE HEARD OF IT, BUT I'VE NEVER PLAYED.
IT WAS A LAUNCH TITLE FOR THE *PIXEL MASTER 2*, ONE OF THE BEST RACING GAMES OF THAT GENERATION. YOU'LL PLAY ONE RACE, THREE LAPS.
START
GOOD LUCK.
MAY THE BEST GAMER WIN.
RACERS, START YOUR ENGINES.

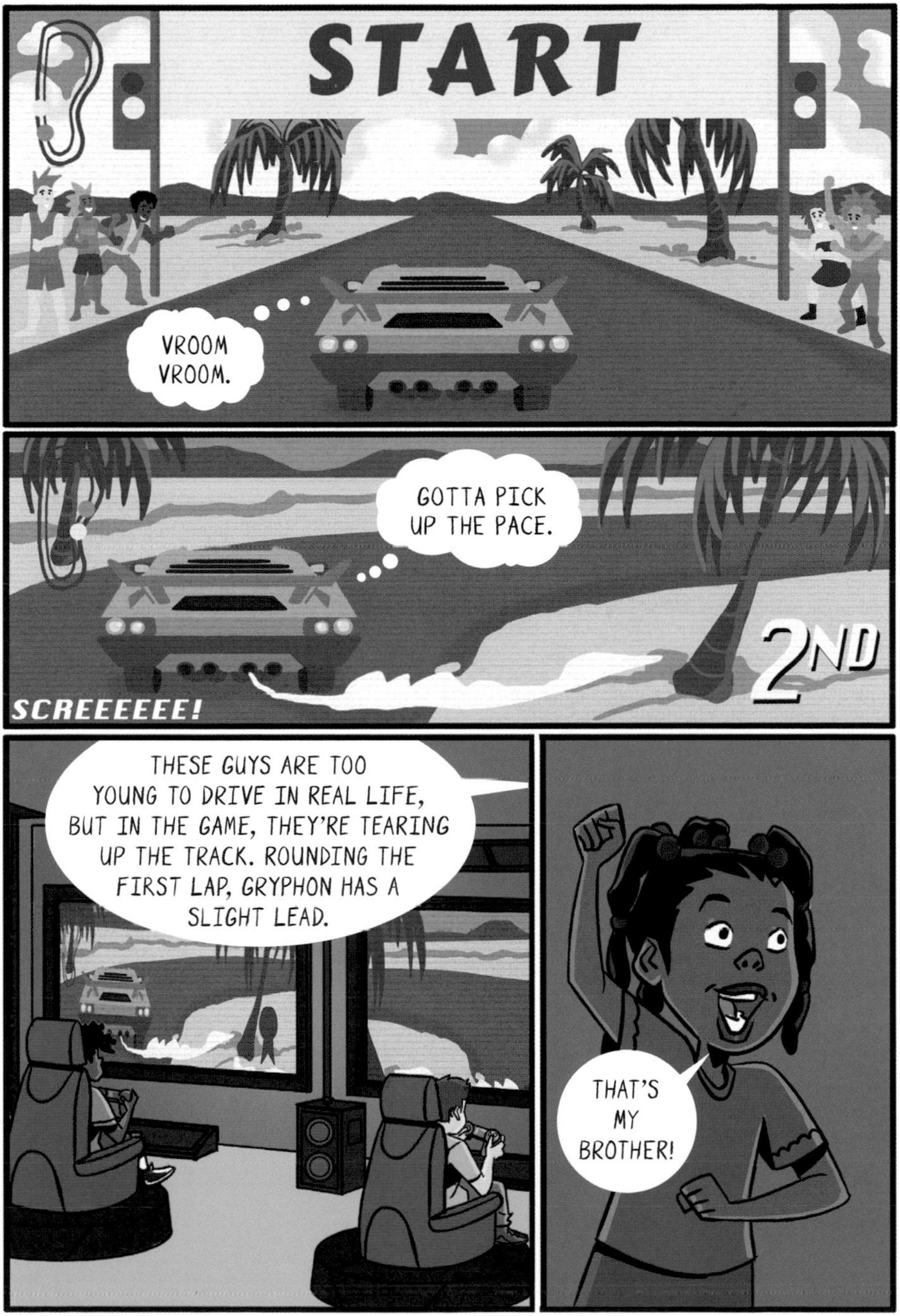
START
VROOM VROOM.
GOTTA PICK UP THE PACE.
2ND
SCREEEEEEE!
THESE GUYS ARE TOO YOUNG TO DRIVE IN REAL LIFE, BUT IN THE GAME, THEY'RE TEARING UP THE TRACK. ROUNDING THE FIRST LAP, GRYPHON HAS A SLIGHT LEAD.
THAT'S MY BROTHER!

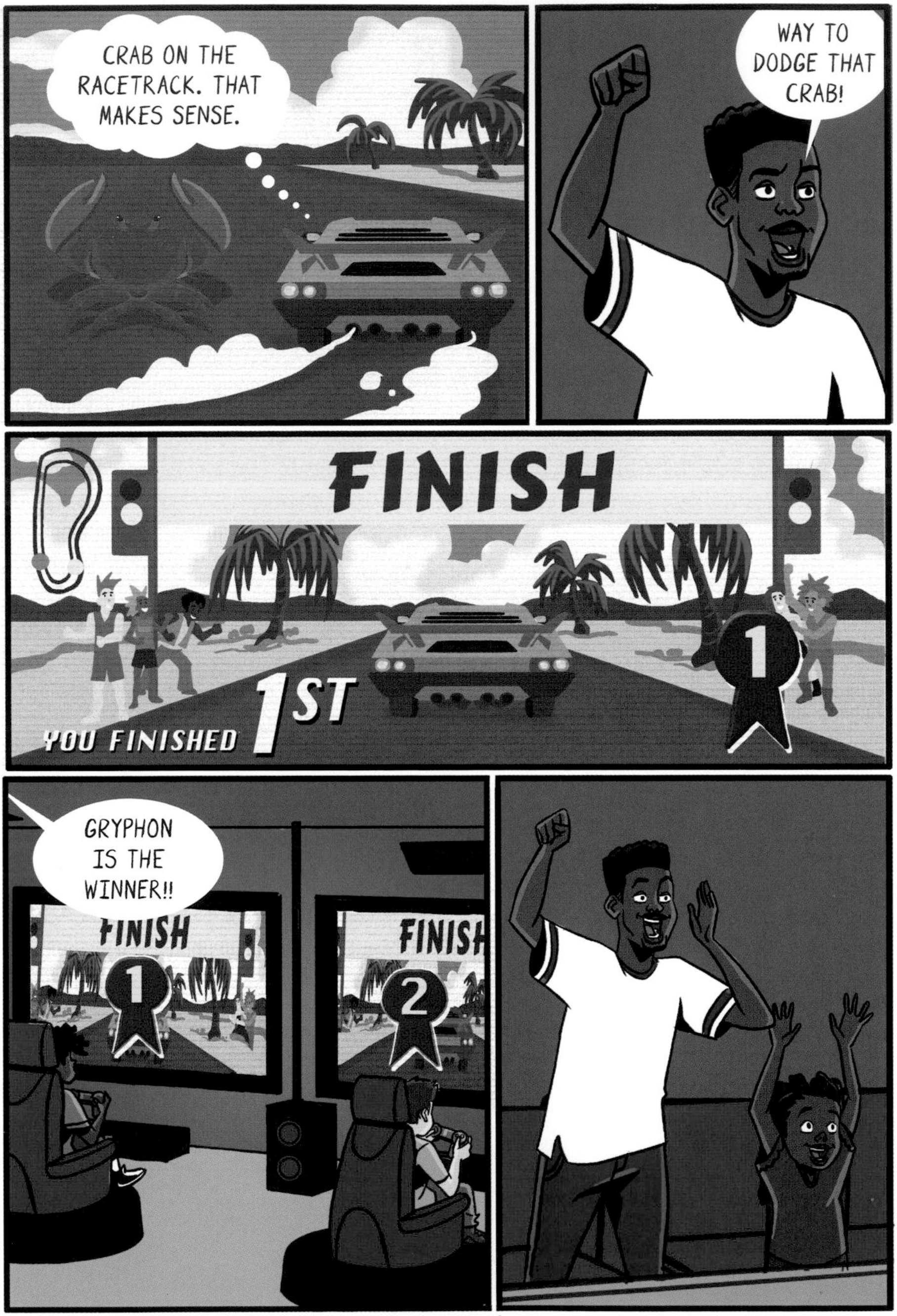
CRAB ON THE RACETRACK. THAT MAKES SENSE.
WAY TO DODGE THAT CRAB!
FINISH
1
YOU FINISHED 1ST
GRYPHON IS THE WINNER!!
FINISH
1
FINISH
2

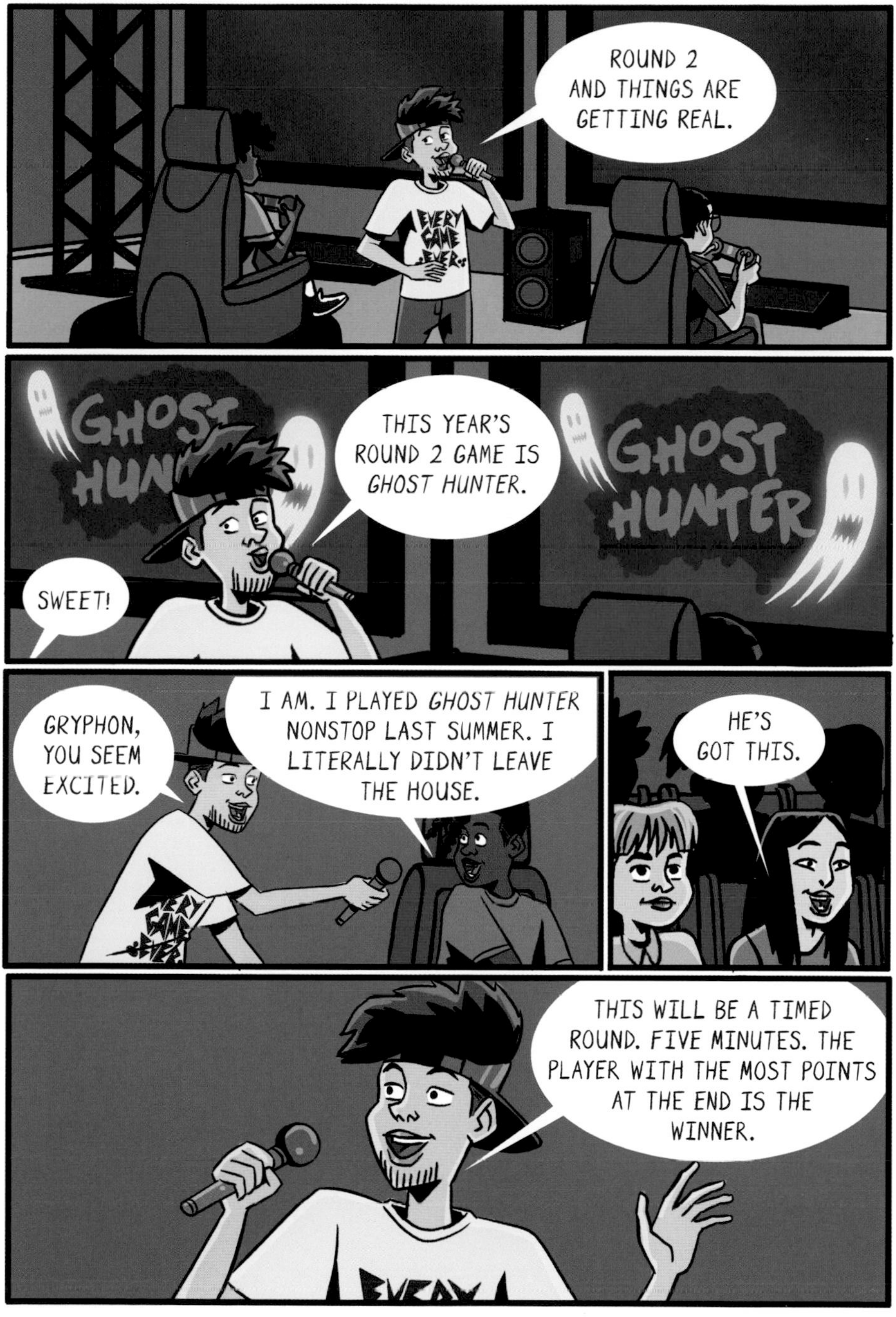
ROUND 2 AND THINGS ARE GETTING REAL.
THIS YEAR'S ROUND 2 GAME IS *GHOST HUNTER*.
GHOST HUNTER
SWEET!
GRYPHON, YOU SEEM EXCITED.
I AM. I PLAYED *GHOST HUNTER* NONSTOP LAST SUMMER. I LITERALLY DIDN'T LEAVE THE HOUSE.
HE'S GOT THIS.
THIS WILL BE A TIMED ROUND. FIVE MINUTES. THE PLAYER WITH THE MOST POINTS AT THE END IS THE WINNER.

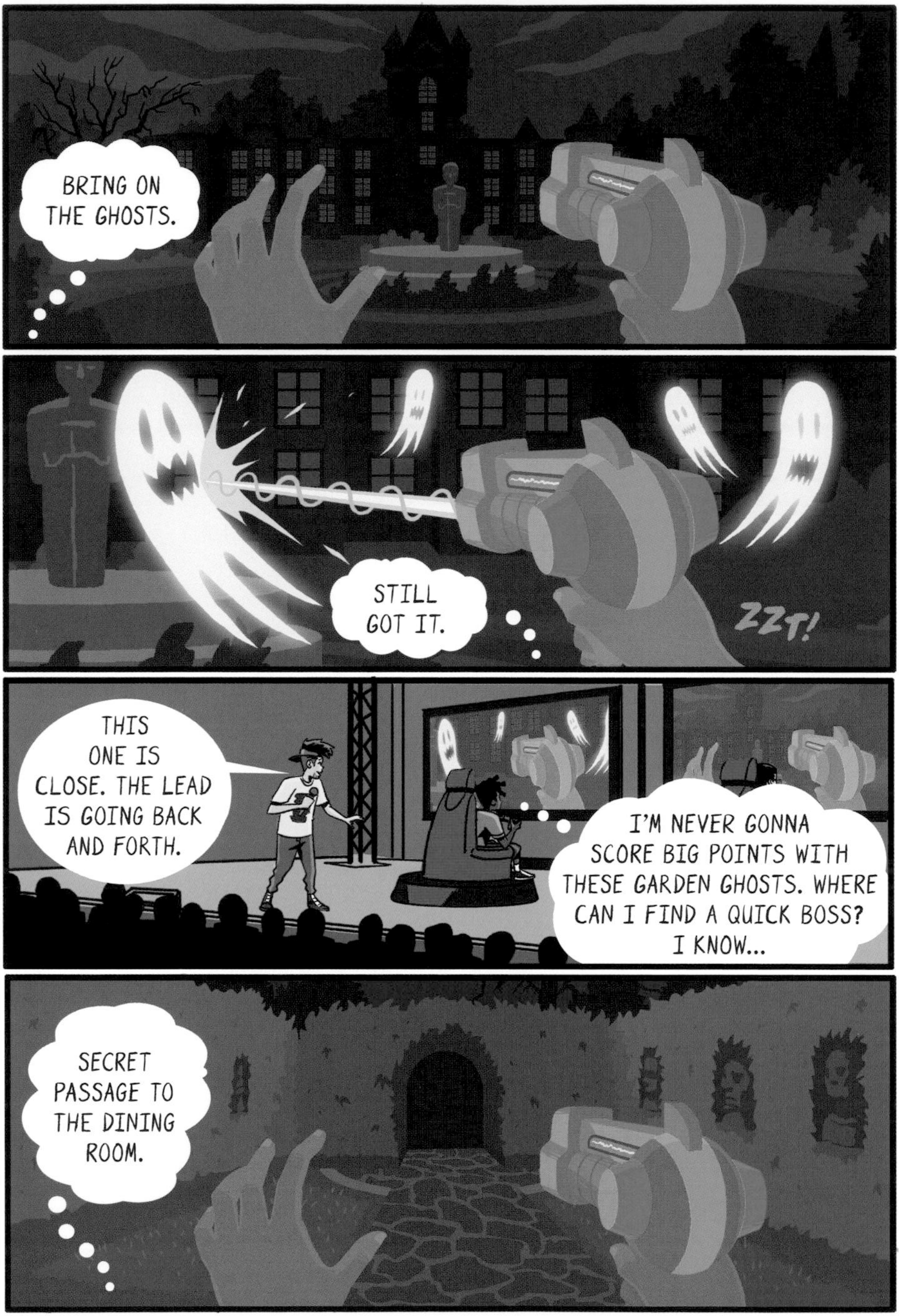
BRING ON THE GHOSTS.
STILL GOT IT.
ZZT!
THIS ONE IS CLOSE. THE LEAD IS GOING BACK AND FORTH.
I'M NEVER GONNA SCORE BIG POINTS WITH THESE GARDEN GHOSTS. WHERE CAN I FIND A QUICK BOSS? I KNOW...
SECRET PASSAGE TO THE DINING ROOM.

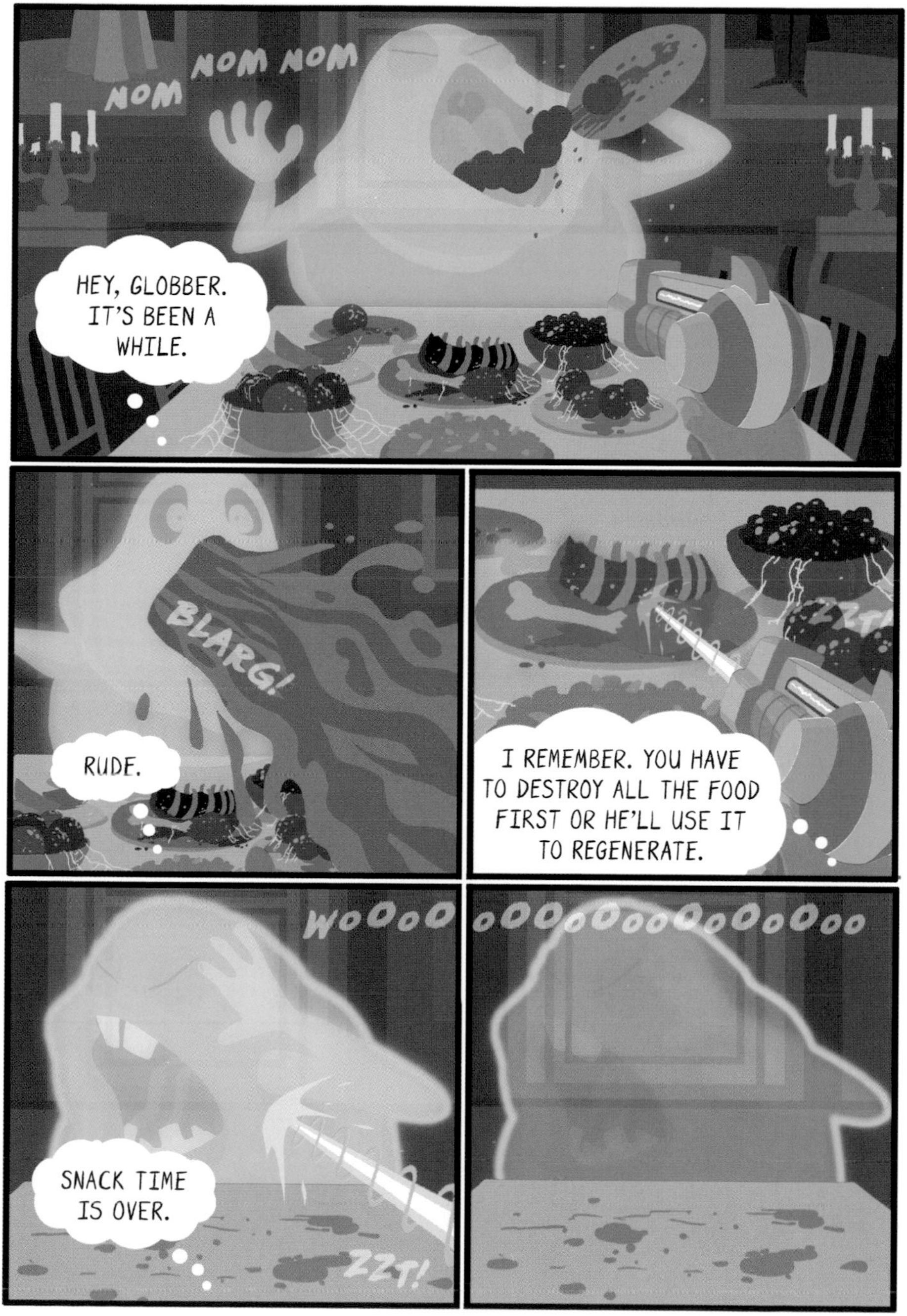
NOM NOM NOM
HEY, GLOBBER. IT'S BEEN A WHILE.
BLARG!
RUDE.
I REMEMBER. YOU HAVE TO DESTROY ALL THE FOOD FIRST OR HE'LL USE IT TO REGENERATE.
WoOoO oOOoOooOoOoOoo
SNACK TIME IS OVER.
ZZT!

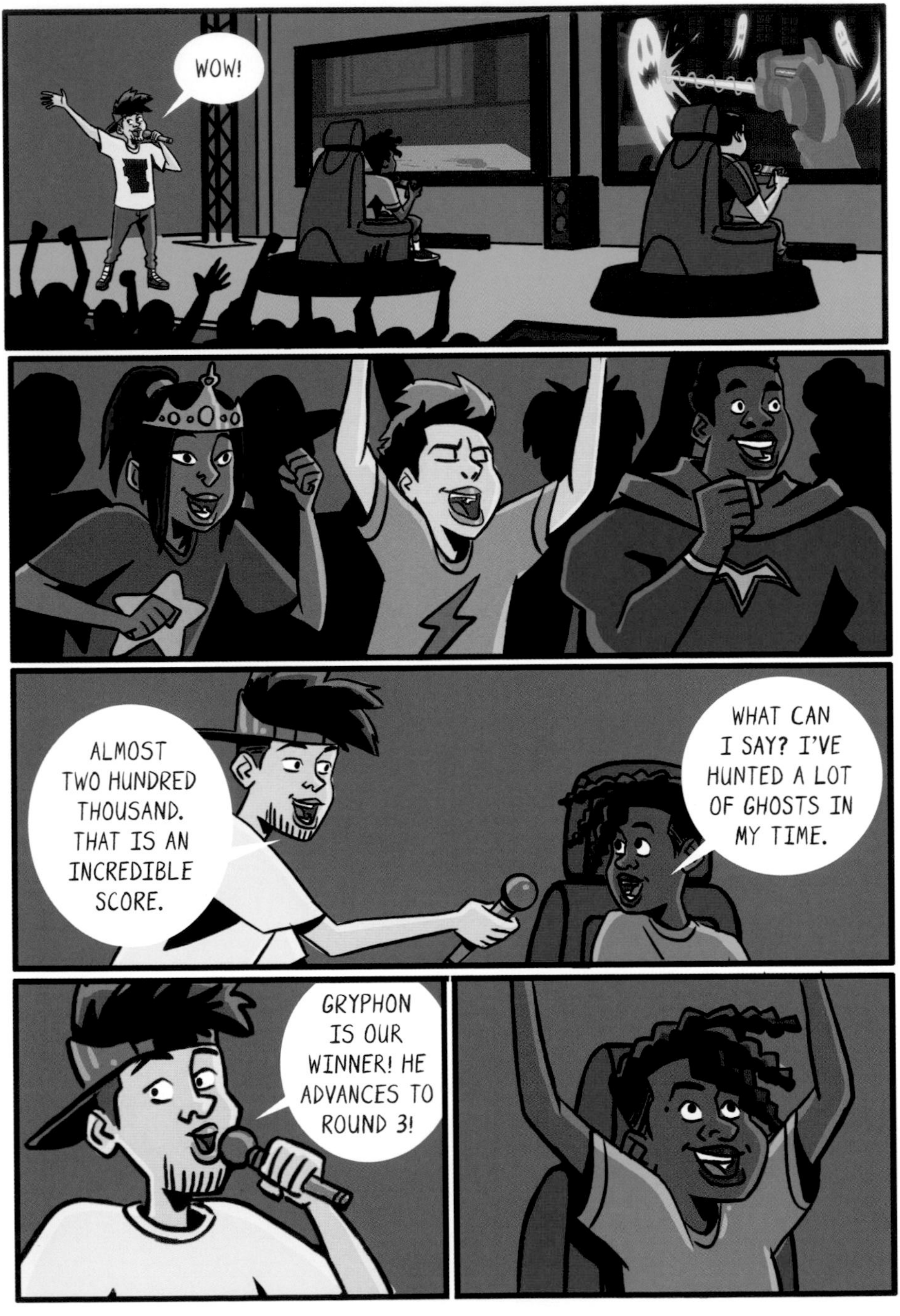
WOW!
ALMOST TWO HUNDRED THOUSAND. THAT IS AN INCREDIBLE SCORE.
WHAT CAN I SAY? I'VE HUNTED A LOT OF GHOSTS IN MY TIME.
GRYPHON IS OUR WINNER! HE ADVANCES TO ROUND 3!

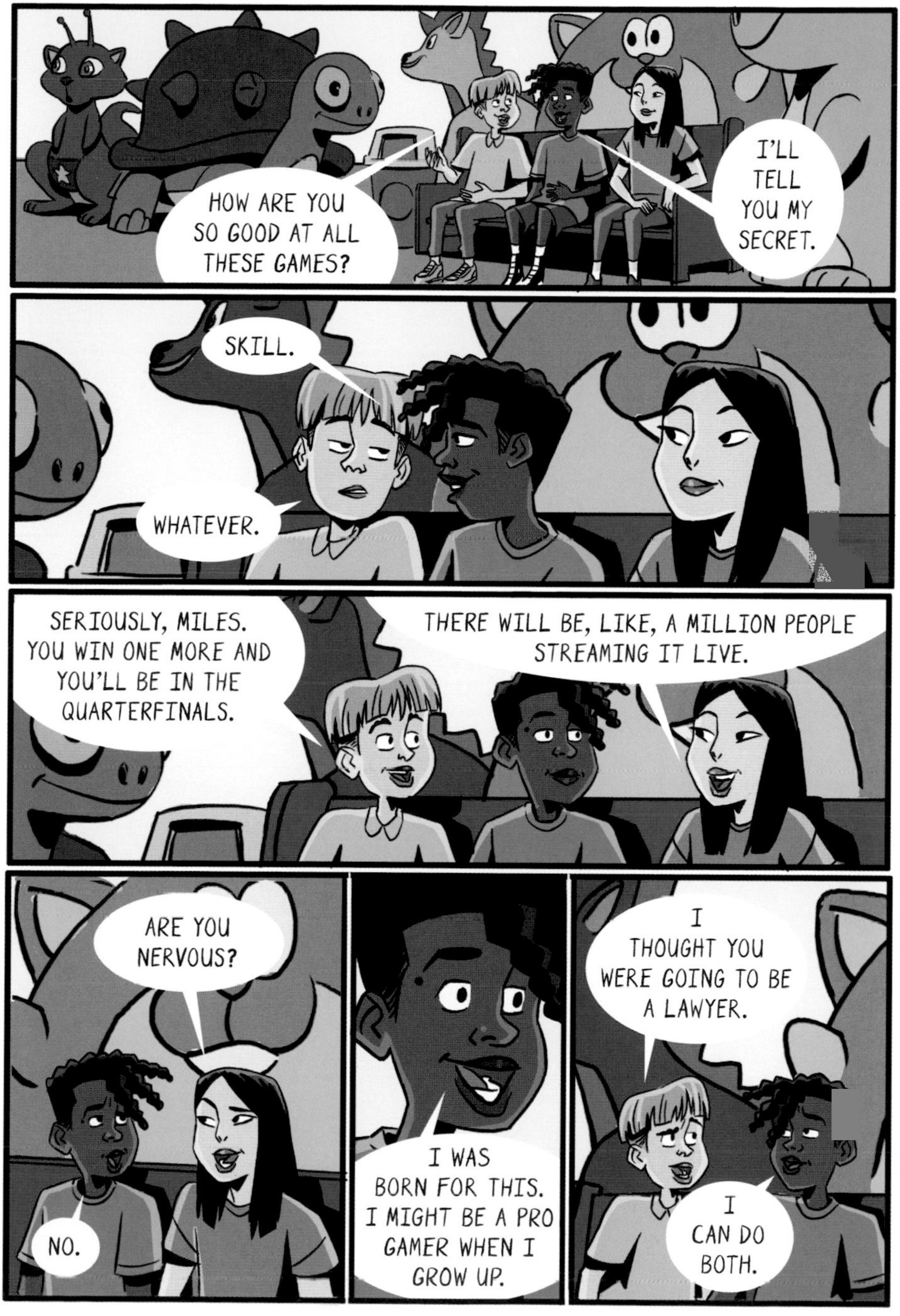
HOW ARE YOU SO GOOD AT ALL THESE GAMES?
I'LL TELL YOU MY SECRET.
SKILL.
WHATEVER.
SERIOUSLY, MILES. YOU WIN ONE MORE AND YOU'LL BE IN THE QUARTERFINALS.
THERE WILL BE, LIKE, A MILLION PEOPLE STREAMING IT LIVE.
ARE YOU NERVOUS?
NO.
I WAS BORN FOR THIS. I MIGHT BE A PRO GAMER WHEN I GROW UP.
I THOUGHT YOU WERE GOING TO BE A LAWYER.
I CAN DO BOTH.

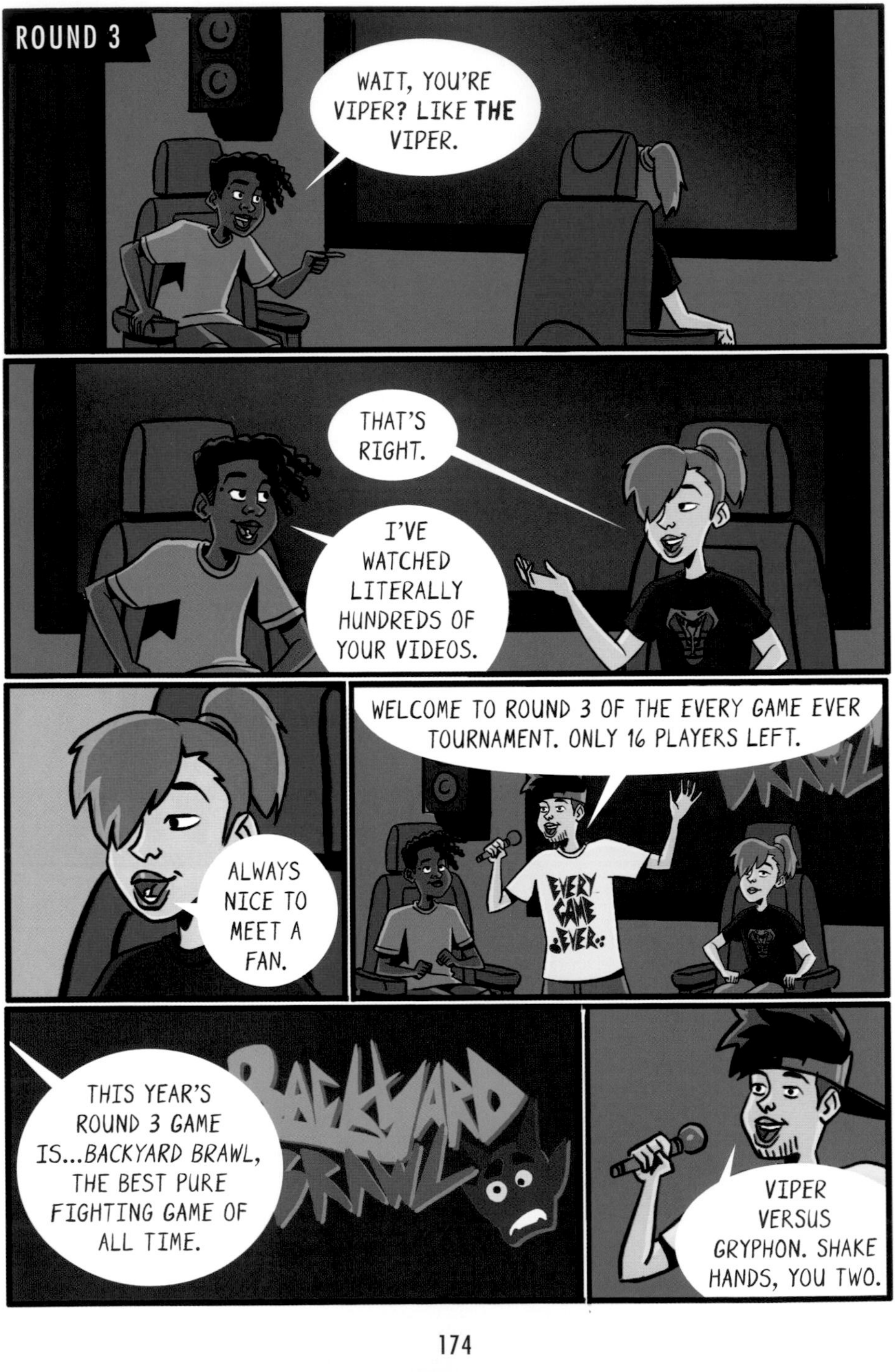
ROUND 3
WAIT, YOU'RE VIPER? LIKE **THE** VIPER.
THAT'S RIGHT.
I'VE WATCHED LITERALLY HUNDREDS OF YOUR VIDEOS.
ALWAYS NICE TO MEET A FAN.
WELCOME TO ROUND 3 OF THE EVERY GAME EVER TOURNAMENT. ONLY 16 PLAYERS LEFT.
EVERY GAME EVER
THIS YEAR'S ROUND 3 GAME IS...*BACKYARD BRAWL*, THE BEST PURE FIGHTING GAME OF ALL TIME.
BACKYARD BRAWL
VIPER VERSUS GRYPHON. SHAKE HANDS, YOU TWO.

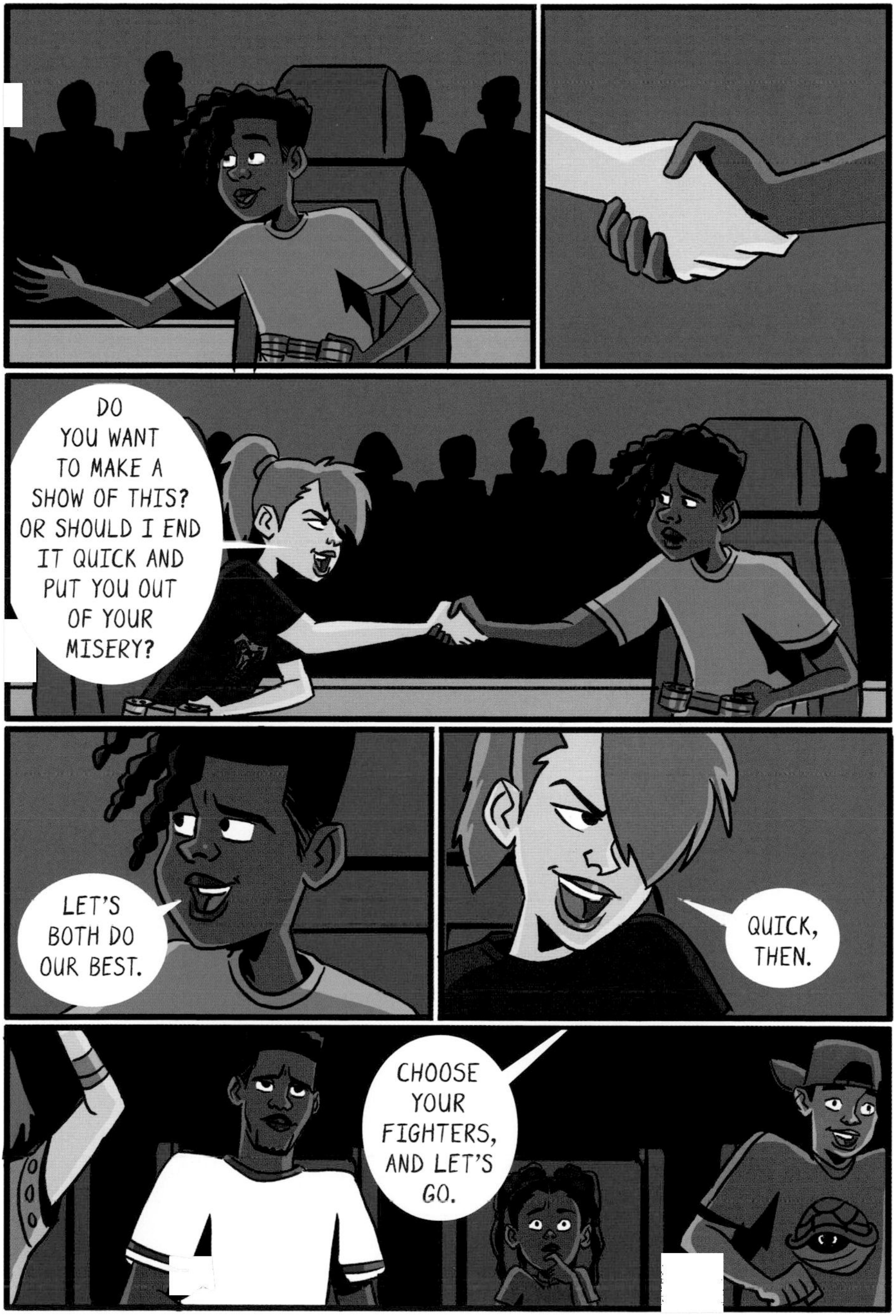
DO YOU WANT TO MAKE A SHOW OF THIS? OR SHOULD I END IT QUICK AND PUT YOU OUT OF YOUR MISERY?
LET'S BOTH DO OUR BEST.
QUICK, THEN.
CHOOSE YOUR FIGHTERS, AND LET'S GO.

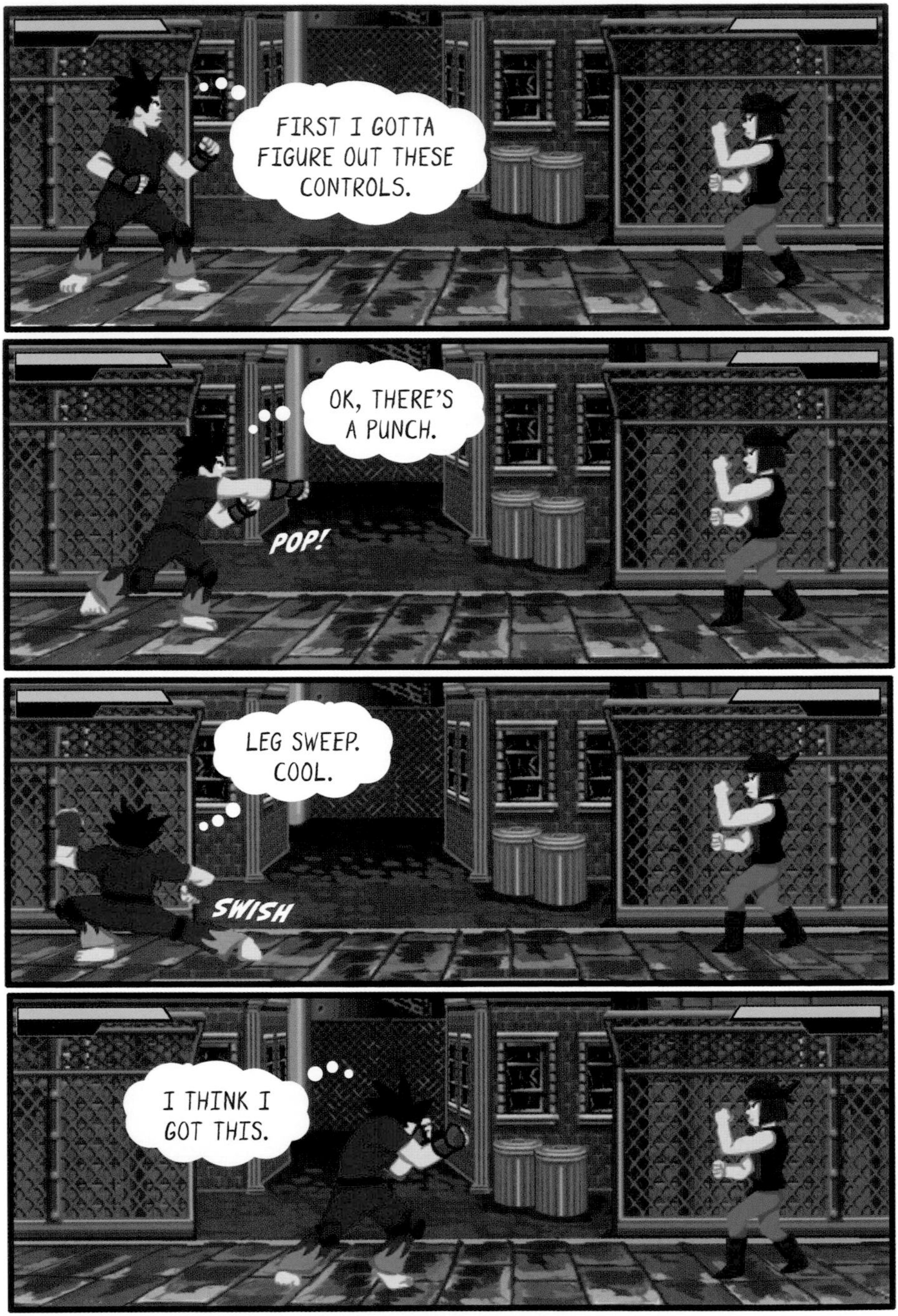
FIRST I GOTTA FIGURE OUT THESE CONTROLS.
OK, THERE'S A PUNCH.
POP!
LEG SWEEP. COOL.
SWISH
I THINK I GOT THIS.

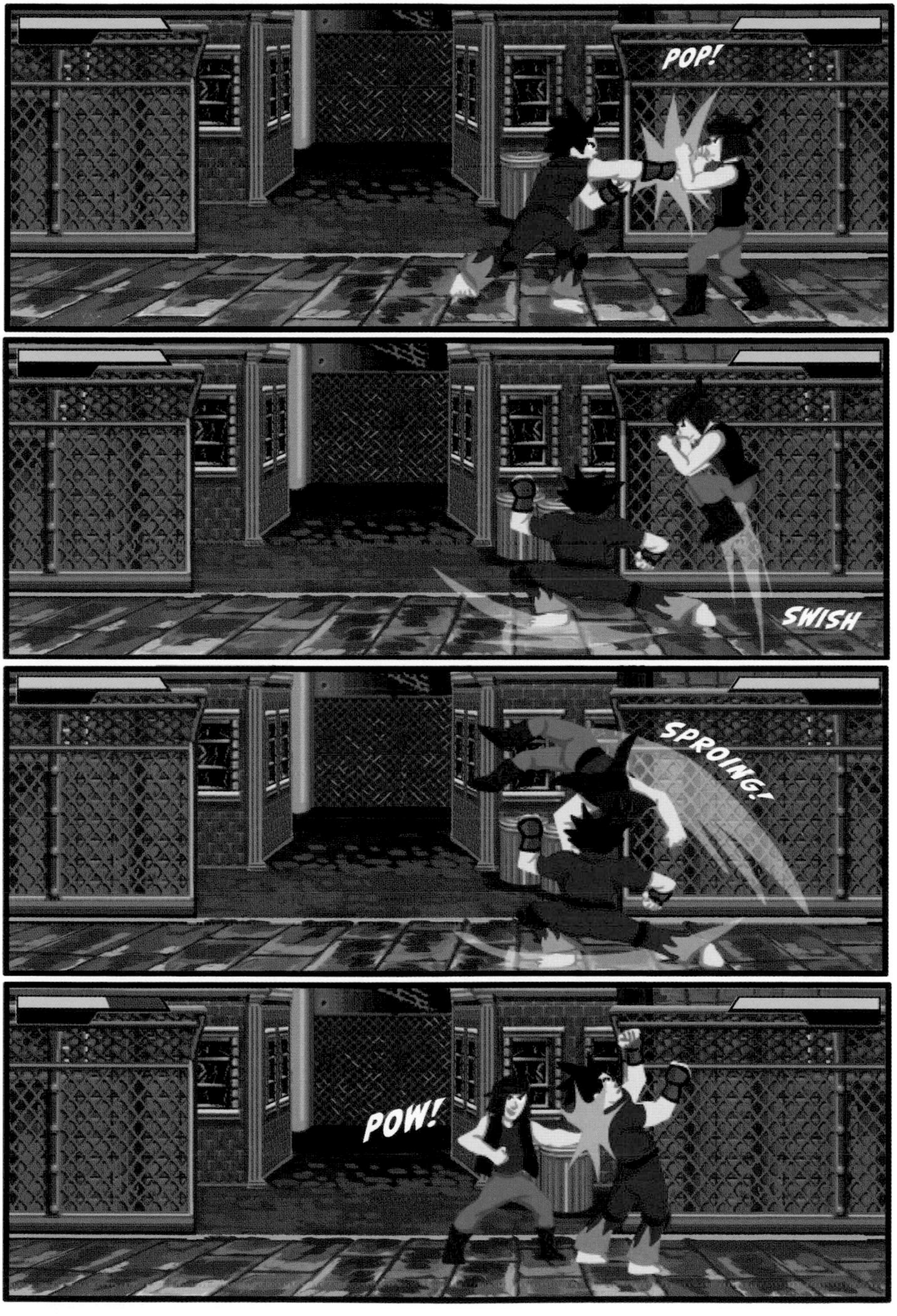
POP!
SWISH
SPROING!
POW!

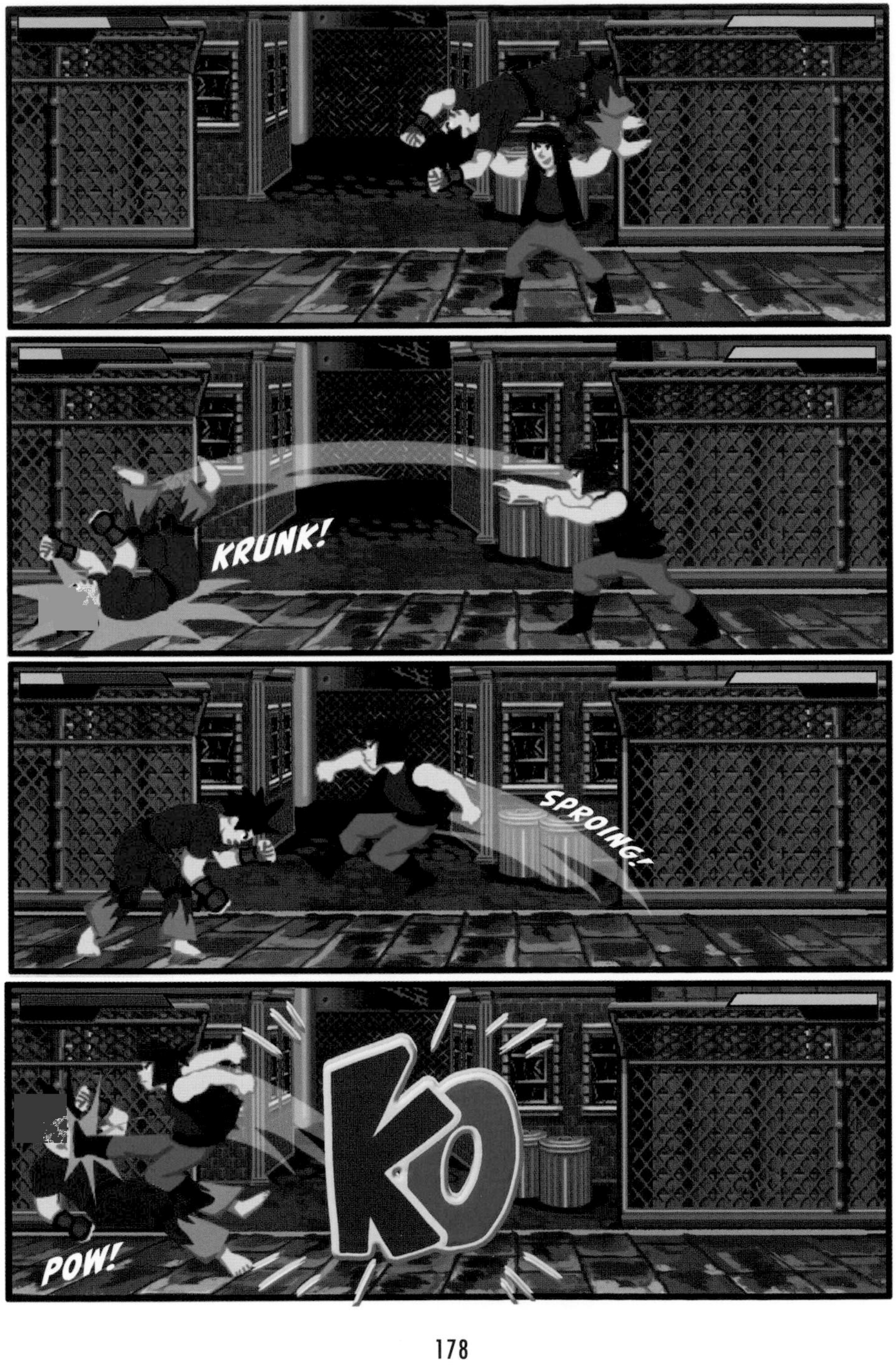
KRUNK!
SPROING!
KO
POW!

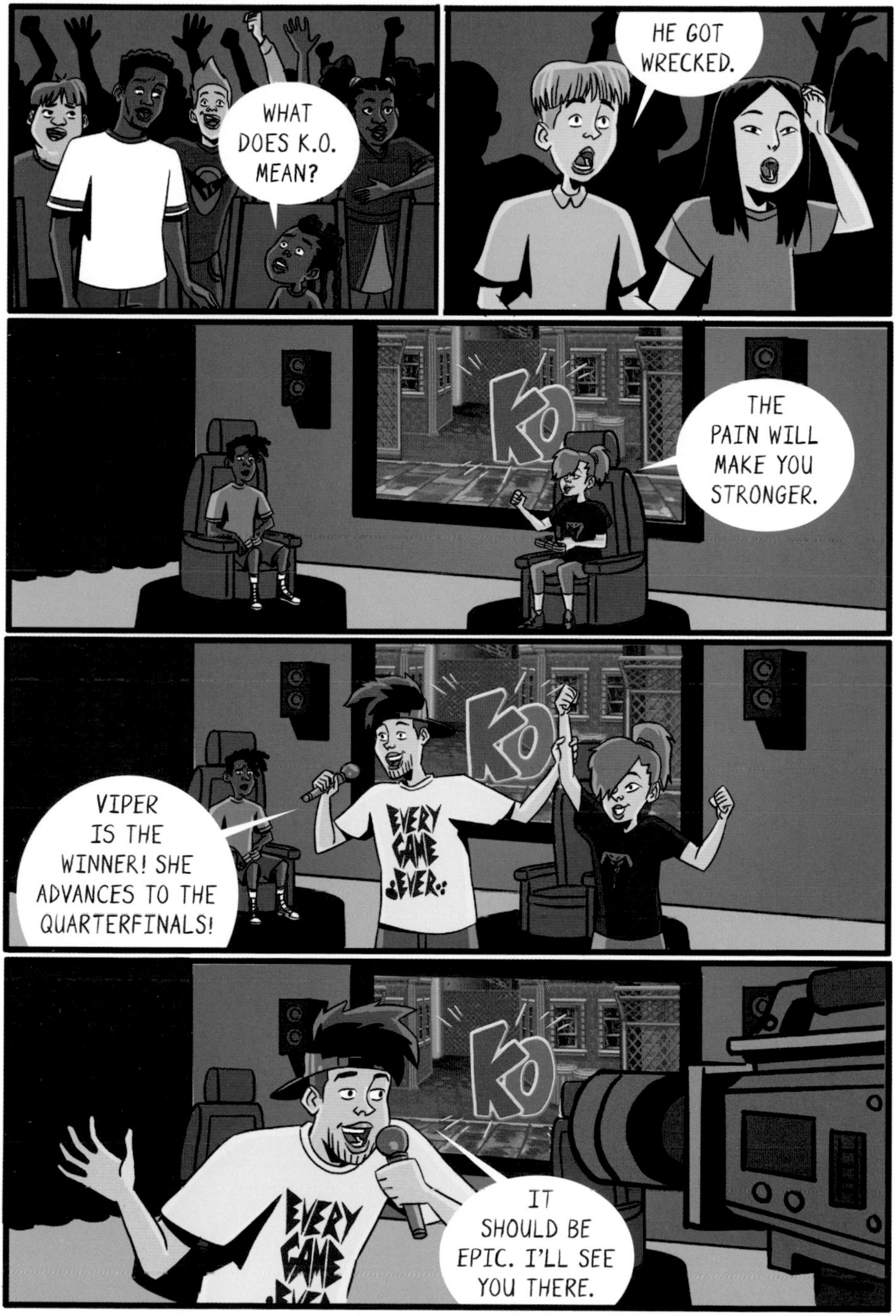
WHAT DOES K.O. MEAN?
HE GOT WRECKED.
KO
THE PAIN WILL MAKE YOU STRONGER.
KO
VIPER IS THE WINNER! SHE ADVANCES TO THE QUARTERFINALS!
EVERY GAME EVER
KO
EVERY GAME
IT SHOULD BE EPIC. I'LL SEE YOU THERE.

CHAPTER 11
DUO

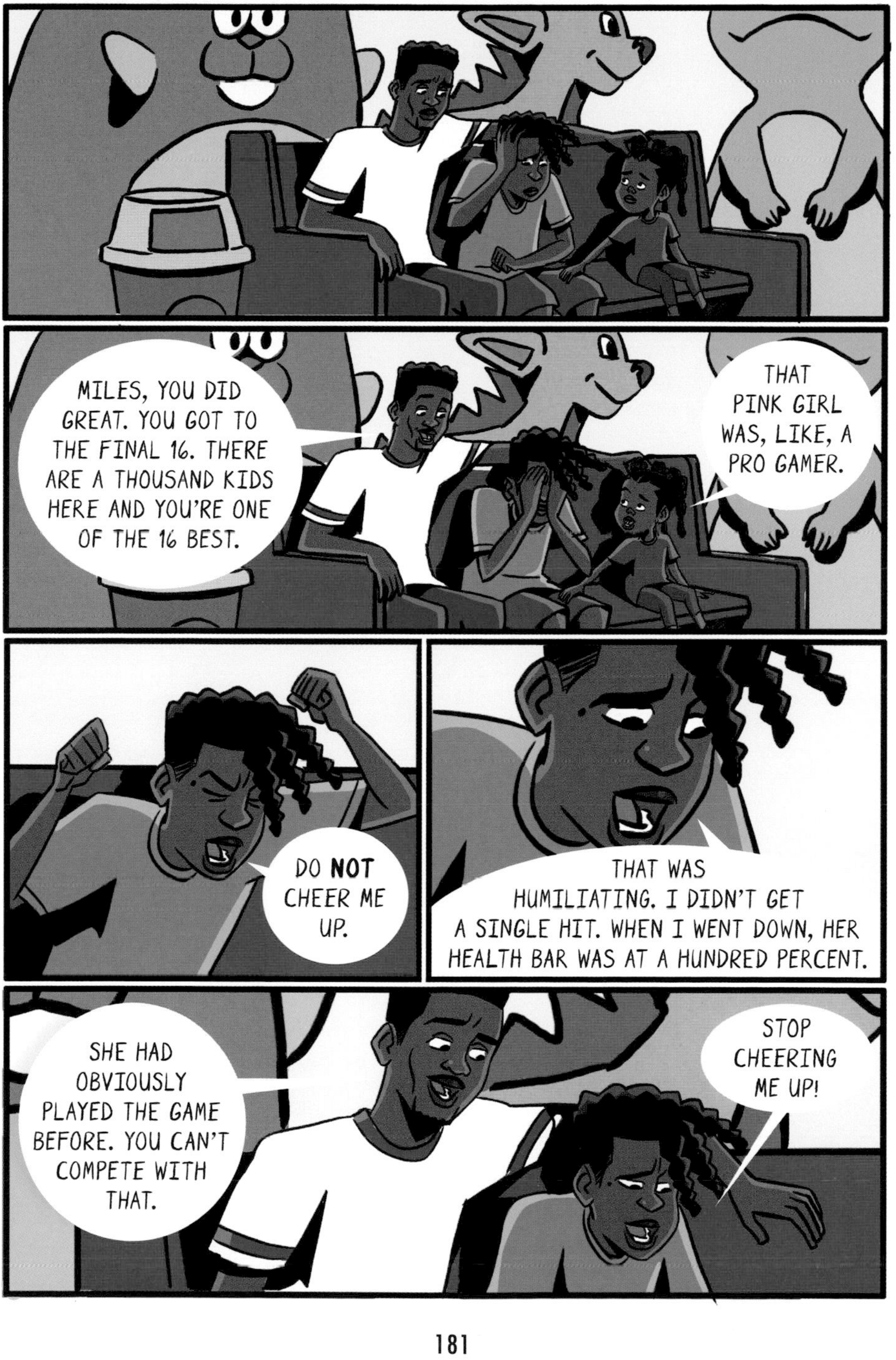
MILES, YOU DID GREAT. YOU GOT TO THE FINAL 16. THERE ARE A THOUSAND KIDS HERE AND YOU'RE ONE OF THE 16 BEST.
THAT PINK GIRL WAS, LIKE, A PRO GAMER.
DO **NOT** CHEER ME UP.
THAT WAS HUMILIATING. I DIDN'T GET A SINGLE HIT. WHEN I WENT DOWN, HER HEALTH BAR WAS AT A HUNDRED PERCENT.
SHE HAD OBVIOUSLY PLAYED THE GAME BEFORE. YOU CAN'T COMPETE WITH THAT.
STOP CHEERING ME UP!

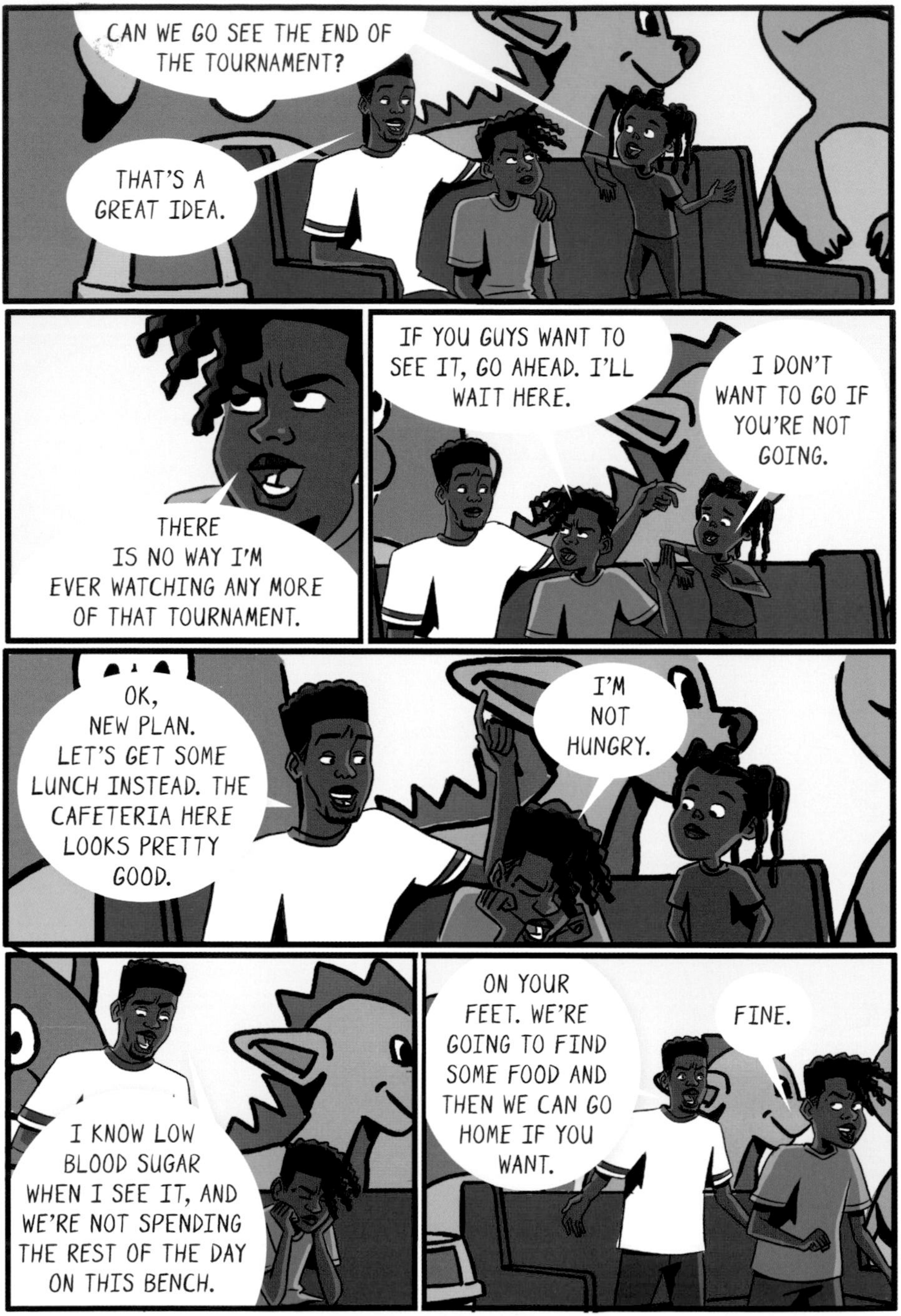
CAN WE GO SEE THE END OF THE TOURNAMENT?
THAT'S A GREAT IDEA.
THERE IS NO WAY I'M EVER WATCHING ANY MORE OF THAT TOURNAMENT.
IF YOU GUYS WANT TO SEE IT, GO AHEAD. I'LL WAIT HERE.
I DON'T WANT TO GO IF YOU'RE NOT GOING.
OK, NEW PLAN. LET'S GET SOME LUNCH INSTEAD. THE CAFETERIA HERE LOOKS PRETTY GOOD.
I'M NOT HUNGRY.
I KNOW LOW BLOOD SUGAR WHEN I SEE IT, AND WE'RE NOT SPENDING THE REST OF THE DAY ON THIS BENCH.
ON YOUR FEET. WE'RE GOING TO FIND SOME FOOD AND THEN WE CAN GO HOME IF YOU WANT.
FINE.

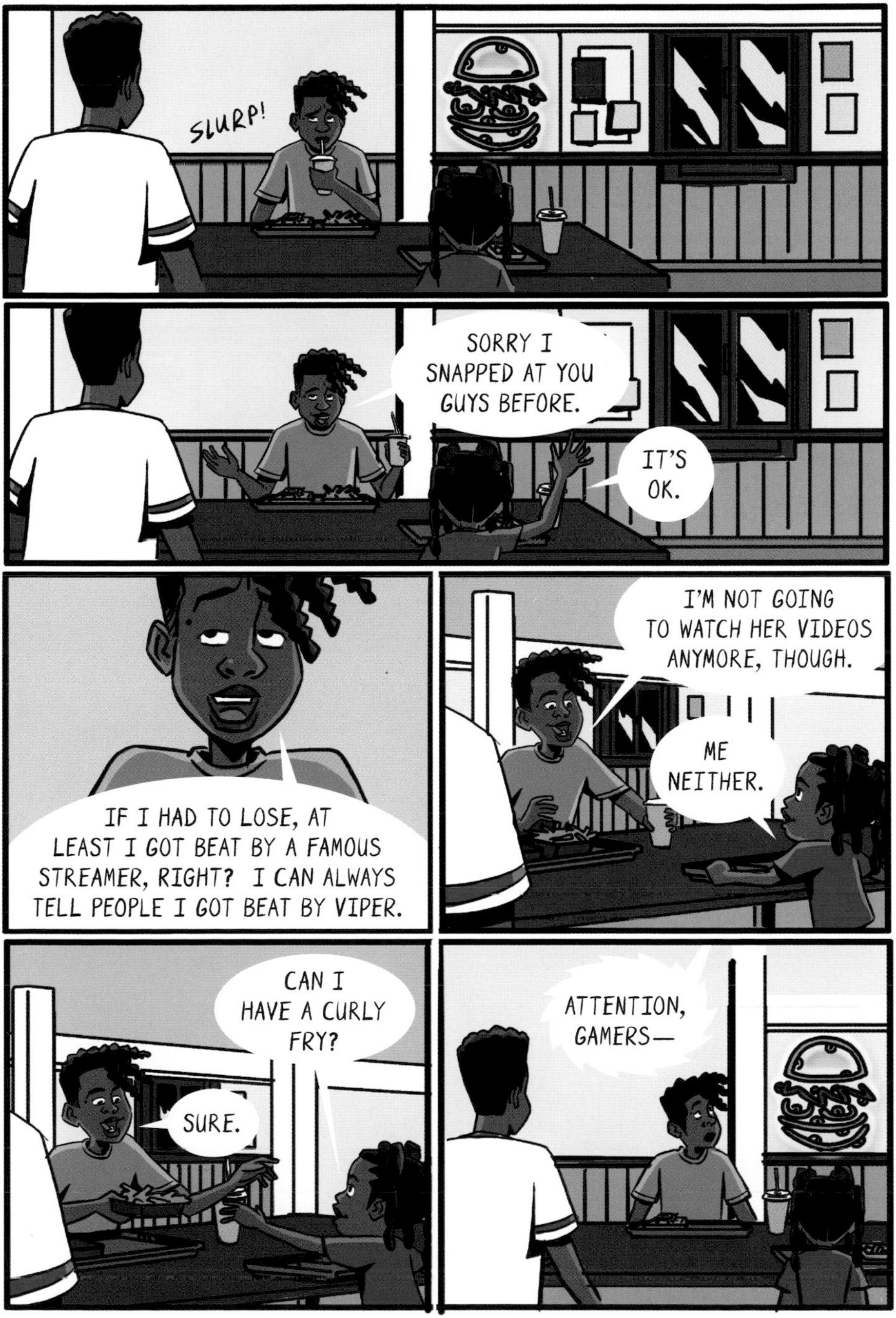
SLURP!
SORRY I SNAPPED AT YOU GUYS BEFORE.
IT'S OK.
IF I HAD TO LOSE, AT LEAST I GOT BEAT BY A FAMOUS STREAMER, RIGHT? I CAN ALWAYS TELL PEOPLE I GOT BEAT BY VIPER.
I'M NOT GOING TO WATCH HER VIDEOS ANYMORE, THOUGH.
ME NEITHER.
CAN I HAVE A CURLY FRY?
SURE.
ATTENTION, GAMERS—

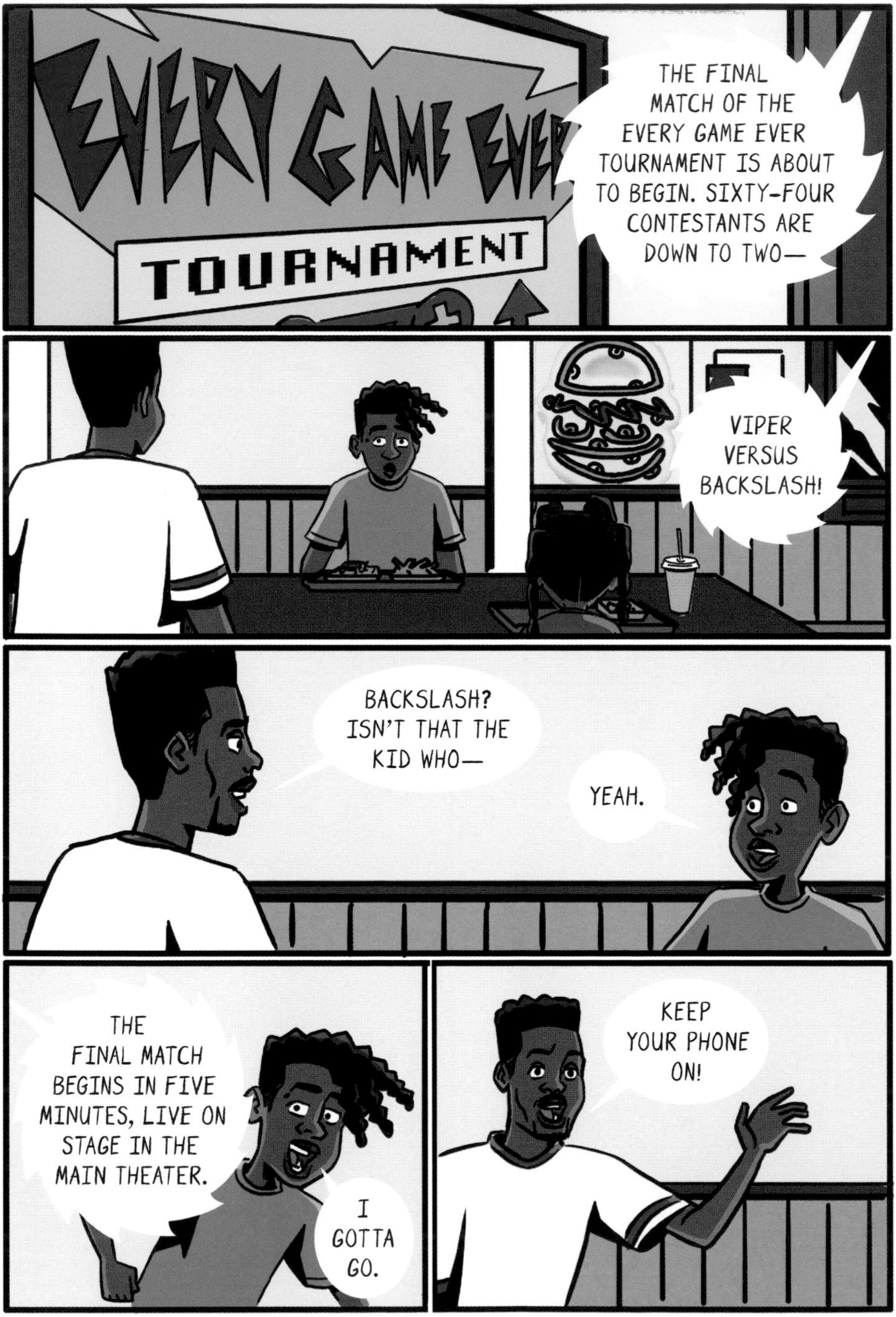
EVERY GAME EVER
TOURNAMENT
THE FINAL MATCH OF THE EVERY GAME EVER TOURNAMENT IS ABOUT TO BEGIN. SIXTY-FOUR CONTESTANTS ARE DOWN TO TWO—
VIPER VERSUS BACKSLASH!
BACKSLASH? ISN'T THAT THE KID WHO—
YEAH.
THE FINAL MATCH BEGINS IN FIVE MINUTES, LIVE ON STAGE IN THE MAIN THEATER.
I GOTTA GO.
KEEP YOUR PHONE ON!

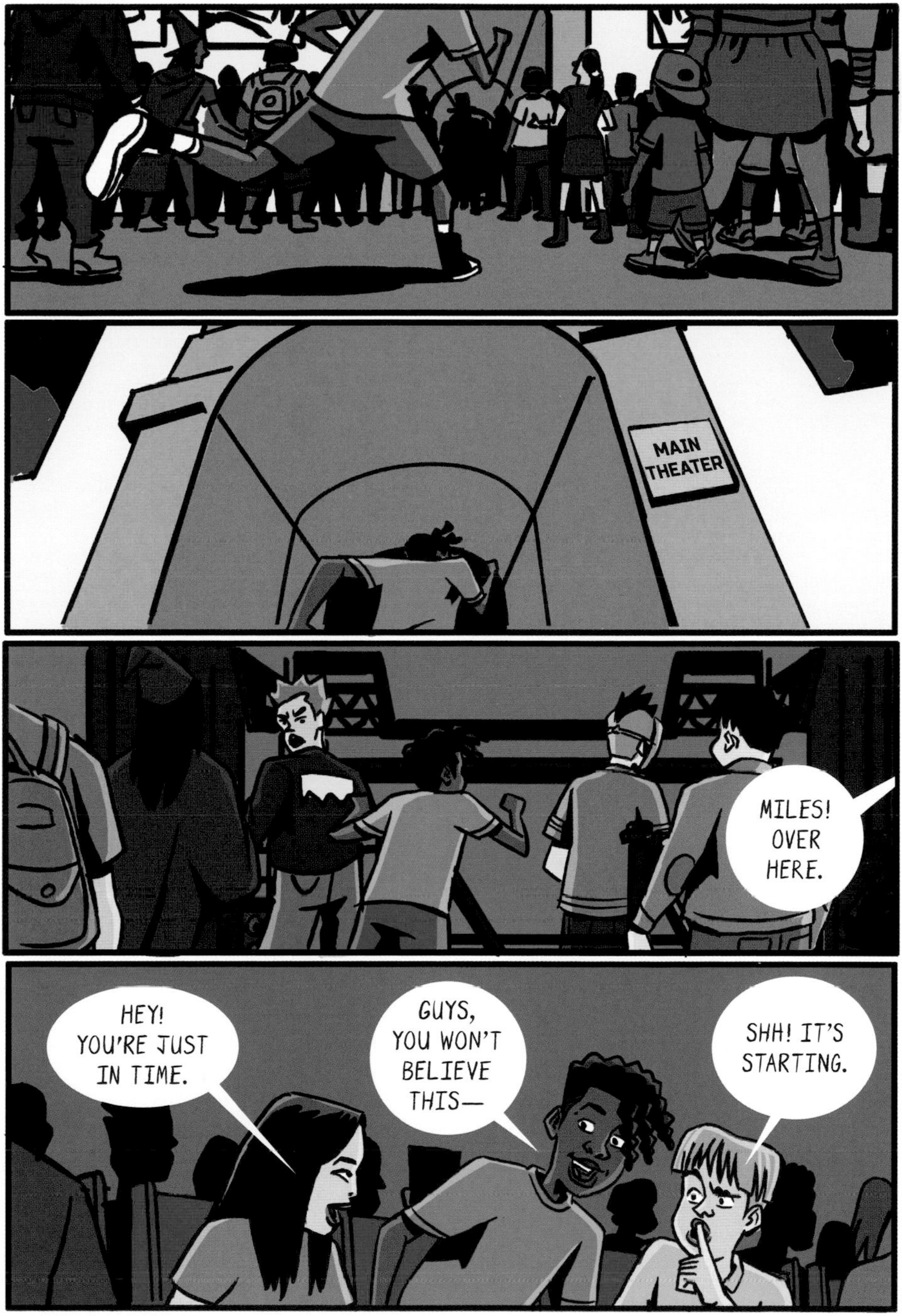

MAIN THEATER
MILES! OVER HERE.
HEY! YOU'RE JUST IN TIME.
GUYS, YOU WON'T BELIEVE THIS—
SHH! IT'S STARTING.

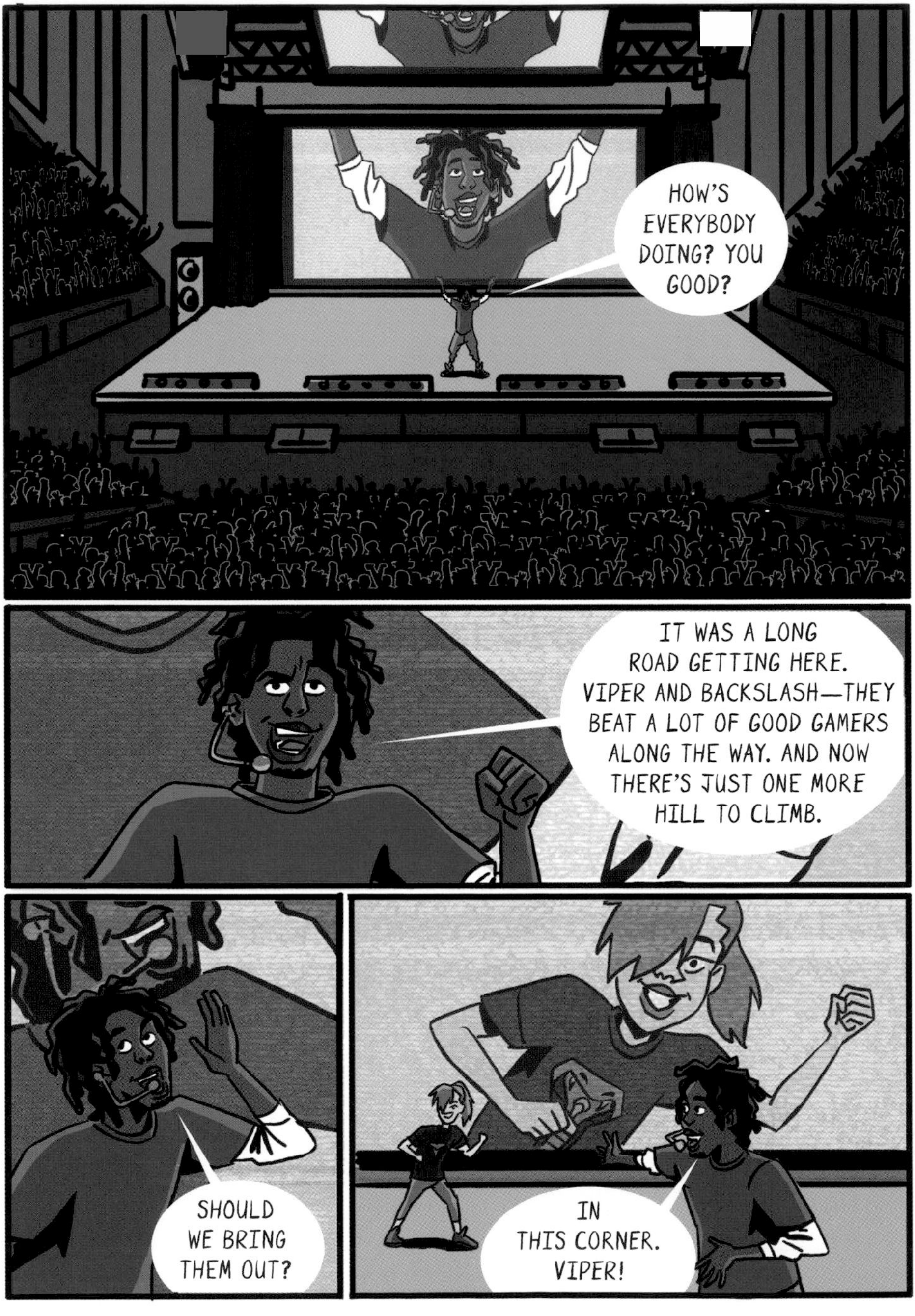
HOW'S EVERYBODY DOING? YOU GOOD?
IT WAS A LONG ROAD GETTING HERE. VIPER AND BACKSLASH—THEY BEAT A LOT OF GOOD GAMERS ALONG THE WAY. AND NOW THERE'S JUST ONE MORE HILL TO CLIMB.
SHOULD WE BRING THEM OUT?
IN THIS CORNER. VIPER!

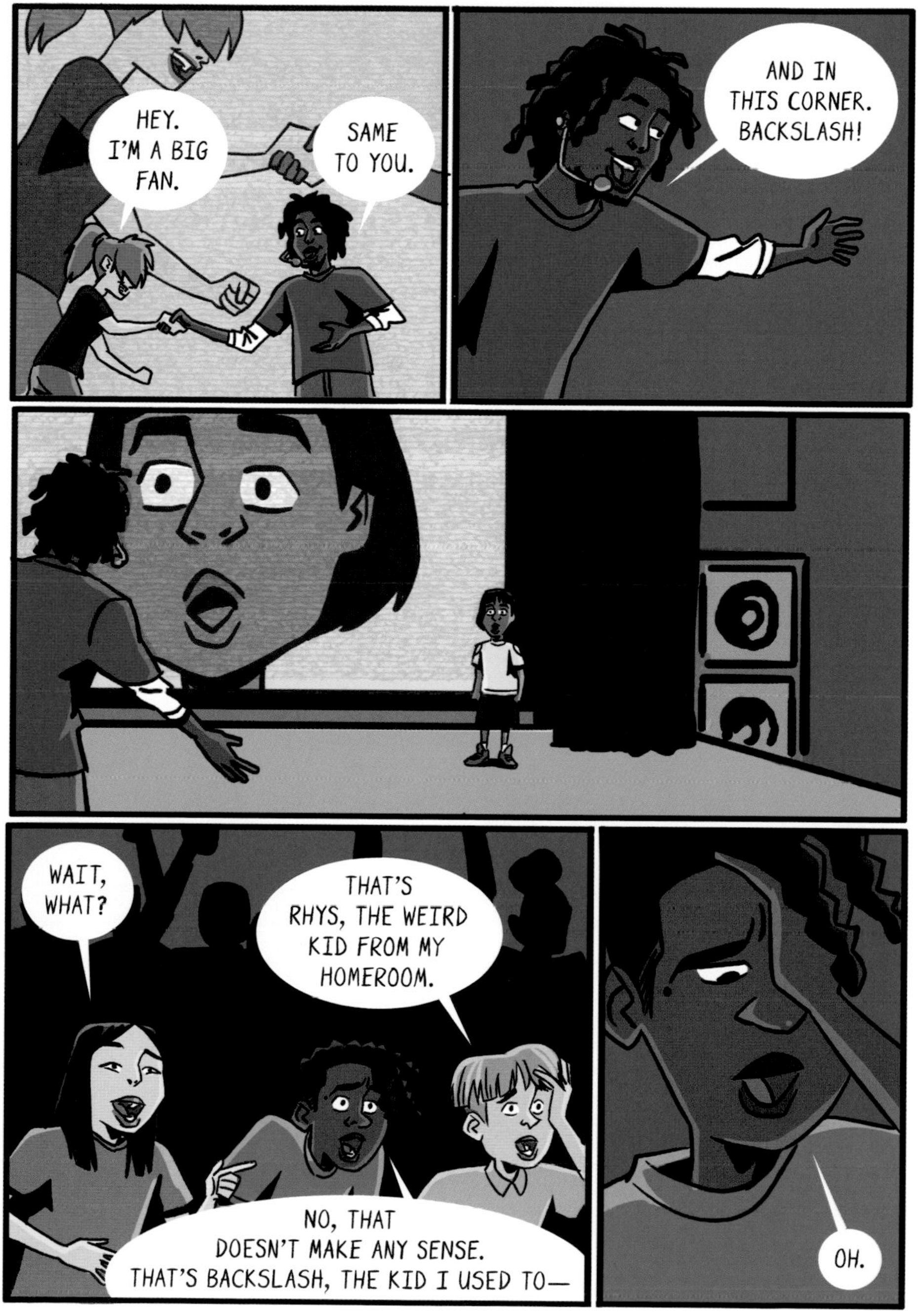

HEY. I'M A BIG FAN.
SAME TO YOU.
AND IN THIS CORNER. BACKSLASH!
WAIT, WHAT?
THAT'S RHYS, THE WEIRD KID FROM MY HOMEROOM.
NO, THAT DOESN'T MAKE ANY SENSE. THAT'S BACKSLASH, THE KID I USED TO—
OH.

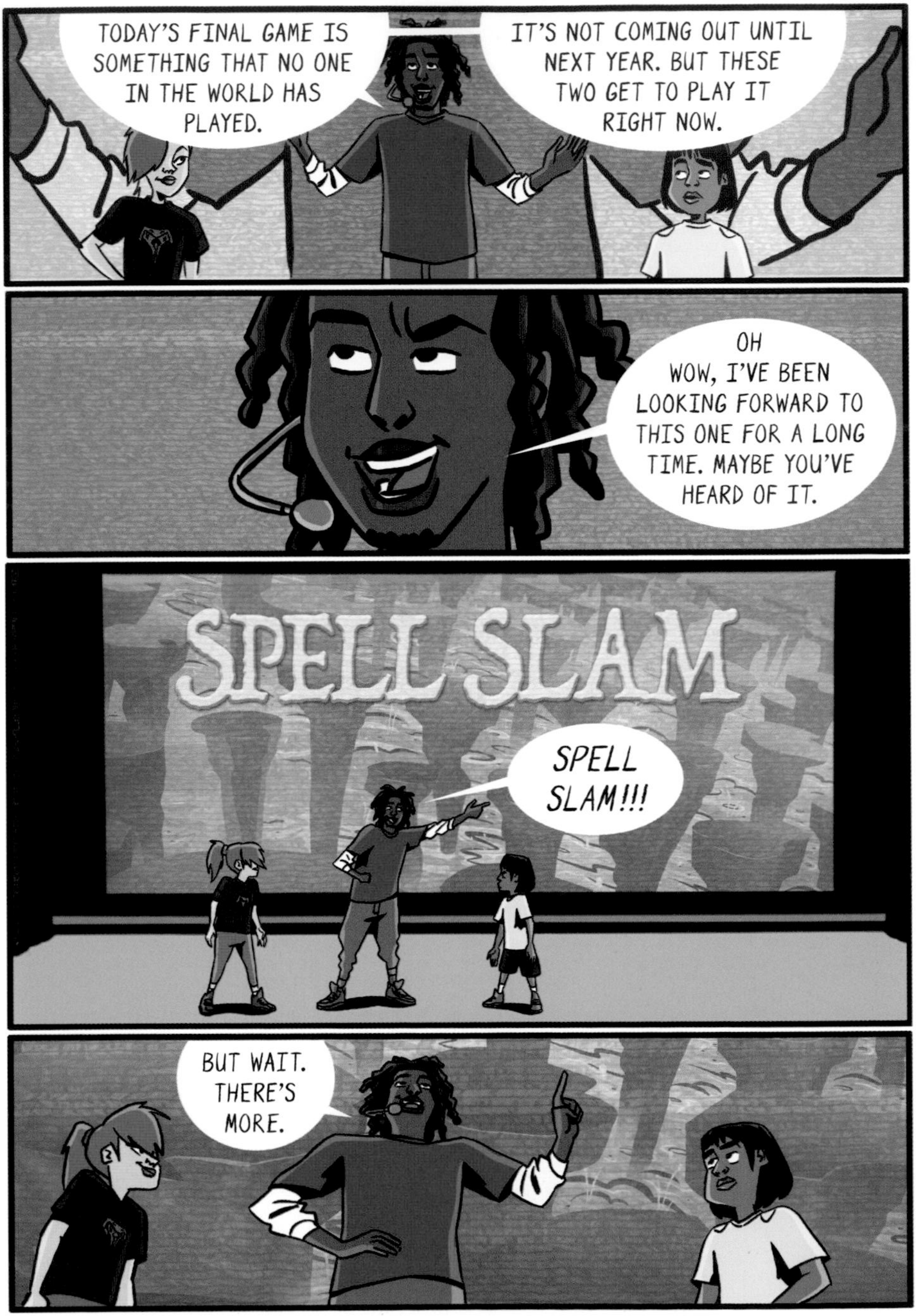
TODAY'S FINAL GAME IS SOMETHING THAT NO ONE IN THE WORLD HAS PLAYED.
IT'S NOT COMING OUT UNTIL NEXT YEAR. BUT THESE TWO GET TO PLAY IT RIGHT NOW.
OH WOW, I'VE BEEN LOOKING FORWARD TO THIS ONE FOR A LONG TIME. MAYBE YOU'VE HEARD OF IT.
SPELL SLAM
SPELL SLAM!!!
BUT WAIT. THERE'S MORE.

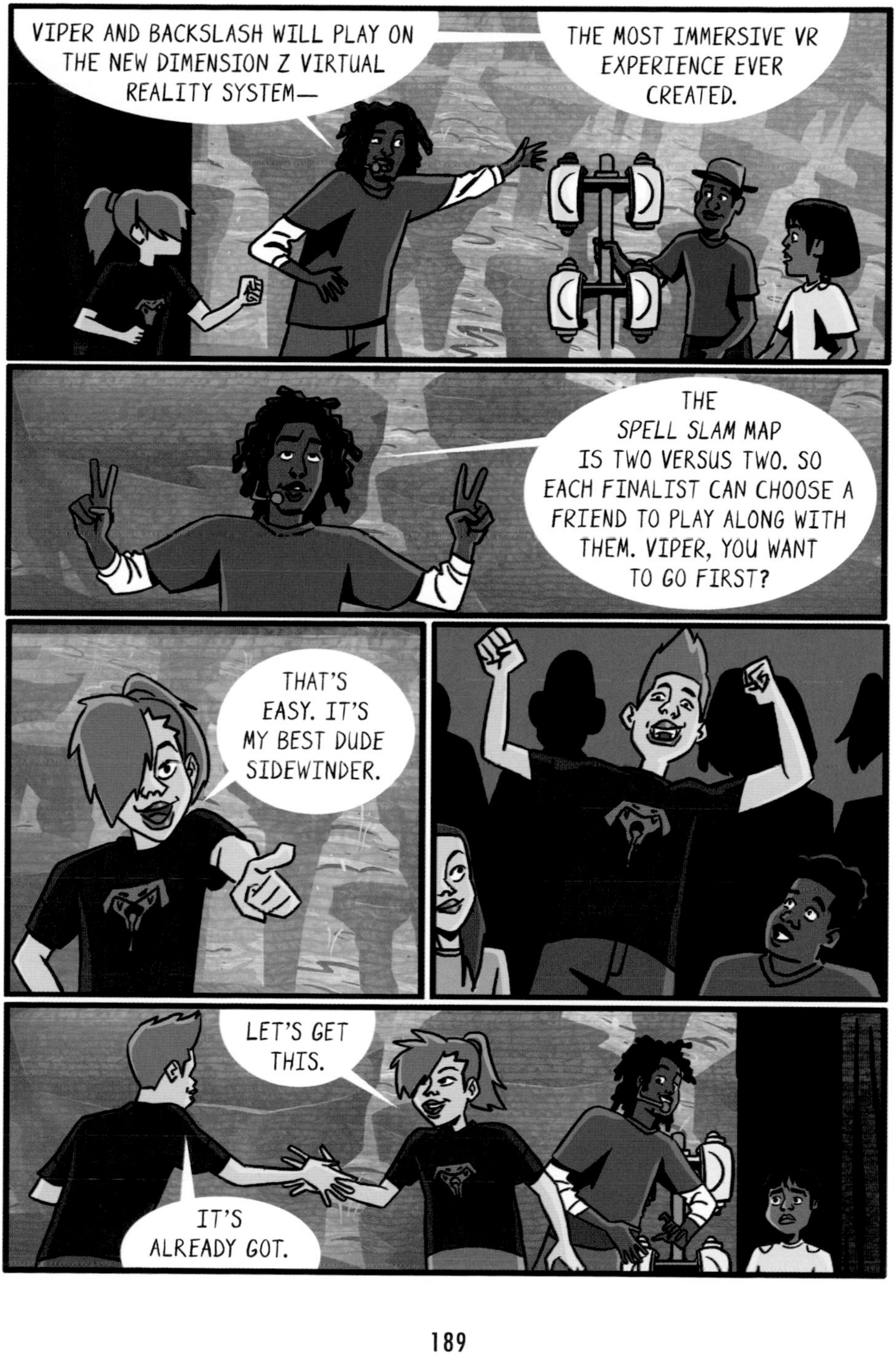
VIPER AND BACKSLASH WILL PLAY ON THE NEW DIMENSION Z VIRTUAL REALITY SYSTEM—
THE MOST IMMERSIVE VR EXPERIENCE EVER CREATED.
THE *SPELL SLAM MAP* IS TWO VERSUS TWO. SO EACH FINALIST CAN CHOOSE A FRIEND TO PLAY ALONG WITH THEM. VIPER, YOU WANT TO GO FIRST?
THAT'S EASY. IT'S MY BEST DUDE SIDEWINDER.
LET'S GET THIS.
IT'S ALREADY GOT.

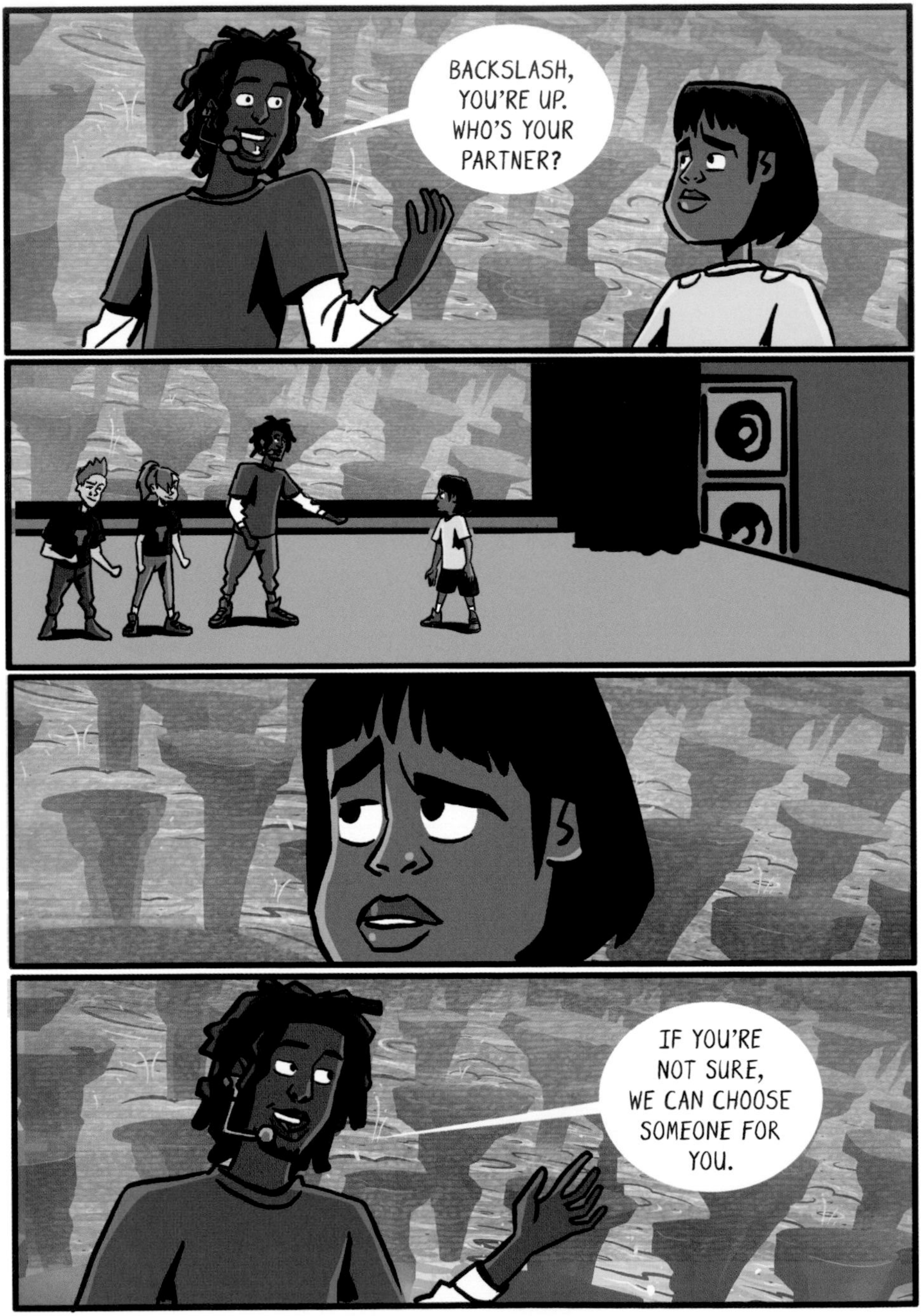
BACKSLASH, YOU'RE UP. WHO'S YOUR PARTNER?
IF YOU'RE NOT SURE, WE CAN CHOOSE SOMEONE FOR YOU.

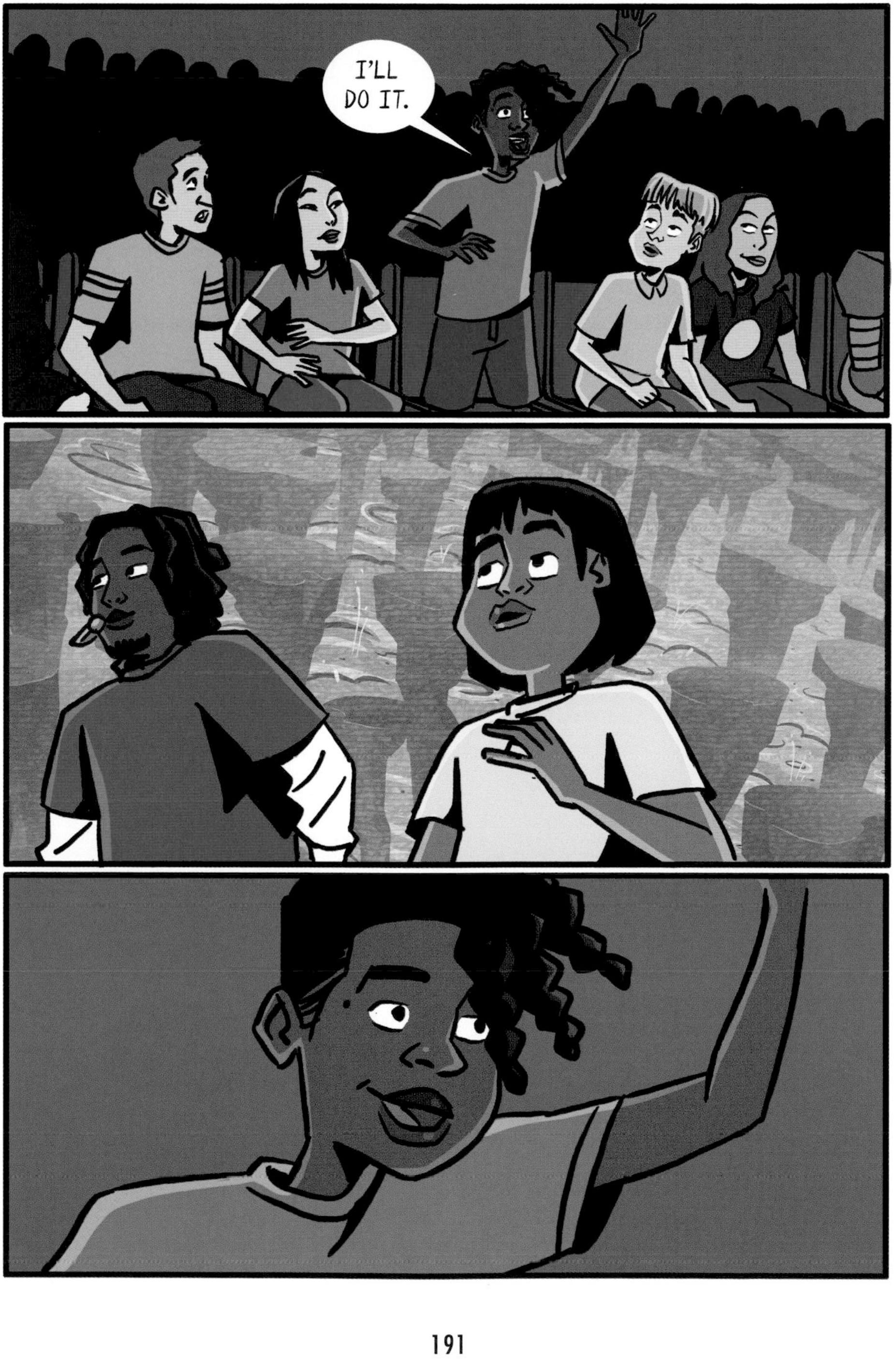
I'LL DO IT.

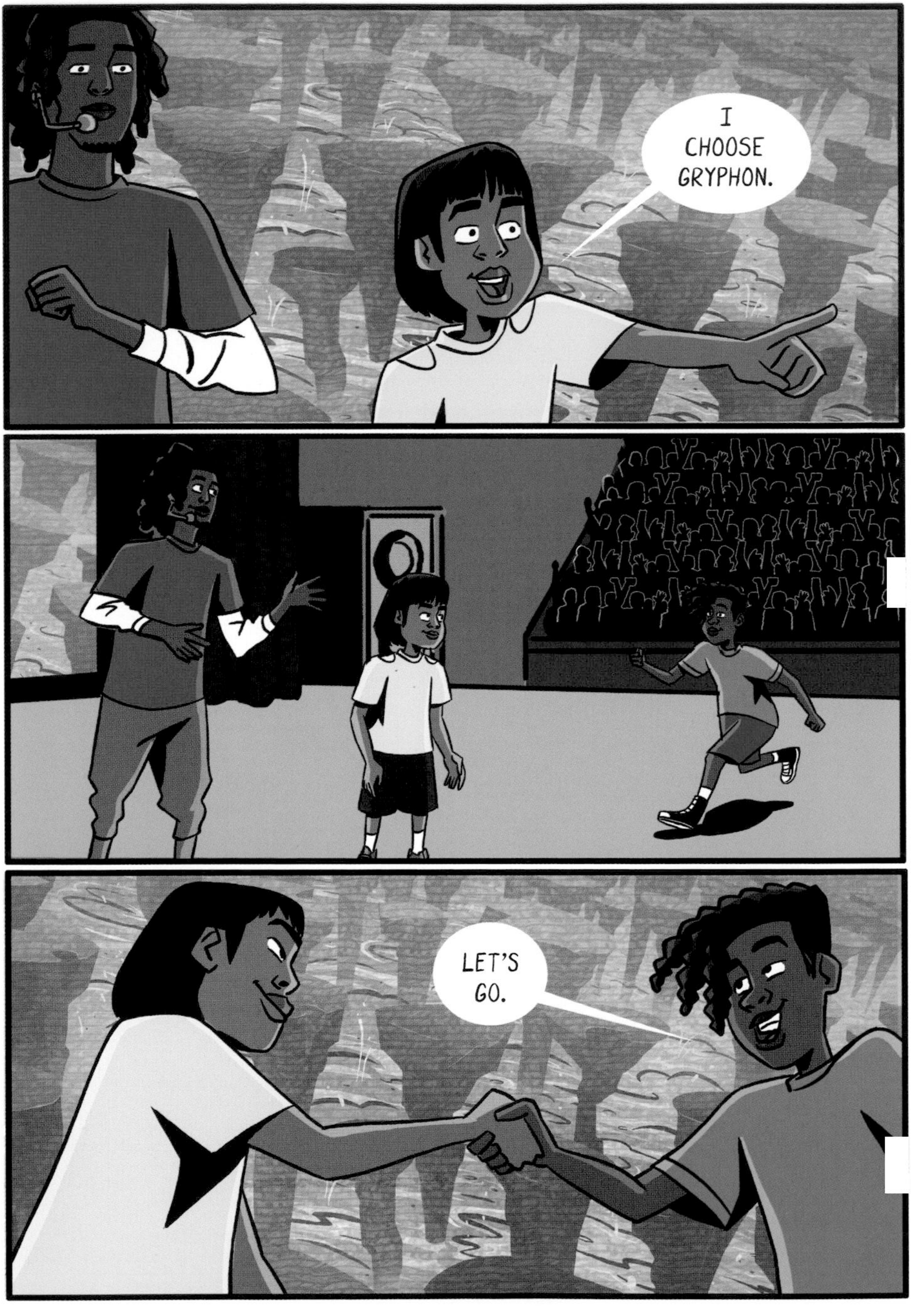
I CHOOSE GRYPHON.
LET'S GO.

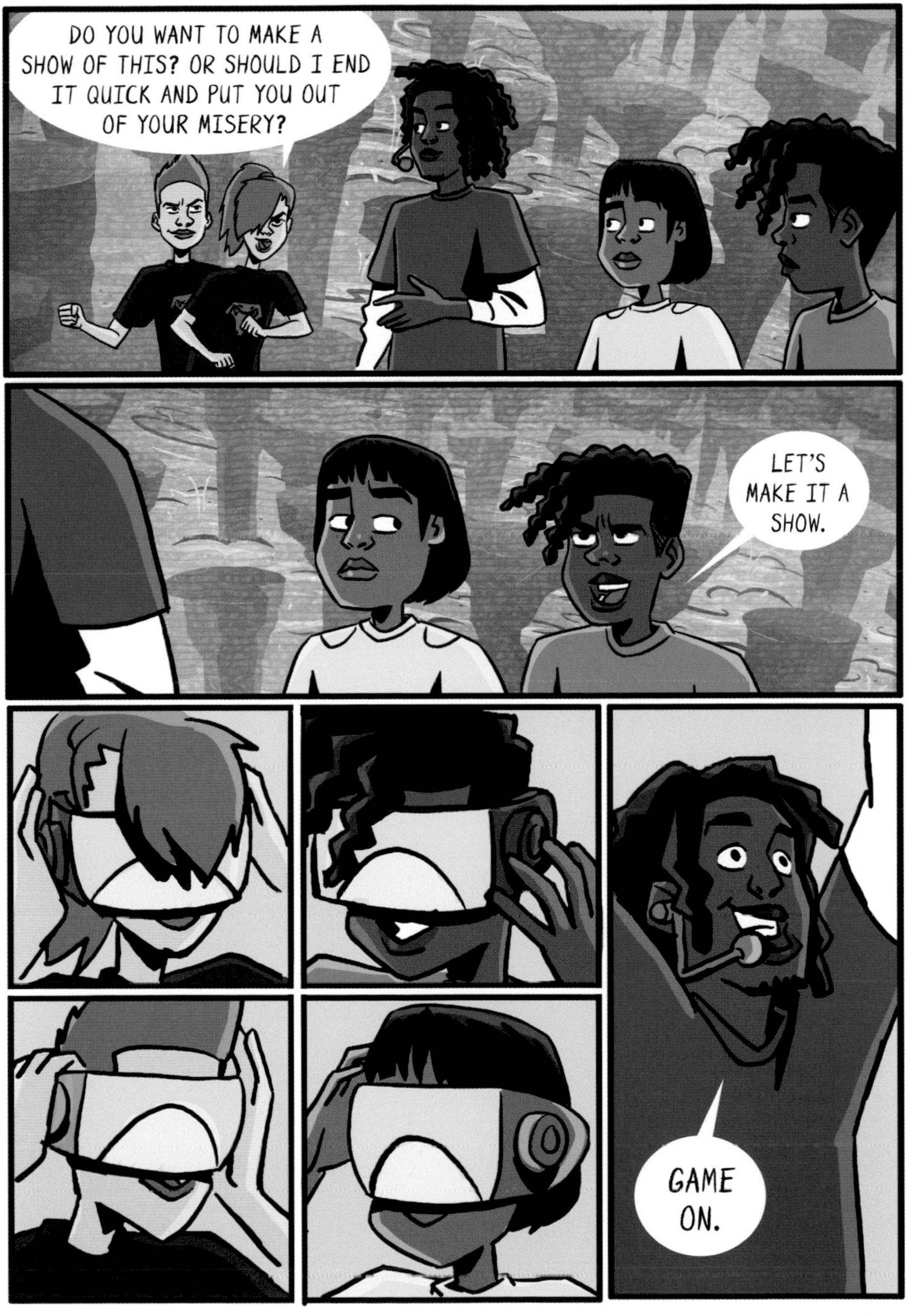
DO YOU WANT TO MAKE A SHOW OF THIS? OR SHOULD I END IT QUICK AND PUT YOU OUT OF YOUR MISERY?
LET'S MAKE IT A SHOW.
GAME ON.

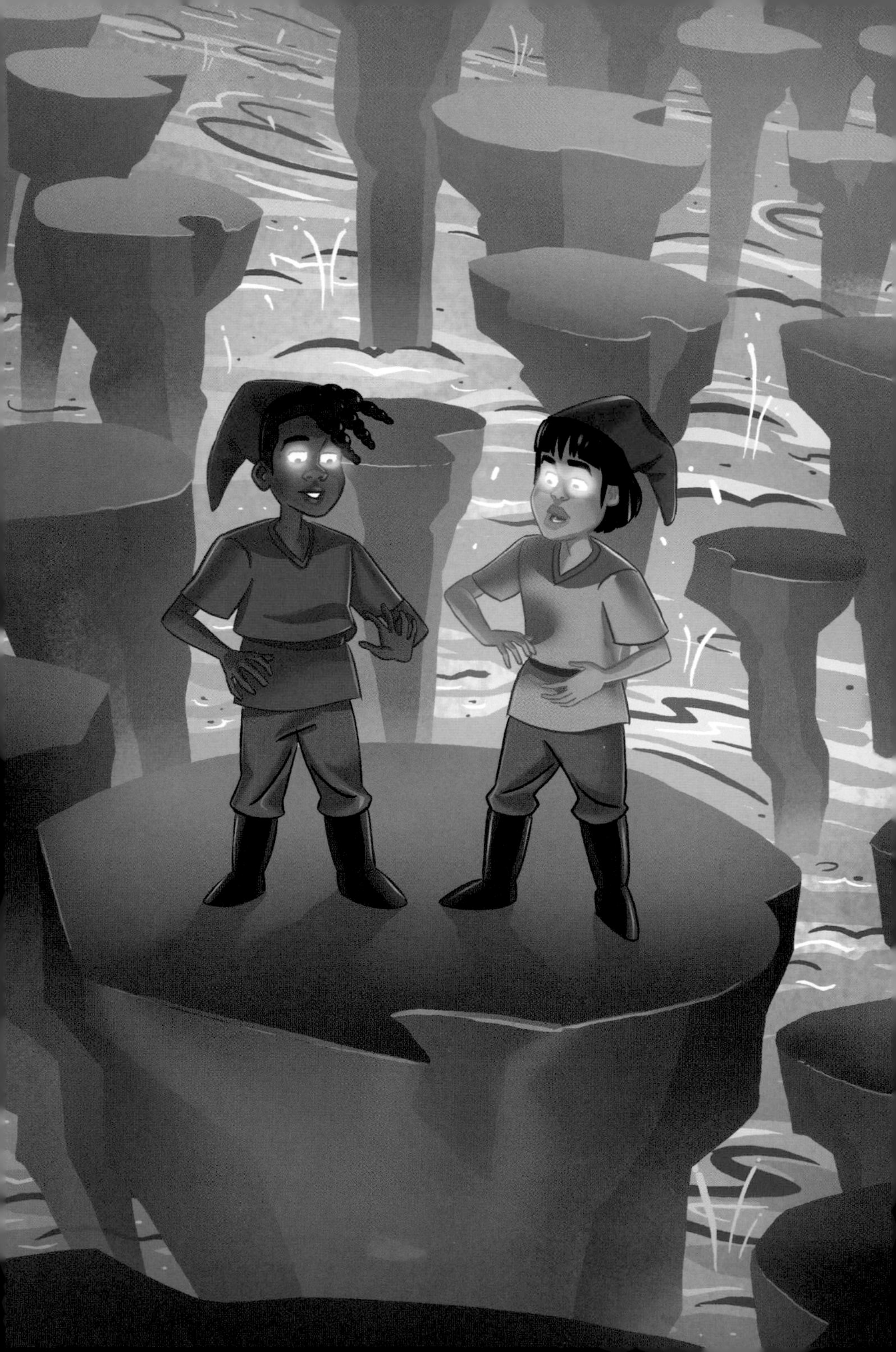

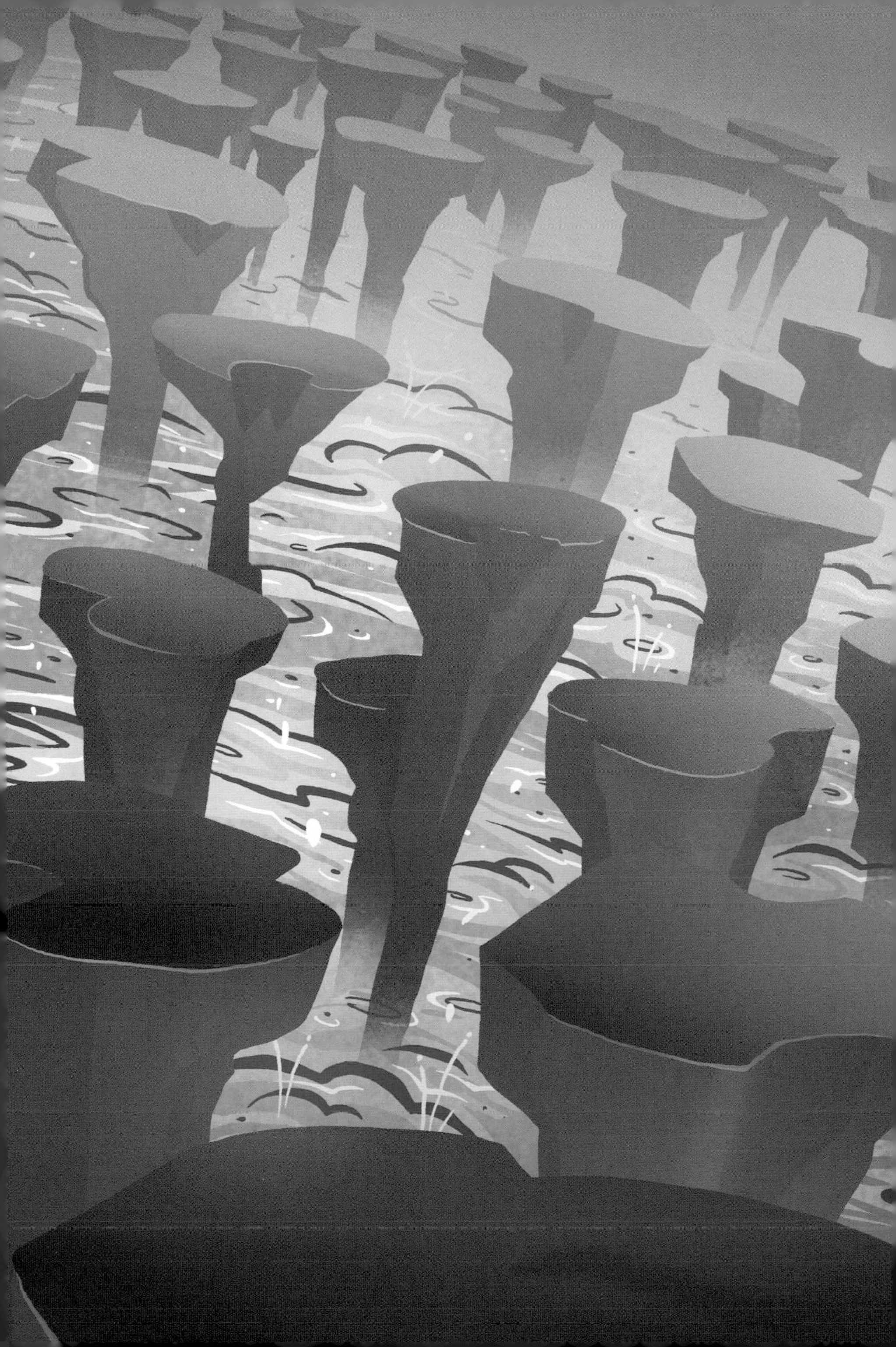

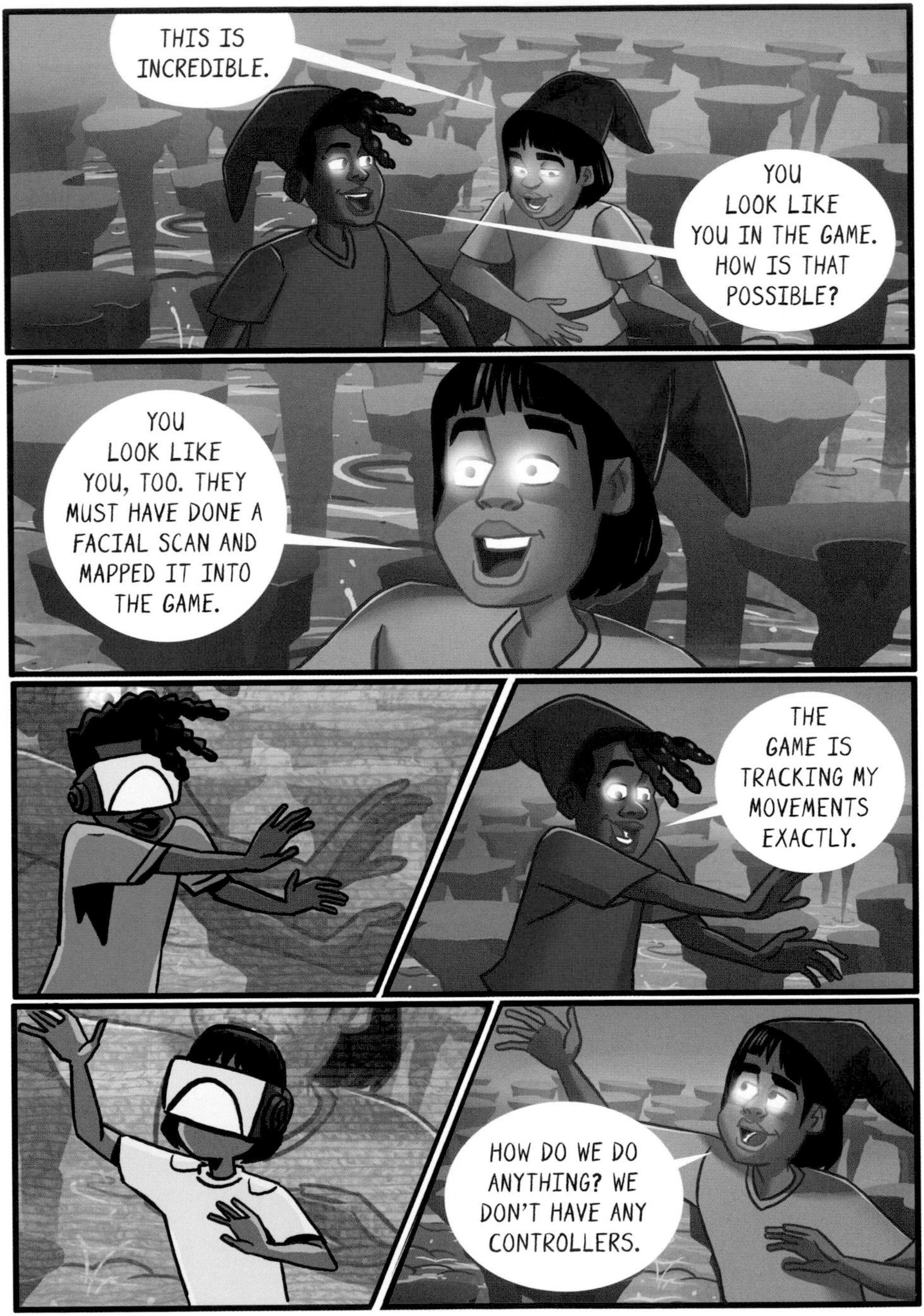
THIS IS INCREDIBLE.
YOU LOOK LIKE YOU IN THE GAME. HOW IS THAT POSSIBLE?
YOU LOOK LIKE YOU, TOO. THEY MUST HAVE DONE A FACIAL SCAN AND MAPPED IT INTO THE GAME.
THE GAME IS TRACKING MY MOVEMENTS EXACTLY.
HOW DO WE DO ANYTHING? WE DON'T HAVE ANY CONTROLLERS.

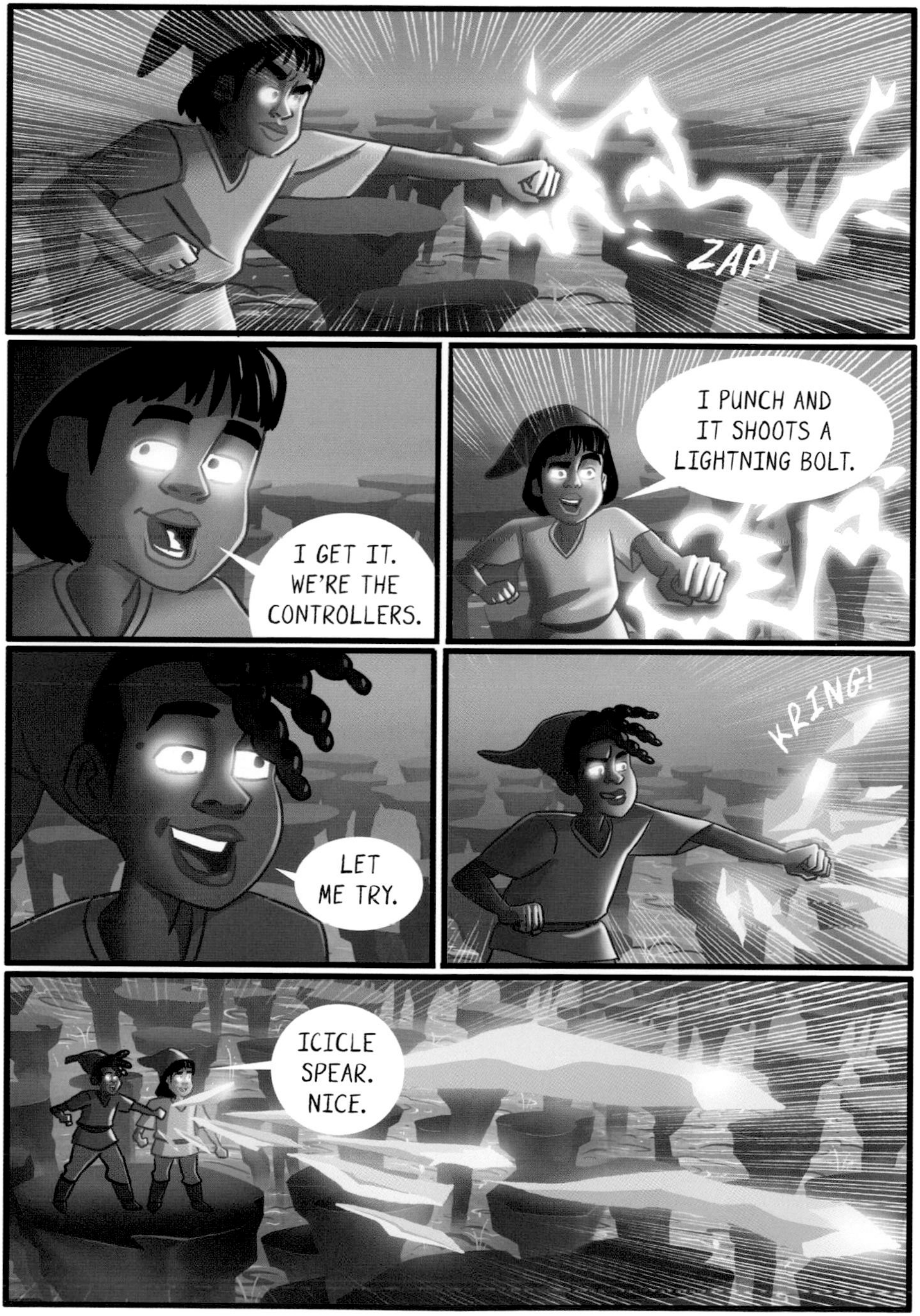
ZAP!
I GET IT. WE'RE THE CONTROLLERS.
I PUNCH AND IT SHOOTS A LIGHTNING BOLT.
LET ME TRY.
KRING!
ICICLE SPEAR. NICE.

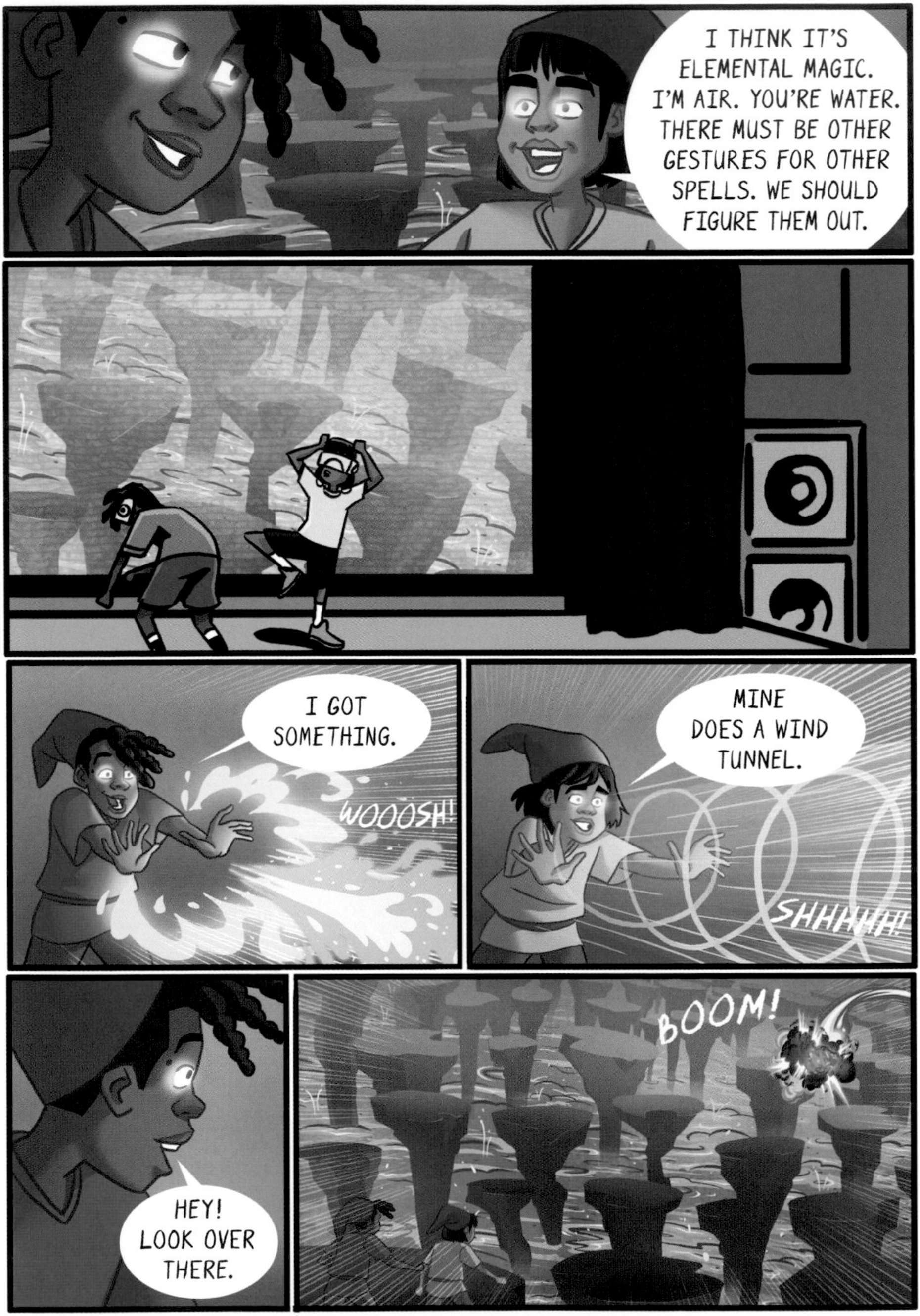
I THINK IT'S ELEMENTAL MAGIC. I'M AIR. YOU'RE WATER. THERE MUST BE OTHER GESTURES FOR OTHER SPELLS. WE SHOULD FIGURE THEM OUT.
I GOT SOMETHING.
WOOOSH!
MINE DOES A WIND TUNNEL.
SHHHHH!
HEY! LOOK OVER THERE.
BOOM!

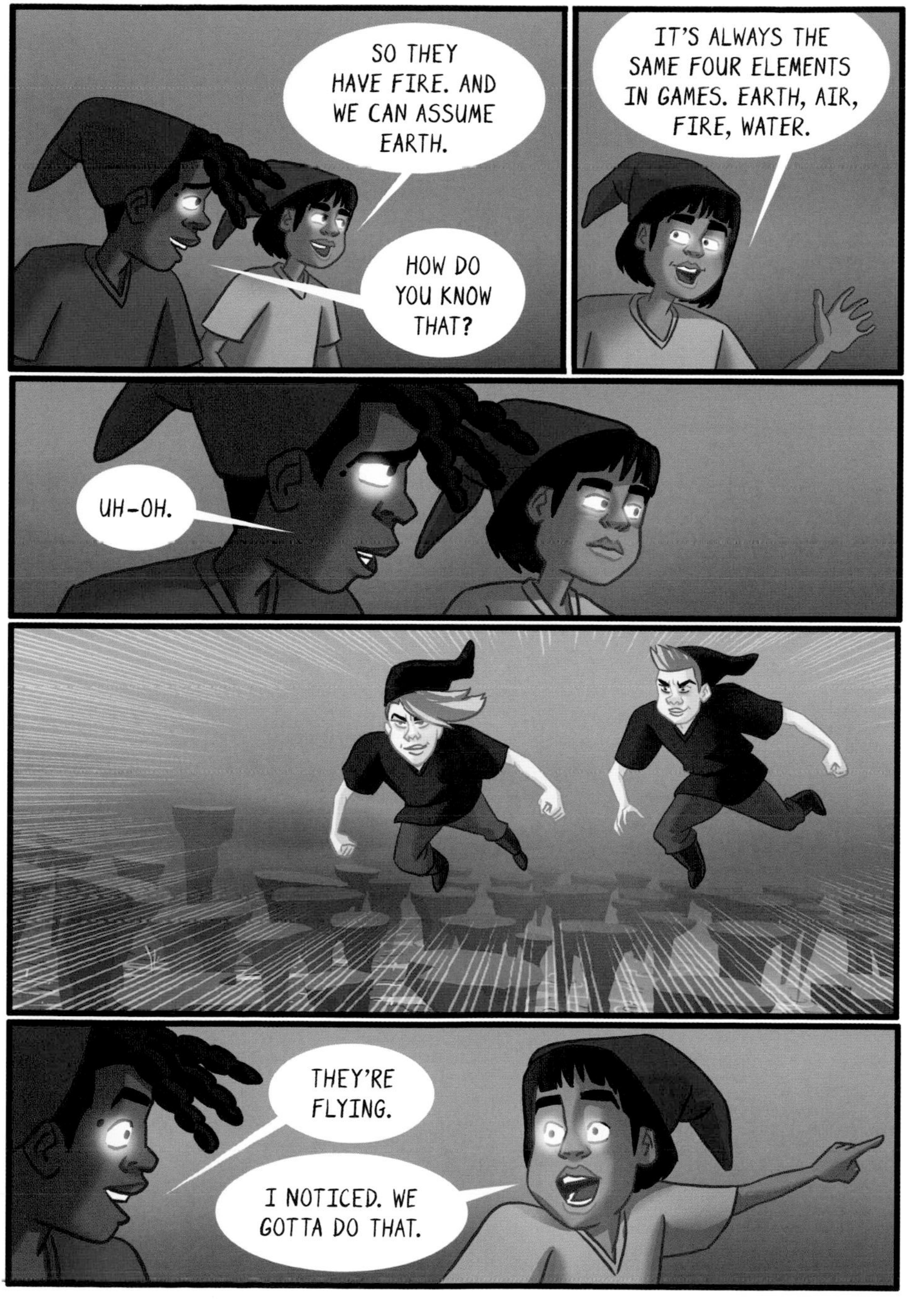
SO THEY HAVE FIRE. AND WE CAN ASSUME EARTH.
HOW DO YOU KNOW THAT?
IT'S ALWAYS THE SAME FOUR ELEMENTS IN GAMES. EARTH, AIR, FIRE, WATER.
UH-OH.
THEY'RE FLYING.
I NOTICED. WE GOTTA DO THAT.

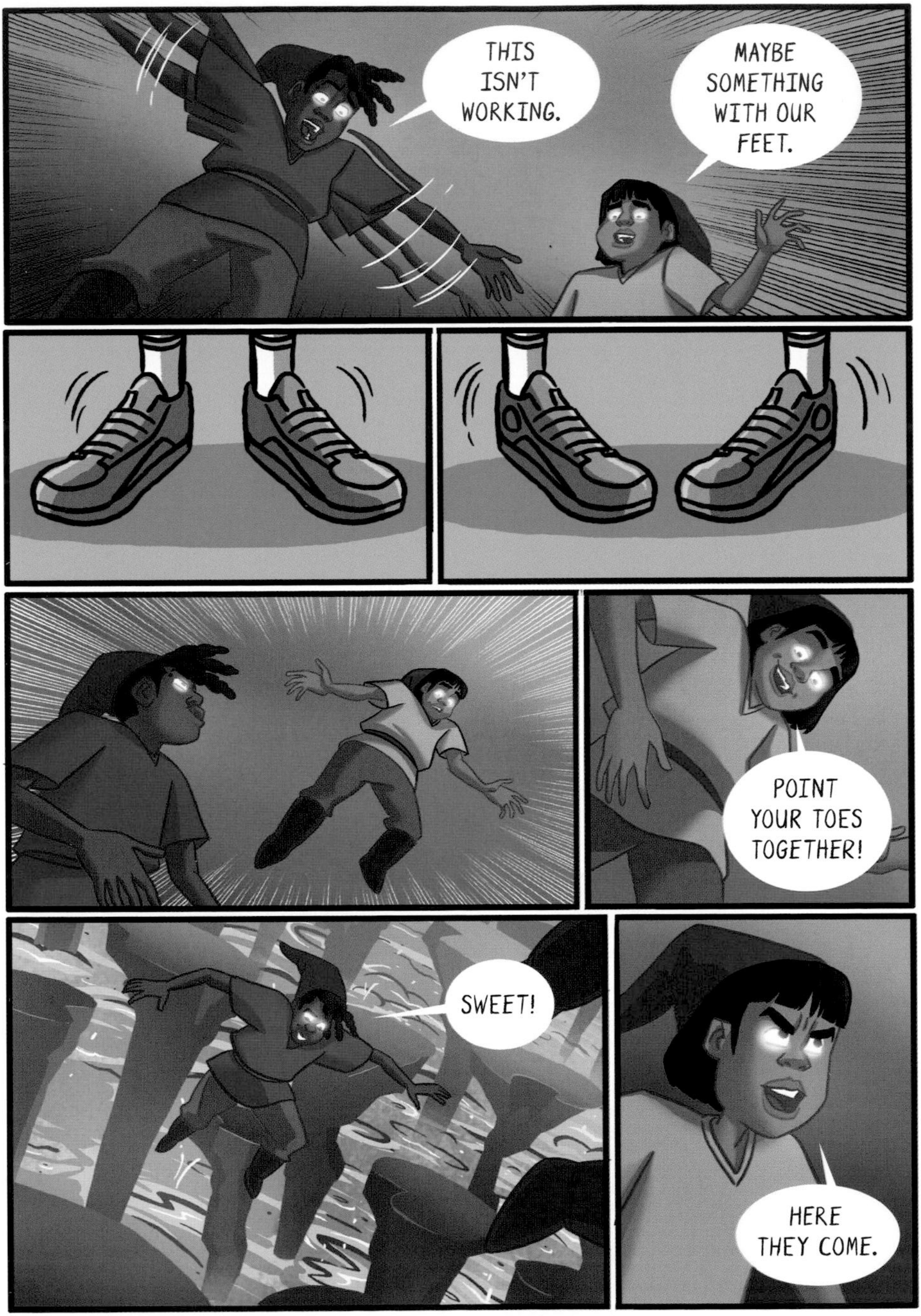
THIS ISN'T WORKING.
MAYBE SOMETHING WITH OUR FEET.
POINT YOUR TOES TOGETHER!
SWEET!
HERE THEY COME.

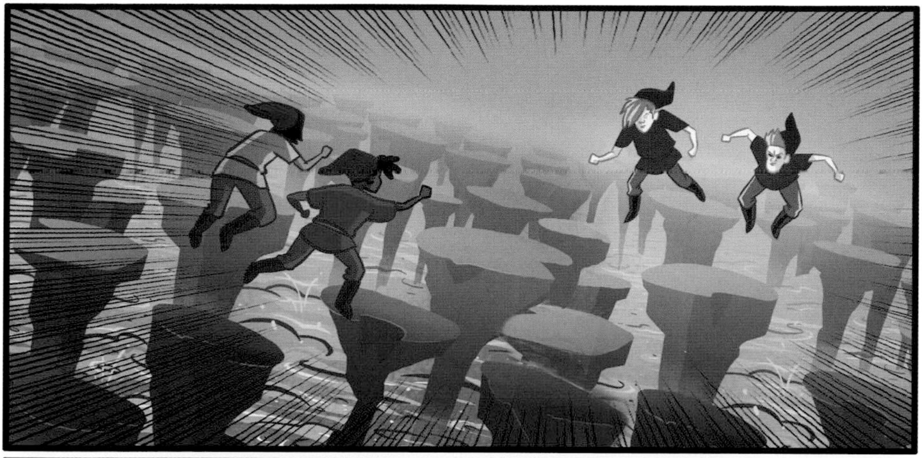

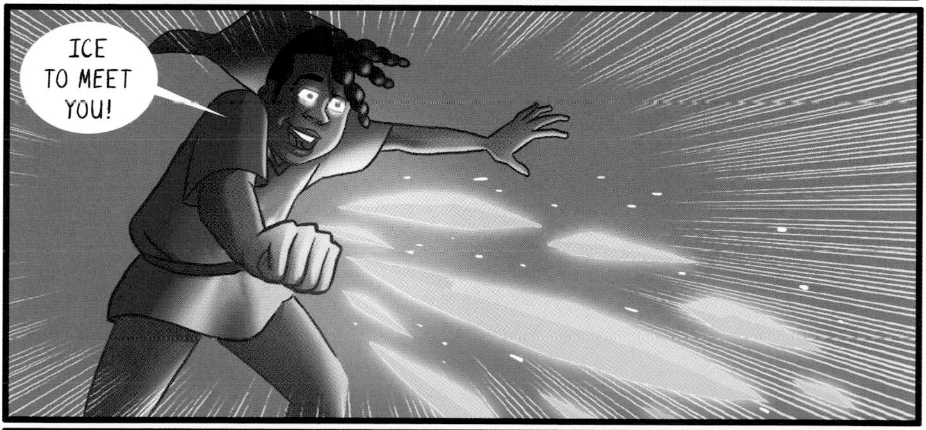
ICE TO MEET YOU!

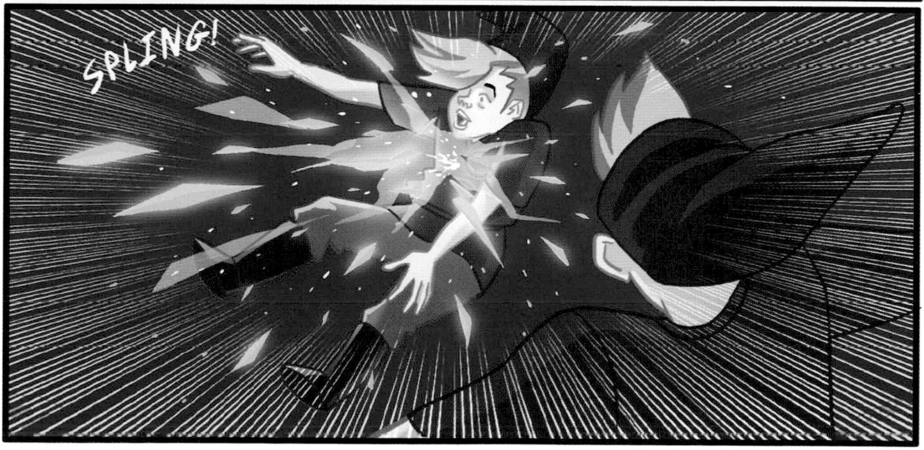
SPLING!

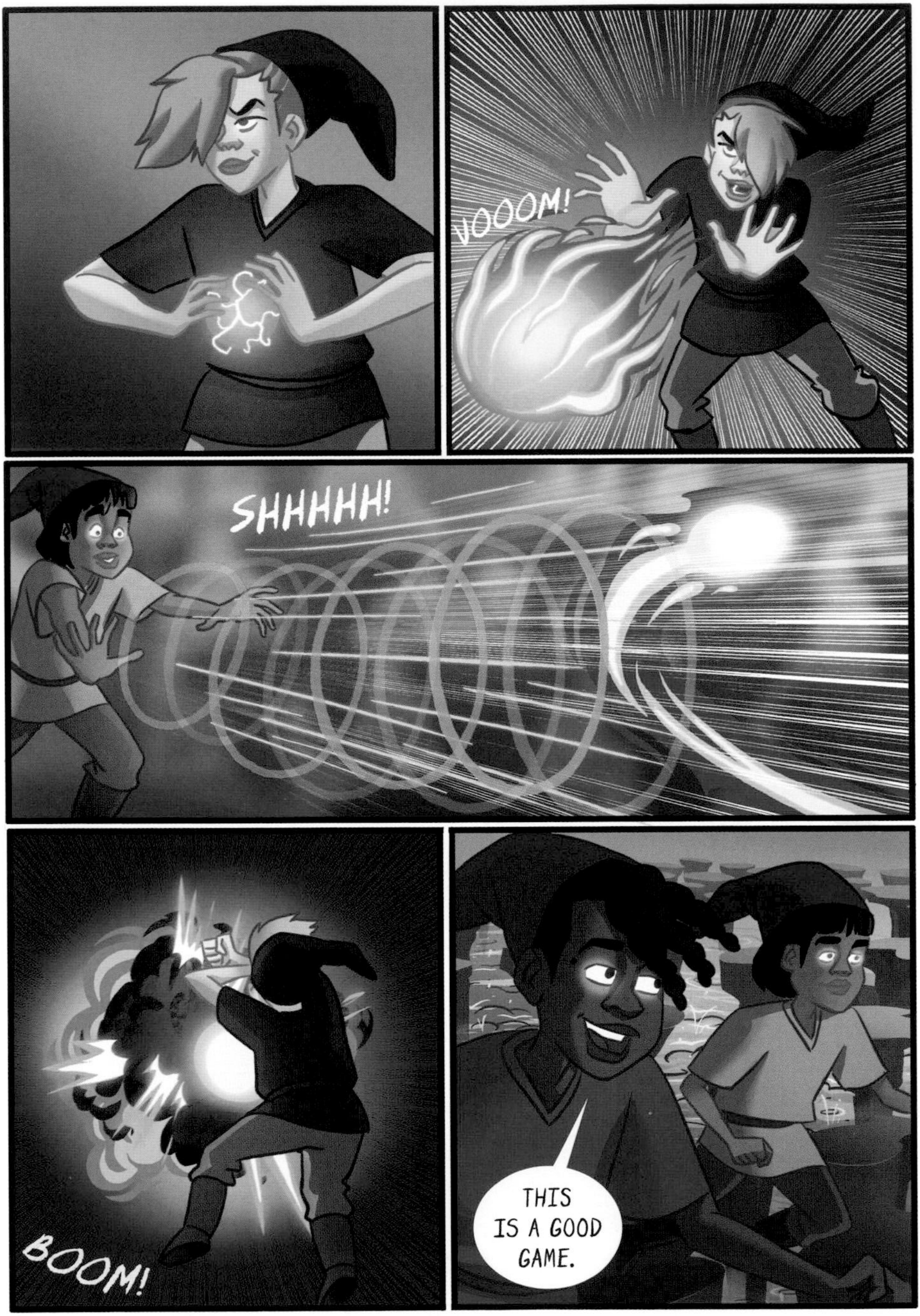
VOOOM!
SHHHHH!
BOOM!
THIS IS A GOOD GAME.

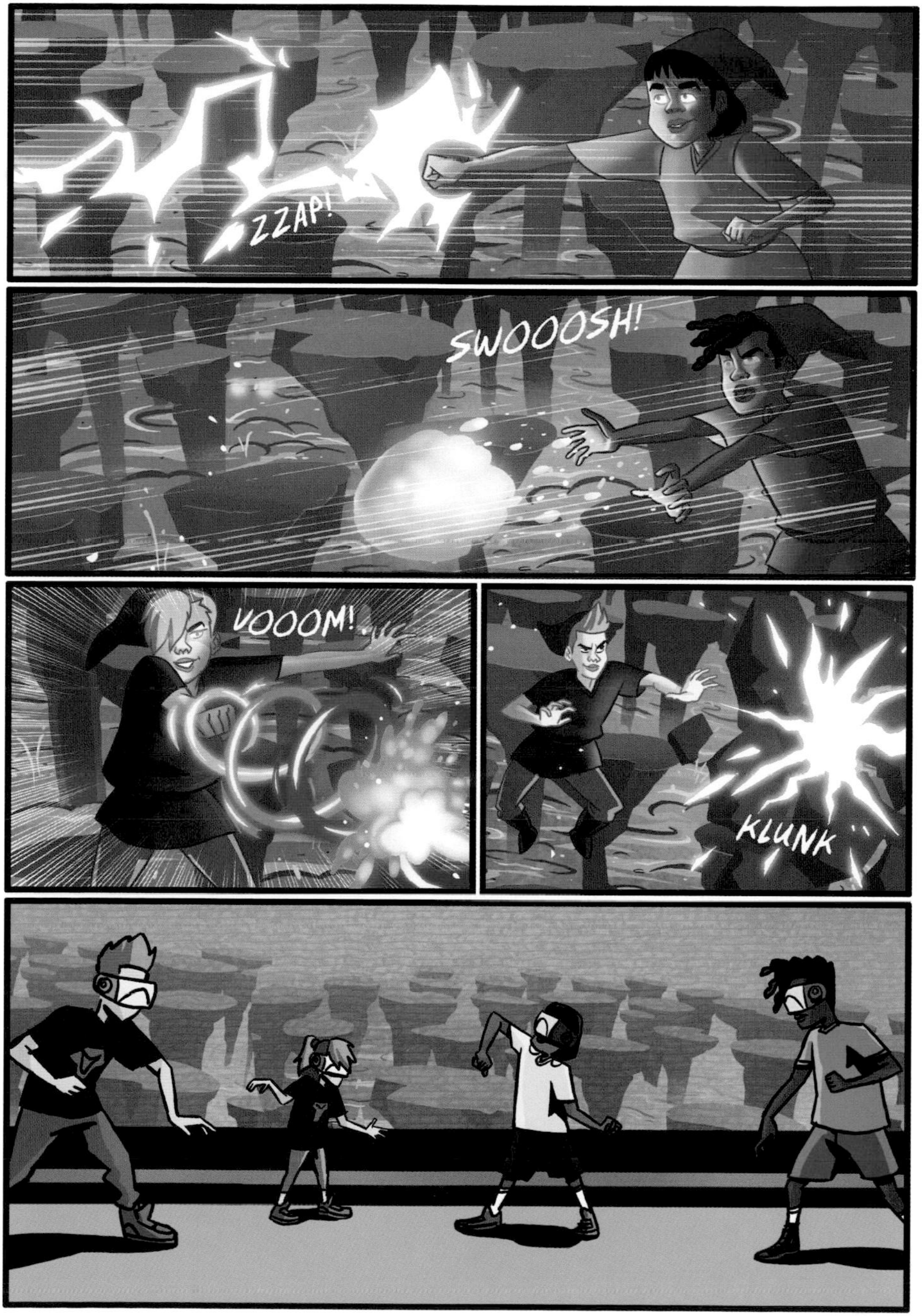
ZZAP!
SWOOOSH!
VOOOM!
KLUNK

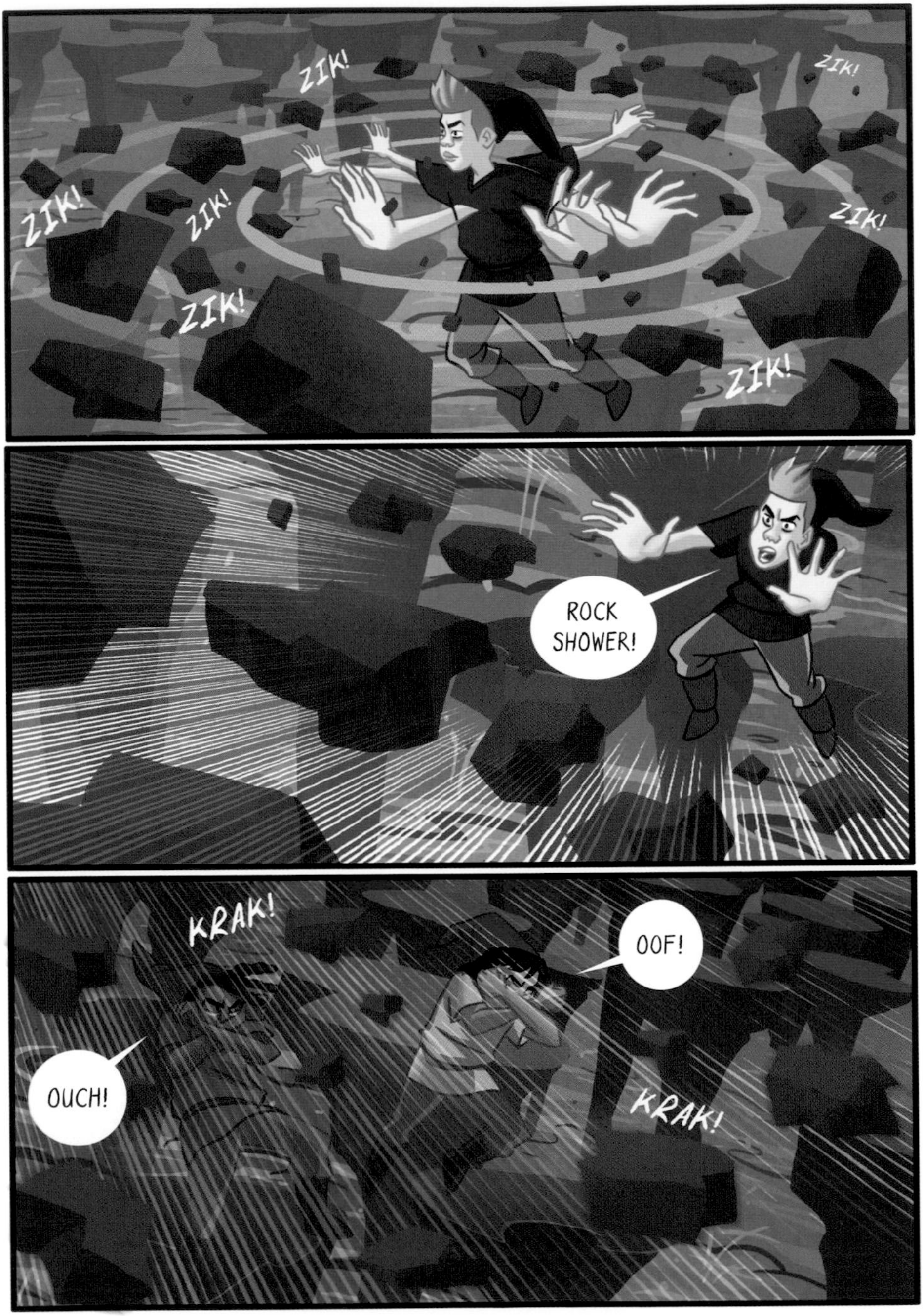
ZIK!
ZIK!
ZIK!
ZIK!
ZIK!
ZIK!
ZIK!
ROCK SHOWER!
KRAK!
OOF!
OUCH!
KRAK!

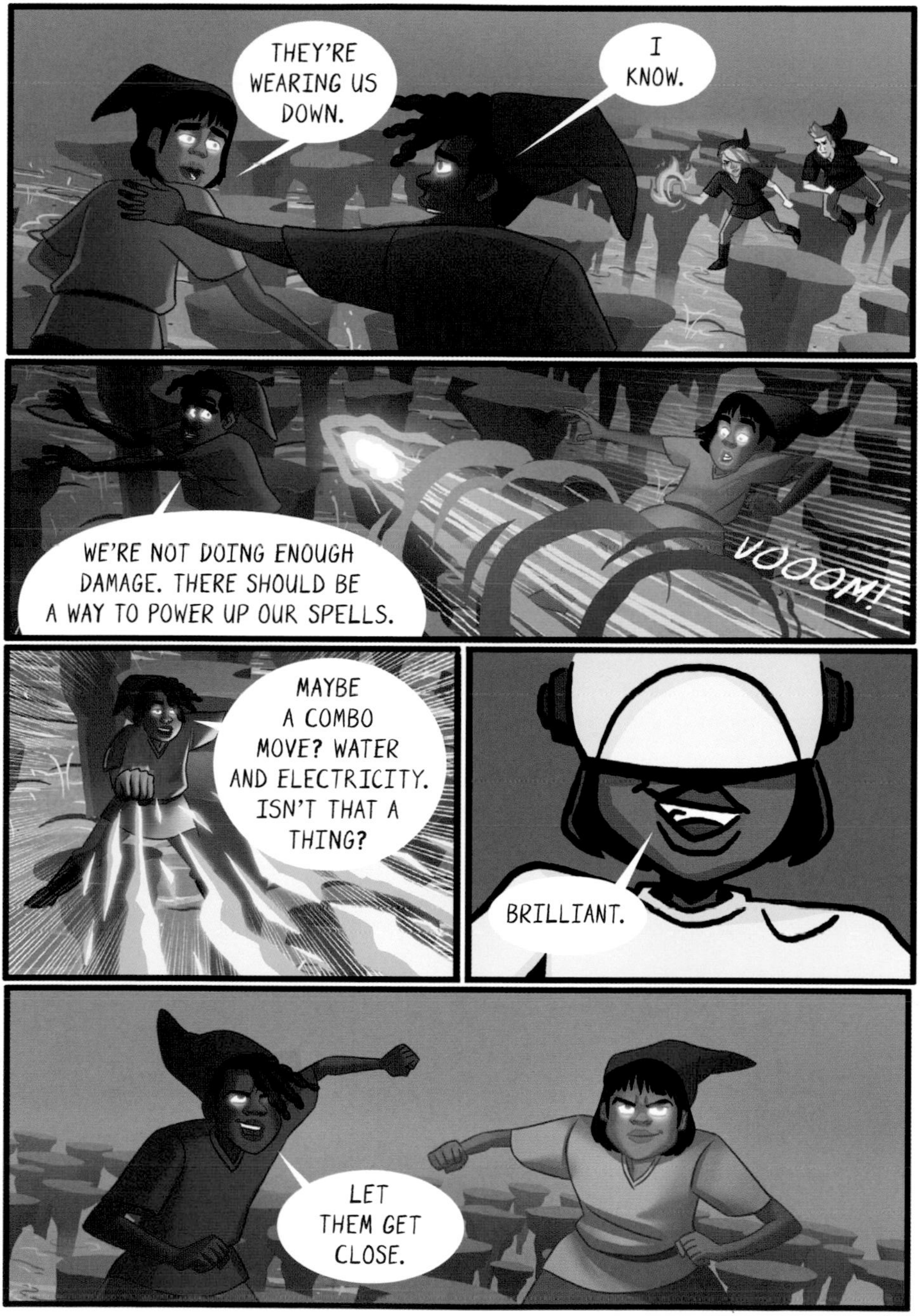
THEY'RE WEARING US DOWN.
I KNOW.
WE'RE NOT DOING ENOUGH DAMAGE. THERE SHOULD BE A WAY TO POWER UP OUR SPELLS.
VOOOM!
MAYBE A COMBO MOVE? WATER AND ELECTRICITY. ISN'T THAT A THING?
BRILLIANT.
LET THEM GET CLOSE.

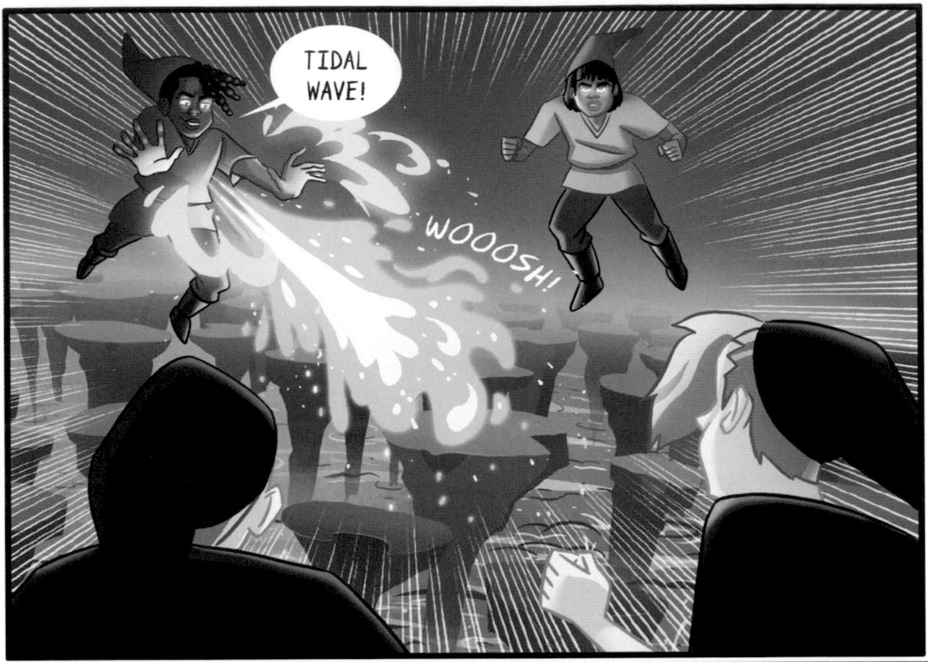
TIDAL WAVE!
WOOOSH!

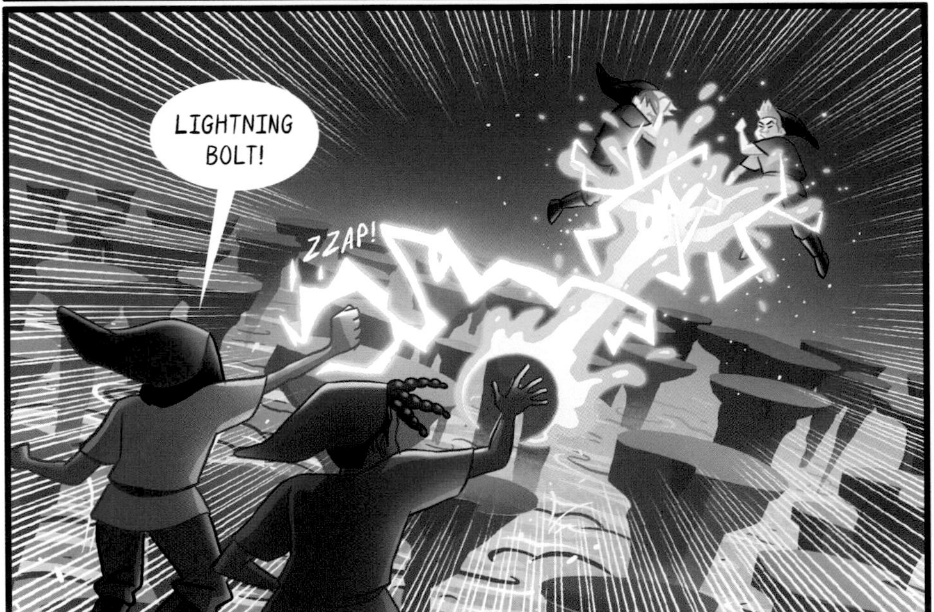
LIGHTNING BOLT!
ZZAP!

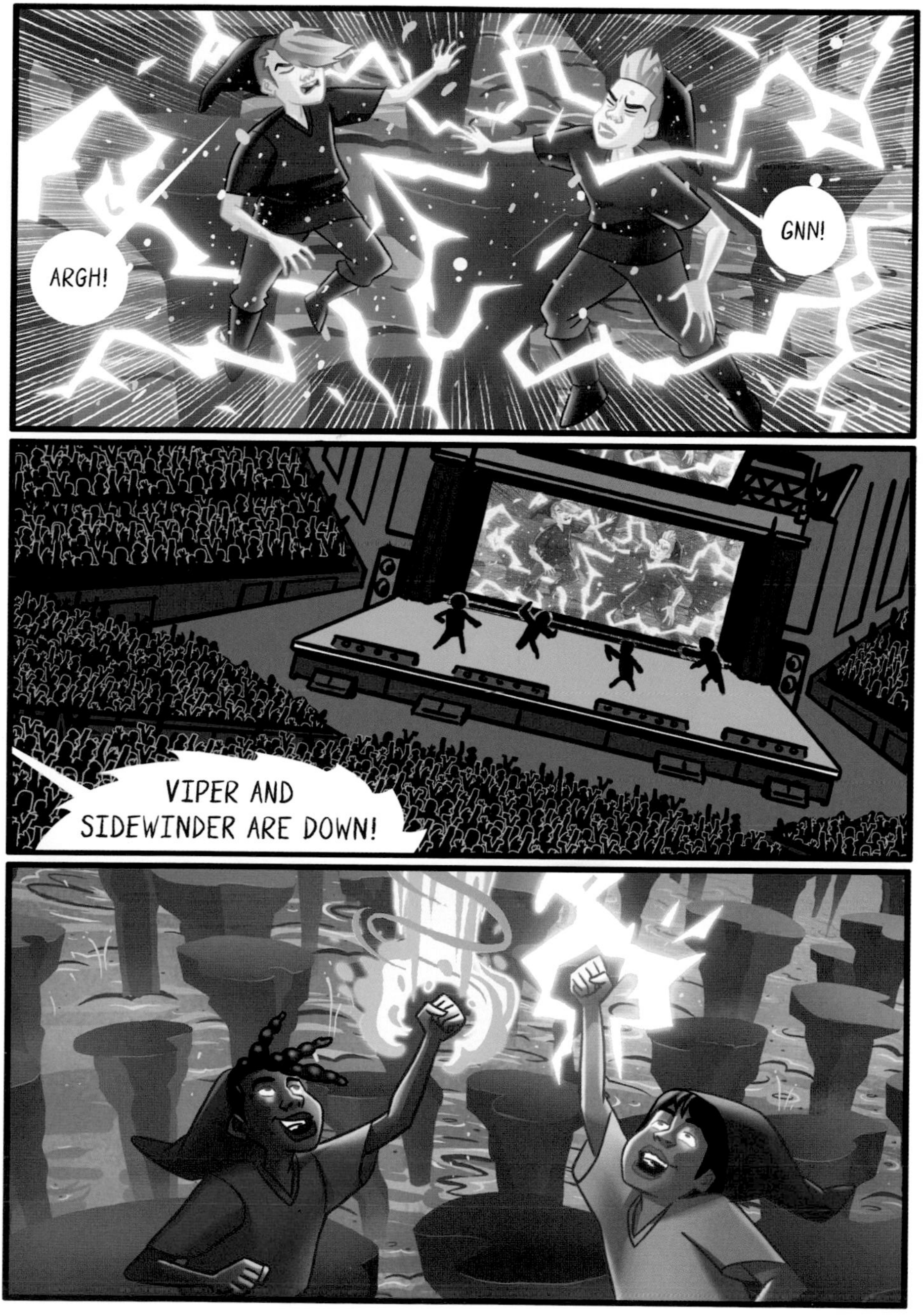
ARGH!
GNN!
VIPER AND SIDEWINDER ARE DOWN!

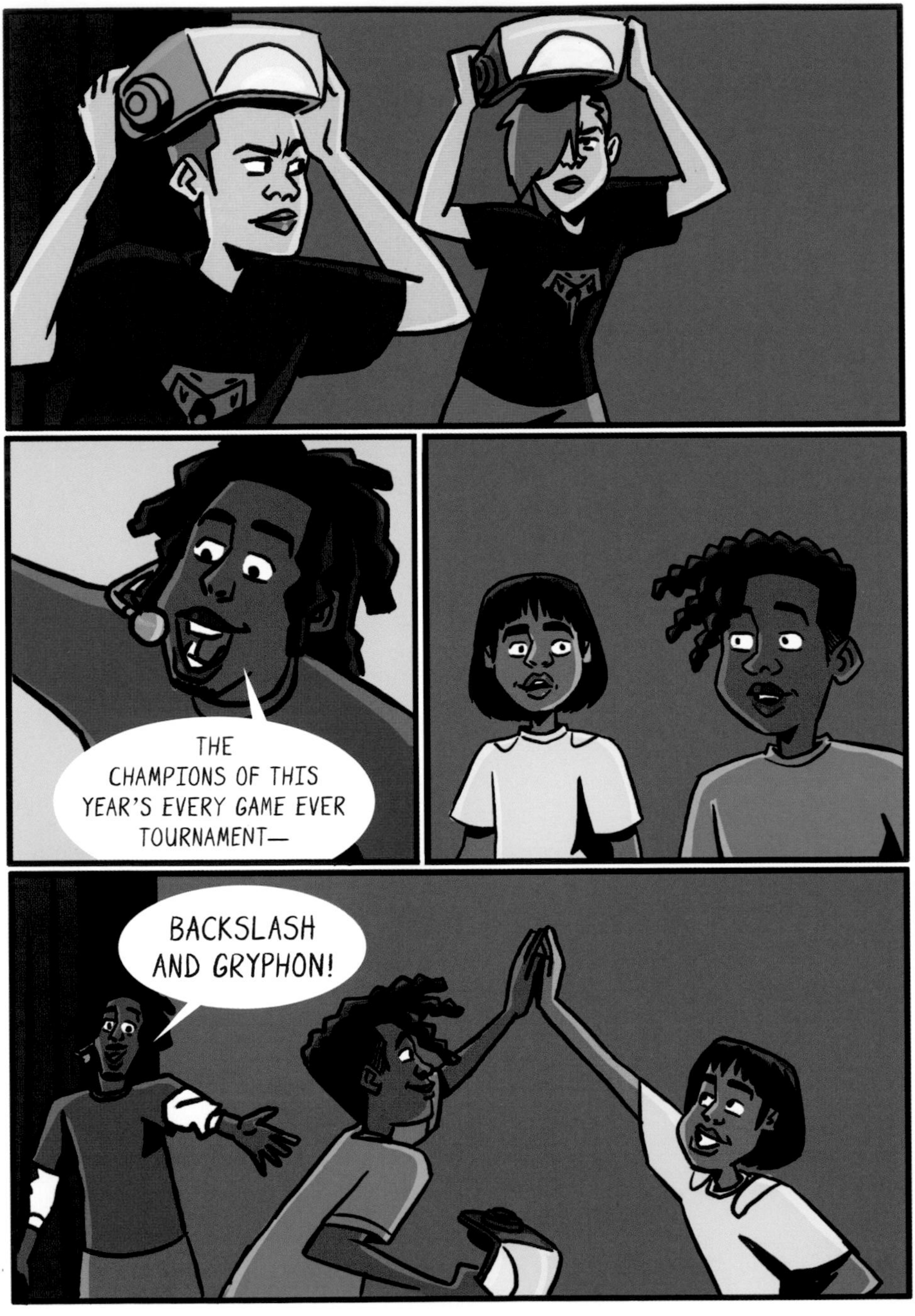
THE CHAMPIONS OF THIS YEAR'S EVERY GAME EVER TOURNAMENT—
BACKSLASH AND GRYPHON!

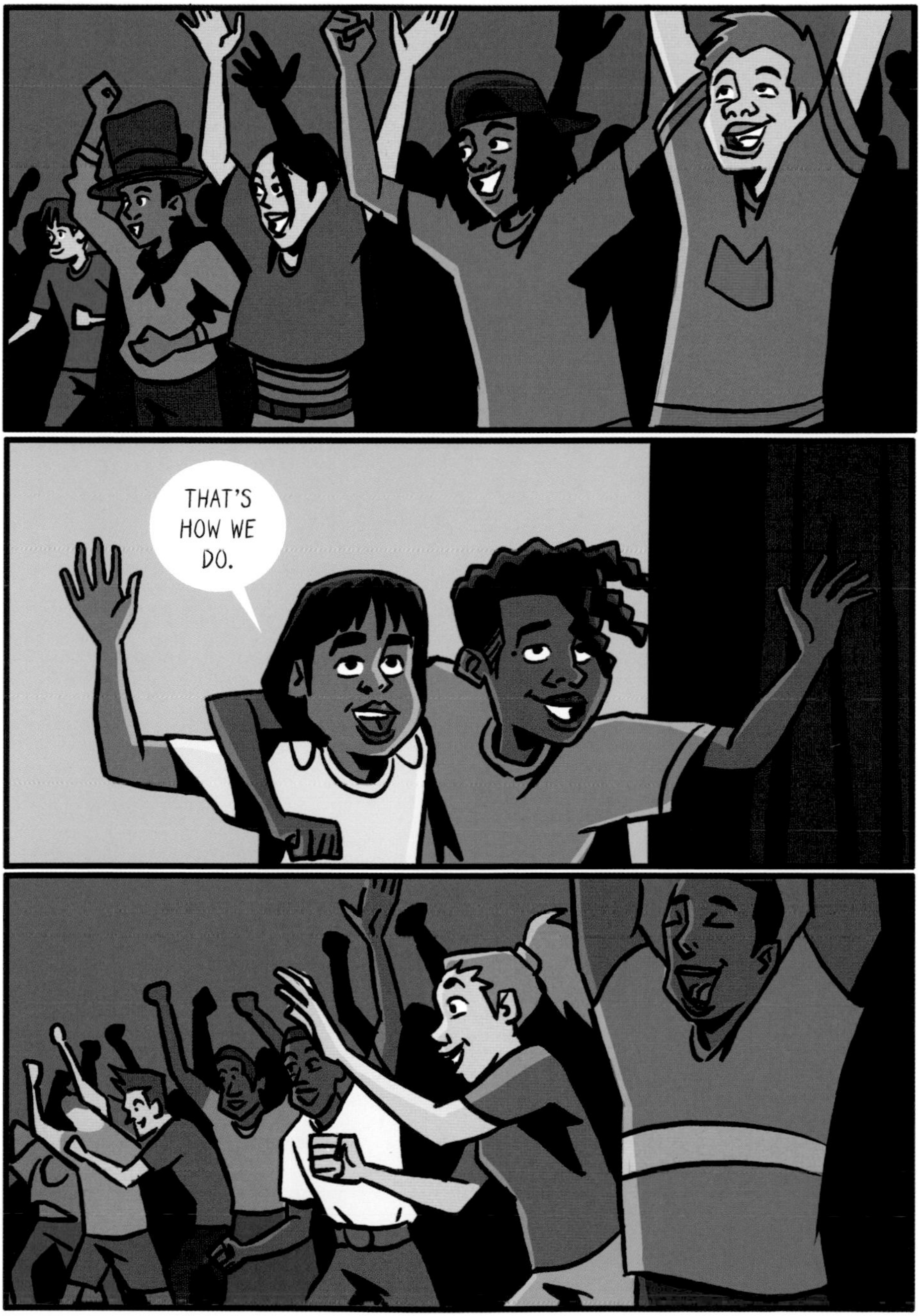
THAT'S
HOW WE
DO.

CHAPTER 12
NEW GAME

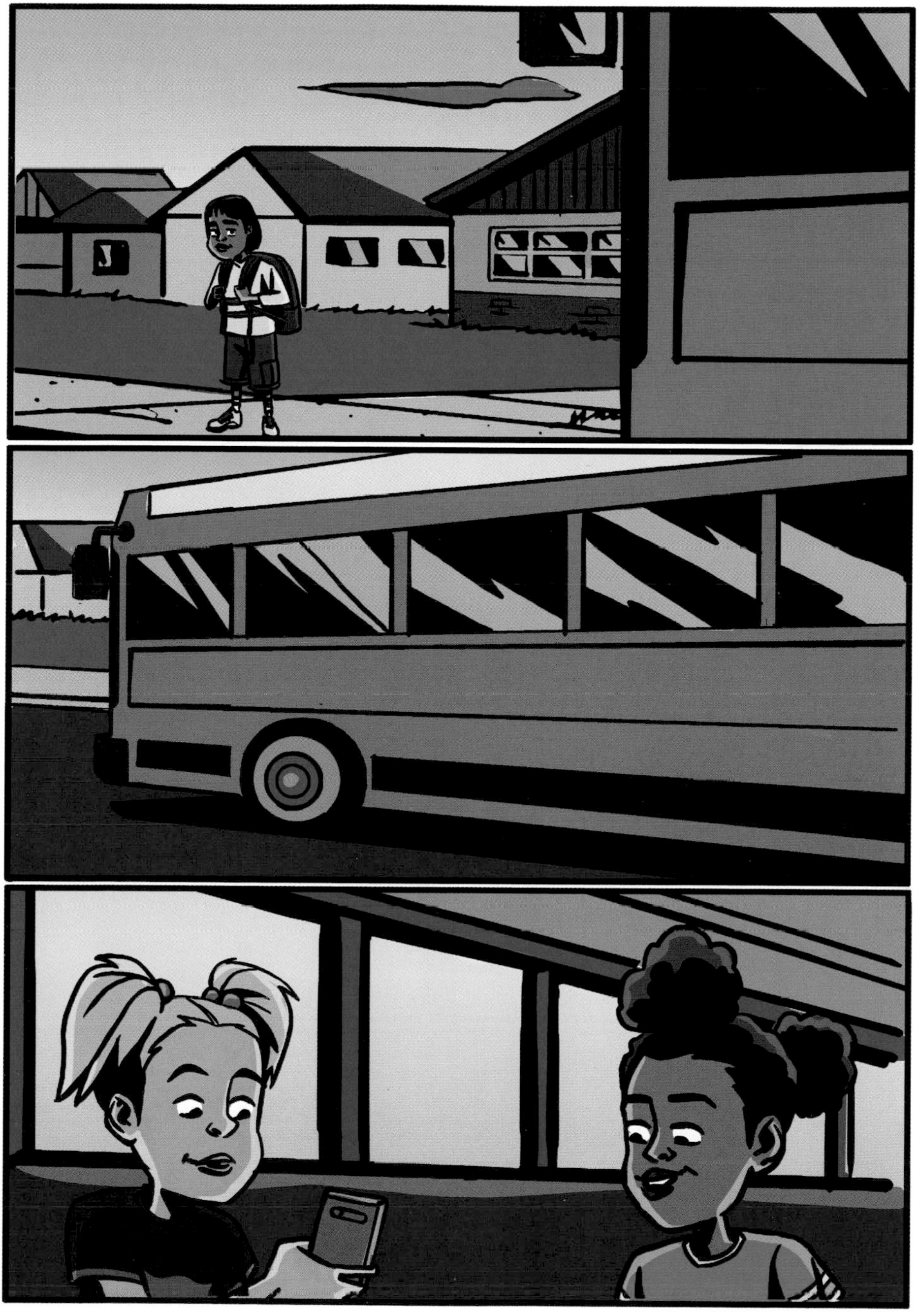

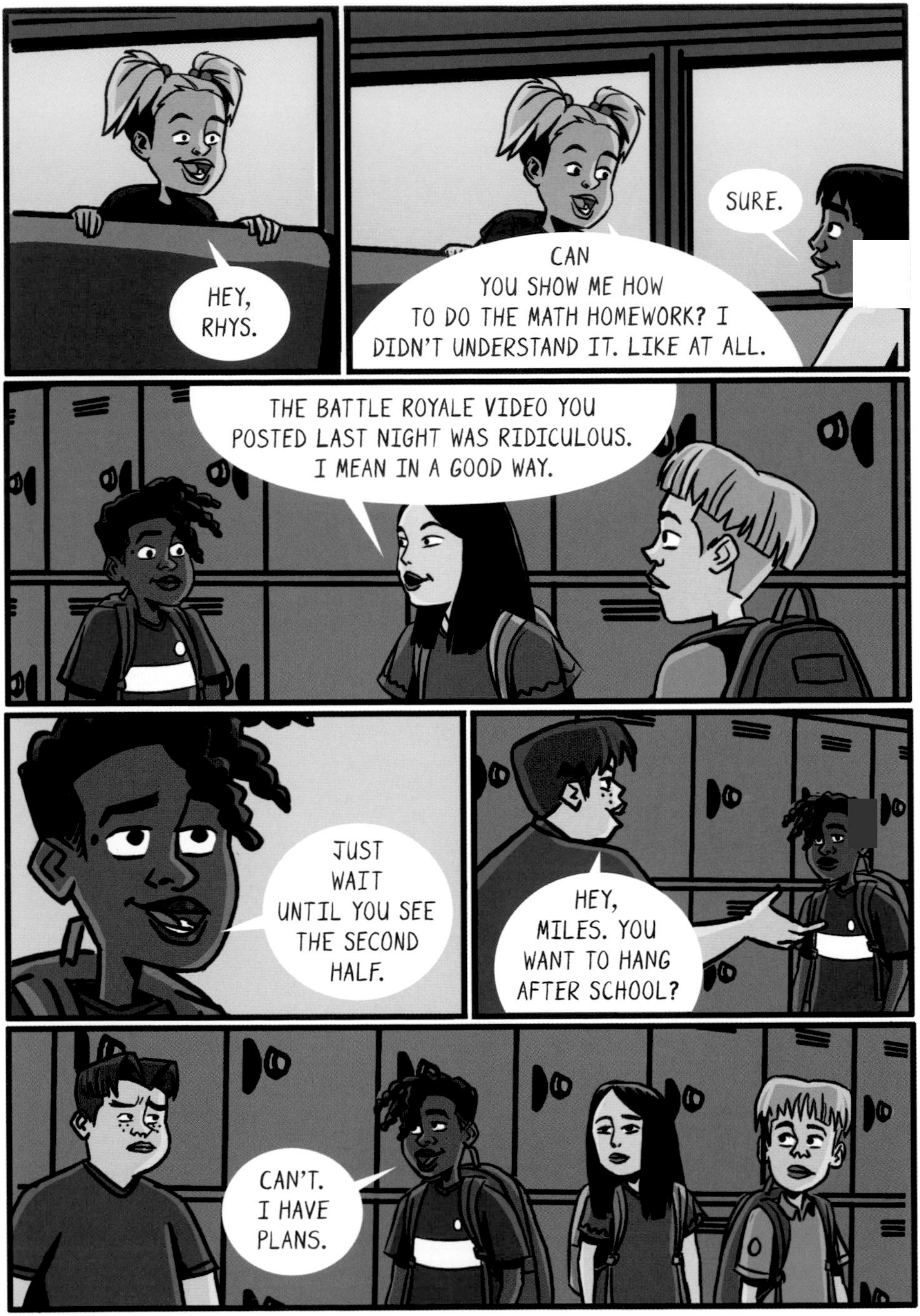
HEY, RHYS.
CAN YOU SHOW ME HOW TO DO THE MATH HOMEWORK? I DIDN'T UNDERSTAND IT. LIKE AT ALL.
SURE.
THE BATTLE ROYALE VIDEO YOU POSTED LAST NIGHT WAS RIDICULOUS. I MEAN IN A GOOD WAY.
JUST WAIT UNTIL YOU SEE THE SECOND HALF.
HEY, MILES. YOU WANT TO HANG AFTER SCHOOL?
CAN'T. I HAVE PLANS.

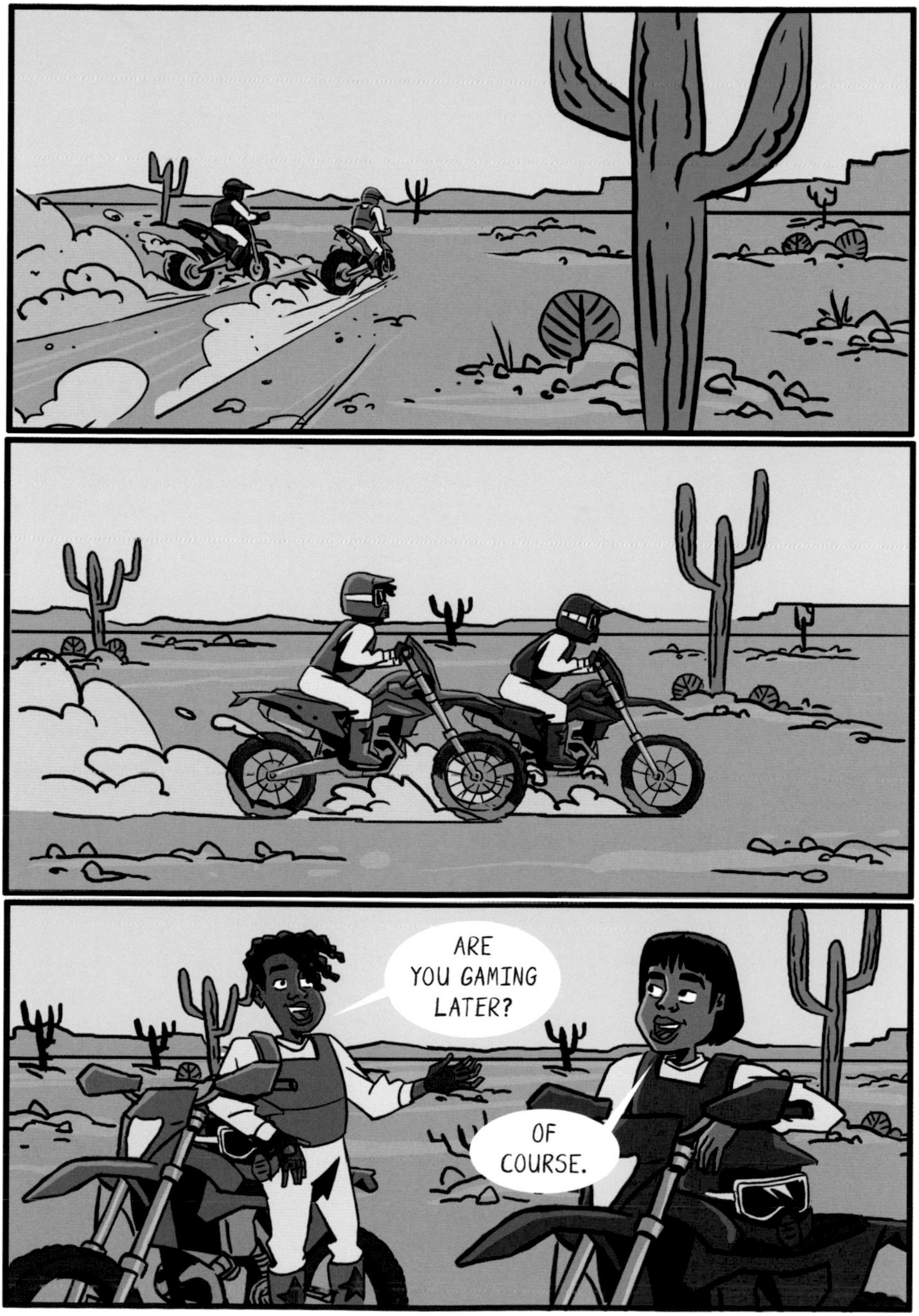
ARE YOU GAMING LATER?
OF COURSE.

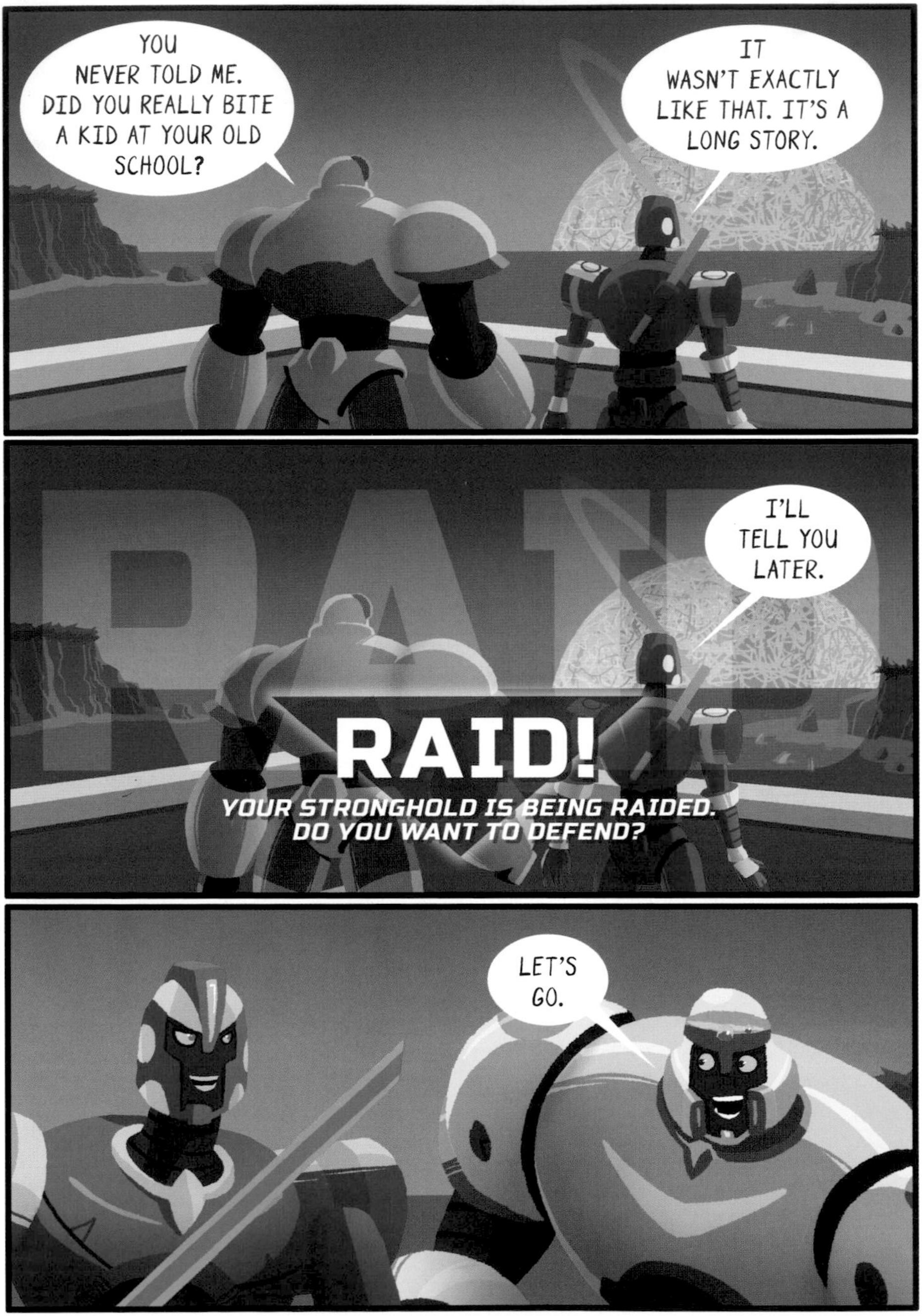
YOU NEVER TOLD ME. DID YOU REALLY BITE A KID AT YOUR OLD SCHOOL?
IT WASN'T EXACTLY LIKE THAT. IT'S A LONG STORY.
I'LL TELL YOU LATER.
RAID!
YOUR STRONGHOLD IS BEING RAIDED. DO YOU WANT TO DEFEND?
LET'S GO.